BIDDING WAR

HIGHEST BIDDER
BOOK 2

CHARLOTTE BYRD

Charlotte Byrd

BYRD BOOKS

Visit my website at www.charlotte-byrd.com

✳ Created with Vellum

"Suspenseful romance!" (Goodreads)

"Amazing. Scintillating. Drama times 10. Love and heartbreak. They say what you don't know can't hurt you, but that's not true in this book." (Goodreads)

"I loved this book, it is fast paced on the crime plot, and super-hot on the drama, I would say the perfect mix. This suspense will have your heart racing and your blood pumping. I am happy to recommend this thrilling and exciting book, that I just could not stop reading once I started. This story will keep you glued to the pages and you will find yourself cheering this couple on to finding their happiness. This book is filled with energy, intensity and heat. I loved this book so much. It was super easy to get swept up into and once there, I was very happy to stay." (*Goodreads*)

"BEST AUTHOR YET! Charlotte has done it again! There is a reason she is an amazing author and she continues to prove it! I was definitely not disappointed in this series!!" (*Goodreads*)

"LOVE!!! I loved this book and the whole series!!! I just wish it didn't have to end. I am definitely a fan for life!!! (*Goodreads*)

"Extremely captivating, sexy, steamy, intriguing, and intense!" (*Goodreads*) ⭐⭐⭐⭐⭐

"Addictive and impossible to put down." (*Goodreads*) ⭐⭐⭐⭐⭐

"What a magnificent story from the 1st book through book 6 it never slowed down always surprising the reader in one way or the other. Nicholas and Olive's paths crossed in a most unorthodox way and that's how their story begins it's exhilarating with that nail biting suspense that keeps you riding on the edge the whole series. You'll love it!" (*Goodreads*) ⭐⭐⭐⭐⭐

"What is Love Worth. This is a great epic ending to this series. Nicholas and Olive have a deep connection and the mystery surrounding the deaths of the people he is accused of murdering is to be read. Olive is one strong woman with deep convictions. The twists, angst, confusion is all put together to make this worthwhile read." (*Goodreads*) ⭐⭐⭐⭐⭐

"Fast-paced romantic suspense filled with twists and turns, danger, betrayal, and so much more." (*Goodreads*) ⭐⭐⭐⭐⭐

"Decadent, delicious, & dangerously addictive!" (*Goodreads*) ⭐⭐⭐⭐⭐

WANT TO BE THE FIRST TO KNOW ABOUT MY UPCOMING SALES, NEW RELEASES AND EXCLUSIVE GIVEAWAYS?

Sign up for my newsletter and get a FREE book: https://dl.bookfunnel.com/gp3o8yvmxd

Join my Facebook Group: https://www.facebook.com/groups/276340079439433/

Bonus Points: Follow me on BookBub and Goodreads!

ABOUT CHARLOTTE BYRD

Charlotte Byrd is the bestselling author of romantic suspense novels. She has sold over 2 Million books and has been translated into five languages.

She lives near Palm Springs, California with her husband, son, a toy Australian Shepherd and a Ragdoll cat. Charlotte is addicted to books and Netflix, and she loves hot weather and crystal blue water.

Write her here:

charlotte@charlotte-byrd.com

Check out her books here:

www.charlotte-byrd.com

Connect with her here:

www.tiktok.com/charlottebyrdbooks

www.facebook.com/charlottebyrdbooks

www.instagram.com/charlottebyrdbooks

Sign up for my newsletter: https://www.
subscribepage.com/byrdVIPList

Join my Facebook Group: https://www.facebook.
com/groups/276340079439433/

Bonus Points: Follow me on BookBub and
Goodreads!

amazon.com/Charlotte-Byrd/e/B013MN45Q6

facebook.com/charlottebyrdbooks

tiktok.com/charlottebyrdbooks

bookbub.com/profile/charlotte-byrd

instagram.com/charlottebyrdbooks

x.com/byrdauthor

ALSO BY CHARLOTTE BYRD

All books are available at ALL major retailers! If you can't find it, please email me at charlotte@ charlotte-byrd.com

Highest Bidder Series
Highest Bidder
Bidding War
Winning Bid

Hockey Why Choose
One Pucking Night (Novella)
Kiss and Puck
Pucking Disaster
Puck Me
Puck It

Tell me Series
Tell Me to Stop

Tell Me to Go
Tell Me to Stay
Tell Me to Run
Tell Me to Fight
Tell Me to Lie

Tell Me to Stop Box Set Books 1-6

Black Series
Black Edge
Black Rules
Black Bounds
Black Contract
Black Limit

Black Edge Box Set Books 1-5

Dark Intentions Series
Dark Intentions
Dark Redemption
Dark Sins
Dark Temptations
<u>Dark Inheritance</u>

Dark Intentions Box Set Books 1-5

Tangled Series
Tangled up in Ice
Tangled up in Pain
Tangled up in Lace

Tangled up in Hate
Tangled up in Love

Tangled up in Ice Box Set Books 1-5

The Perfect Stranger Series
The Perfect Stranger
The Perfect Cover
The Perfect Lie
The Perfect Life
The Perfect Getaway

The Perfect Stranger Box Set Books 1-5

Wedlocked Trilogy
Dangerous Engagement
Lethal Wedding
Fatal Wedding

Dangerous Engagement Box Set Books 1-3

Lavish Trilogy
Lavish Lies
Lavish Betrayal
Lavish Obsession

Lavish Lies Box Set Books 1-3

Somerset Harbor
Hate Mate (Cargill Brothers 1)

Best Laid Plans (Cargill Brothers 2)
Picture Perfect (Cargill Brothers 3)
Always Never (Cargill Brothers 4)
Kiss Me Again (Macmillan Brothers 1)
Say You'll Stay (Macmillan Brothers 2)
Never Let Go (Macmillan Brothers 3)
Keep Me Close (Macmillan Brothers 4)

All the Lies Series
All the Lies
All the Secrets
All the Doubts

All the Lies Box Set Books 1-3

Not into you Duet
Not into you
Still not into you

Standalone Novels
Dressing Mr. Dalton
Debt
Offer
Unknown

ABOUT BIDDING WAR

I never expected to meet the love of my life while auctioning myself off the to the highest bidder.

Anderson West is the heir to a billion dollar fortune and I had to work my butt off for everything I have.

At school, he was my bully.
In law school, he was my rival.
In the real world, we fell in love. Hard.

Our relationship should have been a fairy tale. But his controlling father turned it into a scandalous headline.

The world is full of dangerous men and the most dangerous ones work for the Wests.

After loosing my job, I have to work for his family's biggest rival and play a dangerous game of chess.

When someone comes after me, Anderson takes his life, and I become an accomplice in covering up a murder to protect the man I love.

Is this the end of us or is it just the beginning?

1

JUNE

It's eleven in the morning, and the caffeine still hasn't kicked in. The buzzing din of the office is unhelpful, much like our "state of the art" open floor plan design. No door for me to slam or wall to hide behind. Is this the third or eighth time I've read this sentence? Why doesn't it sound right?

I groan at my computer and roll my chair back. Garrett Edison, my desk neighbor, gives the head tilt of pity. "Why are you stressing about this? It's a letter to the IRS. You've written hundreds of them for clients. It's practically a form letter. What's different about this one?"

It's not that the letter is different. It's me. I'm the thing that's different. But I can't say anything about that to Garrett. No matter how much I adore the guy, he's my sweet desk neighbor. I would never put him in harm's way by telling him the truth.

"I know I'm a corporate attorney, and this should be like breathing, but I'm just having a hard time focusing. Think I need more coffee or —

He snatches the mug from me. "Nope. You have hit the coffeepot so many times this morning that it's making *me* vibrate. What is going on, June?"

My entire life is over, thanks to some miscommunication and gangsters of unknown origin. But I can't say any of that. It would lead to more questions. "I don't know. Maybe I'm not cut out for helping another multimillionaire save a few million dollars on their taxes. It just feels wrong, you know?"

"But you're a lawyer."

"And so are you. What's your point?"

"Didn't they strip you of your morals in law school?" He grins, and he might as well be a breathing dentistry ad. His teeth are so perfect. Garrett is Japanese American and gorgeous. I got over my tiny office crush on him the first week when he arrived. Spinach in his teeth after lunch. Can't. Just can't. Since then, he's been a buddy, and he's never made a move I'd have to awkwardly turn down, so we've been tight ever since.

I still won't read him in on this.

"Most of my morals were already gone by the time law school started. High school was rough," I tease. "But seriously, I have the Peterson presentation due this afternoon and this letter, and I just ... it's like my brain is stuck." Because I was kidnapped, and I'm still kinda freaked out by that. And that's not the worst thing that's happened.

"Sounds to me like you don't need more coffee. You need some fresh air."

"Boston winter fresh air? Have you lost your mind?"

He snorts a laugh. "I saw your running gear in your bag."

I lie, "I went to the gym this morning—"

He laughs hard that time. "Be glad you didn't go into litigation because you are the worst liar I have ever seen. Go for a run. The frosty air will clear your head. Besides, it's almost lunchtime. No one will care if you're gone right now."

I stared at the same sentence I wrote an hour ago. Or five minutes ago. I don't know. Time is a construct. "Yeah, okay. Not making any headway here anyway."

"That's the spirit."

"I want my coffee mug back when I return."

"You can have it back if you bring me a donut from MacGregor's."

I laugh. "Are you kidding me? That is too far for a winter run."

"I find your lack of faith disturbing."

I roll my eyes at his Star Wars reference. "Nerd. Fine, MacGregor's. What kind?"

"Lemon-iced, blueberry-filled, and thank you very much."

Grabbing my bag, I kick his chair on my way past, and he laughs as I grumble, "Blackmailer."

"Procrastinator."

But I'm not procrastinating. I'm distracted. Changing in the ladies room around lunch is weird because the actual running bunnies are changing, too. I'm not much of a runner. Never have been. I've always said that if I was running, it was because I was being chased.

Now, I feel like I am.

Stretching my gear over my body makes my brain freeze up. It's tight. Tight like binds. Like the binds the kidnappers had on my wrists. When I was trapped and helpless and—

Three good breaths, June. You can do three things. Breathe in. Don't let it out. Breathe in again. Hold on. I know it feels like your lungs will burst, but they won't. One more good breath, then let it out slowly. When I do, I'm not in that grimy basement anymore. I'm at work. Changing for a run. No. For a donut mission.

I'd read about the breathing technique being good to get rid of hiccups or panic. Something about how it grounds you. I don't know about that, but it seems to help when I have flashbacks. Can't tell anyone about them. No one would understand. The two people in my life who even know about what happened have never been kidnapped, and I'm not polling my other friends to find out who has been just so I have someone to talk to. That would be risky and I don't plan on telling anyone about that.

Lacing up my shoes, I'm ready for the fresh air, icy or not. The runners are out of the ladies room. Apparently, they fled during my deep breathing meditation. Checking myself in the mirror, I tighten my ponytail and feed it through the hole in my purple knit hat. If I don't bind my frizzy brown hair for a run, it will fly into my face and jab my eyes —

I should have been an eye jabber when the kidnapper grabbed me off the street. But I was so shocked when it began that I didn't have the time to think of it. Didn't have the time to think at all. Before I knew it, he had a knife at my throat.

Shake it off, June. We're fine. No physical harm was done. Breathe. Breathe. Breathe.

Strange the way it hits sometimes. The slightest thought throws me back into the basement I was sure I'd never leave. But put the thought away and jog back to my desk and stash my bag there before bounding out of the office. The elevator trip is short, a quick swerve through the glass and stone lobby, and I'm outside.

It is so cold that the air has needles in it.

But it'll warm up when I do, so I begin my run. The sidewalks are packed with office workers going to lunch, and I'm an idiot running her fool head off while dodging their foot traffic. Doesn't matter. I have to get to MacGregor's. Can't let Garrett down. I have to clear my head. Can't let my clients down. People are counting on me to get this run in.

It's stupid that I have to couch it that way to myself, but I do. I'm much better at being accountable to other people than I am at being accountable to myself. Not that I'm a pushover or anything, but in my head, it makes more sense when I tell myself I have to do something for someone else.

Which is probably why I was okay with going along with Anderson's plan. I still cannot get over the fact that his father caught us in bed together. And stole my money. This has not been my best month.

Where did it all go wrong?

Probably right at the start, when I illegally auctioned myself off to the highest bidder. It wasn't for my time, like a professional escort. It was explicitly for sex. But desperate times call for desperate measures, and I have to leave my job. I hate it so much that I was willing to bang whoever walked into the suite if it meant I got paid enough to leave my job.

He could have been ugly or old or whatever, and I wouldn't have cared. My job is soulless, and I cannot stand the work I do. But I lucked out. My winning bidder wasn't ugly or old. He was Anderson West, my high school bully.

As handsome as he is rich, Anderson had made my teenage years a living hell. But the years have changed him. He isn't the cocky boy who teased me for wearing thrift store shoes. He's grown into a caring, smart man who looks like he lives at the gym.

But then his dad froze his bank account, so he couldn't pay up after that night. Since his father is on him about proving his worth by committing to someone, I pretended to be his fiancée, and it was all going well until his father's enemies kidnapped me. Sure, it was only for a day, but it was the second worst day of my life.

Once Anderson got me back, he didn't tell his father. Instead, he said I was kidnapped, so he needed his bank account unfrozen. His father made him do him a favor—something Anderson still won't tell me about—and then gave him the money to pay the kidnappers.

It worked, and I was incredibly proud of Anderson for his plan. Worried, of course. His father is, by all accounts, a dangerous man in his own right. He owns the entertainment law firm in Boston with a media empire on the side. He has powerful allies and enemies. Not someone we wanted to cross, but he left us no choice.

And then he walked into my apartment, caught us fucking, and stole the money back.

2

JUNE

At MacGregor's, I order Garrett's donut and a bacon maple crème for me. I would have grabbed a chocolate-iced, crème-filled for Callie, my other office friend, but she's out today. She was there the night of the auction and encouraged me to go for it. How could she have known what would transpire after that? I didn't blame her for any of it—I make my own choices. But when I came back from pretending to be sick to cover the time I'd missed, I'd blurted out the whole story to her. She and Anderson are the only two people who know.

She deserves a donut.

As I'm paying, a text notification pops up. Anderson again. I swipe the notification off my screen, take my donuts, and go. Texting him is too close to talking.

Ever since the morning after his father robbed me, I've had all kinds of feelings about him, and none of them are good.

It's too complicated, so I am not ready to speak to him yet. I texted him a few times to let him know I was okay, but that's been it. I know he wants more than that. But I can't give it right now.

Every moment feels like I'm waiting to be grabbed again. Each time someone bumps into me on the street, I'm sure they're going to be the one to press a knife to my throat. When a van slows down near me, I freeze. Can't stop myself from it. But this time, I look the driver in the eye. I want to know who takes me.

Just a money truck picking up at a bank, or so the sign on the truck says. Oh. Maybe I shouldn't be having a staring contest with an armed guard. Keep walking, June.

Back to Anderson, I don't know how to make him comprehend any of this. He was the one to collect me from the kidnappers, so he saw how I was at that moment. But I don't think he gets how much it still affects me. Plus, I was taken because of his father.

How can he not understand that I'm not ready to talk to him?

Love should be easy and fun, right? Not this thing that binds you to a dangerous family. Or is that maligning the rest of his family? I don't know. What I do know is the man who kidnapped me, Andre Moeller, said he did so because Anderson's father, Elliot, owed him a substantial amount of money. Whatever that means to men like them.

So, I leave his texts unread for a while on my way back to the office. I have donuts to deliver. It doesn't help that my phone dings two more times. I know it's him. But I'm not looking. Not right now. I don't need to cater to his wants and needs when I'm the one who was taken.

But I miss him like I miss springtime.

No, no, no. Too complicated. Find a boring accountant or something.

I don't want a boring accountant, though. I want Anderson sans his father's shit. The problem is, when Anderson takes over his family's business, I don't know what happens next. Will he assume the mantle of his father's work and all the seedy parts that go along with that? Or will he strike out and make the business his own, leaving the illegal stuff behind? I don't know, and I can't ask.

He hates what his father is doing. But I'm not sure how deep it goes, and if it's as deep as I suspect, I don't think Anderson will be able to get out of it when the time comes.

Ugh. It's too complicated. All of it. I should just forget about him. Forget about the auction money. Move on and figure out another way to escape my corporate attorney drudgery. I'll be happier for it, or at least, I'll be safer for it.

But I don't want to move on. I still want Anderson West.

I groan internally as my office building looms. It's nice enough and looks like the dozens of other office buildings in downtown Boston. The elevators always work smoothly. It's clean and modern on my floor. Nice enough to impress our high-end clientele.

And so grating that it makes my teeth hurt.

Doesn't matter, though, because it starts raining again, so I dash into the lobby with the bag of donuts tucked beneath my jacket. Between helping the rich get richer and dealing with people like Madi Montague, I hate it. Madi is a senior staff member, so she thinks of herself as in charge of everyone else. Our boss, Wallace, likes that she keeps him informed of the goings-on in the office, so he lets her get away with too much. It's so mundane that I want to run screaming from the building instead of taking the elevator up.

But I hit the button and zip up to my floor. When the metal doors close, I see myself in the reflection.

Holy crap, I look terrible. Red-cheeked and sweaty from the run and soaked from the rain. Well, at least I look like the mess I really am now. No hiding it when I look like this. I think I pounded the pavement a bit harder than I meant to, but that's due to avoiding Anderson's texts, I'm sure of it.

I can clean up in the bathroom, wolf my donut down, and get to work. Can't tell if my head is any clearer or if I'm just going to have to power through, but either way, I can do this. If I can survive a kidnapping, I can survive feeling a little grungy at work for half a day.

As soon as the doors open, though, my stomach drops and I nearly lose the donuts. I force a professional smile on. "Wallace. Haven't seen you all day."

"I've been busy," he says with no small amount of irritation. "I'd like you to follow me to my office. Now."

Oh hell. What is going on? Wallace is never like this. He's older than me by twenty years or so and a quirky uncle type. He's not that angry school principal type I'm seeing in him today. "Uh, sure. Just let me get cleaned up, and I'll meet you there."

"That won't be necessary. Come along, June."

Fuck. Did a client complain about me? Is the IRS getting crabby? I've been at the firm for a few years now, but the work I've done has been good and legal. Maybe hit a couple of legal gray areas, but that's always been encouraged if it saves our clients more money, and none of it has been actually illegal. Just stuff that makes the IRS huff at us.

Are they done huffing? Have they gotten serious?

I try to lighten the mood as I follow him between the rows of desks. I toss Garrett the bag of donuts and don't say a word to him. When he sees who I'm walking with and how bad I look, he winces. Does he know what's going on? Does everyone know what's going on, and I'm the last to find out? Whatever the case, I hope Madi is not in Wallace's office. I can handle getting yelled at, but not in front of her.

Never in front of her.

Wallace, being a boss, has a real office. A nice corner number that I had my eye on the first year I was here. Back then, I figured I'd be with the firm for my full thirty years, so I should keep an eye out for which office I wanted as I progressed in my field. Like most graduates, I was full of hope for the future and love for the law.

Now, my future is cloudy, and the law can go to hell.

As Wallace walks around his desk to his chair, he says, "Take a seat, June. We need to talk."

I lightly joke, "Almost sounds like you're breaking up with me, Wallace."

He gives a thin smile, and whatever it is, I know I am fucked.

3

ANDERSON

"Not at all, Rena. We've been with you every step of the way, and we're not about to turn our backs now," I tell her as reassuringly as possible. Rena Banks is one of our top stars. A Disney child actor-turned-singer and now an incredibly popular influencer, Rena worries over everything. It's a shame she doesn't worry *before* she does stupid shit. "I'm no agent—"

"No, Anderson," she says, suddenly reaching for my hand. "You're better. My agent thinks this will all blow over. You're the only one who said to do an apology video."

I smile politely, give her hand a friendly squeeze, and take my hand back. There are at least three paparazzi in this restaurant, and all of them snapped a shot of her grabbing my hand. As I'd planned. After all, I was the one who called them.

I knew she would flirt with me. Rena, for all her flaws, is affectionate and handsy. Which is why I said we should sit on the same side of the booth. Give the people something else to focus on, like the possibility of a blooming romance, and they'll glom onto it. I would have told Rena before our meeting, but she is a far better singer than she is an actress, and she would have overdone it. Hopefully, she doesn't take my friendliness for more.

I cannot afford any more screwups.

"It's basic math, really," I tell her. "You said some things that people didn't like, so you need to walk it back. Waiting for it to blow over isn't as proactive as you should be. You're an influencer. You're not passive."

She nods enthusiastically. "Exactly. Maybe I need a new agent ... "

"We work with several. I'll send you a list I think could be—"

She bats her big blue eyes at me. "What about you? I mean, it's basically the same thing as a lawyer, right? Except agents have fewer rules."

Not happening. Rena sleeps with her agents. It's practically required. Three months ago, I might have considered it. But I have too many reasons to say no now, and June is all of them. She is everything.

I smile and tilt my head sympathetically, even though I hardly mean it. "A sweet offer, but I must pass. My life is in Boston, not LA."

"I can make it worth your while, Anderson. You get me more than my agents ever have. They're all sharks. I hate it."

A paparazzo is getting bored. Can't let them leave yet. So, I flirt a little. "If they're all sharks, then what am I?"

Her doctor-enhanced, comically large lips twist into a smirk. "Really fucking hot."

I laugh, letting her think her compliment landed. "Appreciated. My point is you need sharks when you're on the West Coast, Rena. They're good for you. I am good for you here, where I can handle your legal matters. Again, thank you for the offer."

She sighs. "Fine, fine. What do I say in the apology video?"

"I already emailed you a script."

"See? You're the best, Anderson." She kisses my cheek. "What a pity you're a lawyer. You're handsome enough to be an actor, you know?"

"Considering some character actors, I'm not sure if that's a compliment," I tease.

She giggles. "You know what I mean. You have a face for film."

A gentle shrug. "If you say so. How about some more champagne?" I ask while I refill her flute.

"Are you trying to get me drunk?"

"Only if that's what you want." I hate playing the cad. I've spent a lifetime doing it, so I know what buttons to press, what sentences to drag out, and what words to emphasize. It would be easy enough to fuck Rena in the bathroom, and that would convince her to go along with whatever I wanted. Business is fifty percent who you know and fifty percent how you make them feel. But no thought has appealed less in the past five minutes. The only woman I want is June Devlin, and playing the cad never got me anywhere with her.

"Mm, I dunno," Rena murmurs in my ear as her hand slides onto my thigh beneath the table. "I make questionable choices when I'm drunk."

Back to business. Bringing up things she bristles at will cool her down. "Hence why you need to do that apology video now. The sooner, the better, in fact. Can't let the people sit on your statement for too long, or you're canceled, and then it's another stint in rehab to make it up to people. You remember how much you hated rehab."

Her bottom lip pokes out in a pout, and she blushes. "Rehab was humiliating. The counselors were no fun, and they kept making me talk about my childhood and shit. I hated it. You have no idea how embarrassing that is."

No more embarrassing than being balls deep in the woman you love when your dad comes in, mocks you, and robs her. Pretty sure I would talk about my childhood forever if it meant I'd never have to mentally relive that moment. The bastard humiliated me, and I mean to pay him back.

Somehow.

I still haven't seen him since that night. Blackmail is an unseemly tool in my arsenal, but it works both ways. Recently, I discovered our family fortune is built on many, many illegal activities. Dad forced me to go on a ride along with his pet enforcer to retrieve some money, and during the meeting with the debtor and his associates, a firefight broke out. The debtor and his friends ended up dead.

I could turn Dad in for that. But I was there, and he is the only person with footage of the firefight in the warehouse. I'd be held responsible for those deaths, same as him. It would almost be worth it to see the smug look on his face fall away. But I don't savor the idea of conjugal visits with June in a prison.

So, I've avoided Dad as much as possible until I figure out a plan. I don't miss him. In fact, it's been nice not seeing him. Our relationship has always been contentious. Nothing I've ever done has been enough for him, not even when I was a kid.

When I had perfect grades, he found fault with my lack of extracurriculars. When I had perfect grades *and* captained the rugby team, he thought I should have also captained the debate team. After managing that feat, he said I should dress better for school.

We wore uniforms.

It didn't matter what I did. Nothing compared to the image of me in his head. So now, all I have left for the man is disdain and resentment. The world would be better off with him in prison, and not only because of our relationship. He's a criminal. When we watched the footage of the warehouse, he didn't bat an eye at the three men who died. They were nothing to him. Which means they are not the first deaths he is responsible for. If I don't get him locked up soon, they won't be the last.

"And here I thought I had your attention, Anderson," Rena coos in my ear as she presses her breasts against my arm, snuggling close.

"Apologies, Rena," I say with a smile. "You mentioned discussing childhood, and I fell into some memories. I'm sure you know what that's like."

She sits back, as I knew she would. "I don't like talking about that."

"And there is no need right now. How is your mom?"

Her smile brightens. "Really good. Thank you for recommending that treatment facility."

"Of course. I am glad they can help her … "

We chat about nothing for a time, and it's easy and convivial and boring as hell. But this is the job. I am being groomed for CEO when Dad retires, which means I take the high-end clients out for lazy lunches and, on occasion, help them in the courtroom. Essentially, I pretend to be their friend until I need to be their lawyer. The job is so simple I can do it with my eyes closed, and there are times when I've done exactly that. But that doesn't mean I enjoy it.

I don't.

In fact, I've grown to hate it. Knowing what's coming as CEO, it feels like every day I'm another step closer to a noose. I cannot and will not run West Media the way my father does. To date, I still do not know what other illegal operations we are into, and I wish I would never need to know any of the details. But I am not naïve enough to think I could just shut it down without repercussions. June was smart when she pointed out that it's probably

not possible to simply step away from whatever
Dad's gotten us into. It'll be a process.

Assuming the law doesn't catch up to us first.

Time to wrap this shit up. "Rena, you seem sleepy. Is
your driver out there, or—"

"Why?" She drunkenly giggles. "Do you want to
take me to bed?"

I laugh. "Pretty sure you're halfway there now,
aren't you?"

She yawns. "Not for sleeping."

"Let's get you home."

"Mm, okay," she purrs into my ear. "West Media
really is full service, aren't you?"

After an uncomfortable laugh, I grab the check and
walk her out to her town car. When she tries to
pull me in, I give a chuckle. "I'd love to come
along, but you have that apology video to do, and I
must have a stern conversation with your agent so
he knows how to do his job the next time you say
something off the cuff like that. As far as your
comment is concerned, when an interviewer brings
up women's rights, what are you going to tell
them?"

She huffs and flatly parrots, "That women deserve
the same rights as everyone else."

"That's right. No more talking about *barefoot and pregnant*, okay?"

Another huff. "But what's so wrong about that?"

"Because equal rights sell, Rena. You want to keep being an influencer, don't you?"

She nods. "Thanks, Anderson. This is why I keep coming back to West Media. You really are the best."

"Anytime. Off you go." I shut her door and pat the roof twice before heading for my car. On my way there, I text June again. Maybe this will be the one she decides to read. It's the hope that keeps me texting her.

No response. So, I call.

She doesn't pick up.

I can hardly blame her. If my father hadn't gotten into debt with Andre Moeller, then June wouldn't have been kidnapped. I wasn't involved with any of that—I didn't know anything about it whatsoever. But if I hadn't pretended she was my fiancée, she never would have been kidnapped in the first place. So, it's my fault in a way.

It was also my idea to lie to Dad about her continuing to be kidnapped, and everything that happened after that lie is definitely my fault. That thought haunts me.

If I hadn't lied about her being my fiancée, then she wouldn't have been kidnapped. If I hadn't lied and said she was *still* kidnapped, then Dad never would have sent me on the ride along with Moss to earn her ransom from him. Those men at the warehouse might still be alive if I hadn't been there. The firefight only broke out because I had shoved my hand in my pocket, and one of the guys saw my gun when I did it.

In that respect, I am guilty of their deaths.

It weighs on me. A lot. But I can't do anything to fix it, and I can fix whatever is wrong between me and June. I have to. I love her.

-

4

JUNE

Wallace takes a deep breath and blows it out quickly. "I am afraid I have to let you go, June."

"You what?" I can hardly believe my ears. I certainly don't want to.

"It's nothing personal. A business decision—"

"What the hell kind of business decision starts with letting go of one of your top attorneys?" I can't keep my outburst in. I'm pissed.

"You are a top attorney. That's why this is so hard for me—

"For *you*? It's hard *for you*?"

He sighs and rubs his bald spot the way he does when he's uncomfortable. "I know this is hard on you, too, June. I hate letting you go, but this is financial. We are cutting costs, and to do that, we have to let some of our people go."

"Why not Madi? Or—"

"If I had a choice in the matter, you would not be my pick."

"If? Are you saying you don't have a choice?"

His lips bunch up. "I don't make all the calls here. You know that."

"Yes, you do … " But he has bosses he answers to, too. And those bosses are friends with Elliot West. West Media often sends their clients to us for their taxes. That's the only way this makes any sense. He's angry we tricked him, and now, he's getting me fired because he's a giant prick who wants everything his way.

Fuck me.

"… so you see, it's just a matter of numbers, and—

"I am worth more than you pay me, Wallace. You know I am. How much have I saved our clients? How much money have I made for the firm? I caught the error Madi made on the Ventriss account. They would have left us if I hadn't caught that, and you know it. You need me here."

"The decision is final, and you cannot argue your way out of it. I know that's hard for a lawyer to hear—"

"Does Elliot West have anything to do with this?"

He freezes up like someone rebooted him. He blinks rapidly, and his cheeks flush. "I, um … I don't know what you're talking about. Who is that?"

"Do yourself a favor and never play poker, Wallace." I get up and head for the door.

"I will write you a letter of recommendation, June. A glowing one. Your severance package will be generous, as well. If you need—"

I whip around. "I needed a job, Wallace."

He winces at that. "I know. I'm sorry."

Stomping to my desk, I force myself to keep it all inside. The hurt, the anger. The betrayal. This was a financial decision, I'm sure of it. Elliot West threatened to withhold his clients from us. Their billing runs in the millions every year. What could I possibly say or do to argue my way over Elliot's favor?

Not a damn thing.

Garrett sees me, and I will not break down in front of him. Not here. Not now. He gently asks, "Hey, what's going on?"

"I'm out." I gather my things.

"Did Wallace fire you?" he asks with a gasp.

"Laid-off is the official story, but yeah."

"Fuck him! He can't do that! Doesn't he know what you—"

"Yeah. He knows." I zip up my bag, ready to get the hell out. "I'll call you, Garrett. Just need to cool down."

He nods. "If I can do anything—"

"I'll let you know." Marching to the elevator, I want to scream. But then I smell Madi's perfume nearby, and I want to run.

"Guess it's really not your month, June," she says smugly.

When I face her, she stands there, arms crossed and smirking. Through gritted teeth, I ask, "How's that?"

"First, that dreadful bout of food poisoning combined with the flu—which no one believes, by the way—and then you get fired." She shakes her head in fake pity. "I wonder if it's karma. What could you have done to deserve this bad luck? Guess we'll never know. Poor thing. Oops. Bad phrasing. With no job, you really will be poor soon. I'd hate to see you out on the street like a common—"

"You have the rest of your life to be an asshole. Take today off."

She gasps. "Excuse you?"

"One of the best parts of leaving this place is I will never have to see you again."

"I was just showing my concern."

"You were showing your ass, and you know it." Where the hell is the elevator?

"You're just upset, June," she says dismissively. "I understand—"

"Oh, Madi. How could you understand anything? You're as simple as the dress you're wearing."

She huffs in derision. "How dare you!"

"Madison." I smile at her, knowing I will never have to again. Hell, I'm almost giddy at the thought. "I would tell you to go play in traffic, but I'm worried you're so intellectually void that you would actually consider it, and I might be held liable, so I'll leave you with this. Your mother should have stuck to her guns when she asked for a back rub the night you were conceived."

The elevator doors open, so I walk in. When I face her again, she stands there, mouth agape. Garrett, some five feet behind her, shouts, "You're my hero, June!" as the doors close.

That felt amazing. I'd been holding that in for years, and for once in my life, I thought of what I wanted to say right in the moment. The feeling wears off by the time I reach the lobby, though. I said what I wanted to when it came to Madi, but there is nothing to say to fix being fired.

Not with Elliot West holds all the cards.

I half wonder if this is why Callie was out today. She's dating one of the firm's board members. Did she know about this, or did he keep her out of the office to prevent her from seeing the carnage? I guess it could be that she's taking a personal day for herself but the timing is too coincidental, and I'm seeing conspiracies everywhere I turn. It's hard not to.

Elliot West is on every recent disaster in my life. First, he gets my payment frozen. Then, he gets me kidnapped. And then, he walks into my apartment like he owns the place and steals back the money I earned. Finally, he gets me fired.

Except, is freezing my payment really the first thing he did to fuck me over?

No. He raised Anderson to be a little monster when we were kids. Elliot never showed him any warmth or love as a child. All Elliot ever did was belittle him. So, when Anderson had a crush on me, he belittled me, thinking that was how to show affection. When

I snapped back at him, it only spurred him on. It messed up our entire dynamic, and he bullied me for years. I hated him back then.

Which is why I was super confused the night of my auction.

I shake my head at myself as I walk home. Thank God it stopped raining because walking home in that would have been so much worse. I am shaking because I'm angry. Elliot is a fucking monster. I want to make him pay. But I don't know how.

He's ruthless. He's rich and powerful.

I'm an unemployed tax attorney with too much student debt.

It's not a fair fight. Not even close. I need an upper hand in this and —

My phone goes off. Another text from Anderson. I don't know what to do. Read it, and let him know I'm alive? Or ignore it and plod on? I could give in to feeling sorry for myself. It's hard not to. But self-pity won't get me anywhere good, and I need to do something. I have to fix a part of my life, or today goes down as an abject failure of a day.

Maybe Anderson will have some idea about what to do when it comes to his father.

I sigh deeply and flick the message open. There's a string of them, but they all say basically the same thing. "I'm sorry," or "This is all my fault," or "Can we talk?" I don't want to talk about us. Things are too complicated between us. I want to talk about his dad, and doing that via text seems like a bad idea. If we meet up, I can steer the conversation to Elliot.

So, I send, "Meet me at Guerrero's Coffee at four."

"I'll be there."

That gives me just enough time to get home, shower, debate for an hour whether this is a smart move, and get prettied up. Before I can tuck my phone away, a raindrop splats on the screen. A freezing downpour begins.

Super.

5

JUNE

Guerrero's Coffee is a quaint little out-of-the-way shop. Being off the main drag, most people walk right past without noticing it. But the charming painted white brick interior and wooden accents make the place homey, and the unobservant are missing out on a real gem of Boston.

I almost feel bad bringing Anderson here. It's like sharing a secret I'm not ready to share with him yet.

That twinge makes me wonder. Not long ago, I'd thought we had something incredible. Something poets write about. But after everything I have been put through because of his father, I don't know.

When I see him, though, he still takes my breath away.

Anderson West is tall and dreamy with muscles. His blue eyes peer deep, and his smile is devilish in just the right ways. When he sees me, he rakes his fingers through his black hair. It's styled casually, but sometimes he smooths it back. I like it both ways. In fact, I like everything about him, which is what makes this so confusing. He wears a fitted black cashmere sweater that looks soft enough to bury my face in and dark blue jeans with black boots. When he stands to greet me, my heart catches in my throat.

I care far more about Anderson than I should. It might be the L-word, but I can't let myself think about that. I have to be in more control than that. After losing control when I was kidnapped, I crave control more than I can put into words.

We have a short, stiff hug before I sit to join him at the small two-top. There are two ceramic mugs on the table, and one sits atop a warmer. I smile at the mug, a question in my eyes.

"I remembered what you ordered from the delivery place the other day and took a swing. Hazelnut latte, right?"

Crap. That's so sweet of him. "Yeah. Thanks." When I sip it, it's perfect. Damn him for making it so hard to stay angry.

"So, why did you finally respond to my texts?"

"Because we need to talk," I say too sharply. Can't help it.

"What's wrong, June? Whatever it is, we can fix it."

"You have ruined my life. Not sure how we fix that."

He pauses, which is satisfying. I'm not used to seeing Anderson caught off guard. His voice lowers as he asks, "And how did I manage that exactly?"

"Well, the first time was when we were kids—"

"And you know how sorry I am for what I did back then."

"And the second time, as adults."

He thinks for a minute. "I will do everything in my power to make up to you what's happened. The kidnapping, the thing with my dad walking in on us and taking your money, all of it. June, there is nothing I won't do to repair what's been done—"

"Elliot got me fired, Anderson."

"I beg your pardon?"

"Your father wants to punish me for what we did," I say with a frustrated shrug. "He wants me destitute and suffering, I guess, and so he got me fired for what we did."

"What *I* did, and what makes you think he could get you fired?"

"Don't do that. I did this as much as you did. I went along with your lie. Don't try to take all the responsibility when I made that choice, too." I might not have much control over this, but I'll be damned if he takes that from me. I went into this with my eyes wide open. The consequences are mine as much as his.

"Fine, but what makes you think he had anything to do with this?"

"My boss all but confirmed it. When I asked him about your father, he sputtered and hemmed and hawed until I gave up on an answer. It was Elliot. I know it in my bones."

His brow lines. Anderson's disagreement face. "My father is powerful in certain circles, but I can't believe he'd come after you. This is personal, and forgive me, but I don't think you rate on his scale of what's personal to him."

"There is no other reason for me to be laid off. I'm a hard worker, I'm there whenever they need me, and I bring in a ton of money to the firm." I grumble, "But apparently, not as much as Elliot West does."

Anderson's hands ball into fists as his jaw tightens. "June, I am so sorry. My father is the world's biggest asshole. He's going to get what's coming to him—"

"I don't think he will."

"Why is that?"

I huff bitterly. "I realize you grew up in an ivory tower, Anderson, but I grew up on the ground, so let me tell you how it works. Men like your father never get what's coming to them. They flit through life, fucking good people over, and they face no consequences. You should be familiar with the dynamic. Have you ever faced a consequence in your life?"

His eyes narrow on me. He spits out, "Once or twice."

"And did the slap on the wrists sting, or did you even notice it?"

"June, I get what you're saying. I'm a lawyer, too, remember? I help rich people deal with consequences—"

"No. You help spoiled brats escape consequences."

He stretches his hands in frustration. "Since when did this become about me, exactly?"

"It's always been about you, hasn't it? Everything in your life is all about you. Hell, even the night you bid on me, it was because you couldn't stand the idea of another man putting his hands on me!"

He sits back, trying to calm down. But I don't want to calm down. I'm pissed off. Anderson is quieter now. "June, I only did that because I care about you. I wanted to keep you safe from whoever might have won. If you —"

"But you can't keep me safe from you, can you?"

"What's that supposed to mean?"

"It's not fair of me to lay this at your feet, and I don't. Not all of it. But the fact remains that the moment you won my auction was the moment my life fell the fuck apart." A hot knot forms in my throat.

"We will fix it. Together. I know you're angry right now —"

"I might never stop being angry when it comes to you."

He winces. "Fine. Be angry. But shutting me out won't fix anything."

"Yeah, actually. It will." I get up and stomp out of the café with Anderson hollering behind me. But if I don't leave now, I never will. I cannot have him in my life. He makes everything so fucking complicated. Tears sting my eyes, but I ignore them as I make my way from the coffeeshop. It doesn't matter how much I care about Anderson, because the end result is the same.

Love does not conquer all.

Just as I'm about to cross the street, a hand grabs my shoulder to spin me around. As I turn, I punch. I'm not getting taken again! But it's Anderson, and he catches my fist in his palm. "Sorry to surprise you like that—"

"Just leave me alone!"

"I can't do that, June."

Tears streak down my face. "Why the hell not? I just want to be left alone! You're not good for me, don't you get that? This is too complicated. It's too hard!"

He looks crushed, and I hate that I've crushed him. But now he knows how I feel. Maybe that's a good thing.

He begs, "Don't say that. You don't mean it."

"I do," I sob. "This has to stop."

"No—"

"Whatever this is, whatever we are, I have to end it. Now. Before things get worse."

"My father will pay—"

"Your father will get away with it. Just like he gets away with everything else. I can't do this anymore. I'm done, Anderson. I don't want a relationship with you. I want to forget I ever knew you."

At that, he stops speaking. He just stands there, dazed.

I can't tell if his silence is a relief or not. But I run across the street and away from him. I have to get home. All I want is to put on my pajamas and to pour a big bottle of vodka into a tub of vanilla ice cream and smash my face into it. It's not just Anderson I want to forget about. It's every damn thing in my life.

6

ANDERSON

I don't know how long I stand on the sidewalk where June shattered me. But it's long enough that the sun finished going down, and it's too cold out here for me to stay. I stumble toward my car in a daze. Her words carved out all the happiness she had put into me. Every bit of June-shaped joy in my heart is gone.

My father has won again.

It's enough to make me drive to his apartment in the city. I want to beat the shit out of that man. He took away my money. He made me complicit in the murder of three people. And now, he's taken June from me.

When she said it was my father, I didn't want to believe it. I tried to push back against that narrative, but every counterargument she threw at me made too much sense. I don't know how he did it. Sure, we send her firm clients, but I didn't think we had that much influence over them. It's startling to consider. But if we have that much influence over a simple tax firm, then where else do we wield influence?

Did this happen because he called in a favor or because he's blackmailing someone? Did firing June pay off a debt someone owes him? If so, what is her destitution worth to him?

Me. It's worth me.

Dad always talks about how smart June is. He did this, knowing she would put two and two together. He left his fingerprints on this for her to find. For her to blame me. He did this to make her break up with me. Son of a bitch, it fucking worked.

My head digs back against my car seat as I sit on the street below my father's apartment. If I go up there now, I won't control myself. It will be brief but violent. I cannot do that to my mom. That woman is a saint, and she is always home. I can't fight him with her around.

I have to leave.

So, instead of storming into his place, I storm into mine. It's a large corner apartment in downtown with floor-to-ceiling windows and an expansive bedroom. Everything is decorated in blues and grays, perfect for relaxing after a long day.

Today has been the longest day.

On the drive over, my day shuttles through my mind. Between the pall of my father hanging over my head, spending too much time setting Rena up with a proper paparazzi pic to deflect her followers from unsubscribing, and getting colossally dumped in the middle of the street, I am so fucking done with today. I take responsibility for the parts I played in getting dumped. It was my idea to blackmail my father. My idea for June to play the role of my fiancée. I own those mistakes. But everything else has been his fucking fault.

And I want him to pay.

The part of this that sits on my shoulders feels like it might crush me under the weight of it. I can't take back what I did. But I also can't make it up to her if she won't see me. I like fixing things. It makes me feel useful. But there is no fixing this. Not really. I know that.

She said she wishes she never met me. How in the fuck do I fix that?

I fling my keys into the bowl on the hall table as soon as I walk in. It feels good to throw things. Maybe I should go to one of those axe-throwing bars. I could fling sharp things and drink cheap beer until I get drunk enough to pathetically call June and beg her to take me back like I'm some kind of breathing cliché. Nah. I'd probably end up dropping an axe on my foot, with the way my luck is.

Pfft. Luck.

I used to think of myself as the luckiest bastard on the planet. Born into wealth and great genetics, there was no pretending to be anything but who I am. A rich, handsome man who is in a position to end up with a lot of power. Women liked me, and men wanted to be my friend. All of that got turned on its axis the day I met June Devlin.

High school feels like a thousand years ago. But I still remember her shy smile. The tentative look in her eyes. The way she walked into the room — confident, but she knew she was out of her element. Appleton Academy is one of the most prestigious prep schools in Boston. She was there on scholarship. And I was the little dickhead who pointed out that she didn't belong there.

I don't excuse who I was then. Sure, I was just a kid, but so was she. She didn't deserve to be talked to the way I talked to her. She deserved kindness and empathy, all the things someone should show a new person. But I didn't hold back. I held court, encouraging my friends to give her a hard time, too. They did until she gave us shit right back.

And that was our four years of high school. Me, attacking. Her, counterpunching. Back then, she didn't know the reason I went after her was I confused name-calling for tenderness. She didn't know my father never showed me anything but his disappointment and mockery. She only knew I was terrible to her.

I deserved her vitriol back then. Every bit of it. But now? We made up over all of that. She said she forgave me. As things progressed between us, it became more than how it started—the auction got things going, but we kept them going.

Until now.

Pacing a hole in my carpet is not going to solve this, but I don't know what else to do. She won't talk to me. She wishes I had never come into her life. June is all I have ever wanted in life, and I can't have her because of my father.

And my couple of screw-ups, but mostly because of him.

My phone rings, and I scramble for it, hoping for good news. I answer without even looking at the caller ID. "June—"

"Not June," a familiar voice says.

I check the ID and it's an unknown number. "Who—"

"It is Moss, your father's—"

"I know who you are," I growl. Moss is my father's pet enforcer. The one who dragged me on that ride-along. The one who shot and killed three men in front of me. "What do you want?"

His Italian-tainted Bostonian accent always throws me for a loop, and the longer he speaks, the thicker it is. "You will come with me to another job. Your father wishes I educate you on the details of the business. Be ready by—"

"No." I hang up.

But he calls again. "We were cut off—"

And I hang up again. That was why I answered this time. I want him to get the message that I am not doing this. I am not my father's fucking errand boy. Especially not today.

Yet, he calls again.

This time, I answer, "Moss, I will not be doing that with you. Never. If Dad wants another errand boy, he can hire one. I am not for sale. My morals are not for sale. If you think I will be handled into submission, you have another think coming."

"But Anderson, he thinks this is a perfect job for you. Nothing like the last one, I promise."

"It will be nothing like the last one because I won't be there. I'm not fucking stupid, Moss. I know why he wants me there. Do not call me again." I hang up and turn my phone off. I hadn't wanted to turn it off in case June reached out, but this is bigger than our fight. Involvement in a criminal situation will end badly for me, and Dad will make sure of it. Last time, he made sure to have footage of the murders. This time, who knows how far he would go to keep me in line?

That's the whole point of all this. He doesn't like it when we aren't under his control. The bastard froze my assets when he thought I was spending too frivolously. I'm thirty years old. He had no fucking right except that my accounts are under the business' purview. We keep everything tied to the business, so in case something were to go wrong legally, then our assets are not available for scrutiny. Or so the theory went.

A mistake I intend to rectify.

But first, I need to get June back. To do that, I have to see Dad. Even if she never wants to see me again, I still owe her four hundred thousand dollars. And I will pay her. The question is, what will it cost me?

-

7

JUNE

My place isn't extravagant, but I have savings, which gives me a sense of predictability in a chaotic world. It's comfy, too. Buttery yellows, white, and a few pops of grass green to make everything feel lively without being loud. It's not much, but it's home.

After a long hot shower full of crying, I slip my pajamas on and root around for the bottle of cheap vodka I bought a long time ago. It has to be in the back of my cabinet. I just know it. Feeling around back there turns up an old cake plate I thought I got rid of years ago and a candleholder I bought in college, but no vodka. So, I try the next cabinet and sure enough, there it is. My security vodka.

I love this brand because, for whatever reason, it works like liquid Xanax. I just have to drink enough of it, and soon, I won't give a shit about anything.

Vanilla ice cream takes the sharp edge off the cheapness of the vodka, so I grab the quart I keep in the freezer for emergencies. But when I peel the lid back, it's almost gone.

I've had a lot of emergencies lately.

"Well," I tell no one but me, "it'll have to do." I pour it in anyway, give it a stir, and plop down in front of the TV for some romantic movies to make me cry more and get it out of my system so I can function like an adult again. The moment the synth piano and sax-heavy opening theme of *Baby Boom* comes on, out come the tears.

The vodka cannot work fast enough.

Baby Boom is an old eighties rom com my mom loved, and we used to watch it around Valentine's Day when she got mad about my dad. She joked that she should have moved to upstate New York and started a baby food company just like the heroine because I made fun of her mushy food. Mom is my favorite person, but a good cook, she is not.

I wish I could tell her what's going on. I wish I could—"

Someone knocks at my door. That's weird. I haven't ordered food. Pretty sure Anderson knows not to show up after everything I said to him. I could check the peephole, but ever since I saw a thing on the news about putting your eye up to peepholes lets bad guys know where your head is, I've been shouting through the door instead. "Yes?"

"It's me, June. Open up," Callie shouts back.

I fling the locks and throw the door open. She's gorgeous always—long, shiny blond hair, deep brown eyes, the kind of body men lose their minds over—but tonight, she looks different. Worried. It panics me. More bad news? "What's wrong?" I ask as I pull her in.

She laughs. "You're asking me that?" She holds up a heavy bag from the grocery store. "I just heard about everything, honey, and I am so fucking sorry, so I wanted to bring you supplies for the night." My heart warms, but that only makes me cry more. She comes for a hug. "Sweetie, I'm so sorry."

"How did you find out? Did he call you?"

She scoffs at that. "I'm not talking to him. Let me get the groceries put away, and we'll talk."

"Okay, you talk, I'll drink."

"Whatever you need." She scoots off to the kitchen to stow whatever she bought me, and I resume my plopped position on the couch. When she joins me, there's a bag of chips under her arm, a pint of ice cream in her hand, a cocktail in the other, and a bag of microwaved popcorn in her teeth. Somehow, she gracefully manages to sit without spilling or dropping any of that. "What's this one?"

"*Baby Boom*. An old favorite."

"I would have figured you'd be on a horror kick. It's your favorite genre. I thought you had to have a go-to splatter fest in mind for such things."

"Not enough horror movies show the girl going after the boy. Figured sappy rom coms will work to get the tears out."

She nods. "Oh. Okay."

"So, is everything alright with you? With your personal day, I—"

She huffs and turns on her seat to face me. "Sweetie, I am so sorry for that. Daniel didn't tell me anything at first. He said he wanted to go out on his boat for the day—"

"I thought you looked tanner."

She shrugs. "He didn't say anything about you getting laid off until we got back home. Said he didn't think it would be good for me to see it happen. God, I'm so sorry, and he is on my shit list for the next week over this. I wish I could have been there for you, June. I hate this."

I blink at her. "Wait, what?"

"Oh my god, please tell me I didn't just break the news about you getting laid off—"

"No! No, no, no!

"Phew."

I laugh and shake my head. "I mean, yeah, I'm pissed about getting laid off. It's certainly not helping things. But I'm upset because I broke up with Anderson today."

"Oh no." She looks heartbroken for me, and I love her for that, but I hate it at the same time. Pity grates on me. Always has. Especially when it comes from the incredibly fortunate. On top of being conventionally pretty, Callie Brown comes from a wealthy family. The kind of wealthy family who summers in the best of New England towns. But I know her heart is in the right place, so I try not to bristle at it. "Sweetie, what happened?"

"Well, I told you about the whole kidnapping fiasco, right?"

"That you and Anderson tried to scam his dad for the money Anderson owes you?"

I nod. "He got the money in cash. Still hasn't told me how he convinced his dad to fork it over, but I know it was something illegal. Anyway, the money was sitting in a bag on the table when we were going at it like bunnies. We had just finished when his dad walked in, said a few choice words, grabbed the money, and left."

"Holy shit, are you kidding me?"

"I wish I were. That's bad enough, but when Wallace was firing me, he kept saying something about not having a choice in the matter, and it clicked. I asked him if Elliot West had anything to do with this and Callie, he didn't say it outright, but he practically choked on his words. Didn't say no. Didn't deny it at all. Just promised me a glowing letter of recommendation, blah, blah, blah. I know this was Elliot. Every fucking disaster in my life has been because of him."

She sighs. "I am so sorry, honey. Is that why you broke up with Anderson? Too complicated?"

"Yes, oh my god, how is it that it took you two seconds to figure that out, but Anderson was still in some kind of fugue state of denial on that?"

"He doesn't want to think he's not enough to overcome the shitshow that is his father."

I huff and sit back. "Yeah, well, I guess I get that. The truth is, it all sort of bubbled out of me and onto him. It's weird to admit it, but I kind of broke up with him on a whim. Like I started down a rhetorical path and couldn't get out of it."

"Do you regret breaking up with him?"

"No. Yes. Both."

She smiles, her eyes still full of pity, but I can't bring myself to care right now. "We all say things we don't mean when we're upset. I'm sure you can walk this back if you want to. That man is in love with you."

I snort in derision. "Hardly."

"Oh, please. Who scams their own father to pay some woman without there being emotions involved?"

"He hates his father. Those are the emotions involved here."

"Not buying it," she says, sipping her cocktail. "But the better question, really, the only important one, is what do you want?"

"I want my job back."

"Okay, what do you want that we can actually control?"

"Figures you'd ask the hard questions."

She smirks and nudges my shoulder. "Come on. Out with it. Do you want Anderson back?"

My heart lurches at the thought. "Part of me does. But part of me wants to run screaming into the hills just to get away from all the craziness he brings into my life."

"Hmm," she says between sips. "You know how they say you should never make any big life decisions during a traumatic event?"

"Yeah."

"You've had, like, seven traumatic events in the past two months or less. Maybe *don't* make any big decisions right now?"

"That might be the best advice I have ever received."

We watch the film for a couple of minutes, before Callie asks, "Are you drinking vanilla ice cream? No judgment."

"I'm drinking vanilla ice cream mixed with vodka. It's mostly vodka. Didn't have enough ice cream to make it good."

"I brought more vanilla."

I grin at her. "Because you're the best person on the planet."

She giggles and jogs off to get the vanilla for me. I chomp on some chips and popcorn, deciding I need chips more than popcorn. It's nice to have her over. Even if she didn't text first—wait.

Did she?

I check my phone. The rain got to it. Crap. "Can you bring some rice in a plastic baggie?"

"Need me to microwave it?"

"No, raw rice."

She leans out past my cabinets. "It's not for hot water bottle purposes?"

"Nope. My phone."

She winces. "Your luck sucks, honey. Thought it might have been for cramps. Be right there."

I wish she were wrong about my luck, but she's not. Today has been utter garbage. Maybe tomorrow will be better.

-

8

ANDERSON

When I wake up in the morning, I'm still enraged at my father, but something else has come over me. I am glad I didn't run up to his apartment and kick his ass. That would not have solved anything, and if Moss had been there, he might have started something on Dad's behalf. That guy is always armed, so it wouldn't have gone in my favor, and Mom would have been beside herself. I made the right call by coming home instead.

It's given me time to think.

Dad responds to very little, aside from verifiable threats and outright violence. But he respects people who stick to their guns, and I am not about to back down over this. I will go to him. Tell him this isn't up for debate. Demand not only that he unfreeze my accounts but also that he gives me the cash. I earned it. Three dead bodies say so.

A wave of discontent threatens to settle over me, but I am undeterred. Time to see my father.

After a quick shower and dressing for the weather, I take the Jag for the four-hour long drive to the New York harbor, where he keeps his sailing yacht. It's the fourth Saturday of the month, which means he will be entertaining clients on his yacht. By the time I arrive, he will be doing the precheck to make sure everything is ready to go by the time everyone shows up. Can't let them see you sweat, he likes to say.

Dad handles everything himself. That's why he wanted a relatively small yacht. No staff. According to him, staff are liabilities on a yacht. If they screw up, then a client could get injured, or worse. Never mind, there are professional licensed and insured companies he could hire for the job. Never mind, they have better reflexes than he does at his age. Nope. He has to do it all himself.

It's the perfect time to get him alone.

As I cross the bridge, I see the harbor isn't frozen over this year. It should be smooth sailing. No surprise there. Elliot West always gets calm waters and easy passage to everything.

Not today.

I park by the docks and jog out to his boat. The Sea Star is so named for all the stars we have helped over the years. Mom's idea. It's as close to kitsch as Dad would allow.

There he is, looking every bit the navy man he thinks himself to be, in his midnight blue wool peacoat. The truth is, Dad avoided all things military easily enough. No draft when he was coming of age, and his father didn't want another sailor in the family. He was so disappointed when Dad bought the yacht.

Grandfather said there was too much death on the water. Had a fear of it after his Swift boat went down in the war. He never spoke about it. I only knew because Grandmother told me once. I didn't understand why he wouldn't go swimming with me and my brother, so I asked. He walked away, but she explained a little.

As soon as Dad sees me, there's a knife in my gut. I hate that he looks pleased at my presence. I would have preferred anxiety on his face. "Ahoy!"

Ahoy— Like he's a fucking waterman. I move to step onto the gangplank and start, "Hey—"

"Hay is for horses, and you know what to say before you come aboard another man's ship."

I barge on anyway. "Not playing your games today."

"By all rights of the water, I can throw you overboard for that, stowaway."

"And by rights of the land, I could have shot you for breaking into June's apartment, so maybe we won't play that game today, huh?"

He snorts a laugh. "You? You'd have to be a better shot than what I saw in the warehouse footage."

I've been in his presence for under a minute, and I'm ready to strangle him. But I will not give him the satisfaction of letting him see me lose my cool. I will remain aloof. It's one of the few things he responds to. "By that comment, I take it we are here alone?"

"Yes. Why have you come to see me here? You've never shown any interest in my hobbies."

"Same to you," I say with too much emotion. Dammit. Shut that shit down. "I came to speak to you alone."

"Oh? Should I be worried?" He says it like a joke. Like I'm a joke to him.

"It must really grind your gears that you've been grooming me for thirty years, and I don't live up to your expectations. Huh. I almost pity you."

"Don't be tiresome, Anderson. Why are you here?"

Tiresome is what he calls me when I've struck a nerve. It's a win for me. "Fine, I won't beat around the bush. Did you get June fired?"

He sighs and runs his fingers along some part of the sidewall. I think he does it to have something to do while not looking me in the eye. "We have a stellar Human Resources Department at West Media. Did you know that?"

"Of course, but—"

"According to them, lying about being kidnapped and taking time off to spend it in bed with your new beau instead is a fireable offense. Strange to think there are consequences to one's actions, hmm?"

"That was my idea. My doing. If you want to fire anyone, fire me."

At that, he makes eye contact. Or rather, he looks into my eyes as he gives the most condescending smile imaginable. "Son, throwing yourself in the line of fire for her? Come now, you must know how pathetic that is. Trying to win her back, are you?"

"You got her fired to stress her out and make her break up with me, right?"

He chuckles under his breath. "She's not one of us, Anderson. The moment someone of her ilk panics about money, they either do anything they can to keep a hold of it or they do something stupid. I see she chose the latter."

"What do you mean she would do anything to keep a hold of it?"

"Of you, if I weren't clear enough for you to follow."

"What money do I have?" I ask angrily. "You froze my accounts!"

He shrugs. "Then I would think you'd do well to remember who your loyalties truly belong to. An unemployed tax attorney or your own flesh and blood. It's really not much of a choice, now is it?"

"So, that's it?" I smirk. "That's the play?"

"What?"

"You're trying to make me choose between you and her. You've always been on me about getting a girlfriend. Someone I can commit to. I brought you June. She didn't buckle under your interrogation in the den. You called her smart. That must have scared you—"

"Don't be preposterous!"

I laugh. "Oh my god. I feel like a fool."

"Well, you certainly sound like one—"

"You knew June would figure out what is going on behind the scenes. All the illegal shit you're up to. If she got close enough to the business, then she would know, right? And you can't control her like you control everyone else. She told me about when you asked her to sign a prenup, and she told you she would be happy to do it. So you know you can't lord your money over her. Which means you had to break us up. If it wasn't going to happen now, it would have been later, I'm sure of it." I laugh again in his face. "You're a coward."

He growls, "Watch your tone with me!"

"No, I don't think I'll be doing that. And you will pay me back. The four hundred thousand cash is mine." I grit out, "I earned it. You have the footage to prove that I did."

"That money was for a non-existent ransom—"

"That money was to be a bridge between us because you sent me to either die or kill someone else for a measly quarter of a million dollars. That's what that man owed you. That's what you sent us out to collect. You were willing to risk me for a quarter of a million. I've seen you blow that on a weekend in Vegas, Dad. So, don't act like that money is anything other than a payment to make me feel better about having you for a father!"

"You are out of line—"

"And you will unfreeze my accounts, as well. We are done with this controlling bullshit. You want me to be CEO? Then treat me like a fucking adult. I not only demand it. I expect it out of you."

"You can expect the moon to be plaid, but that doesn't mean it will happen. Until you fall in line, you will obey me."

Again, I laugh at him. "Obey you? What makes you think — "

He snarls, "You will do as I instruct. When Moss calls you, the missions are not optional. You will come to work on time. You will show Cole the ropes, now that he's joining the company. Anderson, you will be the man the company needs. You do not have a choice in the matter. And until you do everything I tell you to do, you will get nothing. End of discussion." His eyes dart over my shoulder.

I glance back there, half expecting to see Moss with a gun pointed at my head, but it's worse. Clients are coming down the dock. Can't very well talk about any of this in front of them. I whip back around to him. "This isn't over."

But he smiles, so fucking pleased with himself. "It was over before it began. Don't forget who owns you, Anderson. Ta."

I wave at the clients, smiling. But quietly, I tell him, "I am going to make you pay, Elliot. Safe trip. I'd hate for you to drown."

At that, he scowls. "You know not to say that word on a boat."

"Oh, right. How silly of me." I smile and trot across the gangplank. "Good luck and goodbye."

"Anderson!" he shouts my name like a curse word.

I know the old sailor superstitions. If I have to use them to get under his skin, so be it. Instead of answering, I give a friendly wave while I jog past the clients and back to my car.

9

ANDERSON

The drive home feels longer than the drive to the harbor. I'm not sure how, but it does. Maybe because I feel deflated somehow. He's right. He has all the cards. What the hell do I have? A bad attitude and no plan.

I hate being at his mercy, but it's been this way ever since Grandfather died. When Dad took control of the family, our money was bound up with his as a protection against liability. Allegedly. My inheritance from my grandparents is tied up in my trust, which slowly leaks money over the years. It's designed to help me not blow through it, but that means what I have now is a pittance compared to what I'm owed. I don't get the remainder until I turn forty, the age they deemed to be when someone is responsible.

Not to mention, I work for my father. Sure, I've been groomed for three decades to take over at the company, but that's not set in stone. He is in charge of how much I make. My vacation time. My sick time. Hell, even my retirement, so I'll be feeling the sting of his presence the rest of my life.

Fuck.

Not only that, now that I'm thinking about it. He also owns my apartment. How in the hell did I go along with all of this? In hindsight, it's crazy. But back when I agreed to all of this, it seemed like the smart thing to do. To protect the family's assets by tying them to the company. It was the logical thing to do. My cousins, my brothers. That's how generational wealth is passed down. By protecting it.

I never knew my father was some kind of criminal. Hell, I still don't know exactly what he does on that end of things. All I know is he risked my life for peanuts and expects me to thank him for the privilege. I punch the steering wheel in anger without thinking, and afterwards, I am glad I didn't set off the airbag. Though I'm not sure if I could. Feels like I could have—my hand aches.

Okay. Obviously, I'm not thinking clearly and that's exactly what I need to do. What do I want? June. My accounts. Her cash. How do I get them? That's where I come up short.

I have to get June her money. That comes before everything else. I cannot stand the thought of her hating me, but even if she does, I still need to pay her. She earned that money.

Whatever happens after that is up to her.

I'd like to figure out how to get her job back. I know she hated that place, but if she was angry enough to break up with me because she lost that job, then it means more to her than she lets on.

The problem is, tallying up my problems is not a solution. I have no idea how to fix any of this, and I am not good at being powerless. My skills lie in power and money, and I have neither at the moment. Perhaps that's where I need to start. Power truly comes from money, so that's my goal. Get my money back. Somehow.

Okay, new goal. Come up with a plan. No. Come up with a good plan.

Yeah, that was the problem with the other goal. I forgot the word good. Sure. That's it.

Rolling my eyes at myself, I park in the heated underground parking of my apartment building. I've been on the road for over eight hours today. But I'm wired. Too frustrated to feel anything other than annoyance and hunger. I'll grab a power bar and hit the gym on the first floor to burn this off. Nothing like a good workout to get my head clear. A clear head is better at planning. Some of my best ideas have come to me while I was on the indoor rower. Today will be no different.

A cute blonde in the elevator tries to flirt. "Haven't seen you around much, 522."

I recognize her from the building, but I have no idea what her apartment number is. The only thing I know her from is the gym, because she's there all the time. Thankfully, she's already sweaty and in her workout gear. I'll have the gym to myself. I give her a friendly smile. "My girlfriend keeps me busy, so I'm not around much anymore."

Her smile dies. "Oh. Lucky girl." She gets off at the third floor. "If she loses that title, come by and see me sometime. 301."

The doors close, and I'm grateful, because I didn't know how to tell her I am not interested. Not even if I were single. Though, I suppose, technically I am single. But it's temporary. This breakup will not stand. Probably.

What if June meant it, though? Doesn't matter now. Even if June never wants to see me again, I still wouldn't be interested in the cute blonde. I'm done with women like her. Maybe I'm judging her harshly, but I want a woman with more character than that. Hitting on someone you know is taken is hardly a good sign.

Finally, I reach my apartment door. When I throw it open, there's a letter on my floor like someone slipped it through the slit at the bottom of the door. Reading the letter, I'm ready to punch a hole through the drywall.

I have thirty days to vacate my apartment.

Clearly, I've pissed him off. My hands are shaking out of anger. I check my accounts on my phone. Still frozen. Which means I have the cash I keep in my safe—wait. Let's check.

The safe is behind a picture on my bedroom wall. Obvious, but useful. It's a fingerprint safe, but if anyone could break into it, they probably work for my father. The door springs open at my touch, and there inside is my cash. About two grand is snuggled up next to my handguns. Certainly not enough money for an apartment. Not with first, last, and deposit to consider.

If he's willing to go this fucking far, do I even still have a job?

I log into my work email, and since that's working, I'm still employed by West Media. At least I have that going for me. I shoot off an email to HR about getting my direct deposits sent to a new account. It's the first step in divorcing myself from Dad's tyranny, and there are many steps to go.

But I'm going to take them.

I'm going to take all of them.

A plan solidifies in my mind. He wants me to obey?

Fine. I will. I'll do all that he asks. I will become the ruthless asshole he wants me to be.

His games are nothing. Not in the grand scheme of things.

What he doesn't understand is, June and I are the real goal. Not the company. Not the family fortune. None of that. So, I will play along and be the protégé he's always wanted me to be.

The one thing a lifetime of waiting for his approval has taught me is how to hold my breath. I will wait him out. When the time is right, I will get my revenge and June's money. No matter what it takes.

10

JUNE

Why in the hell haven't I heard back from my interviews?

I hit the ground running this week. Callie had given me a pep talk when she came by Friday night, and she pointed out just how awesome I am at my job. And I am. I'm the best at what I do. I have the credentials, and I even have Wallace's glowing letter of recommendation. Since he laid me off, it's easy enough to talk about my lack of employment. A little uncomfortable, but that's how it goes. I'm a good interview, too. I know how to chat people up, get them interested in what I can do, all of that.

So, why in the hell hasn't anyone called me back? No emails, no texts, no nothing. It's unnerving to think I'm not as in-demand as I thought. Especially since I'm about to walk into another interview.

This one is at Chase and Gordon. A smaller firm, but I don't mind that. They cater to old money clients, those whose ancestors did things like found Boston and New York. People who have hospitals and schools named after relatives or themselves. They are big deals to both Boston and to history.

The building is small and old, but renovated and quite classy. They keep things stately and traditional. A little stiff for my tastes, but I can adjust. I *will* adjust if it means I have a job again.

My interview is with Vera Chase. Her assistant types something into her computer, then smiles and stands. "Follow me, Ms. Devlin."

Must have gotten the message, Vera is ready for me. I grab my bag and follow her down a narrow hallway. "These older buildings have so much history to them." Mostly a history of claustrophobia, but I will adjust. I have to.

"Oh yes, we love it here." She pauses at the door at the end of the hall. "Good luck."

"Thanks."

She opens the door for me, and the office is far more modern than I had expected. Quite large, brick interior, but everything else is brand new, from the state of the art treadmill by the window, to the three monitors for her computer. The wall appears to be a screen of some kind. Behind the glass desk is a woman in her mid-fifties, with short hair and a warm smile. Her pantsuit is black and sleek like her hair. She stands to greet me, "June, please come in. Have a seat."

I sit across the desk from her. "Love your office."

"Thank you. Love your resume."

I chuckle. "Thank you."

"This shows that you are more than qualified to join Chase and Gordon, but we like everyone to mesh well here. So, tell me about yourself."

"I'm a Boston native and I love it here, but I don't mind traveling for work. I recently scored a big account with—"

She holds up her hand. "Sorry, I should have been more specific. I meant to say, tell me about *yourself*. Not your job. Not your ambitions. But *you*."

Oh crap. Personal things. Let's see. Recently kidnapped, recently fired, and recently single.

"I like horror movies and American nineties music."

At that, she smirks. "Why horror?"

"When it's good, it's unpredictable. Like life. I think horror is probably the most honest genre of film. And women usually come out on top."

She chuckles. "And American nineties music?"

"It's kind of chaotic."

She laughs. "Chaotic?"

"The lyrics are either deeply personal or bordering on nonsensical. The production values are as good as anything we have now, but a lot of it still sounds raw."

"So you don't mind a bit of unpredictable chaos?"

Like my life recently? "In small, controlled doses, it's good."

That's good to hear, because things can get a little out of control here sometimes. We have clients of every age, every background, but our legacy clients demand a hands-on experience. Let me cut the crap —they expect to be coddled. Is that something you're comfortable with?"

I smile at that. "Every one of my clients at my old firm had the same expectations. It's my wheelhouse."

"Okay, I'm going to level with you. This isn't going to do me any good when it comes to negotiating your pay, but you're perfect for this role, and we are desperate for a new associate. You can expect to hear from us."

"That's great! I am so glad to hear that." This is exactly what I need. Chase and Gordon have a great reputation.

Vera walks me out and shakes my hand by the door. "Be seeing you, June."

I can't keep the smile from my face. "See you soon, Vera." For the first time in years, I actually have a skip in my step. After treating myself to a latte, I get home and hop into the shower to relax. I can't believe I got a job at Chase and Gordon. It's small, but prestigious. It will look great on my resume, and I can make some fantastic connections. More than that, it will irritate Elliot once he finds out I'm employed again.

It's perfect.

I get into my cozy loungewear and pour a cocktail to celebrate. This is amazing. I have to text Callie —wait. Email notification on my phone first. It's from Vera! I click it open and scan fast for the offer.

But it's not an offer. They're going with someone else.

No. I'm not taking this lying down. I call Vera up, hoping her assistant won't block me. To my surprise, Vera answers it herself. "June, how can I help you?"

"You left me with the impression I was your selection. It's been two hours. What happened?"

She takes a beat. "Are you going to make me say it?"

"Yes. Please."

"Okay. I am only telling you this because I like you, and if it were up to me, you would be my hire. But you're being blackballed, June."

I knew it. I fucking knew it. "How? Who?"

"I mentioned to a legacy client of mine that we'd be hiring you, and they said if I hired you, they couldn't do business at Chase and Gordon. He said he would tell everyone at the club about it, too. After that, I was bombarded by a bunch of our legacies. All of them would pull out of Chase and Gordon if you were on board here. I'm sorry, but my hands are tied."

It's all I can do not to start crying. "Thank you for your candor, Vera. I appreciate it. It's more than I got at my old firm."

"You're a great attorney. I'm sure you'll land on your feet."

"That's what I keep hearing. Best of luck to you."

"You, as well. Take care."

We hang up, and I'm beside myself. I didn't know Elliot would take things this far. He's wiping me out of my industry entirely. I'll have to move to some city where no one has ever heard of Elliot West, and where in the hell is that? Bangkok? No—he probably has a tailor there. Fuck! What am I going to do?

How am I going to pay my bills with no income? I don't have the money from the auction, I don't have a job. How long will I have an apartment? Or food? A quick check of my bank accounts tells me I have three months of living expenses covered. What about after that?

In the back of my mind, I hear my mother's voice. "You can always come home."

Except that I can't. I promised myself I would never do that. It's not that I don't love my family—I do. But they are like chaos. Good in small doses.

At my old firm, I thought I was building relationships with people. My clients loved me. But it wasn't enough. None of them would pick me over Elliot. Who would? Other than Anderson.

I take a deep breath. Just thinking his name resurrects the ache in my chest. I miss him. I don't want to, but I do. And if I reach out to him now as a jobless loser, I'll seem even more pathetic than I feel. Besides, he's too handsome and too much of a playboy to stay single for long. He's probably moved on already. I'm the last person he's thinking about right now.

Home vodka isn't working for me. I'm going out for a drink.

I get dressed and doll myself up. Maybe I can pick up a new friend for the night. Someone who looks nothing like Anderson West.

11

JUNE

My head is full of spinning, vodka-fueled thoughts at Manny's Bar. It's an average neighborhood spot with a mix of bankers, doctors, mechanics, and realtors. Dark wood floors glisten from a mix of low lighting on two-for-one shots spilled during happy hour. It's not too loud, not too packed. I have a book on my Kindle, and even the stools are comfy with a cushioned back support. Perfect.

I'm two and a half Cape Cods in when a guy at my left asks, "This seat taken?"

"No, go ahead." My gaze remains on the TV.

"I'm Neil."

I turn to him, and I'm pleasantly surprised. Sandy blond hair, smiling brown eyes, and a dimple on his left cheek. Holy crap, he's cute as hell. Very cornfed

Iowa farmer fantasy vibes. And he looks nothing like Anderson. "I'm June."

He has a movie star smile to boot. "Nice to meet you, June. What're you reading?"

"A mafia novel."

"What's it about?"

I can't tell him I'm reading this novel to figure out if Elliot is involved with the mafia, but honestly, that's the only reason I'm reading it, so I only pay attention to the details about the mob. I've skimmed everything else. Couldn't tell him the plot if I tried. "Just a Godfather rip-off. Everyone wants to be the don, I guess. What do you like to read?"

He gives a sheepish grin. "It's kind of nerdy, but I like sci-fi novels."

"Sci-fi is good. Some of the best films come from sci-fi novels. The original *Jurassic Park* still holds up. Plus, one of my favorite films skims right along the border between sci-fi and horror."

"What's that?"

"*Aliens*."

He laughs. "Can't believe I met a fellow nerd here. Thought this bar was too classy for that."

I wink at him. "We're everywhere."

He chuckles, and after that, the conversation flows easily. Until it doesn't. "… so, June, what do you do?"

Crap. "I am a tax attorney. Or I was until recently. Got laid off."

"Oh, I'm sorry to hear that."

I shrug. "What do you do, Neil?"

"I'm a hedge fund manager at Bryce-Connolly."

Wow. That's a huge bank. "Do you like it?"

"Overall, sure. It's what I always wanted to do once I knew it was a job. A career is important, but it doesn't tell you about who someone really is, and I'd like to know more about you. If you're up for it."

He's cute, friendly, doesn't have any obvious ties to the mob, didn't tease me and bully me into tears when we were kids, so Neil is definitely a step up. "I'd like that."

"Maybe we take one of the booths in the back so we can hear each other without yelling?"

I chuckle and nod, then grab my drink, and we make our way to the booths in the rear of the bar. They're nice leather things that curve around a small round table to give the illusion of privacy. Neil sits a tad closer than I expected, but that's not a bad thing. I like that he's open about his interest in me. So much better than a man who plays games. "Tell me, Neil, aside from being a sexy hedge fund manager, what else do you do?"

He gives a teasing smirk. "You think I'm sexy?"

"Wouldn't have said it otherwise." Normally, I am not this forward. But my three Cape Cods have empowered me.

He's taken aback, and his brows lift with surprise, but he's not put off by my forwardness. Instead, he comes a little closer. "Aside from being a sexy hedge fund manager, I've been spending a lot of time getting to know Boston."

"Where are you from originally?" Say Iowa.

"Nebraska—

"Oh, I was so close!"

He laughs. "Where did you think?"

"Iowa. You look like every fantasy farmer from a romance novel."

Oh my god, he fucking blushes. I'm not sure I've ever seen a man do that. It's strangely erotic. "Well, thank you for that. Maybe I should look for the women who read those—"

I raise my hand. "I've read a few."

His blush fades as he grins. "You know something, June Devlin?"

"What?"

"I am awfully glad I walked in here on a whim tonight."

"So am I."

He nibbles at his bottom lip for a moment while his deep green eyes glance at my mouth. "I'd be remiss if I didn't ask to kiss you."

"If you asked to, I'd say yes."

He closes the gap between us. His voice darkens. "What if I didn't ask? What if I just took your mouth like it belonged to me?"

"Guess you'll have to try and find out."

He lets out a satisfied grunt before slanting his mouth over mine. It's a perfectly good kiss. I taste his hard cider on his lips, and when his tongue grazes at me, I feel like I'm supposed to let him in, so I do.

But it's wrong. It's all wrong.

It's not Neil's fault that it's wrong. I'm the one with the problem. He's not Anderson, and maybe things are too fresh, but kissing someone else feels off. I can't help but back off and wince as I do it. "Sorry, uh —"

"I got pushy. I'm sorry, June."

"No, no. You were fine. Great, really. You're a heck of a kisser, actually, but it's me. I just got out of a super intense relationship, and that felt strange for me."

Just what every guy wants to hear. A woman hung up on her ex, blathering on about another man. "I'm sorry. I shouldn't be putting this off on you. I should go — "

But he snatches my wrist and smiles when I look back at him. "June. It's alright. We all have exes and weird situations. I'm not upset. If you want to go, I understand, but if it were up to me, you'd stay."

Somehow, that makes me feel better. I sit back down next to Neil. "Didn't want to make it uncomfortable for you by talking about him."

He smiles kindly. "I'm guessing he messed you up pretty good, huh?"

"Yeah. It's a whole thing. I don't want to get into it if that's okay."

"Of course. Whatever you like. And thanks for staying. Boston is a tough town. I haven't met a lot of good people yet."

I chuckle. "We are not exactly known for our friendliness. It's more like once you crack into a

Bostonian's hard outer shell, you'll have a friend for life. You have to do the shell cracking first."

"So ... you're like your oysters?"

"Something like that."

He gets a funny look in his eyes. "Can I see your phone?"

"Uh, sure. I guess." I pass it to him.

He fiddles with something and then hands it back. "There. Now you have my number. I know you're dealing with whatever with your ex, but if you ever feel like you need your shell cracked, text me."

Oh my god, he is impossibly cute. "I'll consider it." Maybe I should give the kissing another try. He was quite good, and I need to kiss one guy for every week I was with Anderson. I heard that's the ratio. But I don't know when to count our weeks together. From the auction? From when I pretended to be his fiancée? It's been a while, but not that long. Let's call it eight weeks. So, I need to kiss eight guys.

I think I'll start with Neil.

"You mentioned everyone has their ex drama. Do you want to share yours?"

He sighs, and I hate that I made his smile fade. "My ex drama is exactly that. Drama. She loved it, and I can't stand it. I like things to be simple. Straightforward. Opal did not. She liked to complain about everything, and if there was nothing to complain about, she made stuff up. It got old fast. When I left Nebraska, I cut off all contact with her. I don't need that in my life, you know?"

I nod. "That sounds exhausting."

"What about you? What's your ex's drama?"

Ha, ha, ha, no. How to clean this up so I don't overshare … ? "The usual stuff, I think. He has an overbearing, manipulative father who is way too involved in his life. He tries to control him, and it became too much for me to deal with."

He winces. "That's rough. When families overstep, you never know when to say something, or if that will make things worse between you … it's awkward."

I wish it were only a matter of awkwardness. "Yeah, so how are you liking Boston?"

When he smiles, I fight a shiver. He's so freaking hot. Way out of my league, yet he's here with me. He murmurs, "I'm liking it more and more by the minute."

"Neil?"

"June."

"Any chance we can try that kiss again? I want a do-over."

His eyes dip to my mouth again before meeting my gaze. "I'm a big believer in second chances."

"Good." This time, I kiss him. It's still strange like my body keeps telling me I'm kissing the wrong man. But it's also the kind most people crave their entire lives. I should want this. I should want him. Technically, I have seven more guys to kiss before I'm over Anderson. But for now, practicing with Neil is a good start.

-

12

ANDERSON

Nothing kills time like working with Moss. It's been a few weeks since June unceremoniously dumped me, and I've put my plan into action. I am being the best son I can be, which includes ride-alongs with Moss. The good news is I've been able to form some sort of bond with the incredibly dangerous man. I'm pretty sure he would protect me against most foes.

The bad news is that he is completely my father's pet beast. There is no getting between them and no making Moss slip up. He won't tell me anything Dad has not allowed. Still, though, spending time with him isn't all bad. We have a good working relationship.

Probably because I let him take me to his favorite strip club in Jersey. This man loves naked women dancing almost as much as he loves a strip club buffet. I'd berate him for having such low-class tastes, but in all fairness to him, I have never had better chicken wings than those at Pink Coyotes.

Moss picks me up at my building in his gray SUV. It makes me feel better about things. We're not going to collect on debts. That's done in his black one. Likely, we're going to *remind* people of their debts or make our presence known in certain areas of town. It's a dick-swinging thing Dad has Moss do to ensure people haven't forgotten about him and the services he offers.

Today, we are billboards with guns.

It's not my favorite thing to do, but it's better than collections. I hate collections. People get squirrely. Nothing has gone as badly as the first job I did with Moss. There haven't been any more murders. At least, as far as I know. So, I'll take dick-swinging over collections any day.

I hope we don't run into anyone running the same game we are. That's always tense.

As I get into the passenger side, I smile at Moss, ever the amiable fellow. He grins at me. Moss is a bald white man with the build of a former linebacker. He's gotten a bit of a belly on him from a love of pasta and beer, but the man is as solid as they come otherwise. Tall, too. He has a few inches on me. His Italian-ish accent pops out as he says, "You are in a good mood today, ah?"

I nod. "I am. The weather is holding out, and that cute blonde from the gym gave me her number." A lie, but a carefully crafted one.

"This is good!" He guns the engine, and we're off. "It's good, but my Marianna will be heartbroken."

I laugh, shaking my head. "Pretty sure if that's all it takes to break her heart, she is in for a world of disappointment."

He nods, still smiling. "The heart wants what the heart wants. Even at ten years old, my daughter is boy crazy. How does this happen?"

"Were Caterina or Angela like that at her age?"

"No. Caterina wants to be scientist. Always serious, always studies. She is sixteen and so pale from books and no sun. Angela likes girls. But she was never girl crazy. Only my Marianna. But she says she does not like boys. She likes *men*."

"I hope your house is as well-armed as your vehicles, then."

He laughs and nods. "Oh yes. We are prepared for when the men come for Marianna. They won't make it past my gate."

So, he keeps guns at home. Not at all surprising, but good to know. Before I can build up to another probing question, though, he has one of his own.

"Your father and you, things have been tense, yeah?"

I nod. "But I think it's getting better."

"Why do you think so?"

He asks some version of this every time we do a ride-along, so I am not surprised by the question. It's his — or Dad's — way of getting me to say out loud what they want me to believe. It is a mind control technique that I've read about in a few books on cults recently.

But if I agree too easily, it will sound as fake as it is. So, I bite back the argument in my mind and keep a level smile on my face while I lie through my teeth. "I've come to believe he isn't wrong about everything. The family, for all our flaws, has certain ways of doing things. I could fight against that and make my life hell, or I can accept that we have flaws. Right now, I am striving for acceptance."

He affectionately smacks my knee, and his hand returns to the steering wheel. "You are a good son, Anderson. This is what I tell your father. That you just needed a chance to come around."

Even the knee-smack is textbook cult behavior. I said the thing they wanted to hear, so I get a reward of something they think I want. They think I want to be one of the boys in the in-group. And I do, though not for the reasons they think I do.

I want into the in-group to dismantle the whole goddamn thing.

After researching everything I could about the mafia, cults, MLMs, and every other controlling group I could think of, I settled on cults as the blueprint for how Dad operates. It's not so much traditional mafia operations. I've never seen anyone kiss a ring or call him any of their typical titles. Dad gets off on control. Total control. Which is more cultish than the mafia. Once I made that connection, it's been easier to operate as a spy.

Now that I know what he wants to hear, I know what to say.

It helps that, for all his murdering, Moss is a likable man. That likability lets people drop their guard. It's easy to do, and I find myself accidentally doing so from time to time. But that works in my favor, too. As long as he thinks I'm being straight with him, I won't get a bullet in the back of my head.

No, not the back. Moss prefers to shoot people in their face.

He grunts and juts his chin at a man walking into a convenience store. "You see him? He is not supposed to be here today."

"The white guy in the blue coat?"

He nods. "He owes."

Shit. "But we're not prepared for that kind of thing—"

"No. We are not." The gray SUV has armored doors just like the black one, but Moss usually keeps only two guns in it. The black SUV is practically an armory on most days. Despite this, he pulls over in front of the convenience store.

"What's the plan, Moss?" This is definitely off-book. I don't like to admit it, but I'm sweating this.

"We will say hello." He unbuckles his seatbelt. "Come on."

I don't like it, but I don't get to say no, either. Not if I want to be the good son.

To my relief, he doesn't go to the rear of the SUV where the guns are. Evidently, we really will just say hello. Walking into the convenience store, I see the wariness in the owner's eyes. He's a Chinese man, and when he smiles at Moss, it is nothing but nervous.

To my surprise, Moss asks him something in Cantonese. I shouldn't be surprised by Moss anymore. The man comes off as a street thug, but I've heard him speak Russian, Italian, Cantonese, and German in the past few weeks. When he chooses the music in the car, it's always classical. As much as he appreciates the low-rent world of strip clubs, he's also a fan of the opera.

When Moss laughs, the Chinese man does, too, so I smile and nod along. The owner sees us to the back through some plastic flaps that serve as a divider. It's colder back here and dark, but with Moss in front of me, I worry less about a hail of bullets and more about a fistfight breaking out.

Instead, it's a poker game.

The man in the blue coat sees Moss and bolts out the back door. I step to chase him, but Moss puts his arm out to stop me. I follow his lead and shrug it off. The owner says in English, "He loses a lot. That's why we like him. You didn't have to chase him away."

Moss chuckles, his massive shoulders bouncing. He pulls out a wad of hundreds and peels ten off. "This make up for it?"

The owner nods once. "Thank you, Moss."

"Keep him out. He is persona non grata in your games until he pays."

Another nod.

Moss tells me, "Let's go."

Once we're back in the SUV, my curiosity gets the better of me. "Has Dad said anything to you about me?"

"Only that he wants you to join me in doing this. Has he spoken to you about it?"

"Just that day on the boat. I want to make things up to him, Moss. I've never understood my father, but I'm starting to. Any suggestions?" *Anything you can tell me that might give me leverage?*

He purses his lips and shakes his head. "Mr. West likes cooperation. He rewards it. Keep cooperating, and you will be rewarded."

"Things are sketchy at work, too," I tell him, sitting back in faux-resignation. "So, I've been applying to places in New York just to see what I'm worth. You know, fishing."

He nods. "A man should know what he is worth."

"That's just it, though. Dad keeps blocking me, calling in favors to get my interviews canceled. I have stellar credentials, and I get no callbacks. Nothing. So, I don't get to know what I'm worth. That seem fair to you?" I will drive a wedge between them with the flimsiest of things if I have to.

He makes a noncommittal grunt. His favorite sound, I think. "It is not for me to decide what is fair for another man's child. I raise my girls a certain way. He raises his boys a certain way. I do not judge."

Dammit. "I'm thirty, Moss. I'm not a boy."

"Aye, no, but you are still his son. You will always be his son."

Biologically, yes. But in reality, no. Not ever.

13

JUNE

Sunlight creeps in at the edges of my curtains, and I want it to stop. But with a huff at myself, I throw the covers back to get started with my day.

I don't want to. In fact, all I want to do is stay in bed all morning. And afternoon. Evening, too. But I did that yesterday. Today is a day for action.

Being unemployed does not suit me. I like having a purpose. A direction. I didn't like using my energy to make the rich stay richer, so this is an opportunity to figure out something else.

A new path.

I have to think of something.

If I'm not busy, I start thinking. Thinking is bad for me. Thinking leads to remembering, and remembering leads to things I don't want to recall. My family, for one. The camp incident, for another. Getting kidnapped — nope. I'm not going to think about any of that.

Work. Career. Paycheck. The respect and admiration of my peers. Things I can manage. But how do I keep my head above water when I can't get back into my field? Just thinking about getting back into tax law, it feels like there's a weight on my chest.

If I'm not interested in making things better for rich people, then what the hell am I doing in tax law? It's not as simple as that, and I know it. But it feels like it is, and right now, I want things to feel better than that. Maybe I can try something else for a while, like vodka.

Okay, vodka won't pay the bills, but it'll sure make me feel better in the short term. Short-term is all I can focus on. Everything else is too painful, and then, there's the Anderson of it all. Ugh. My career and my love life are fragmented and raw. An open wound on my psyche. I just need a fucking break. I can't take another day of beating myself up over everything.

Instead, I slip on some cold weather running gear, grab my wallet and keys, and head out the door. If I can't think of anything else to do, at the very least, I can go for a run. It doesn't cost me anything if I don't stop anywhere, and it clears my head better than most things.

Running through my neighborhood is always great for stress relief. I have fairly low rent compared to the rest of my area, but it's still almost three grand a month. The neighborhood has improved over the years, but some of the older businesses remain strong in the face of gentrification, which gives the area a quirky but old Boston feel to it. I love it.

I really hope I don't have to move. Yet.

My footfalls are steady though while I wind between commuters. I've reached a good pace with my runs now that I have plenty of time to practice. It's a net positive so far—running helps with all the ice cream and vodka calories. I don't even get shin splints anymore. But that might have something to do with the lack of heeled shoes in my life lately.

On my run, I buzz past my old bar. O'Mulligan's was home to my misspent youth, or so I like to pretend. The truth is, I worked there through college, and I loved it. Only ten years older than me, the boss, Kelsey O'Mulligan, was the third-generation owner of the place, and he pretended to be a bad influence on his bartenders while simultaneously working harder than any of us. His father, Liam, had died of a heart attack right before I came on board, so Kelsey inherited the place pretty young.

To my surprise, Kelsey is behind the bar right now. Screw the run. I'm going to say hi.

I pop in, and the familiar bell jingle overhead makes me feel like I've come home. Kelsey's head automatically pops up—it's early for a customer to be in, so he was just rolling silverware. He brightens in an instant. "Well, if you aren't a sight for sore eyes! Get over here!" He dashes around the bar for a hug.

"I'm all sweaty—"

"And I'm not?" he teases. He gives the best hugs. Kelsey is six feet tall, but he feels much taller. Has one of those larger-than-life personalities that lights up a room. Bright ginger hair with a big, bushy beard and sparkling, sweet blue eyes, he's the pale Viking type who looks like he'd be more at home raiding a village or chopping wood than fetching drinks for strangers. He grins. "How the fuck are you, June?"

"Oof, loaded question ... " When I walk in, the worn copper-topped bar is on my left, with the dining area on the right, and booths line the interior far wall. O'Mulligan's is on a corner, so it has two glass walls that overlook the sidewalk. It's a big space and worth a tremendous amount of money, but Kelsey vowed he would never sell. He wants to pass the place on to his kids. "Looks like the place hasn't changed much."

"We got new napkins, but that's about it. Come on in. Let me buy you a drink. Still appletinis?"

I laugh. "I've graduated to vodka sodas."

He winces before rounding the bar again. "Next, you'll tell me you're into Fernet Branca."

"Nope. I'm not there yet." I pop onto a stool across from him. "How are things with you?"

"Great! Monica's pregnant again."

"Congratulations!" I know he's always wanted a big family. "Number three?"

He laughs and passes me my drink. "Five."

"Five? Jeez, man, let that woman rest!"

He laughs again. "There was a set of twins in pregnancy two, so only four pregnancies." He pauses. "For now."

"How many are you aiming for?"

"Don't really have a number in mind, but I wouldn't mind having eight or nine kids."

Yikes. "That's a lot, man. I'm glad it makes you happy."

"What about you? Any little ones running about?"

"Hell no!"

He laughs. "That's … adamant."

"Sorry—they're great for anyone who wants them. But my life is way too turbulent to have to think about kids right now."

"Turbulent?" He returns to rolling silverware while we chat.

I sigh. "Don't let me dump on you, Kelsey. You're—"

"A bartender. Comes with the territory when it's early like this. What's going on, June?"

I give up. "I got laid off because I pissed off the wrong people, and now I'm getting blackballed out of my industry. It's not great."

He cringes. "That's terrible. I can make some calls—"

"No, no, no. Thanks, though." O'Mulligan's has been a neighborhood fixture for over forty years, so he has the pull to do something like that. But it's nothing like the pull Elliot West has, and I'd hate for him to try and shutter O'Mulligan's just because Kelsey tried to help me out. "I came in here to see how things were going and check in on you. Not for a favor."

He smiles. "If you ever change your mind, let me know. As far as me? I'm great." But then his smile falters. I wouldn't have picked up on it if I hadn't worked next to the man for years.

"What's up, Kelsey? I don't want to hear *great* out of you again until you mean it."

He laughs a little too sharply and shakes his head. "You know how it is, June. When you hire kids, they move on. They graduate, or they move, or whatever. It's hard to keep good staff. I like hiring young people because they have the energy for the job, but they don't stick around. Just had a bartender quit on me last night because she's relocating to Los Angeles." When he says the city's name, he makes the same face most Bostonians make when they mention it. A grimace twisted by confusion as if asking why anyone would move someplace hot and sunny. "Miss having you here. You were one of the longest-lasting bartenders I had."

I chuckle at that. "I'm stubborn. Remember when I was working doubles during finals week?"

"Was that the time you poured a whole pitcher of beer on a guy for grabbing your butt?"

I laugh. "No, that was March Madness. During my doubles and finals week, a guy kept dropping his napkin whenever I'd walk by so I'd pick it up and he could look down my shirt. So, I went to the bathroom and wrote, 'Fuck you' in black eyeliner over my boobs right where he'd see it when I bent over next, and—"

"Right! I had Bruno drag him out. But I remember there was more to it than that."

"He waited until Bruno went on break and snuck back in when we were busy to come at me, but two of my usual guests saw him coming and tackled him. He got arrested."

"Oh yeah," he says with a nod. "Forgot all about that guy."

"Still the same rowdy crowd during hockey season?"

He chuckles. "Yep. It's been busy lately. Still get the college kids who can't handle their liquor and the business people who overtip to show off. You're welcome to take a shift—"

I laugh and sarcastically tell him, "Sure, sounds like a plan." But then it feels less sarcastic. I could use a job. I loved it here. And I don't want to run through my savings as fast as I have been. Plus, I'm going stir-crazy.

"Ah, well. Thought I'd ask—"

"I'll do it."

His crystalline blue eyes light up. "Wait, are you fucking with me?"

"I'm serious, actually. Not like I'm doing anything else. Might as well make some money."

"You're so hired!"

I laugh. "You're serious?"

"Wear something black and be here by three."

Grinning ear to ear, I nod. "You're on."

14

JUNE

I can't believe I'm going to work a shift at my old bar again. And with Kelsey! I thought he'd sell the place or something. Bartending is a tough business to be in long-term, but I guess if it's in your blood, you don't quit. It's not in my blood, but it'll be fun and pay the bills for now. Right?

Doesn't matter. I'm going to try it out for a night and see how things go.

Digging through my closet, I find a low-cut black blouse that will work. Bad for the weather, but perfect for increasing my tips. I go a little heavy-handed on the makeup because that's what patrons like, especially after a few too many. Nothing garish, but a bright red lip and a little extra eye liner never hurt anybody.

Nervously, I stop for a triple espresso on my way in. I don't want to be the one dragging the team down with my lack of energy. All the other bartenders are younger than me, and I'll die of embarrassment if I'm the one slowing us down. I even slept in this morning just to be sure. Can't disappoint Kelsey. He's taking a chance on me, and I appreciate that a lot. Feels like no one else will.

Once I'm at the bar, though, it's strange. I double knot my black half apron around my waist and get started taking orders, and it's like I never left. At first, it's after-work office workers—the martinis and vodka tonics crowd. Back in the day, they were a nice way to start a shift. Generally pretty mellow.

Then come the younger office workers. The ones who went home to freshen up before coming to the bar. In other words, the single businesspeople. No one is waiting at home for them, so they'd rather go out and try to hook up. It can be a rowdy crowd, but usually, they're just good tippers who appreciate a drink special.

After that, it's the college kids. Oh, so many college kids. They slow us down because checking IDs becomes more of a thing. Most are good about it, and the ones who aren't are the ones we don't want to stay. From behind the bar, I smile at one in particular when I keep a hold of his fake ID. "You're forty-eight?"

His eyes nervously widen. "Uh, yeah. I know I look young for my age —"

"That's interesting because according to your license, you're thirty-eight."

"Um, uh, well, I'm bad at math."

I snort a laugh at him. "That's not all you're bad at. Go on. Get out of here."

"You can't talk to me like that! I am thirty-eight —"

But I motion for the bouncer to come by. "Tell it to Bruno."

"I want to talk to the owner! Is he the owner?"

"I'm Bruno," my favorite bouncer growls in his baritone voice.

When the kid turns around and sees a former footballer with forearms the size of his own thighs, he bolts out the door.

Bruno grins at me, and I smile back. "Thanks."

"Anytime, Devlin." He returns to his post by the door.

A dipshit at the end of the bar snaps his fingers at me. He's been trying to impress his date by ordering wines he mispronounces, and she seems bored. I plaster a smile on and grumble to Kelsey. "Duty snaps."

"Don't be afraid to snap back."

I nod and trot to the dipshit. "How's the tempranillo?"

"It's dry," he says with a curling lip.

"Tempranillos *are* dry."

"Well, I don't like it. Too harsh on the palate. Bring me something better."

"You got it." Beneath the bar, we keep a bottle of Manischewitz to soak maraschino cherries in, so I pour him a glass of the soaked cherry juice. It's the sweetest thing I have ever tasted in my life, like liquid candy. Generally appropriate punishment for people who annoy us. "Try this."

He sips it, and his eyes light up. "This is excellent. What is it?"

Of course, he likes it. He has the palate of a teenager. The man ordered a well-done hamburger to go with his wine. To avoid him googling it correctly, I tell him, "Manisck-He-Wiss. It's German. In fact, you might want to stick with German wines. A lot of them have a similar profile."

"Thanks."

Kelsey, having seen what transpired, asks, "Another happy customer, eh?"

"You know me. I'm all about making them happy."

"Think the sugar rush will let him sleep tonight?"

I snort a laugh. "Not my problem, and by the looks of things, not hers, either. I've never seen someone so bored."

"I've never seen someone chug the Manischewitz cherry juice."

"It's the juice box of adult children."

"Million-dollar idea."

I laugh, and another patron flags me to her, so I pop over. "How can I —"

"These fries are not well done. Did you even ask for them to be well done? How hard is that to remember?" She's a snotty sorority girl with her friends. Pretty sure she just wants to whine and show off.

Strangely, I am completely unbothered. "I did, in fact. But I'd be happy to ask them to burn some fries for you."

"I didn't say burnt —"

"Well, that's the next step after that level of doneness, so it's really your only option at this point."

She makes a dissatisfied gasp. "I want them well done! Do your job! It's not like it takes brain cells to get fries right!"

I take her plate of fries away, and she looks startled. "I'll bring you a fresh order. Be right back!" Dumping the fries, I put in an order for burnt ones and return to Kelsey to barback for him until they're ready. "You know the nice thing about rude people?"

"No, I really don't."

"That you don't mind if we're rude right back to them."

He laughs. "I certainly do not."

"It's funny, though. I don't even care that the sorority girls are being bratty little bitches or that idiot is chugging kiddie wine. This is so low stress here compared to my old job."

"Really?" He flips out a dozen shot glasses and fills them with the requested variety of shots in under a minute. "How so?"

"No one here will scream at me for losing them several million dollars and shout about how they'll sue me if I can't get them a tax break on their new yacht."

"Guess that does add a certain amount of calm to your day, eh?"

I nod enthusiastically and make a tray of gin and tonics for the stock brokers in the corner so Melina can whisk it away. "Seriously, this is the least amount of job stress I've had in years. I kind of love it."

"If you want the gig, June, it's yours."

"I'm in. For now, I mean. You remember—"

"I know. You want to work in your field. But you see how swamped I am. I'll take all the help I can get."

I smile and deliver a basket of nearly black fries to the sorority girl. "Here you are."

"Thanks," she bites out at me before turning to her friends.

The rest of the night goes on like that until it's near closing time, and I am wiped out. But it's a good tired. The kind of tiredness you have at the end of a long day when you know you've accomplished something. As I'm wiping down the bar, I try to think of everything I need to do to solidify my employment. "Oh, Kelsey, I don't think I gave you my email—"

He laughs. Hard. "Why would I need that?"

Then, I laugh at myself. "Guess you don't. Oh my god, a job with no email? I'm in heaven." I know that it's not—not by a long shot. But this feels like the easiest job in the world. It's not that I don't take bartending seriously. It's just that my old job was nothing but high stakes. At the bar, I can smile my problems away.

In walks Callie, and I am delighted to see her. "Hey, girl! Drink's on me." I pour us some cocktails and sit with her on the other side of the bar.

"I cannot believe you're doing this."

"What else am I supposed to do? You know why I'm here."

She nods. "I think it's great, June. But what about long-term?"

"For once in my planned-out, high-pressure life, I am not planning ahead. No thoughts about long-term. I am going with the flow and working just enough to pay my bills. I am taking a break from the career stuff, and I am completely at peace with it. And life in general, to be honest. In fact, I think I've reached some kind of homeostatic Zen state. I have never been so relaxed and calm as I am right now." Maybe my smile is a little smug, but I kind of feel sorry for Callie, who is still stuck in the rat race.

"What about Anderson?"

Tears spring out of my eyes like fireworks, and I lose my shit. There goes my calm.

15

JUNE

After Callie's millionth apology text, I finish getting ready for the next day's shift. I know she didn't mean to upset me. But she accidentally asked a question I'm not prepared to answer.

I brush my hair and wonder what the answer really is. What about Anderson? The truth is, I just don't know. Things are messy, and I end up with my brush tangled in my hair when I think too hard about him. As if I needed another sign.

Once I finish getting ready, I'm out the door and at the bar before I know it. It's early, so there're just a few people at the bar. Kelsey introduces me to the new regulars. They seem great. Things flow easily at the bar again—even easier than the first night, actually. Kelsey notes, "You're having fun, aren't you?"

I chuckle. "Yeah. I am. How can you tell?"

"You look happier today than you did when you came in here that first day."

I smile and shrug. "Part of it is I'm enjoying myself. Part of it is knowing I'll be able to pay my bills. And the other part of it is this place is like a sabbatical or something. I'm not stressed out by work for the first time in years, Kel. It's wonderful."

"Glad to hear it." He pauses to serve some cosmos to two cougars on the prowl. "Think you'd be interested in picking up some more shifts? I know you said you only wanted a couple to get your feet wet, but your feet look pretty wet, June."

I want to say yes. But I know better. "I'm good for now. But if that changes, I'll let you know."

He nods and attends his side of the bar while I take care of mine. It's like a dance, and all the steps come back to me easily. I really am enjoying myself, much to my surprise. Never thought I'd return to tending bar. Not in a million years. But it's like a vacation from my real life, and a desperately needed one.

Here, I'm not the failed tax attorney. I'm not Anderson West's ex. I'm not the woman who faked a kidnapping after really being taken. At the bar, I'm just June. A decent bartender with a nice rack and an easy smile. My recent string of questionable choices doesn't matter. Only that I keep the drinks coming.

It's easy to get swept up in the rhythm of the bar to ignore how overwhelmed I've felt. Working here is comfortable, like an old college sweatshirt. Rough around the edges but familiar in all the right ways. Maybe that's the real reason I lost my shit with Callie last night. She mentioned Anderson, and all of a sudden, I couldn't breathe anymore. It brought everything back at once. As much as I felt overwhelmed by the circumstances that broke us up, though, I missed the shit out of him when she said his name. It was like a weight on my chest.

I still miss Anderson. And I still don't know what to do about him.

But I can't think about that right now. Right now, I'm slinging drinks. It is wall-to-wall, and we are packed. Some hockey game is on, so all the fans and haters are in the bar, cheering on their teams. Thankfully, most of them are beer drinkers, so it's faster than mixing drinks. Just gotta pour, for the most part. That, and tapping the kegs, Kelsey drags up.

Every seat in my section is taken but one on the far end, which gives me a space to feel like I can breathe. But when I turn around, it fills up a moment later. Dammit. I am still having fun, but there's a certain zombie-swarm feeling to the proceedings. Like we're surrounded, and instead of, "Brains!" these zombies cry out, "Beer!"

I can't even make my way to the new patron yet — too swamped with others' orders. But I need to keep him happy, so before I can even make eye contact with the newbie, I ask, "What can I —"

"June, it's me."

I blink over at him and get hit by a fifty-thousand-watt smile. "Oh my gosh, Neil? What are you doing here?"

"When you texted me earlier, you said you were picking up a shift here —"

"Right, right. I forgot." I gesture around me. "It's a little hectic."

"Don't let me slow you down."

"You're on deck. What can I get you?"

"Right. I'm in your section. Um, a porter —"

"Coming right up." I pour him a Mayflower and deliver. "On me."

"You don't —"

"Yeah, I do. I'll be busy for a while if you want to hang out until my break or something?"

He grins. "Yeah. I'll be here."

God, he's cute as hell. "Good." I get back to work, stealing glances at Neil all the while. He wears the heck out of his deep green cashmere sweater. It's stretched tight over his muscles, showing him off without being showy. When we had texted, he'd wanted to go out, and I had to tell him I couldn't do it. The fact he showed up for me is really sweet.

He has such a different demeanor than Anderson.

Anderson probably would have just paid me to stay in with him or something equally over the top. Instead of doing something heavy-handed about my lack of availability, Neil showed up for me. He's this cute, sweet, normal guy. I haven't had that in a very long time. Even the guys I dated before Anderson weren't thoughtful enough to show up and support me.

It's weird to think of missing Anderson while also considering beginning a new thing with Neil. Feels like having a foot in two worlds. At some point, I'll have to choose which world to be in, but not tonight. Tonight is for work. And after work, tonight is also for some fun with someone new.

After the rush, I get a break and find a quiet corner with Neil. He balks at my basket of fries. "Come on, that can't be dinner."

"I ate a proper dinner before I came. The fries are to get me through the rest of the night."

He chuckles. "So, how are you liking it here?"

"It's fun, actually. I've missed this place."

"Oh?"

"I used to bartend here when I was in college."

"You're just full of surprises, aren't you?"

He doesn't know the half of it. I laugh. "More than I care to admit."

"Well, in case you're interested in going back to your day job, I just found out my bank is looking for an attorney."

I could work for a bank. But, "Thanks, but for now, I'm happy here. Things are tighter financially, but I have not been this relaxed in years. My boss doesn't even have my email. He doesn't text me at all hours. No one is crying about millions of dollars. The worst I get from the patrons is a pinch on the ass, and I have full permission to beat the shit out of them if they do, which is a huge step up from the worst I've gotten as an attorney."

He raises a brow at that. "Some client got handsy with you when you were doing their tax stuff?"

I huff. "A client got offended when I told him I had no interest in starting an affair with him, so he tried to get me fired and disbarred."

Neil laughs once. "What? Fired is one thing, but disbarred? How?"

"He's a judge. He has friends in places he doesn't deserve to have friends." I shrug. "It went nowhere, thankfully, but when some people have too much money, they lose their minds."

"That's wild."

I nod. "So, for now, I'm happy to stay put."

"Understandably." He sighs and gets a wistful look in his pretty green eyes. "Sometimes, I have this fantasy that I've saved up a bunch of money, and I open up a sunglasses hut on a hot beach in the Caribbean. No stress, no bosses. Just me, the beach, all the oysters I can eat." His wistful expression goes slyly blissful. "Paradise."

"That sounds amazing."

"Funny. I never thought I'd end up in Boston, of all places. But you never know where life takes you. I try to be open to every possibility. Live in the moment. Life is stressful enough without trying to control everything, you know?"

"Amen to that." I feel like Neil really gets what I'm going for. "Never thought I'd hear surfer philosophy out of a hedge fund manager from Nebraska."

He grins, and his dimple deepens, capturing my attention. "Surfer life has an appeal all its own. One day, maybe."

"I —"

But then my phone goes off to tell me my break is over. "Gotta get back."

-

16

JUNE

"I'll stick around if you don't mind. I'd like to walk you home. Make sure you get there safe."

"Are all of you Midwestern guys so chivalrous?"

He smirks. "Only the ones who were raised right."

I giggle and get myself back to work. It's still a madhouse, and I might have taken a little too long with Neil in the corner, but Kelsey doesn't mention it. In fact, all he says is, "Thought I might have lost you tonight. Looks like someone's head over heels."

I laugh and shake my head as I pour a Bud. "Definitely too soon for me —"

"Not you. Him. I haven't seen a guy that smitten since I met my wife."

"You really think so?"

He nods once. "Watch yourself with that one. He is very into you."

I cringe at that. "Damn."

"That's a bad thing?"

I duck under the bar for a tray as Kelsey reaches over me. Can't believe we still move in sync as well as we do. "I'm fresh out of a relationship. Not sure I want someone smitten with me. Especially someone as sweet as Neil. He's a really good guy, newly from Nebraska. I don't want to be the Boston bitch who broke his heart."

"Understood. Want Bruno to chase him out of here?"

"No, no. Nothing like that. I just need to be careful with him. Make sure I don't lead him on, that kind of thing. No big deal. I'll handle it."

Kelsey nods, and we go back to slamming drinks out for the crowd. With my boss' words ringing in my head, I'm torn. On the one hand, I like that Neil is sticking around to walk me home. On the other hand, I don't want him to think we're a thing. I like kissing the guy. He's easy on the eyes. But letting myself get close to someone the way I was with Anderson is out of the question for a long, long time.

As the hockey game heats up near the last period, two fans of the opposing teams get into it. The bar is too clogged for Bruno or Marcus to get there in time, so Neil steps up. I can't hear what he says to them, but he brings the guys to the bar and buys them a round to keep the peace. They go to their separate corners after that, and I mouth, "Thank you!" to Neil. He gives a shy smile and returns to his booth.

"If you don't marry him, I might," Kelsey says.

When things wind down, Neil hangs out at the bar, but when they pick up again, he returns to the quiet booth at the corner. I appreciate that he's trying to make sure I get more people in my section. More people, more tips. He's so thoughtful. It's a nice change from the boyfriends I've had before. Harry, who I had to remind, it was Valentine's Day. Derek, who balked at eating pussy but wanted blowjobs. Neil isn't like them at all.

Honestly, he's unlike anyone I've ever met.

At the end of the night, I say my goodbyes, and Neil helps me into my coat. It's such an old-school gesture, and I find it endearing. He even opens the door for me on our way out. The frosty air hits my lungs hard. "Oh, wow. It's colder than I thought."

Without a word, he takes off his scarf and wraps it around me, tying it comfortably around my neck.

"This will help."

"Thanks, but what about you?"

He gazes over my face and smiles. "I'll think warm thoughts."

"Me, too." I grab his collar and pull him to my lips. When he brushes over mine, there's such a spark, and it flashes through me, warming me from the inside out. Okay. I might not be ready to start something with Neil, but I'd like to be. Just as we break the kiss, snowflakes fall. It's a perfect moment.

But then another icy breeze hits.

Even with his heat on my mouth, I shiver. Neil says, "Let's get you someplace warm. I'd suggest my place, but I'm getting it painted."

"We're not that far from mine."

"Perfect."

As fresh, clean snow falls, we trundle through the streets of Boston. It's late, so there're fewer cars on the road and more people out. The night owls are my people once again. From servers to dancers, only us weirdos walk the night. But with Neil at my side, I feel a lot less vulnerable.

"How come you jumped in the middle of that fight tonight? That was really dangerous."

He chuckles, shaking his head. "They were hot. Had to cool off. Not all that dangerous."

"Come on! They were huge dudes, shouting at each other and ready to swing."

"They reminded me of these two bulls we had back home, and—"

"Bulls? Like cows?"

He laughs. "Bulls are cattle. People use cattle and cow interchangeably, but it's debatable. Anyway, these two bulls hated each other. They'd always almost get into a ruckus, but once we turned them into steers," he snaps his fingers, "docile like little calves. You just have to know how to take the fight out of a man."

"I'm sorry, but I thought bulls and steers were the same thing."

"A bull is an uncastrated male. A steer is castrated."

"And all that castration talk doesn't make you want to cringe?"

He grins and shakes his head. "Nah. You get used to it, growing up on a ranch."

"Wow. So, like, you grew up extra rural, huh?"

"You could say that. We raised beef and had a small garden plot for the family. Just a few acres of vegetables, no big deal."

"I kill house plants. A few acres of vegetables is a big deal."

He laughs again. "I find that hard to believe. You couldn't hurt a fly."

"Pretty sure the only thing I ever hurt is feelings."

"You? No."

"Ask my exes. I think they'd disagree. I was born with a sharp tongue. Got it from my mom."

At that, he pauses. "My mom had a mouth on her, too. Never liked it. She was always … pushy. That's why I went away to school. Just needed to get out of the house, you know?"

"Very much. I could have lived at home for college, but I chose the dorm. I had to get out." He nods sympathetically, and before I know it, we're at my building. "This is me. Wanna come up for a nightcap?"

"I'd like that."

So, we walk into the lobby area. It's not much more than a hallway, really. Off to the left is the mail area and to the right, the elevators. Neil presses the button, and while we wait, he comes closer. I don't mind it. He smells amazing. When he lifts my ponytail out of the way and kisses the side of my neck, I'm surprised. But it's nice. Then he spins me around and kisses my lips. This kiss is hungrier than before. Less gentlemanly and more aggressive. I'd be all for it if I weren't wiped out from the night. Still, though. The kissing is nice.

When his hand snakes up my shirt, though, I put the brakes on.

I back off just a little. "Neil, that's—"

But he kisses me again. Okay, as long as he keeps it to kissing, that's fine. I don't mind it. In fact, he's a very good kisser, and I find myself getting lost in it until his cold hand goes up my shirt again.

I give him a playful shove. "Neil, come on. We're not doing that right now." Where the hell is the elevator?

"Yes, we are," he says calmly as he cups my breast over my bra.

I shove him a little harder this time, but he doesn't back off. "Stop."

But a sinister smile twists his once-handsome face. "You're not going to tell me what to do."

His words shoot fear through me. "What's gotten into you?"

"You invited me for a nightcap. I know what that means, June."

"Fine. Then you're uninvited. Leave. Now."

But instead, he pushes me against the wall. Hard. But I'm close to the wall, so it doesn't hurt much. "Don't make me repeat myself. You do not tell me what to do. *I* tell *you*. Do you understand?"

Fuck.

17

ANDERSON
EARLIER THAT NIGHT

I s it healthy to watch your ex at work? No. Is that going to stop me from doing it? Also no.

It didn't take long for me to figure out where June has been working. Not when I've been randomly circling her building every other day when I'm not working with Moss. She hoofed it to a dive bar, and since June is not much of a drinker normally, I tailed her just to make sure she was okay. Seeing her behind the bar instead of in front of it was a shock. But she looked completely at home there, laughing with drunks and chatting up the staff like she'd been born to it.

Like she had this whole other life that I knew nothing about.

It's odd to think about. Did she hide this from me when we were together? I don't see how. It must be a new development. Maybe she just fits in everywhere she goes. Must be nice.

Working with Moss has had a stiff learning curve.

I don't mind it. Not really. He's been good at teaching me the ins and outs of the work, and I pick up things fast. But still, I am out of my element. There is no way around it. Hopefully, the next ride-along will go as smoothly as June's new job goes for her.

It's like watching Mozart conduct or a deer frolic. Someone doing the thing they are meant to do in the world. She is nothing but gracious smiles and easy laughter, even when she's buried by drunks. Watching from across the street is peculiar. But under Moss' tutelage, I've learned how to look like a tourist. It's a great disguise—just dress oddly for the weather and try to take pictures with my camera and curse up a storm when it doesn't work, which is an easy way to use your zoom to see whoever you're spying on. No one in Boston likes tourists, so no one even notices me.

I am careful not to stick around for too long, though. I keep a few changes of clothes in my car, which is parked around the corner. Every once in a while, I change something I'm wearing or add a new layer, and boom, I'm a whole new tourist. With the weather getting colder, it's the perfect excuse to cover more of my face.

Standing around all night is weird. I'm being obsessive. I know I am. But I miss the shit out of June, and I need regular reminders why I'm putting myself through the crazy shit with Dad. It's for her. It's all for her. I have to pay her back. I have to get her back. That's all there is to it. She means everything to me.

Even if I mean nothing to her.

I'd go into her bar if I thought she wouldn't have me kicked out. So, if watching her from afar on my nights off is what I have to do to stay focused, then that is what I'll do. And I do not like the way *Green Sweater* is looking at her. Like he's as focused on her as I am.

He sits in her section and she approaches him like she does all her other patrons. But then she looks at him, and there's a spark in her eyes I haven't seen in far too long. My jaw and fists clench. I hate that she's sparking with him. But maybe she's gunning for tips. I can't judge how she makes her money. That's not fair. She's doing the best she can.

When she takes her break with him, though, bile rises in my throat.

She's moved on. No, maybe they're just friends. Maybe he's gay. Yeah, he looks like he could be — he's twirling the end of her ponytail while they talk. Probably not gay. And as close as she's sitting to him? Those coy glances. No reason for that other than her being into him.

She used to give me those coy glances. Shit.

The first thing to hit me isn't loneliness. It's something akin to anguish. Regret, maybe. The regret that I didn't know how to fix things before they reached this point. Loneliness doesn't hit all at once. Not in my experience. It never hits. It creeps in, dragging depression and aimlessness with it. Loneliness is slow. Regret is a speedy motherfucker, and right now, it's overwhelming. The loneliness will come later, I imagine.

June is moving on, and I have no clue how to stop her. Or even if I should. I'll still pay her, of course. *Green Sweater* has nothing to do with what's gone on between us. I know I shouldn't push my way back into her life. I should let her have her new happiness without me dragging her down. She deserves better than to be involved in the illegal, nefarious shit my dad is into. June deserves the world.

I can't give that to her. Not anytime soon. So, I won't stand in the way of her happiness with *Green Sweater*. It's the least I can do right now. When the time comes when I can give her the world, I'll try again. But it will have to wait until I've extracted West Media from Dad's illegal dealings. Until then, I have to make peace with the fact that she will have guys buzzing around her. She's a smart, gorgeous woman. Of course, she'll attract guys. Especially working at a bar.

Backing off is the logical, kind thing to do.

So, why haven't I walked away? I couldn't walk away from June if I wanted to. But I won't interrupt. I won't make a scene or bug her. She can have all the guys she wants. I'll obsess quietly and from a distance.

At the end of her night, *Green Sweater* leaves with her. He ties his scarf on her—cheeseball move—and they kiss. Well, shit. She likes the cheeseball, apparently. That's a dagger in the heart if ever there was one. Then, they walk toward her place. Fuck, is he staying over? So soon?

Okay, it's not that soon, but still.

I can't believe she's going to sleep with him. It's unthinkable for me. But clearly, I'm more involved in this than she is. After all, I didn't dump her. She dumped me.

They pause at her building, and she invites him in. Yep. They're fucking. I'm guessing it's their first time, based on how they've been all night. Things are tentative. New. They both looked like they had butterflies in their stomachs all night. I need to stop watching them through the glass doors, but I can't tear my eyes away.

I should be happy for her. But I'm not that evolved. I want to stop her from doing this. Instead, I stretch my fists and decide to leave. Nothing good comes from me sticking around for this. They're going to get into her elevator, and then I'll go.

Just then, something shifts on his face. No more butterflies. Purely lupine. I really do not like this guy. I would have thought June had better taste in men than someone who looks like that when her back is turned. But then again, how would she know? He looks like a smug son of a bitch when she's not paying attention to him. Like every frat boy, I beat the snot out of in college. He thinks he has this in the bag, and well, he's right. Clearly.

I am so twisted up over all of this that I don't notice her body language at first. When he kisses her this time, she's not into it. I squint to see, but that doesn't help, so I pull out my phone for a zoom. He's reaching up her shirt, and she's not happy about it. In fact, she gives him a girlie push to make him back off.

I have never been so relieved—wait. They're kissing again. And she seems okay with it. Dammit. This is not what I needed. He's going up her shirt again, and this time, she pushes harder, then tells him off. Thank god—wait. He's not leaving. Is this some kind of sex game between them? Like she plays the chaste innocent, and he plays the wolf? I'm torn. I want to go in there and stop him from bugging her, but if this is a game between them and I rush in there, I'm a stalker, and she'll never talk to me again.

But, if it is a sex game, why does she look scared? Is that a part of it? Shit. What do I do?

18

JUNE

"Neil, you need to go. My neighbors will—"

"They're asleep. It's after midnight, June. No decent person is up this late." He smirks pointedly as he comes in for another kiss.

"I'm not kissing you ever again. I want you to leave. Now!"

"I'm not going anywhere until I get what I came for." He chucks my chin with his finger. "If you don't fight it, this will go much better for you."

But I push him back. "Leave me alone!"

"It's okay. You haven't disappointed me, June. Don't worry." He smiles, and it sends ice through my veins. "I like a woman with some fight in her. It's always better when they fight back." He lunges forward toward me.

As soon as I move to hit him, he catches my wrist in an iron grip. I try for the other fist, and he catches that one, too, and laughs at me. Then Neil slams me back, keeping my wrists pinned against the wall. The slam makes me a little dizzy, and with my wrists pinned, I panic and try to kick him. But he's too close, pressing himself against me. I try to propel myself off the wall and fail. He's just too heavy with muscle. He growls, "Go ahead. Squirm. I like it."

I can feel how much he likes it. His hard cock digs against me, dry humping through our clothes. This has all been foreplay to him. It's like the good, sweet-natured Nebraska boy thing was a mask, and behind it, a grotesque monster. There's a darkness in his green eyes. Kind warmth has been replaced by frozen hate.

He grinds against me again, and I want to vomit. He's disgusting. I want him arrested. I gasp, "Leave now, and I won't call the cops. Just stop."

He nuzzles against my cheek and whispers, "Stop? Why the fuck would I do that? You think I'm afraid cops will believe a bartending whore over a pillar of society?" Then laughs and bites my earlobe hard enough to make me wince.

I try to bring up my knee for his groin, but he's still pressed too hard up against me, and I can't kick him there. I'm close to crying, and I don't know if that will make him stop or make him angry or if he'll even notice. But I'm not sure I have a choice. I'm freaking the fuck out, and my eyes are welling up. "Please just go away."

"Stop with the fucking whining, June." He grapples with me for a moment until he has one hand on both my wrists, and his other hand goes to my throat. Just bracketing at first, but the longer he speaks, the tighter his grip gets. "I am so sick of you bitches, thinking you can tell me what to do! You think you can do whatever you want, don't you? Lead a man on all night long. Tell him you're into him, and then invite him up. But the moment I start to take what's mine, you get cold feet. You can't treat me like that, June. I'm gonna show you."

I scratch out, "Neil, please—"

"That's more like it. You're sexier when you beg. Let's see how sexy I can make you." His grip locks on my throat, and I try helplessly to move out of his grasp. Can't breathe. Used the last of my air to beg. Regretting that now. I don't want the last name I say to be his. I'd rather it was Anderson's. Fuck. He snarls, "Beg to breathe, bitch."

I can't say a word. No air. Clarity strikes as my clock ticks down. I shouldn't have broken up with

Anderson. He'll never know how I feel about him now. More regrets. Didn't think my last moment would be filled by them.

"Oh, come on. You can do it. Beg me again, and I'll let you breathe."

Can't even make a choking sound. Why is it called lightheaded when all I can see are black spots? The air sounds hollow somehow. Strange, that. The black spots morph into absolute blackness, and I sink into it. Sinking is the last thing I know.

Can't see anything. Can't feel anything. But I hear something in the distance. The distinct squeak of sneakers on a hard floor. Scuffling. Curses. Thuds. Some kind of wet sound.

This isn't hell. Or heaven. Where the fuck am I?

My eyes flutter when I try to open them. Can't focus at first. When my eyes start to hone in on something, it's the slightly yellowed ceiling in my apartment lobby. As soon as my focus comes back, I choke and cough against a bruised throat.

I'm against the wall on the floor, sort of wedged up half on my back. Coughs catch me so hard it feels like I'll burst blood vessels in my eyes or fracture my ribs. One cough hits so hard that my head rattles back. I have to roll over onto my hands and knees to keep coughing without knocking my head into the wall or the floor. Feel like a cat trying to hack up a furball. The coughs are spasmodic, but eventually, I can suck air down without another coughing fit. Movement draws my eyes to the mailboxes across the hall.

Anderson is straddled on Neil's chest, punching the ever-loving fuck out of him. I don't know if I'm hallucinating this. Maybe Neil killed me, and this is some kind of fantasy my brain is feeding me to help ease my transition. I read about that kind of thing somewhere.

But then Neil scrabbles out from under him and kicks Anderson in the ribs before he can get up. What the hell kind of comforting hallucination would do that? This is really happening.

I cringe back from the fight, still sitting on the floor but bringing my knees up. The hall isn't so wide that I couldn't get dragged into it.

Anderson tries to get to his feet after that kick, but Neil slams his fist into his face, knocking him back against the wall of metal mailboxes. But that only catches Anderson's back, almost helping him to his feet. He ricochets off it, using the momentum to carry him forward. Anderson pivots around to Neil's side and dips, jabbing him in the stomach with a low uppercut. They're too close to each other for Neil to punch him again. But he brings his elbow down on Anderson's shoulder.

They move so quickly that I'm not even sure if I'm seeing things right. So much is blurry at the edges. Wherever I look is in focus, but the space around it fuzzes. I blink a lot to clear my vision, but that's not the problem. Whatever Neil did to me is, and my vision hasn't righted itself just yet.

At some point, their match is back and forth, one shoving the other across the space. Neil lands against the wall next to me, then launches from there to attack Anderson before I can grab his leg to stop him. They're too fast for me to help. All I can do is watch.

This isn't the trained elegance of a boxing match or even a sloppy bar fight. Each blow is brutal. Animalistic. They aren't playing by any rules. They're trying to kill each other. I shriek at them to stop, but my voice is so hoarse I hardly hear it. And it wouldn't matter anyway.

They aren't going to stop until this is over.

Neil jams his knee at Anderson's groin, and it takes the focus out of him. Neil seizes the chance and knocks him to the floor. He jumps onto Anderson's chest, straddling him the way Anderson had done to him. But the moment he rears back to punch him, Anderson hooks his hand around Neil's neck and yanks him down, taking away any advantage he had by being on top. Anderson rolls them over. Neil collides with the wall, but he's on his feet almost as fast as Anderson.

For a moment, they pant at each other. But neither is ready to stop. Not by a long shot.

Neil lunges first, head low, arms out, ready to embrace Anderson in a violent tackle. But Anderson sees it. He turns to his side, so when Neil tackles him, he thrusts his elbow on the back of Neil's head. The crack of it echoes as Neil staggers. He blinks rapidly like he's gotten his bell rung.

Anderson grabs a fistful of his hair to slam Neil's head into his knee. Neil almost crumbles, but Anderson shoves him upright and punches him so hard that he whacks his head into the wall. Blood gushes from Neil's nose as he slides down the wall, unconscious.

Instantly, Anderson is at my side. He asks something, but it sounds like he's underwater. Sweat glistens on his upper lip. His handsome face is bruised up, and I think he's going to have a black eye. My poor guy. He waves his hand in front of my face. I can't quite hear him right, but I read his lips, "How many fingers?"

"Three," I squeak out.

He closes his eyes in relief and wraps me in his arms.

19

ANDERSON

Holding June is exactly what I need right now. Doesn't matter that we're in her apartment building lobby. Doesn't matter that we're not *together*. Holding her is the only thing in the world that matters. That bastard will never touch her again.

My fist throbs along with the rest of my body. *Green Sweater* got in some great shots, and he's strong. Whoever he is, he's either had training or he's been in a lot of street fights. That was way too close for comfort.

During the whole thing, I was kicking myself for not taking Moss' offer of a small side piece. He had said, "It does not hurt to carry a little gun. You never know who might need to catch a bullet." Motherfucker was right about that. I'll have to ask him for some training, too. I don't like how close this was, and it's been way too long since I took any kind of martial arts classes.

,June's shaking, and it breaks my heart. I don't trust my voice not to waver, but I have to start a conversation to get her to calm down. "You're sure you're okay?"

"Yeah," she hisses out in a strange whisper. It's all she can do. He ravaged her throat.

I lean back and stare at the bruises blossoming there. The shape of his hand on her throat makes me sick. I cannot believe I let it get that far. That I almost walked away. He would have had her on her back and worse. That sick fuck would have killed her. I'm sure of it. The only question is before or after he did what he wanted to her body.

"Don't," she hisses.

"Don't what?"

"Don't look at me like that." Tears spill down her cheeks.

I hold her close. "Baby, I'm so sorry. How did I look at you?"

She sniffles hard. "Disgusted."

At that, I freeze up. "I am disgusted with him. Not you. You did nothing wrong, June. Nothing. Do you hear me?"

She cries harder, and I wrap her up in me again. Her every sobbing shake destroys me. It takes a long time for her to calm down, and I hold her the whole time, just glad to be here for her. I can't stop thinking about what would have happened if he'd gotten her alone. My imagination runs wild with the thought like it's trying to punish me for not stopping him sooner.

She mumbles something, but I don't catch it. When I lean back, her eyes are so red that it guts me. She breathlessly says, "I don't know how this happened."

"*Green Sweater* is a piece of shit."

She frowns. "*Green Sweater*?"

"I don't know his name."

She almost smiles at that. "Neil. He's a hedge fund manager at Bryce-Connolly. That's what he told me, anyway."

"Well, Neil, the hedge fund manager at Bryce-Connolly, is a piece of shit."

She snorts out a laugh at that before her face crumbles into tears. "I thought he was a nice guy. I'm so sorry, Anderson."

I know I shouldn't keep asking questions. Her throat must be killing her. But she sounds so guilty for something, and it's weirding me out. I can't stop myself from asking, "Sorry for what?"

"I shouldn't have gone with him. I should—"

"Stop. June, please stop. It's fine. We're not together. You don't owe me an explanation for your dating life, and you didn't deserve any of this. You did nothing wrong."

She wipes her wide eyes, but more tears fall. "I shouldn't have gone with him because I'm in love with you."

My voice catches in my throat, and my heart stutters. "I'm in love with you, too, June. I always have been."

She cups my face in her hands, and we meet in the middle for the gentlest kiss imaginable. She gives a small smile. "Didn't want to hurt your lip worse."

But I'm still hazy from our love admissions, and that kiss was not enough to slake my thirst for her. "You can do whatever you want to my lip."

She giggles, but then more tears come. Right. It's been a fuckup of a night. Our emotions are all over the place, and she might be saying things she doesn't mean or will want to take back in the morning once she's calmed down. I won't push her on any of it. Instead, I hold her again. That doesn't seem like crossing the line, and it feels amazing after everything we've been through.

Once she calms down some, she quietly says, "I got a job."

Oh shit. She hasn't figured out I've been watching her. Best to play dumb. "Really?"

"I'm bartending back at the place I worked in college."

No wonder she looks so at home there. "That's great. I'm happy for you."

"Thanks," she says numbly.

Her breathing has evened out, and I want to test out pulling away so we can get this handled. Need to call the cops and get Neil arrested. I also need to talk her into getting checked out at the hospital. Something tells me she's going to be stubborn about that. But I'm worried if I pull away, she'll fall apart. Instead, I wait until she pulls away. "Think you can stand?"

"I don't know. I was blacked out … I don't know for how long."

"Let me call an ambulance—"

"No."

I close my eyes in frustration. "June, you should get checked out."

"I'm bruised. I'll heal."

"If you think you can't stand, then we should get you to the hospital."

".Just need some help, I think." She starts to get up, so I give her a hand. Once she's straight and not wobbling, I feel better. "See? I'm okay."

"You're sure?" I still haven't stopped holding her hand to brace her.

She smiles at that. "Yeah. I am. Are you?"

"I'm fine—"

"You look like you were in a car accident."

"Well, you sound like you swallowed rocks."

She gives me a screwy look.

"Thought we were pointing out the obvious."

She snorts a giggle, and then her face falls. Her eyes have settled on Neil's slumped body. He hasn't budged since I knocked him out. Thankfully, the blood stopped streaming down his face and chest. June shakes her head at him, then holds it as if that will stop her from spinning. "I can't believe I thought he was a nice guy."

"Wolf in sheep's clothing."

"He made it sound like he was this sweetie from a farm in Nebraska. I don't know how much of that was bullshit or if he was for real. How ... how does anyone trust anybody?"

I put my arm around her. "In my experience, it takes years of being a certified asshole, turning over a new leaf, buying a woman's time for a night, and then having your dad turn her life upside down before a woman will trust you."

She laughs at that, and I am relieved to hear it. Her laugh is choppy and a little deranged after everything she's been through tonight, but it's still June's laugh, and there is no better sound in the world. She leans her head on my shoulder. "You're right, though. I do trust you, Anderson."

I don't even care that her head is bearing down on one of my bruises. Is it a bruise? Feels worse. Did that fucker break my clavicle? Doesn't matter. I have June. For now, anyway.

"We should call the cops."

She sighs. "Yeah. I guess so." She stands up, quirking her head to the side as she stares at Neil. "He doesn't look right."

"What do you mean?"

But she kneels next to him, shocking the hell out of me. If I were her, I wouldn't get anywhere near that piece of shit.

"Don't stand so close to him, in case he wakes up."

"I don't think I have to worry about that."

"What are you talking about?"

She quietly murmurs, "He's blue, Anderson."

That drops me next to her. The sheen from the blood on his sweater isn't moving beneath the lights. His chest isn't rising and falling. Warily, I lift his hand, and it limply slaps to the floor. She's right—he is faintly blue. If he's faking this, he's dedicated. Playing dead is a smart tactic when you're down. He's a good enough fighter that this is likely his plan. If so, his next swing will be a kill shot.

"June, get behind me."

She stands up and moves behind me. "What are you doing?"

I gulp and press two fingers to his throat, ready for him to strike.

But he can't strike. He's dead.

-

20

JUNE

Anderson quietly mutters, "He's not just blue. He's dead."

I blink so many times there might as well be a strobe light in the lobby. My brain doesn't want to wrap around this. In fact, my brain doesn't want to comprehend anything that's happened in the past hour. I want to go back in time to the moment Nice Neil kissed me outside of O'Mulligan's and get a do-over of the night.

This cannot be happening.

"Well, it is."

"Did I say that out loud?"

Anderson nods once. "You're shaking again. Do you need to sit?"

But I've lost all my words. Instead, I lean against the wall, and a shaky "How?" rises out of my soul.

He gulps and gestures to the wall behind Neil. There's a deep dent in the plaster. And a streak of blood down from that spot. I hadn't noticed it before. Anderson fingers the hole some, then says, "Pretty sure it's a stud."

I frown up at him. "That's the weirdest thing to say about someone who attacked me—"

"In the wall, June," he says patiently.

It's all too strange to think about. "You're fine, though."

He frowns at me.

"You're bruised and battered, but you're alive. I don't get how he's dead, and you're alive."

"When I punched him, I think the impact sent him careening back against a stud in the wall. Hit him just right at the base of his skull ... that's why he stopped bleeding. No more heartbeat." He gives Neil a shove forward, and sure enough, there's a ton of blood down the back of him.

A wave of nausea strikes, and I have to turn away. I've never been squeamish before. Blood has never bothered me. I've seen lots of bar fights, and god knows, when I get my period, there's plenty of blood. But this is different. This is someone I was making out with. Someone I had ... well, not feelings for, but someone I liked. At first, anyway. "Oh god."

Quietly, Anderson says, "We can't stay here forever, June."

"I know that!" I hiss at him. I'm not actually mad at him — I'm grateful beyond imagining that he was here. It's just that it's impossible for me to cobble my thoughts together right now, and I don't know what to do.

Okay. Lawyer hat on. First of all, thank god there's no doorman. He'd see this ... no. He wouldn't have. If I had a doorman, Neil would have waited until we were in my apartment to start his shit. He would have strangled me or found some other way to kill me after he raped me. Or before ... he didn't seem to care what order he did things in — the bastard had his hand on my throat before he ever got anywhere. Maybe he is a necrophiliac.

Was. Maybe he *was* a necrophiliac.

I shiver thinking about it. Point is, I am so fucking glad I don't have a doorman, because I'd be dead right now. Whatever Neil wanted from me doesn't matter. He's the dead one. Not me. And we have to deal with his body in a safe, legal way.

I take a breath. "We should call the police."

"No."

I blink at him for a moment. "No?"

Anderson scrubs his hand through his hair, and I hope he's not spreading Neil's DNA. "Think about it, June. What happens if we call the police?"

I frown. The words come out numbly. "They come and ask us what happened. We tell them exactly what happened because neither one of us is in the wrong here. They tell us to get to the hospital to get checked out and probably tell us not to leave the city until their investigation is over, and when they find out we've told the truth, everything is fine."

He gives me the saddest smile. "It is sweet that you think it would go that well."

I have the strangest feeling he's being patronizing, but I don't think he means to be. Right now, I'm dazed, and I know it. Maybe he's thinking more clearly than I am. I can't tell. But I want his input on this. "How do you think it would go?"

He sighs, staring at Neil. "The police come and ask us what happened. We tell them because we're innocent enough, right? But I took karate and Muay Thai as a kid. Great for defense, but not so great when it comes to a dead body because now it looks like I'm a hothead who got out of control—"

"How would they even know that? You're being paranoid."

"I won awards at state," he says with a shrug. "I stopped doing it before I got to high school, but it's not that hard to figure out that I've had some training. That will be used against me. My dad, for all his important friends, has important enemies, too. Even if the cops didn't want to come after me, some of Dad's enemies would just to prove to my father that they could. There are a thousand ways this will go very, very wrong, June."

I close my eyes. "Why does everything we do have to revolve around your father?"

"Because he—"

I hold my hand up. "That was rhetorical."

He nods once and sighs. "Even if this went best case scenario like you talked about, it'll be plastered all over the news for a long time. This will haunt me forever. Goodbye to state office. Goodbye to a possible Senatorship. My trajectory, as sketchy as it is now, will be destroyed by this piece of shit." He kicks Neil's thigh in anger, and the body slumps over, earning a sneer from Anderson before he turns away. "Not to mention what'll happen to you. Do you really want to be tied to Neil every time someone googles you? Is this what you want to be known for?"

I can't think about that right now. My mind sorts through how this will affect me. Mine ranges in trauma, though. Not in career destruction ... or will it?

I don't know. This is going to be a lot to unpack with a therapist one day. I know it will. Right now, the man who attacked me is dead. That's a good thing. Especially given what he said about other women ... he made it sound like I was not the first he'd done this to. Did he leave a trail of bodies in Nebraska? I doubt I'll ever know for sure.

My voice still sounds rough. "What do we do, then?"

He sighs. "I got a guy."

A spike of chilled sickness jerks through me. Did he really just say that? I stare at him for a few seconds, open-mouthed. "You got a guy? One that helps you with dead bodies?"

His lips smooth into a line of impatience. "It's this, or we call the police and blow our lives up, June."

On the one hand, I don't want this to get out. Anderson has a good point. I don't want to be the woman attached to the death of this monster. I don't want my face on the news, and I certainly don't want this to be what I'm known for. It's bad enough that Elliot has fucked me over. It's not fair if Neil gets to, too.

With all that's happened, I'm unemployable in my field. I'd hate to be unemployable everywhere. Kelsey would stand by me, but I don't want to be the sideshow freak at the bar, either. People are weird — they'd come to get a drink poured by me just because of this. They'd ask all kinds of questions because drunk people have no filter. They'd ask, what did Neil do? Do I think he deserved to die for getting a little handsy? Do I like it when guys are rough with me, and he just took it too far?

He's dead, and I'm alive, so in a lot of minds, that makes me a murderous bitch who should have gotten what she had coming to her. A lot of people will take a man's side no matter what, and if I have to spend the rest of my life defending what happened here, I'll have to move and hope this doesn't follow me, or I'll lose my mind. No. Just no. Neil's corpse does not get to chase me out of my hometown.

On the other hand, I also don't want to be involved in a crime. Right now, we haven't done anything wrong. The moment he makes that call, though, we've mishandled a dead body. Three years in prison, as far as I remember from law school. I do not want to go to prison. I would not do well in prison. A gray prison jumpsuit will not suit me.

Committing a crime to cover up a non-crime feels like a bad idea. But so do all the other outcomes, and we're running out of time. At some point, a neighbor will come through here, and what the hell do we do then?

I sigh. "Make the call."

21

ANDERSON

Once the call is made, there's no going back. I know that. But going forward legitimately is uglier than going forward illegitimately, and I don't have the stomach to be attached to *Green Sweater* for the rest of my life. He's garbage. I won't wear his stink forever, and I'll be damned if I let June. This is going to make things weird for me with Dad, and I'd rather things be weird than be in prison.

I dial up Moss. "Sorry it's so late. I got a hankering to catch some haddock. You up for a boat trip?"

His smile is evident in his rough voice. "I'll bring the gear, you bring the beer."

"I'll text you the address where you can pick me up." I hang up and send him the address.

"That ... that's it?" June asks, her voice still shaking.

"Yep. That's it."

She looks ill. "Seems like there should be more to it than that."

Gently, I put my arm around her. "You okay?"

She simply looks at me.

"Yeah, I know. It's a dumb question, but I don't know what else to say."

That earns her smile. She leans against me a little, and fuck, I've missed that. "I know. I don't know what else to say, either." She stands there, letting me hold her for a moment. But when a thought hits her, her body gets stiff. "Can I ... I really want to go shower. Forever."

"Eh, not just yet. I want to do this by my guy's book. He knows what to do. Sorry."

Her lips press tightly together, but she nods. "How ... how have you been? Since when do you have a guy for things like this? What's changed?"

Everything. "We'll talk about all of that later. Don't really want to get into things like that when we're about to be interrupted."

"He's that fast?"

"Lives near here. I expect him soon."

Something else makes her go stiff again. "Am I … I know you wouldn't put me in harm's way, but should I be afraid of this guy?"

"I would never let him touch you, June. And he's only violent when he's told to be."

"Sounds like a charmer."

I laugh. "You might be the first person to describe him that way."

Just then, Moss barges in with a black duffel bag in hand. Dressed in head-to-toe black, as well, complete with a black skullcap. Good for the weather and for witnesses at a distance who will think he has black hair instead of being bald. One of his many tricks for getting away with illegal activities.

He sees June, noting her petrified expression, her mussed clothing, and her throat bruise. He sees me, looking disheveled. Then he sees *Green Sweater*. His lip curls in a sneer. "The haddock was an asshole, uh?"

"You can say that again."

He nods once, then kneels and opens his duffel bag. He passes gloves and a spray canister to June. "Miss, if you would, please spray every surface in this room with that. A light mist will do the trick."

She blinks and takes the items, putting on the gloves. It's like she's on auto-pilot—she does exactly what he says with no questions asked.

"You get to help me." He unrolls a carpet from the duffel bag. I have no clue how he fit it in there. Then he lays plastic sheeting onto it. We make a *Green Sweater* burrito, and I try to ignore the crunch of bone when Moss kicks the bundle to ensure it's snug. Or just to get his own knock on the guy. I'm not sure. Then he hoists the bundled roll onto his shoulder and carries it out to his van.

He returns a moment later—or maybe it only seems like it's just a moment. My brain is getting foggy with post-fight letdown. When he returns, he has a cart with potted plants in vases, wooden stands, cleaning equipment, and bottles of water. He passes me rags with some sort of chemical on them. "Wipe any blood or sweat anywhere you touch. Make it clean."

"What are you going to do?"

He grins. "What I do." He holds up a potted plant in a vase and a wooden stand, and I could not possibly be more confused. But I follow orders because he's saving my life. Still, I steal glances while he works. I might need to know how to do this on my own one day.

Moss wipes down the blood where *Green Sweater* knocked into the wall and busted the plaster. Once it's no longer red, he sets the wooden stand on the ground where *Green Sweater* died. He places the potted plant on top of it. With a gentle push, he knocks it into the wall in a rough approximation of where his head went into it. The sound alerts June, but when she sees what he's up to, she resumes spraying. Potting soil is everywhere, thanks to the shattered vase. It covers anything we might have missed spraying. When maintenance hears of the broken potted plant, they'll clean it up, and no one will think twice about the broken wall.

After setting that up, he sets out a few more potted plants on stands to make it appear as though the building manager had tried to class the place up. It also makes the sight of a solitary broken vase not that out of the ordinary. Genius.

"Pity there is no camera here," he grunts.

"A pity?" I ask, shocked.

"If there were, I might have told you to call the police. Cameras are the best witnesses when you do nothing wrong. You are a good man, Anderson. I know you did nothing wrong."

If only a jury of my peers would believe that. If only that mattered to the evening news. I huff. "Well, we work with what we've got, right?"

He smiles and nods. When his eyes fall on June across the hall, he quietly asks, "How bad did it get?"

"Bad. But not that far."

To my surprise, he crosses himself like a grateful Catholic. "She is fortunate you watch over her. Especially in a building with no security." Unfortunately, he has a point.

Once I get my life back, I'm moving her to a better building. Mine, if at all possible.

Moss interrupts my hopeful thoughts. "I will need your assistance with the haddock. It is a two-man job. He is a large catch."

I nod once and turn to June. I do not want to leave her right now. It feels like the wrong thing to do. She's been through so much. She shouldn't be alone right now. Hell, I shouldn't be alone right now. But I suppose Moss is a kind of company ... but June. She looks so lost. Her eyes are wide, and I know she's sprayed that mailbox half a dozen times. She's dazed, maybe in shock.

"Give me a minute."

He nods once. "But we will have to go soon. You're sure there were no witnesses besides the two of you?"

"If so, they would have called the cops by now. It's the weekend. People are out or asleep this late."

"Very good timing."

Lucky me. I walk to her, crossing the killing field to reach her. There is something unsettling about walking through the space where I killed a man. Like I expect his ghost to come at me or something like that. I have never been superstitious in my life, but for some reason, it feels sacrilegious to be walking where he died. Odd, that.

"June?"

She jumps and lets out a squeak. Right. Don't sneak up on the woman who was just attacked. I'm an idiot.

"Sorry for that. We have to go handle the—"

"Haddock?" she asks.

That's my girl. Catching on fast is a specialty of hers. "Yeah. But I want you upstairs—Moss, should she do something special with her clothes or anything?"

To my surprise, he keeps his voice soft when speaking to her. It's like he's trying not to spook her after everything she has gone through tonight. "No. Nothing special to be done. Wash like usual. Throw away after wash, if you like, miss."

She doesn't make eye contact with him, but she nods all the same. "I'll go up … do I need to spray anything else?"

I glance at Moss, who shakes his head. "No, baby. You can go up now. Thank you for your help. That was brave."

At that, she gives me a mildly annoyed look. She whispers, "I didn't have a choice. He's scary."

"Right now, though, he's on our side. Let's be glad for that."

Her smile comes in at the edges. It's only a little, but it makes me feel better. "Yeah. I guess so."

I might be pushing it, but I have to try. "When this is done, I'll come check on you, okay?"

"I'd like that."

Three simple words that mean the world to me. I shouldn't be thinking of my love life right now. I killed a man. That has weight, and it should. But just hearing that she wants me to come to see her after everything is said and done is enough to make my heart lighter in spite of *Green Sweater*.

"It'll be a while. Sleep if you can."

Her impertinent laugh tells me that's not happening.

I escort her to the elevator and watch as the doors close. Moss says, "We must hurry. Haddock stinks fast when dead, I do not want my van to reek of death."

22

JUNE

I can't stop shaking. I hadn't noticed it until I tried to press the button to my floor. But my finger shook so badly that it was blurry. Once I managed to press the button, the doors made Anderson's face vanish, and that made the shaking so much worse. By the time I reach my door and try to put the key in the lock, I can't.

I force myself to take a deep breath, but the air passing through my throat hurts. There's a lump there. Hot, nagging. Telling me to cry. But if I do that now, then I'll never get into my home. I close my eyes and feel the lock with my fingertips. Gentling the key's tip into the hole, the notches on the inside feel familiar as metal fits into metal.

Home. I am home.

I am safe.

The thought makes me laugh maniacally as I turn the doorknob. Am I losing my mind? Maybe. But it doesn't scare me like I thought it would. After everything I've been through tonight, a little madness feels appropriate.

Necessary, even. How the fuck else am I supposed to get through all of this?

Nothing makes any sense. Madness might save me for a while.

Well, madness and a shower.

I head for my bathroom, then clarity strikes with a vengeance. I bolt for my front door, throwing all the locks and the chain. In all my years of living alone, I've never forgotten to lock at least one of them behind me, and *tonight* is the time I pick to do so? Fuck.

I'm not in my right mind, and I know it, but I have to do something, or I'll hurt myself. I know that, too.

So, I force myself to walk more carefully to the bathroom, avoiding doorframes with my elbows and stepping the particular way I do if I'm sloppy drunk. Minding each footstep like it could be my last. Once I reach my bathroom, I turn on the shower and wait until it heats up to test the temperature instead of just climbing in blindly like normal. Don't want to burn myself, and this old building's hot water is the hottest I've ever had anywhere I've been.

But when I look in the mirror and start to undress, I freeze up.

His hand is on my throat. Purple already. I don't normally bruise up this fast, but his grip...

Can't think about it. I turn my head away from the mirror. I don't want to see Neil's hand on me. Don't want to think about that ever again. I know I'll have to. Tonight ... it won't just go away because I want it to. But right now, I don't want to think about him. Or his hand. Or the way he pressed himself against me through our clothes. The sick, dirty feeling creeps over me again, and I turn to retch into the toilet just in time to miss vomiting all over my counter.

The one good thing about a small bathroom, I guess. Everything is within easy reach.

I rinse my mouth out and contemplate taking my clothes off. But it feels ungrateful to take them off. They protected me. Suppose I hadn't had my clothes on ... if ... if anything had gone differently tonight, I'd be dead right now. I know it in my gut. He wouldn't have left me alive.

I retch again at the thought, then climb into the shower, fully clothed. It feels good. Safe. Protected. But soon, it feels like wet clothes, and slowly, I take them off. Scarf first —

Oh, my fuck. This is Neil's scarf.

CHARLOTTE BYRD

I fling it out of the shower as fast as possible and burst into tears. He had given me that scarf tonight, and I thought that was the sweetest thing. I am a fucking fool, and nearly a dead one, all because some guy told me exactly what I wanted to hear.

With startling lucidity, it hits me. Anderson has never told me what I wanted to hear. He has always been straight with me, even when I didn't want him to be. That is how I know I can trust him. He might come from the worst kind of father, but he is honest with me. And he has the world's best timing. God, if he hadn't shown up tonight ...

Why did he show up tonight? I never did get the chance to ask him. Was it just good timing? Did he happen to walk by and see — no. I'm not that naïve. He was watching me. He had to be. And if I ask him, he will tell me. He won't lie. He's Anderson West. There are gruesome things he's capable of, but lying to me is not one of them.

And if I'm honest with myself, I don't even care that he was following me.

Our breakup has sucked. I physically hurt when I am not with him. Call it codependency, but I don't fucking care. I love that man. I am so grateful that he was here tonight that the method of his arrival doesn't even ping my bad guy radar. My bad guy radar got a hard reset tonight.

My clothes are soaked through, so I pry them off of me to attempt to get clean. That sounds nice and good and like something I haven't had in a long time. I scrub my hair and my body a few times before getting out. Doesn't feel like enough to be clean again, though. But if I keep going, I'll destroy my skin. Even with all the humidity in the air from the rain and wet snows we've had this year, it'll dry out fast from indoor heating.

Rubbing lotion on my skin feels odd, so I give up after a forearm. I don't want long, lingering strokes on me. Not even from my own hand. Instead, I dress in my softest pajamas, wring out my wet laundry into the tub, and toss it into the laundry bin before padding out to the kitchen.

Once I get there, I realize I was in the shower for over an hour. When was the last time that happened? I have no idea.

I'm a little more stable on my feet now, so I worry less about falling or bumping into things. I'd love some cheese, but using a knife seems like a bad idea at the moment. More stable, yes, but I might be prone to clumsiness with my still-shaking hands. Instead, I make a cup of tea and some dry toast to settle my upset stomach.

Nibbling at the edges, my mind wanders like it's being nibbled, too. I have a bad case of the ifs. If I hadn't gone out with Neil, none of this would be happening. If I hadn't kissed him, he wouldn't have felt entitled to me. If I hadn't flirted with him in the first place, Anderson wouldn't have committed murder.

Of course, it wasn't murder. It was self-defense. But would anyone believe that? He's my ex. He saw me with another man after he stalked me home. I know exactly how a prosecutor would pose the facts to a jury. The dry, hard, facts of the case do not add up to Anderson's freedom.

Dry and hard. Like my toast. Blech.

I dump it into the trash and reach for my emergency chocolate I keep in the back of the cabinet. It's a bag of chocolate chips, perfect for having just a little or a lot. Tonight, I might eat the whole bag. No, not tonight. This morning. Fuck me, when did it get so late?

Pouring a glass of wine to accompany my chocolate chip bowl, I take another deep breath. The scent of syrah is calming for some reason. Maybe it's knowing about the impending warm buzz that does it. I dunno. All I know is I have wine and chocolate and Netflix, and I'm going to use all of this to phase out for a while.

I settle onto the couch with my junk food and click on the TV. Scrolling delays my drinking and snacking, so I pick something at random and let it flash before my eyes while I mindlessly consume. It's better this way. I'm better this way. Senseless. Empty. Hollow. My only goal is a temporary vegetative state. I don't want to feel anything anymore.

From the moment Neil got forceful with me, all I have felt is terror. And I am exhausted from hours of that. I set my wine glass down next to my chocolate chip bowl and wriggle into the couch cushions until I'm lying down. Sleep might not come, but right now, it sounds like a welcome break from the terror. After five minutes with my eyes closed and a mental battle with the memory of Neil, I know sleep is not going to be my friend tonight.

23

ANDERSON

"You love her," Moss gruffly declares as the docks come into view.

I can't tell if that's a good or bad thing in his book. If I say yes, she can be used against me. If I say no, then I'll look like a lunatic for killing *Green Sweater*. I refuse to call him Neil, even in my head. Not to dehumanize him and, therefore, justify what I did. What I did needs no justification.

It's that a man who does what he did is no man. He wasn't human. He was a monster in a human suit. No actual human can do what he did to June, and he was so bold about it that I'm sure it wasn't his first time. To attack her in a shared hallway, in full view of the street through the glass doors … that was no man. That was a beast.

But I sit next to another beast, and he left a declaration hanging. So, I confirm, "I love her."

He cheerfully nudges my thigh. "Love is a good thing, Anderson. It makes all the things we do worthy of doing them."

"Is that how you justify your line of work?" I can't take the sting of judgment out of my words. It's there. And I don't have it in me to care right now. He helped me tonight, but Moss was there on the second worst day of my life. He made me complicit in the murders of three people. I won't forget that.

He takes a moment to respond. "I do what I do because I am good at what I do. It is why you called me."

Not wrong at all on that score. "But the rest of it … the killing in my dad's name. What makes that okay in your mind?"

He shrugs. "Some people need killing."

I want to argue, but considering we're hauling a corpse I made, I don't have much of a leg to stand on. "Yes, some people do. But people who merely owe money? That seems like a flimsy reason."

"You ask these things like your father is the first man to employ me. Is that what you think?"

I've never considered it. "I don't know."

"He is not. I have worked for others. Others who were … less scrupulous than your father. Men and women who wanted me to punish people for slights. Whether or not they were real slights, it did not matter to them, only that their enemies were punished. Brutally." He pauses. "I became good at what I do. Word got around. Your father … he is not a good man. But he is better than some. I came to work for him because the people I hunt for him have done wrong by him. Yes, even just money. Money is a resource. Would you hit a man who stole your food?"

"Only if I were starving, and my father is certainly not starving."

He shrugs again. "Resources are resources. But he has never sent me out for someone because he thought they insulted him. He has never sent me out to attack an innocent. It has been over ten years since I was sent out for no reason at all. I have your father to thank for this."

He used to attack innocents? Fuck. I don't want to think of that on top of what happened tonight.

"I know you love her because you would not have done this otherwise, Anderson. You are measured. Careful. You think before you act. This is why I come to help you tonight. If you were hotheaded, I would not have. He attacked her, did he not?"

Numbly, I nod. "Bastard had her by the throat. He was going to do worse to her."

"I saw the bruise." He looks like he wants to spit. "A man who attacks a woman that way, he is a coward. A weakling. If you have to force yourself on her, you never had her. A woman must give willingly." His hands grip the steering wheel tighter. "If any man touches my daughters that way … "

"I'd prefer not to try to imagine what you'd do, Moss."

He huffs a bitter laugh. "You and I are of the same mind, I think. But once I got a hold of him, it would last for weeks if his heart was strong."

And again, I am filled with the urge to never fall on his bad side.

The dock is on the outskirts of town and empty for now. It won't be for long, though. Hobby fishers start early, even in this frigid weather. This isn't a commercial dock, thankfully, or it would be swamped by now.

He parks, and we get out, each taking an end of our *Green Sweater* roll to carry it to his boat. It's at the end of the dock, so by the time we get there, my muscles burn with fatigue. It has been a long fucking night, and dead weight really is somehow heavier than living weight.

We toss him over the side into the boat, then climb in. Within moments, Moss has us on the water, tooling out deeper. We're both quiet, and I know why I am, but I'm not sure why he is. I'm wiped out from the night and thinking about the fact we're about to dump a body I made. But Moss isn't usually silent. It's eerie.

When I make eye contact, I almost expect an attack from him. But he's smiling. So, I ask, "What is it?"

"I did not need your help with the body."

The words are jarring. Of course, he didn't. He hoisted *Green Sweater's* body over his shoulder like it was nothing back in June's building. He knows how to dispose of a body. Why the fuck am I here instead of with her?

Is he going to kill me?

I look for any kind of weapon while not making any fast moves. "So, why am I here, Moss?"

"A test. To see how far gone you were when this happened."

That might have been the last thing I expected to hear. I give up my search for a weapon to look him in the eyes. "Huh?"

He chuckles. "When I came, you let me take control. Let me handle things, let me tell you and her what to do. You both needed tasks. You were not ready to handle this on your own. You came with me willingly, even though you wished to stay at her side because you knew someone else knew more than you. It was to show you that you still have things to learn, and I still have things to teach you." All mirth drains from his face. "So do not think to cut me off anytime soon, understand?"

The man is a fucking mind reader. He knows I want out from under Dad's thumb. He knows I don't want to be in on the ride-alongs. He knows I have plans to end Dad's illegal dealings, and he doesn't want to be fired anytime soon.

Right now, I'm angry with him. I should be by June's side. Holding her, getting her take out, whatever she needs. That is where I belong. Instead, he has me doing his grunt work.

But …

Moss, for all his condescension, isn't wrong. I do need to learn things from him. I would have botched trying to hide *Green Sweater's* body. Without a doubt, I know that. And the only time I saw June stop shaking was when she was spraying whatever that chemical was. He gave her something to concentrate on. Me, too. Condescending or not, it was useful. *Moss* is useful.

And once Dad is out of the picture, I have to keep him happy or end up in a carpet myself. He's showing me what happens to people he deals with. He has since day one. The ride-alongs are useful to Dad because we get things done for him, but they're useful for Moss, too. He's been showing me his skillset, so I know who I'm dealing with because he knows Dad's plan is for me to take over, and he wants a secure position with me.

"I won't cut you off, Moss. I might not like everything Dad does, but he's not stupid. He hires the right people for the job. When I have his seat, you'll retain yours." Until I figure something else out.

He grins and claps my shoulder. "I like you, Anderson. You are better than the last man I worked with."

And what the hell happened to him? Staring out across the blackwater, I have a feeling I know. "How am I better?"

He points to his temple. "Absent here. A moron, too dumb for my own good. Nearly got us arrested twice." Then he shakes his head. "He liked disco music and always insisted on playing it on the job. Disco!"

"What, like The Bee Gees?" I ask with a laugh.

"And Donna Summer and KC and the Sunshine Band and Sister Sledge, but the worst was ABBA. So much ABBA."

I snort a laugh, thinking about the big bad killer bopping to disco, and I can't make the picture work. "That is hard to imagine."

"You let me listen to my music. I like that very much. You are considerate when we travel. Much improvement." He kills the motor. "Ready?"

I gulp against a dry throat. "Thought you didn't need me for this."

"It's your first body. I will not take that honor from you. Come. We weigh it down."

I hadn't noticed the cement block at the far end of the boat because it was covered by a tarp. Apparently, we are on his body-dumping boat. It seems this man has a mode of transport for every occasion.

We chain the cement blocks to the body. He swears it doesn't take all that much to weigh a body down, but I worry it's not enough. "You do not trust easy, but I do this for a long time now. No one will find him. Not out here. Not ever."

With that, we fling the blocks overboard, and when enough of them are over, their weight drags the carpet overboard, too. Moss spits in the water after him. "Good riddance."

I spit, too, because he's right.

—

24

ANDERSON

Once the body is gone, I feel things. The cold, for one. It's beyond brisk out on the open water. Some part of me had gone numb after *Green Sweater* was dead. Maybe my mind tried to protect me from the severity of my actions … I don't know. But I start to feel better once I see the docks again.

The docks mean I can put this behind me and check on June.

We disembark and get into his van fast. When he cranks on the heat, it's not enough. The freezing cold has finally cut into me, and I cannot get warm. Something tells me I won't be warm again until I see her face.

"You did well, Anderson," Moss says. "Your father will be proud."

"Proud that I murdered someone?" Saying it out loud makes me want to vomit.

"Ees not murder. You were right to call me — police … they do not take these things well. But it was no murder. You did what you had to do to protect the one you love. The haddock brought it on himself."

I'm not sure if the approval of an actual murderer is what I should be looking for, but at the moment, it soothes the guilt I have a right to have. I know I did the right thing. It wasn't even a conscious call to make, truthfully. Once I saw him put his hands on her in a way she didn't want, I went on autopilot, and I wasn't about to stop until he was down for the count. Truth be told, before I knew he was dead, I'd begun to plan his death for what he'd done to June.

I sigh at the thought of her. Fuck, she looked so fragile in his grasp. My strong June, weakened by a beast. My equal, gasping for air … no. Not my equal. June is better than me in every aspect. I would give her everything just to have her back in my arms again. That's what makes the night so foggy.

I have only a vague recollection of when she went down. My last thoughts before I was on top of his chest and pounding his face were, "She better be alive." I'd never been so terrified in my life, and I couldn't check on her. I had to eliminate the threat, or she would have never been safe again. And if she had died from him choking her …

My mind would have snapped. I know it. As it was, I was close to going feral. During the fight, I nearly bit his throat out. Any weapon in my arsenal was an option. Teeth, nails, hair pulling. All of it was on the table. I sank into some primal part of my mind. I didn't care anymore. If she was gone, so was I.

But then I heard her keening rasp, and it brought me back to myself.

She was alive. No one else mattered.

There were no consequences to my actions in my mind. No fear of repercussions at the moment. Laws and rules and decorum did not exist in my head. Once he started to choke her, I couldn't have told him my own name. I knew nothing but destroying him. I had sunk so low into my caveman brain that hearing her rasp buoyed me straight back into myself, only now, I had something to fight for.

"We are here."

I blink awake, realizing I'd fallen asleep on the car ride back to June's place. All my thoughts had been of the fight and of June, and I'd nodded off. I take another breath to fill my lungs and clear my head, but it won't be properly cleared until I see her. "Thanks, Moss. For everything."

He smiles and nods. "Anytime you need me, Anderson, you call me. For anything."

I smile and nod back. "Same." Then I get out and into the frosty night air. He leaves, still driving the speed limit, using turn signals. As Moss puts it, break one law at a time. That way, you never attract undue attention to yourself. He's right—I have much to learn from him.

Just as I reach for the door to her building, I catch a whiff of freshly baked something. A plume of flour puffs up into the air down the road. A bakery, already hard at work at three-thirty in the morning. It makes my mouth water, and I'm sure June hasn't had anything good to eat since I was gone. She has a hard enough time keeping herself well-fed under the best of circumstances.

I stroll to the bakery, and at first, they won't open up. But I flash a hundred-dollar bill through the glass door, and that gets them moving. Overpaying for things tends to open doors. I get two coffees, a dozen bagels of different flavors, and some cream cheeses so she has decent food in her place, and I tell them to keep the rest as a tip, then head back to her place.

I'm at her door before I can think, but suddenly, I'm nervous. What if she realized I was stalking her? What if she takes back saying she loves me? What if she hates me for killing someone in front of her?

Even though he deserved it without question, not everyone responds well to that. When Moss killed three people in front of me, I hated him for it. But my hate didn't change things, and neither would hers.

Even if she hated me for the rest of my life, I'd still be in love with her.

With that thought in mind, I knock. The slides of several locks sound out, but before she undoes the final one, she softly calls out, "Hello?"

"It's me, June."

That gets the chain undone. She opens the door, and I do my best to look her in the eye instead of at the bruise on her throat. She looks so tired, like she needs ten years of sleep.

I hold up the bag. "Got coffee and bagels. Thought you might be hungry, or—

She opens the door wider and gives a meek smile. "You don't have to bribe me for me to let you in."

I chuckle at that and walk into her place. It's a quaint apartment decorated in Grandma chic because her grandmother used to own it. But I can't take any of the sights in. She's the only thing I want to see.

Setting the bag on the breakfast bar on my right, I turn to look at her after she re-locks everything.

June still looks fragile but in a different way now. No, not fragile. Traumatized. So, I redirect her to help. "Hungry?"

"Coffee sounds wonderful right now."

I smile and nod, happy I know the way to her heart. "Hazelnut latte. I hope that's okay."

June smiles and nods, taking it from the bag. She takes a sniff of it first and appears pleased before she has a sip. After that, her shoulders droop. "The warmth is good on my throat. Thank you so much for this."

Of course, I brought her bagels. Something chewy and crispy when toasted. Something hard for her to swallow. Dammit. "I can go out and get you oatmeal or something if that's easier for you to eat."

She demurs, shaking her head. "A bagel sounds like heaven right now."

"But can you swallow it? I should have thought about that—

"I'll be fine. Promise."

We get our bagels prepared—mine, a sesame with dill cream cheese, hers, a blueberry with lemon cream cheese—and take them to the couch in the living room. For a moment, I picture what it'd be like to live with her. To be together always. Domestic bliss things, like cleaning a house together or cooking dinner together. Simple things. I love the thought. So much better than what we've done together tonight.

Between bites, she asks, "How are you?"

"Pretty sure that's my line, considering. But I didn't want to make you talk if you don't have to."

She gulps her untoasted bagel down. It doesn't seem to hurt her much — no wincing. But it still looks like work. "Talking is okay. And I have no idea how I'm doing right now. It's like, I'm fine one moment, and then it all comes crashing at me. You?"

"Can I tell you something stupid?"

"Always."

"I'm mad I didn't get to kill him on purpose."

She laughs sharply at that. "That is stupid, and I totally understand."

"Fuck, it's good to hear you laugh."

"You're the only person who could make me smile after everything."

It lifts my heart to hear that. "June, I know tonight has been traumatic and fucking awful." I brace myself to say what I need to say. Doesn't make it any easier. "But if, at any point, you want to retract telling me you love me, I understand. It's been an emotional rollercoaster, and —

She pops forward and kisses me softly, then presses her forehead to mine. "I'm not taking it back. I meant what I said. Did you?"

"Yes."

She sits back again, smiling this time. "Good."

"Do … do you want to talk about it?"

"I'm not sure. You were following me, right? That's how you were there in time."

If I admit that, will she change her mind? Doesn't matter. I'm not lying to her ever again. "I'd hardly call it being there in time, but yeah. I was."

"Anderson, you saved my life, so you were there in time." She sips her latte, thinking. "And I understand following me. It's okay. I'm not mad. Our breakup has sucked. We do iffy things when we're in pain. I get that."

"You're being way too understanding."

She smiles. "A flaw of mine, I think."

"Yeah, maybe." But I'm smiling when I say it.

June sets her food aside to give me her full attention, so I do the same. Her eyes are red and swollen from crying. Her throat still wears that purple bruise. But she's still the most beautiful woman I have ever seen. After all she has been through — the auction, the kidnapping, getting fired, and now this—she's still smiling. She is so much stronger than me, and I am in awe of her.

"I don't want to be broken up anymore, Anderson."

My heart wants that to mean what I think it means, but I need clarity. "What do you want?"

"You. In my life. I want you to be my boyfriend again. Or for the first time. We weren't real specific before, and—

I lean and kiss her in a flash. This is exactly what I want, and I can't believe I'm getting it. I slant my mouth over hers, sliding my tongue along the seam of her lips, and she lets me in. My heart leaps into my throat.

Throat. Fuck.

I pull back to my side of the couch. "Sorry. I got carried away."

"Don't be sorry." She crawls to my side, straddling me. "I want you, Anderson."

"*Want*?"

For an answer, she pulls her pajama top off and kisses me. And because I'm weak, I let her. I am of two minds at the moment. I don't know if this is what she needs right now. But I can't be the condescending prick who tells her what she can and can't do with her own body. Not after what she's been through tonight. Her body, her choice.

That said, I don't know if I can be monster enough to take advantage of her vulnerability. But am I taking advantage? She's instigating this. I know she's emotionally wrecked over everything. I am, too. Shit, is this going to fuck me up?

My raging cock, on the other hand, has no qualms about any of this. The traitor.

Her small hand pries at my clothes and the touch of her skin on mine wipes out all doubt. If this fucks us up, we'll be fucked up together. I clasp her ass with one hand and stand up with the other so her legs wrap around my waist. We kiss as I carry her to her bed. I need this. I need her. How can I even think of denying her anything she wants?

Clothes fly off us both in all directions until we are skin-on-skin. I lay her down before me, and as much as I'd love to spend an hour worshipping her with my tongue, I need to feel her tight body around me. She pulls me on top of her, spreading her thighs for me and cradling my body there. Our kisses are fevered and messy, something between a kiss and a giggle. My heart pounds faster than anything. I'm simply too giddy to have her with me again.

I brush my cock over her to make sure she's wet before I enter her. No more pain for my love. Only pleasure. Once I start, though, it's nearly impossible to hold myself back. She must be on the same page —she juts herself up to me for more. Our bodies wave at one another until we are locked in together, sweetly moaning. Hers is almost a purr, and instantly, I'm addicted to the sound.

We kiss and stroke and groan together, every movement, every sound, perfection. I love her with my whole being, and I want to show her with my body. When she looks up at me with that mystified smile, I know I'm giving her one, too. Everything between us is simply too good. Nothing could ever be this incredible again.

Until the next thrust. And the one after that. And so on.

She wraps her legs around me tightly as she comes, and her pussy clenches on me like she never wants to let me go. I don't want her to. I work her into a frenzy. No more words out of her. Only more of those delicious sounds.

Her face flushes red as her head digs back into the pillow, baring her throat to me. I see evidence of the unworthy man on her there, and knowing he could have never had this, I work her harder. He could never earn her love. Could never make her come. It's petty of me, and I don't care. I beat him in every possible way, and it makes me feel like a conqueror.

Once her body goes limp, I'm convinced she's about to fall asleep. But not my June. She pushes me until I roll onto my back for her, and she straddles my cock, riding me. Just when I think she'll zig, she zags, and I love it.

She lays on my chest, and I hold her to me as we gently roll against one another. I'm so deep inside of her that I'm lost, and I can't think of a better thing than being lost inside of June. Her body pulses on me again as she tenses, and her climax brings mine forward. She kisses me as she comes, and her taste tips me over the edge. June makes me come deep inside of her, and there is nothing else in the world. Just her and me and this moment. I want to live here forever.

25

JUNE

I wake up, twined in Anderson. His arms, his legs. The poor guy has so many bruises on him. I didn't realize just how bad things had been in the fight until he was naked. His ribs, collarbone, and shins, not to mention his handsome face. He's all scuffed up and purple in spots, but none of it slowed him down once he knew what I wanted.

Sex after trauma can be a mistake. I know this. I went into it with my eyes wide open. But I didn't care. I needed him. Needed the comfort of his body, his way. The feel of him set something deep inside of me at ease. Making love had never felt that right, not even after he rescued me from my kidnappers.

Even now, I want him again. It's sometime in the morning—the sun is at just the right angle to tell me that. I hope he doesn't have anywhere to be because

I'm not waking him for anything. Not even my own libido. Instead, I snuggle back against him, relishing the warmth of his body.

He makes me feel protected and cherished when he spoons me. I love the feel of his skin on mine. Languid heat flushes through me, and it's hard not to press back against his morning wood. Here, I'm safe. Here, I'm loved. Last night feels a million miles away, and I am so damned grateful for that. Anderson has made me grateful for everything.

I'm alive, thanks to him.

When he clutches at my waist and pulls me closer in his sleep, I love it. It's like I'm his teddy bear or something. I comfort him as much as he comforts me. This is what love is supposed to be. Will things be complicated? I'm sure of it. As long as his father breathes, it'll be complicated. But we can face anything together. Last night showed me that. I only hope I can be there for Anderson if ever he needs someone the way I needed him.

I'll do my damnedest.

He kisses the back of my neck, and it sends shivers through me. His sleepy voice is so deep that there are even more shivers. "Good morning, baby."

"Good morning."

"I don't know about you, but I could really use a fucking shower."

I giggle at that. "Had one last night before you got here, but I wouldn't mind another. If that was an invitation, I mean."

"You are permanently invited to all of my showers." He kisses the back of my neck again and presses his hard cock against my ass before he takes a deep breath of me. The simple act of him breathing me in turns me on. Like he's some kind of animal, scenting his mate. He growls, "Your skin is so soft there."

I ache for him again. This man is everything I want. Softly, I murmur, "You might like it better, soft and slippery. Shower?"

He lets out a groan. "Yeah. Shower."

We manage to make our way there before falling into each other's mouths. He fumbles with the shower knob as we make out, so I turn us and set the temperature where I like it. With him behind me again, he lifts my hair and nibbles on my shoulder. Heat pools between my thighs in response. The water is hot enough, so I yank back the curtain, and we barely make it into the shower before he has his hand on my pussy.

"So fucking wet for me already," he murmurs before he kisses me. He's right. I'm practically drenched. His finger glides right in while his thumb works my clit. His work makes me shudder. But then he pulls back. "Not yet." Anderson drops to his knees and lifts up my left leg over his shoulder for access. Thank god there's a grab bar in the shower, or I'd fall over.

No, not thank god. Thank Grandma. Nope. Don't want to think about that right now.

I cling to it for dear life while Anderson sucks my clit. His finger still shuttles in and out of me, and I'm already on fire for him. I chirp out, "Just like that. Don't stop!"

He doesn't. I think he'd never stop if he didn't need to eat food at some point. His finger hooks against my G-spot, working me there. Fire pours through my veins as I come, and my back arches so hard he almost loses his grip on me. Just as my orgasm ends, he turns me around and thrusts his cock into me. A thick arm wraps around my waist to hold me up.

He's a man possessed, pounding like a demon. It feels so fucking good that another climax builds fast. Anderson reaches around and works my tender clit. I'm shaking against him, unable to speak or think. I can't do anything but come for him again. I'm screaming, and my body jerks in his grasp as I come all over his cock, but he doesn't drop me, and he doesn't quit. He's only too happy to make me squirm and cry out for him. I hear his gloating huff behind me. "That's it, baby, just let go!"

I do. I couldn't stop if I tried. He milks another one from me, with his cock dancing on my G-spot from behind. Spots burst before my eyes as I go yet again, and my rasping throat begs for relief, but there is none to be had. Not until he's done with me.

After that last one, he pulls out and turns me to face him once more. He lifts me up with my legs around his waist and presses my back against the hot, wet tile as he enters me. His hair is wet, and his face is red with labored breaths. An intense stare from his crystalline blue eyes drives me closer to another orgasm as he works me over. I can't help it. I am addicted to this man.

He pours himself into our kiss and swells inside my body. That added edge makes me come again, but it's softer this time. A pleasurable sigh throughout my body instead of a semitruck crashing into a brick wall. He drives into me with a wicked shove as he comes, too.

If last night was making love, this was the other thing.

He pulls out, and after that, we hold each other under the water. After a few silent minutes, he softly says, "I don't know why girls like the shower to scald them."

I snort at that. "I don't know why boys like to keep offices frigid."

"Touche."

"Anderson?"

"Yes, June?"

"I'm glad you came back."

He holds me tighter from behind. "I will always come back for you."

It makes me smile. Right now, I have exactly what I want in the world. His arms are around me, and a bag full of fresh bagels is on my counter. Life doesn't get much better than this.

Until I kiss him again. Then, it gets way better.

But he wanted a shower, so I force myself to back off. I know how good it feels to get clean again after … everything. Part of me wants to ask what he did with the body. But another part doesn't want to know. The less I know, the better, I think. Can't be blackmailed with what I don't know.

A wild thought hits me. I couldn't be forced to testify against Anderson if we were married. It's a silly thought, really. But it trickles at the edges of my mind, all the same.

Before I can tease it into conversation, though, he turns the shower off, and we towel dry. Standing in front of the mirror, I catch the shape of a hand on my throat. So I quickly turn around. Hadn't realized

Anderson's eyes were locked on my naked body. When I turn, his eyes fall on my tits, so he lets out a growl.

Every negative thought I had a moment ago evaporates.

I bite my lip and look up at his eyes. "Catch me if you can." I streak for the bed, but just before I make it, he catches me with one arm beneath my waist, and my momentum carries me forward, bent.

He presses himself against me like that, then steps us forward until my shoulders are on the mattress. "I caught you. What do I win?"

My heart thumps in my chest, and I am breathless. "Whatever you want."

"Good answer." He picks me up and tosses me onto the bed as if I weigh nothing at all. Then he climbs after me until he's got me on my hands and knees. His fingers trace my anatomy, and a sound rumbles in his throat. "Still wet for me." He licks up my low back. "Good girl."

What the hell is it about those words that get me? I whimper from all of it, hoping for more. Chills dance up my spine as he spreads me wide for him. This time, there's nothing gentle about any of it. Once he notches in, he shoves forward, keeping my ass up and my head down. I bounce back at him, just as eager for more. I don't know how he's able to get hard again so fast, and I don't care. I'm just grateful.

With every thrust, I shake. Every retraction, I pray he's not close. He hammers me into the mattress, but I meet his every movement. Pleasure coils through me faster this time. Bigger, too. He makes me lose my breath, and I'm right there when he pulls my hair tight for leverage, and I shatter on his cock with a wail. His other hand grips my hip tight to him as he comes, too.

I cannot get enough of Anderson West.

-

26

JUNE

I'm groggy by the time I realize it's way past noon. We've eaten little more than each other for hours. At some point, he warmed me a ginger orange bagel in the microwave and made me eat that, claiming I needed to keep up my strength. Then, he showed me why I needed to keep up my strength.

He's been as insatiable as I am.

A sleepy ache is lodged between my thighs. I stretch out like a cat in a warm square of light on a cold day. It's toasty in my apartment, just as I like it. Even better with him in bed next to me. I want nothing more than to lie here for days and bask in the afterglow of enthusiastic lovemaking and fucking and everything in between.

But something nags in the back of my mind. What the hell is it? We're not thinking about last night yet. Not ready for it. Not now, anyway. I put a pin in that thought for later. Haven't heard from my family in a while, but that's a good thing. No worries there. Callie hasn't texted in a few days, but she mentioned she was traveling with Daniel, so that's not a big—

My job. Fuck! I have a shift.

It's not a warm square of daylight I'm basking in. It's a streetlamp's light pouring into the window. "Shit!" I reach over for my phone to text Kelsey and find I'm seventeen minutes into my shift.

Anderson sits up like a zombie in a horror movie. He's physically awake but not mentally. "What is it? What's wrong?"

"I have to get to work—"

"Are you fucking kidding me?"

Kelsey calls, and I want to answer, but I need to think, so I let it go to voicemail. I feel awful doing it.

"Why the bloody hell would you go to work after last night?"

"Because of last night."

He frowns. "Huh?"

"You're too asleep for your lawyer brain to kick in, aren't you?"

It takes him a moment. "You want to go to work as an alibi?"

"If I go and pretend like nothing is wrong, then no one will come looking for me when people notice Neil is missing."

Anderson scrubs his hand over his face, then through his hair. "Ah. Yeah, I guess I am not awake yet. That's a smart plan ... unless someone figures out we did this, and then it'll look like you're callous as hell to a jury."

I laugh, shaking my head. "I'll take my chances."

He nods. "Okay. But is it okay if I come with you? I won't interfere or anything. I'll keep to myself. But the thought of not being able to see you right now ... it makes me crazy. I need to know you're alright. Like, at all times. It's obsessive, I know, but I'm not letting you out of my sight. If I can't come in, I'll watch from across the street."

I laugh harder this time. "My sweet little stalker."

"Sue me."

Instead, I kiss him. The kiss gets good fast, and before I know it, I've pulled him on top of me again. But my body reminds me of all the times we've done it in the past eighteen hours, and this is probably not a good idea. He groans, then pulls back. "You have to get to work, and my cock is sore, so—"

I giggle. "Aw, poor baby. I should kiss him and make him better."

"You saucy vixen." He nips at my bottom lip and sits up. "Go on. Time for clothes."

"That sounds like punishment."

He laughs. "Yeah, I know. Especially since I have to wear last night's clothes."

"Nope. There's some of yours still in my closet."

"You didn't toss my shit after the breakup?"

I shrug on my way to there. "I couldn't do it. Felt like tossing you out, and I wasn't ready for that."

He strides up behind me. "Oh, thank fuck! I was not looking forward to wearing bloody clothes to a bar."

"If you don't stop pressing yourself against me, we're going to make your cock sorer."

"There're all kinds of things I can do with my mouth—"

"Go get dressed!" I point deeper into the closet, and he laughs at me. I experiment with a few ways to hide the throat bruise and settle on some makeup along with a jaunty short scarf tied in a cute bow. This way, my shirt can frame my cleavage, and I can keep my injury to myself. Minutes later, we regretfully have clothes on, bagels are in hand, and we are running out the door.

As we get into the elevator, he asks, "So, do you make all your tips from cleavage?"

I snort a laugh. "Maybe not all of them, but a lot of them. Judging me?"

"Not at all. Use the assets you have to make your money. Brains, boobs, whatever."

"My thinking, exactly."

Just before the doors open, he says, "Just so long as you know those are mine."

I laugh at him. "Pretty sure they're mine, actually."

The doors open, but he doesn't step out. "Okay, technically, they're yours. I just don't want to share them with anyone but us."

"Me, either."

"They can look, but don't touch."

"It's not that kind of bar, Anderson."

That seems to mollify him. "Good."

The mad dash to work is tricky. It must have snowed today because the sidewalks are icy. Twenty minutes of haphazard slips and dodges of cars and foot traffic, and soon, we're in front of the bar. The place is hopping, so when we bustle in at the same time, no one notices. He just looks like another patron trying to cram in. Happy hour has swamped the place.

"I'm sorry, I'm sorry," I shout over the din as I duck behind the bar and tie my apron on.

Kelsey looks both annoyed and relieved to see me. "You're almost an hour late. You're killing me, Devlin."

Those words. Why did he have to say those words?

I must look stricken because he softens his glare. "You alright?"

I shake myself out of it. "Yeah." I try for a lighthearted laugh and fail miserably. "What makes you ask?"

But Kelsey knows me too well to buy it. He also knows now is not the time to grill me. "Great. Then let's go."

I work the crowd, one after another. It's packed tight, but the guests keep it quick and succinct, and I am utterly grateful for it. Not chatty types, not soccer moms, no evil college kids. Just order after order in a constant stream. Kelsey and I do our dance behind the bar while the servers do theirs in front of it, and I can tell they're relieved I'm here. I am, too.

I almost wasn't. Not if Neil had his way about things.

When that thought clicks in, I instinctively search the crowd for Anderson. He's in a far corner, simply observing. Sometimes, he's on his phone. I'm not sure if he's pretending to be busy or if he actually is. Whatever the case, I am so glad he's here. I wasn't ready for him to leave my sight, either.

As things slow down, people get chattier. It's like they knew not to do it when we were too busy, which is a remarkable amount of consideration for a group of drunks. One, who keeps glancing down my shirt, says, "You have a sexy librarian thing going."

Can't tell if that's a thing or an insult. But I give him a bright smile anyway. "Thanks."

"Can I get your number?"

"Aw, you're sweet." And I keep making other guests' drinks.

"That wasn't a no," he presses on.

I keep my bright smile plastered on my face. "Yes, it was."

He laughs, shaking his head. "Damn. Gotta boyfriend or something?"

"I don't date."

He sits back, intrigued. Like I just threw the gauntlet. Shit. "Now, see, I don't think that's a thing.

That's just something girls say when they're not interested."

"Some might take that as a hint."

He laughs hard at that. "Never been good at hints."

This guy is getting on my last nerve. After last night, my tolerance for pushy men is negative a thousand. I want to threaten him with what happened to the last man who bothered me. But that's a recipe for disaster, and I am smarter than that. "Do you need food or a beverage?'

"No, I—"

"Then have a nice night." I turn my back on him and work the other end of my side of the bar. Kelsey knows what that means, so he takes over with that guy to keep him from bothering me. My boss is the brother I always wanted. I know what they say about jobs that talk about their work families. Work isn't where your family is, blah, blah, blah. But if I could pick a work family member, it'd be him.

-

27

JUNE

Throughout the rush, Anderson stays in his corner booth, still scrolling or reading or whatever on his phone. His presence is reassuring in the extreme. Every time I look his way, I feel better. Not that Kelsey would ever let anything happen to me at work, but it's definitely not the same thing as having my boyfriend watch over me.

After everything we have gone through, it would be easy to think of myself or us as cursed. The past few months have been the most tumultuous time of my adult life. The thing is, even if we are cursed, even if the universe is trying to tell us we shouldn't be together, I don't fucking care at all.

Anderson West is mine. I am his. End of discussion.

When I see his profile in the low bar lights, my breath catches in my raw throat. He's so handsome that it's hard to think about anything other than our day in bed. And in the shower. And in the kitchen. We pretty much banged in my entire apartment today on each available surface. Every step I take is a reminder of our athletics.

Good thing I can do my job on autopilot on a sex hangover.

I love that he's willing to just hang out without me talking to him, all so he can watch over me. It's so sweet of him, and I know it comes from a place of love. Anderson would never try to control me or manipulate me. He's not that guy. I feel so safe with him.

The fact he followed me around for a little while? Water under the bridge. In the grand scheme of things, it's nothing.

His father, on the other hand, will be a challenge. I'm sure of that. He's done nothing but attempt to insert himself between us. I don't look forward to dealing with him again.

Except, I also kind of *do* look forward to it. Elliot West is a challenge, and after last night, I know I can take him on. I have survived worse than him, and I will keep surviving.

Having Anderson near and staying busy for hours also helps keep the Neil thoughts at bay. He had a cornfed, Midwestern thing about him, and thankfully, that is not a common look in Boston, so I don't see too many guys who remind me of him. Whenever my thoughts veer in that direction, I steal a glance at Anderson and feel better in an instant.

We hit a lull, so Kelsey starts everyone's breaks. Since I was late, mine is short. Fair enough. I duck into the bathroom fast so I don't waste the whole break in there. While inside, I check my phone out of habit.

Lo and behold, I have an email I never expected. Reading the name on it stops my heart and mind all at once. Andre Moeller. The man who kidnapped me sent me an email. What in the ever-loving fuck is going on?

I read the name a hundred times. There is no legitimate reason for my kidnapper to email me. None at all. He stole me — rather, he had me stolen on his own behalf — in order to get Elliot's attention regarding a debt Elliot owes him. I was nothing more than a pawn between those two men. It is obscene for him to reach out to me. I should just erase the email and forget it ever happened.

I'm shaking from just reading his name. I am certainly not about to do him the courtesy of reading his email. The bastard had me threatened at knife point, tied into a van, dragged to some frightening basement, and tied to a chair, all before making me eat a meal with him and having a seemingly civilized conversation with him. The man is an absolute sociopath. I knew it from the first ten minutes of our conversation. It was bizarre and messy, and I never want to see that man again. Especially after he had his goons lob me into a trunk for transport after that. During the whole ride to our destination, I was certain I was going to die. They were going to shoot me or dump the car into a body of water, and I'd drown. Utterly terrorizing.

Instead, Anderson was there to take me home. But the point stands. He gave me the scariest twenty-four hours of my life. I owe Andre nothing.

So, why in the hell would he email the woman he kidnapped? I'm starting to feel like the cat that curiosity killed. If I open an email, what's the worst that can happen? My phone gets a virus. Big whoop.

I huff at myself and open the email.

Job Opportunity — Lawyer.

Hello, June. I am sure I need no introduction. I wanted to reach out regarding a unique position within my organization. It is my belief you are the perfect candidate for the role. Your credentials and your resume tell me of your capabilities. I need a good lawyer like you.

Your situation has made you the black sheep of your industry, but I find black sheep are the best workers, and considering who has made you into one, a collaboration could be mutually beneficial. I need someone of your talents, and you strike me as the kind of woman who would want revenge. Professionally speaking, of course.

If you are interested, my contact information is included here. We can arrange an interview as soon as possible. I look forward to hearing from you soon. —Andre"

Strange. An email should answer more questions than it asks.

Andre knows my credentials. He's seen my resume, and he knows I am being blackballed by Elliot. And he knows I'd like revenge on him.

How in the fuck does he know any of this? I want to scream. I want to break something. Andre wants me to be his fucking lawyer? After he kidnapped me? The gall! I knew he was a damned sociopath, but does he think I'm one, too? That I could forgive and forget what he did to me?

It takes all the strength I have not to punch the wall. Instead, I drag my fingers through my hair to self-soothe. It's not enough. Not by a long shot. Aghast does not even begin to describe how I feel. It's too much, this has all been too fucking much! On what planet is this appropriate behavior?

But then I realize the concept of appropriate is likely foreign to Andre. When we'd eaten together, his every sentence was a calculation. He tried to sound sincere when he was sympathetic to my plight, but the sheer act of *trying* to sound sincere made it all ring false and hollow. The man has no human emotions. Only motives. Only goals.

So then, what is the point of trying to get me to work for him? What could possibly be his motivation? Is there a goal I can help him reach?

He said that thing about it being mutually beneficial…I assume he means between him and me. If that's the case, does he plan to put me up against Elliot in some situation? I'm a tax attorney. It's not as if I go to court. None of this makes any sense.

Unless … is he trying to dodge taxes? Does Elliot have some friend in the IRS breathing down Andre's neck or something? I know he has friends throughout the government. Andre seemed to hate Elliot almost as much as I've grown to. If Elliot is wielding the government at Andre, then I might be able to help him that way—

What the fuck am I thinking? How could I possibly help that asshole?

I close my email and tuck my phone back into my pocket. There is no dimension in which I will ever help Andre Moeller, may he rot in hell.

-

28

JUNE

It's been a day, and I still haven't responded to Andre's email. I'd thought to tell Anderson about it, and we'd have a good laugh, but the more I thought of telling him, the worse an idea it sounded. If I tell him, then he will give me shit for considering it.

And I am considering it.

I know it's crazy. In school, no one ever said, "Don't go to work for the man who kidnapped you and used you as a pawn and terrified you for a day." I think they thought that went without saying. Or it's so insane that no one had thought of it at all. But right now, I'm not sure if that's good advice.

If Andre wants revenge on Elliot, why shouldn't I help him? I want it, too.

When I met Elliot, he thought Anderson and I were engaged, so within moments of meeting him, he brought up a prenup. I called his bluff. After I offered to sign it, he admitted he didn't have one on him. I thought that would be the end of things, case closed.

But then Andre entered the picture by having me kidnapped on the very night I met Elliot.

The two of them used me as a pawn. Anderson did everything he could to get me back, and he did, circumventing his father. I think that might be what pissed him off about me initially. That his own son worked around him instead of heeding his advice. Doesn't matter now.

Since then, everything with Elliot's been a shitshow. So, why shouldn't I use Andre to get some revenge? The man is a sociopath, but does that stop him from being useful? Some might argue that would make him more useful. A man without scruples is a handy tool to have around. Like the big scary guy who helped Anderson with the—

"No," I tell myself out loud in my bathroom. "Stop. We don't think about that right now."

I've had to have those talks with myself frequently. Maybe it's a symptom of a fracturing mind, but it helps for now. I choose to focus on one sociopath at a time. Now, the only question is, am I seriously thinking of doing this?

I want to talk to Anderson about it. He's a great sounding board, and he knows more about these people than I do. But he won't approve. That much, I know. He wants me far away from danger, and on that, I agree. But if I can work with Andre in a legitimate capacity in an office somewhere and make Elliot West pay for all the shit he's put me through, I'd be a fool not to take the chance.

Besides that, Andre might pay well. I could stop bartending and still keep my home. Not that I don't love bartending, but I'm not that young anymore, and I've been out of the game for a long time, so the late nights are wearing on me.

It can't hurt to go to a harmless interview, right?

Screw it. I'm in, and I'm not telling Anderson until I know more about all of this.

I email Andre back, and within an hour, I sneak back into my bathroom to read his response. With Anderson in my bedroom, I can't read this in front of him. We agree to an interview at his Boston office tomorrow at ten. For the first time in a long time, I am excited professionally.

The next day, Anderson goes to work, and I tell him I'm running errands for the day since I'm not going to the bar tonight. He kisses me goodbye, and I feel bad for not telling him the absolute truth. But he would have tried to talk me out of it. We would have had a fight. I don't want that. Not when we're reuniting. It feels too soon for that kind of drama. And we've both been through enough trouble to last a lifetime.

I'm not going to stress us both out over what is probably nothing.

I lock up behind him and wait fifteen minutes to make sure he didn't forget anything. If he comes back and I'm in my grown-up clothes, he'll be curious. I dress and do my hair and makeup before running out the door. Andre's office isn't terribly far, so I walk it and will change into my heels in the lobby of his building.

It's a ten-story art deco high rise, probably constructed in the early 20th century, if I had to guess. Classy, but with the potential to have plenty of secret ins and outs, like his building in New York. At least, I think it was in New York. I'd been blindfolded during the trip there. That building had bulletproof glass and tamper-proof systems to keep Andre safe. I wonder what safeguards he's kitted out this building with. The man is nuts, and he is extreme when it comes to his own safety.

In that regard, I'm jealous of him.

The lobby is just as pretty as the exterior, also in an art deco style with ornate trim on every surface and a chandelier so gilded and radiant that it would make the Pope blush from its opulence. Everything is gorgeous except for the security team at the entry. They wand over me and search my bag. I'm a little surprised by the frisking, but it's completely professional.

When they ask me who I'm here to see, the one I'm speaking to has no reaction. But the other guard's eyes widen. Is this a trap of some kind? No backing out now, I guess. The collected guard says, "You'll take the elevator at the end of the hall."

"What floor?"

He smiles. "There is only one button in that elevator. It goes to the penthouse suite."

"Oh." More and more, this is feeling like a trap. But why would Andre trap me when he can have his goons come and get me at any time? He wants me here willingly for some reason, and I have to take him at his word that this is for a professional matter, don't I?

Who am I kidding? I'm here for revenge on Elliot.

The truth is, coming here feels like taking my power back. I didn't tell Anderson, in part, because he would argue against it, and I don't want to hear another man telling me what to do. Even if he thinks it's for my own good. I honestly just want to do what I want to do, regardless of anyone else's opinions of it.

Since the night I sold myself at auction, men have been running the show, and I've had to react to their behavior. Their wants, their needs, their motives. Anderson bought me that night. Why? Because he wanted to protect me from the men I'd opened myself up to. Kinda sweet, kinda bossy. Then there was Elliot, who cut him off, which meant he couldn't pay me. Andre stole me away. Anderson rescued me. Elliot stole my money and had me excommunicated from my industry. Neil tried to rape and murder me. All these men, telling me what to do … I'm sick of it.

I love Anderson, and he means the world to me. But sometimes a woman's gotta do what a woman's gotta do. In one way or another, I've had my autonomy taken from me by men over and over in the past few months, and I am done with all of that. They can react to me from now on. I might not have much power over them, but I do have power over my own fate.

I smash the penthouse button, stand a little straighter, and wait to see what Andre has to tell me. If I like it, I might say yes. If not, I'll walk. Either way, it's not up to him. Or Elliot. Or Anderson. This is my choice and mine alone.

So, why do I feel like I'm going to throw up?

-

29

JUNE

When the doors open, I'm almost disappointed. Part of me thought I'd walk into a room where Andre would turn around in a high-backed chair while stroking a white cat. Instead, he's at the elevator to greet me himself.

Andre Moeller is a medium-framed, impeccably dressed white man in his fifties, by my estimation. He has sparkling green eyes and brown hair with silversides. Not a speck of scruff on him to cover his classically handsome face. He's even wearing the imitation of a friendly smile as he shakes my hand. "June, I am glad you could make it."

I throw on a smile, too, since this is the ruse he's using. "Same here. Shall we get started?"

He nods and gestures for me to enter the main portion of the suite. It's set up like a living room with a bar—complete with a bartender—near the exterior wall of windows. All art deco styling, even down to the ottomans and the end tables. A plush gray rug sits beneath the couch to delineate the seating area. He sits there, so I take a nearby chair.

The bartender comes by to take our orders, and Andre's bijou request surprises me. It's an old cocktail made with London dry gin, orange bitters, sweet vermouth, and green chartreuse, so if the bartender has all of that back there, my Tom Collins shouldn't make him blink. It doesn't.

Andre smirks. "Not too many your age drink Tom Collins."

"Amazing how many young bartenders stare at me blankly when I order one, but it's a classic, and it's delicious."

"Did you acquire the taste for them by working at that dive you're moonlighting at?"

That's the thing about Andre. He always knows far more than he should. "No, actually, I used to have to make them for my grandmother, and I started stealing sips of them when I was nine."

He grins. "You've always been a little wicked, haven't you?"

"I have, indeed. And you? When did you come into your rambunctious side?"

"Now, now, cheeky girls get the paddle."

I don't even know what to say to that, but an unexpected laugh pops out of me, which makes him smile wider. The bartender delivers our drinks, and I settle back into my chair. The drink is perfect, no complaints. But I'm not here for drinks with a friend. "Andre, might I speak plainly?" I nod toward the bartender.

"My staff is compensated well enough to keep their mouths shut regarding any and all matters." He leans back toward the bartender. "Riley, dear. This is the young woman I had kidnapped not long ago."

Riley smiles and waves at me as if Andre had told him I had a golden retriever or we'd met on a boat. It's not startling information to him. Merely information. What kind of work environment is this, that hearing he had kidnapped me is normal to Riley?

It seems no interaction with Andre is ever going to leave me feeling okay.

He returns his attention to me. "Speak as plainly as you like, June. I prefer it."

"Alright, then. What in the hell were you thinking by emailing me?"

"I was thinking I need a good lawyer, and I'd recently met one, so I thought to email her." For him, it is as simple as that. Just emailing a good lawyer. His words are matter of fact. There is no malice or spite in his eyes. No consideration of my feelings or thought that this could be in poor taste. Just business.

I'm not sure if that's comforting or not. "And this revenge you speak of?"

He tuts at me for that, and I've apparently crossed a line. "First things first, as they say. Let us begin with an apology." He sips his drink.

"If you expect me to apologize —

He laughs. It's deep and real, and there is no pretense like his polite laughs from before. "Absolutely not, June. It is I who owes the apology for the circumstances under which we met. That was unfortunate business. But it was only business. Nothing personal against you at all. I wish things had not gone on the way that they did."

"Oh-kay —"

"You see, Elliot and I have had our share of issues for many years, and I required leverage against him. Little did I know his thoughts regarding you. We have been on the outs for a time. It is neither here nor there, but suffice to say, you are no longer on my

CHARLOTTE BYRD

radar. Especially if you were to come to work for me."

"I see. Well, that's good to know, I guess."

"How are wedding preparations going?"

Oh, shit. Okay, he knows some things but not others. That's a good thing, I think. If I tell him we're not getting married or that it was all a ploy … no. Best to let him think nothing has changed. That might be why he wants to hire me in the first place. To give him an inside look at the West family.

"Slowly, to be honest. With things going sideways professionally, I've been too preoccupied with trying to get my career back to where it should be to focus on the wedding."

He nods sympathetically. "I do not imagine having a future father-in-law quashing your professional aspirations puts the wedding into focus. Have you considered whether he is doing this to force you to be a stay-at-home wife for his son?"

I nearly snort my Tom Collins when I laugh. "Um, no. I hadn't given it much thought."

"Tell me of your last job. I'd like to know all about your experiences there."

Thank god. Normal interview topics. "I helped high net worth individuals save tens of millions in taxes. I know the tax codes inside and out, and I am very good at using them to help my clients retain their wealth. It's something of an art to me, especially since I remain within the bounds of the law. I enjoy the challenge."

"I had the impression you do not like helping wealthy people keep their money."

Our last conversation had let me be more forthright than I knew was wise. Plus, I imagine he's heard all kinds of things about me through his network of spies. So, I smile through that. "Certain wealthy people should not be allowed to keep their money, in my less than humble opinion. If someone, say a CEO, uses his money and influence to blackball someone out of her own industry to settle a pointless grudge, for instance, I do not think they are worthy of their fortune. But that does not change the fact that the challenge of working within the law to do so is something I enjoy."

He grins. "You have a keen mind, June. I like that. And I like you. I want you to come to work for me. You'll have fewer clients to work on and less work to do, and I'll top your last annual salary by…twenty thousand," he says with a shrug.

Holy shit. "Twenty thousand more?"

He sighs and rolls his eyes. "Not enough, is it? How does forty thousand more sound?"

I laugh too sharply. Is he outbidding himself?

"Fifty thousand more, my final offer. Well, that and a sign-on bonus as an apology for how we met. Say twenty thousand for that difficult day?"

Oh my freaking god. I can't jump up and down with excitement. That might ruin my chance at bargaining with him if I decide to do this. The inclination is to say no. As fun as it's been to entertain the idea of all of this, it is fraught with difficulties. Like explaining to my boyfriend that I'm working for his family's enemy. Doesn't seem like a smart idea.

But again, I am tired of all these men telling me what to do.

My mouth is parched, so I gulp my Tom Collins as coolly as possible. "Can I have some time to think it over? This isn't an easy decision."

"Why not?"

"Let's be clear, Andre. You kidnapped me. You're the longstanding enemy of the family I am marrying into. It is complicated. Surely, you see that."

He mulls it over. "I suppose so. I'd like an answer within one week."

"Agreed. If I said yes, where would I work?"

He smiles. "Wherever I need you."

A charming non-answer if ever there was one. I want to press him for more information, but I feel like I've come here and gotten no answers at all. Pushing Andre is a recipe for disappointment and possibly danger, so it's just not worth it right now.

"Very well." I set my glass down. "You'll have my answer within a week. Does Riley work where I'll be working? Because that was the second-best Tom Collins I've ever had."

"Second best?" the young man sounds offended.

But I smile at him. "The best I've ever had was made by me."

Andre laughs. "I do believe she's calling you out, Riley."

Riley laughs, too. "I'd be happy to learn from a master."

"We'll see, I guess."

Andre walks me to the elevator. "I do hope to hear from you sooner rather than later, June. We have much business to attend to."

"Time will tell." If he can give non-answers, so can I. The elevator takes me away, and I'm not shaking. I feel steadier than I have since what happened with Neil. Whatever happens, I've got this.

30

JUNE

Carla's Diner is a little out of the way place near the bar, making it the perfect place to meet Anderson after my shift. It looks like an old-fashioned diner—bright red vinyl seats, chrome on everything, and a jukebox in the corner —but the place is too new for any of it to be vintage. The checkerboard floors make me nostalgic for a time I never experienced, and I'm not sure why. But there's something wholesome about the facade.

In short, it's the perfect place to disappoint him.

We sit in the booth furthest from the door, to avoid the cold draft every time someone walks in, and peruse the menus. Nervously, I tell him, "Thanks for agreeing to a late-night date. Sorry I couldn't get out of my shift any earlier."

He smiles. "Of course. I'm happy to see you whenever I can."

After ordering—me, the greasiest breakfast platter they have, and a milkshake and fries for him—the nervousness kicks up a notch. There are no more distractions, no other reason to delay telling him about Andre's offer. But I can handle this. I have been through much worse than disappointing my boyfriend.

Still, I stall. "How's work?"

Anderson sighs, his gaze drifting out one of the many enormous windows overlooking the street. In profile, he looks so worn down, and I hate that for him. "I am so tired of working for my Dad, June. It's really getting to me. And the stuff I do with Moss … I can't stand it." But then his attention zips back to me. "I don't regret that connection. Let me be clear about that. I know what it would have cost us both if I didn't have him in my back pocket, so don't think I regret it—"

"It's okay, Anderson. I know what you meant."

Typically, the pregnant pauses in our conversations were comfortable and easy. This one is not. We're both trying to talk about Neil Night, or as he calls it, *The Green Sweater Incident*, but right now, in public, we both know better than to say anything directly. We had agreed that nothing incriminating gets said publicly, so that sometimes stifles our conversation. It's unavoidable, much like occasionally discussing Neil.

He nods and gulps down some coffee. "The thing is, I don't see a way out, and it's getting to me."

I would love to give him a change of topic onto something more positive. Like that, his girlfriend got a phenomenal job offer. But he won't see it that way, and I'm too chicken shit to say that. "Callie thinks Daniel is going to propose."

His brow knits together, and he lets out a confused laugh. "Um, great, but that was a hell of a subject change."

I shrug. "I didn't know what else to say. You seem so down. I thought I'd give you some good, unrelated news."

He smiles warmly, taking my hand in his. "Thank you for that, June. I appreciate you trying."

When our food comes, I'm still trying to figure out how to tell him about Andre's offer. I shouldn't want to take it. It feels like a huge mistake. But there's an undeniable appeal to the job, and my curiosity about it burns every time some creep at work takes too long of a glance down my cleavage. I don't have to sling drinks anymore. I can go back to my real job. Or, in this case, I can do something better.

Thankfully, my cheese omelet is to die for, and I can't stop scarfing it down. Anderson notices. His lips curl in amusement. "Might I try a bite?"

You can order your own. "Sure, go ahead."

He takes a respectable-sized bite that is entirely too large for my liking. "Oh, you win dinner. That is so good." Then he goes back to his fries.

Part of me is jealous that he can survive on protein bars to make up for the fries and booze and milkshakes he loves. But part of me is just plain mad at him for being able to when I cannot. I'd feel like shit if I ate his enviable diet all the time. Meanwhile, he sits there with visible abs, not worrying about how he'll feel tomorrow or bloating or, god forbid, losing an ab. Even if Anderson's money is all tied up because of his Dad's bullshit, he can still do whatever he wants.

Well, so can I. "I got a job offer from Andre Moeller, and I'm thinking of taking it." Shit. I am too tired to keep secrets, apparently.

He drops a fry into his ketchup and wipes his fingers clean of the grease and salt. Then he sips his coffee and sits back, staring at me like I have two heads. "I'm not sure I heard you right. Can you say that again?"

"You heard me, Anderson. Don't play coy."

"No. I cannot have possibly heard you right because what I heard sounded like you're thinking of taking a job with the man who kidnapped you and scared the fucking daylights out of us both just to piss off my father. I know, deep down in my soul, that you could not possibly be considering such a ridiculous thing because you are my incredibly smart girlfriend who knows better, so please, June. Repeat yourself."

"He emailed me. I went to his place. He made the offer, which is far more money than I had made at my last firm, and I'd have less than half my old workload. Plus, he wants to give me a bonus for the kidnapping to smooth things over in that regard—"

"Do I get a bonus, too?"

My frown is so deep that it hurts. "Excuse me?"

"Yes, you were the one kidnapped, but I am the one who—"

"Don't even, Anderson. Your rough day of trying to find me is nothing compared to what I went through, and that is such a false equivalency that I am not going to justify it with any more of a response than that."

His next exhale is closer to a hiss than breathing. "Apologies. That was untoward."

I nod and sip my coffee, feeling every minute of my day right now. This conversation is just beginning, and I'm already praying for it to end. I circle the rim of my mug and muse, "The biggest bonus of all is how much your father would hate it."

He bitterly laughs. "Silver lining, I suppose."

Another pregnant pause hangs in the air between us. I hate this. I hate it so much. I wish he would just jump on board already. "This is a huge opportunity—"

"Then I am extra sorry you'll have to turn it down."

I blink at him. "What was that?"

"You absolutely cannot take a job with Andre Moeller."

"Okay, first things first." I sit up, leaning forward because I am ready to jump out of my seat to scream at him, and this is the only way I can stop myself from doing exactly that. "You are my boyfriend. That means we enjoy each other's company and make some decisions together. That does not mean you get to tell me what to do. Ever. Second, you need to consider this from my side of things. I cannot get a job in my field anywhere else, thanks to your fucking father, and as much as I love playing bartender, I am tired of making a living off my cleavage, Anderson. I want to be back in my field. This is the only way to do it."

"Bullshit. Other firms will hire you, but you gave up too soon on your job hunt because it was easier to go back to the familiar than to keep trying—"

"Oh fuck you, Anderson! I went back to the bar because I have fucking bills to pay! I know you don't get that concept because of your family money, but for me, it's working my ass off or starve!"

He closes his eyes and takes a beat. "I'm sorry. I was out of line—"

"You think?"

His jaw feathers under the strain of gritting his teeth. "I was out of line, and that does not change the fact that you cannot work for the man who kidnapped you, June."

I laugh, too angry to think straight. The words come out slowly at first. "You're still trying to tell me what to do? You and your fucking ego! You think I will give up on my career, my livelihood *for you*?"

-

31

ANDERSON

This conversation is a fucking nightmare. I shake off her accusation. "Not for me. For you. You cannot go to work for him *for you.*"

"Oh, what, in the condescending bullshit, is this?"

I cannot believe she's being like this. It's like she can't see the forest for the trees. In hopes she'll actually listen to me, I soften my voice. "Do you honestly think it is a net positive for your mental health to work for the man who kidnapped you?"

"You did not ... " She laughs again, shaking her head, and somehow, I have made her angrier. Lucky me. "You did not just try to make it sound like your objection to me working for Andre is about my mental health. You're not upset because you're worried about me. You're upset because you don't like Andre—"

"Can you fucking blame me for not liking the man who kidnapped my girlfriend? For doing anything in my power to stop you from being near that man?" Dammit, I have to watch my volume in here. Carla's Diner isn't packed, but it's busy enough that discussing kidnappings too loud is a bad idea.

"What the fuck ever, Anderson." She drags her fingers through her hair, forgetting she has a ponytail and tugging on it. After a wince, she yanks her ponytail down and rubs her scalp as she speaks. "Look, bartending has been a great way to keep me from dipping too far into my savings, but I still am. I need to make more money. More importantly, I would like to use my brain again. And my degree, which I'm still paying student loans on. Your father blackballed me everywhere in town. I am out of options. I would like you on board for this, but I am not asking for permission."

"I never said you need my permission—"

"No, you didn't. You just told me I couldn't take the job."

My head tips back in frustration. Thankfully, the booths are overstuffed, so I don't hurt myself. "June. This conversation is pointless."

"Right now, it's feeling very pointy."

I huff a laugh. "Yeah, okay. Look, I'm not trying to upset you or tell you what to do. You know that's not who I am. You're right. I don't like Andre. I fucking hate him. I don't want you to work for him. Partly because I hate that guy but also because I don't think you need to be around him. Ever."

"Why are you trying to stop me from getting a good job?"

"That's not what this is!" There goes my volume again. But I don't care. It's like she's being purposefully obtuse on this, and it's not like her. "For the love of god, think about this from my perspective." I lean in to keep my voice down. "Andre kidnapped you—"

"Yeah, I was there."

"To make a point."

"So?"

I close my eyes and huff again. If this keeps up, I'll be hyperventilating. "He is the kind of man who kidnaps random people for the sole purpose of making a point to someone who has gotten on his nerves. That is one step away from something Moss or my father would do. Is that the kind of person you want to work for?"

That sparks something in her eyes, and I can't tell if it's good or bad. "God, you still don't get it, do you?"

"Get what?"

"What's that like, Anderson? To walk through life, getting to be choosy about the kind of people you work for? What privilege—"

"You did not just fucking say that to me." I can barely contain my anger right now. Volume? Forget it. "My father has me tied in knots around his finger, all because I tried to be able to pay you what I owe you. I have to go on ride-alongs with Moss—yes, *that* guy—to keep my father happy, because if I don't, he will ruin me. He will destroy everything I am and what little I have to my name. Every moment of every day, I have to be ready to do another job for him, whether I want to do the job or not. I am at his beck and call. I did not fucking choose that, June. You think getting blackballed by my father is bad? Try being blackmailed by him."

She grips her coffee mug with shaking hands. "Then you, of all people, should understand what it's like to be out of options, shouldn't you?"

I want to rage right now. I want to stomp out of the diner, march to my gym, and blow off all this steam. But I can't. It's not the mature thing to do, and I can't afford my gym membership any longer, thanks to my father cutting me off. Instead of any of that, I rub the scruff on my chin and try to calm down.

I will try a different tactic. "June, you are the smartest person I know. And I think that's part of the problem."

"What's that supposed to mean?"

"Being smart means you understand how things work and can see the paths in front of you. The implications, the fallout, you know all of it. You know how things work. Right?"

"What's your point, Anderson?"

I hate when she says my name like that. Like it annoys her to have to say it. "Since you are so smart and you understand the game, it makes it easy for certain things to escape your eye. You know the big picture, but the details aren't clear."

"Get to your angle—"

"Do you think it's possible Andre did this to drive a wedge between us? That kidnapping you wasn't enough? That the real way to get under Dad's skin would be to have you on his staff?"

She pauses, her brows creased in confusion. "You think Andre is doing this to annoy your dad?"

"Why else would he?"

She sets her coffee mug down and carefully places her palms on the table as if trying not to do something else. "That's it, isn't it?"

"What's it?"

"You tell me I'm smart, then you tell me the only reason Andre would hire me is your dad? In your mind, it couldn't be because I am good at my job, right?"

Fuck. Abort! Abort! "I so did not mean it that way, and you know it. You know I think the world of you—"

"As your girlfriend, sure. But as a lawyer … ?" She shakes her head. Her words are calm and measured, and it's disturbing because I can tell just how pissed off she is right now. Internally, she's nuclear. Externally, she's a solid block of ice. It is disconcerting. She says, "I don't know what you think of me professionally. But that little slip says volumes."

How the fuck do I dig out of this hole? Think fast. "Back in school, you were the best. At everything. It was grating how good you were. How you were always at the top of the class, always the know-it-all. I might not know how you are at your job these days, June, but I still remember the girl who always kicked my ass in class. I don't doubt you're still that girl in the office."

Her expression loosens. No more gripping things, no more grinding her teeth when I speak. Thank fuck, it worked. "Good. Then you know Andre wants me for my brains and not for upsetting your father."

Oh my god. This conversation is going nowhere. "Exactly why couldn't he want you for both of those things?"

A faint light of recognition flashes in her eyes. "Andre wants me for my brains. Me taking the job? That's to upset your father. And to pay my bills. Really, it's a win-win all the way around."

I cannot believe her right now. "You're seriously thinking about taking the job, aren't you? This hasn't been some hypothetical, has it?"

"I'm still undecided."

But I hear it in her voice. She's made the decision. Un-fucking-believable. "Why did you tell me any of this? And I want the real reason this time."

"You're my boyfriend."

"What kind of boyfriend can't at least voice his opinion when he sees his girlfriend doing things that will damage her psyche?"

"The kind of boyfriend who is using that flimsy excuse to get her to do whatever he wants when, really, he's just using it as a smokescreen for his personal reasons."

My head drops into my hands, and I'm unsure how to maintain my composure. I stretch my neck, crack my knuckles, and attempt to make eye contact with the woman currently driving me up the fucking wall.

It doesn't help that she looks sexy as fuck when she thinks she's winning an argument. Hell, that was half the reason I was happy when I heard she was going into law as a profession. I knew she would walk around being extra sexy all day long, probably in one of those tight skirt suits and high heels. Maybe some silk stockings, too. Her hair up in a tight bun, just begging to be unleashed, and dammit, I'm getting sidetracked.

I have one more trick up my sleeve. "You're right."

At that, she looks baffled. "I don't follow you."

"Isn't that what you want to hear? You're right. I'm wrong."

"What is this?" She's too intelligent not to be suspicious. "What am I right about?"

"I have personal reasons for wanting you not to work for Andre. It's true. In fact, all my reasons are personal." I take her hands in mine, and to my surprise, she doesn't jerk away. "My reasons are personal because they are all about you, and you are my person. I hate Andre for what he did to you. I won't apologize for that. He stole you away in the night. He terrified you." I whisper, "You saw what I did to the man who put his hand on your throat. Imagine what I would do to the man who stole you from me?"

She doesn't speak. She merely stares up at me, mystified.

I clear my throat and go on, "If I had the chance, June, Andre would never see the light of day ever again. And now, I'm looking at possible office holiday parties with that man. So, no, I don't want you to work for him, and yes, it is personal. I won't pretend otherwise. And on top of everything else, I firmly believe this is not good for your mental health. That is personal to me too. I will always look out for you even when you don't want me to. Together, not together, it doesn't matter to me. You matter to me. You are my person, and everything that happens to you is personal to me."

Her eyes glisten in the neon lights of the diner, and as much as I hate seeing her cry, I feel triumphant. I've finally gotten through to her. Thank god. Slowly, she pulls away and drinks her coffee. Relief washes through me, and I can breathe again. Then she utters, "I am out of options, Anderson. I'm taking the job."

-

32

JUNE

They say civility is the leash on every man's inner beast. Right now, Anderson's leash must be choking him. He snarls like an animal and snaps, "You have got to be fucking kidding me!"

It is all I can do to sit still right now. I want out. The air is thick with our anger, and I can hardly breathe. I have been through some shit lately, facing down men who had goals contrary to my own. When I was kidnapped, I tried—and failed—to fight off my attackers. When Elliot West broke into my apartment to steal back his money, well, I didn't do much of anything because I was in the middle of sex with Anderson and was in too much shock to speak. You don't exactly expect your boyfriend's father to walk in on you during sex in your own apartment. When Neil attacked me, he was a cross between annoyed and rapey, and I tried to fight back then, too. None of them were angry with me. Not like this.

But Anderson? The man I care about being truly angry with me? I have only one frame of reference for it, and it's not good.

I know he's not my father. I know he's not about to start hitting me. But I can't help but shut down under the onslaught of his anger. He has never put his hands on me in anger, and right now, it almost doesn't matter. My reaction is the same. Shut down and hope it stops. Be quiet, and it'll stop sooner. Just don't say a word, and he'll ignore me.

"June, talk to me."

I can't. Not right now. It's like my voice evaporated. A weight sits on my chest, my thighs, my back. It's grinding me down, just like when I was a kid. But now, there's no place to hide. My heartbeats drum in my ears and my skin. I'm in hell.

Please, something make him stop.

Except, I am the thing that has to make him stop. I'm not a child hiding in a closet anymore. There's no running from my problem, no mom to run interference. I'm a grown woman. It's up to me to end this.

I have been through hell and back so many times that I have frequent flier miles. I can do this. More than that, I have to do this. I love Anderson. He doesn't know anything about my parental PTSD because I have never told him. So, he doesn't know why his rage is shutting me down. That's not fair to him. I have to do this.

My voice comes out in a rasp. "Stop yelling at me."

He frowns, cringing back. "June, I'm not yelling at *you*. I'm yelling at the situation. I love you."

Right. Of course, he does. He loves me, he loves me, he loves me. I have to hang onto that thought. I want to tell him why I went quiet. But I can't. Not right now. It doesn't feel helpful because it'll drag out a whole slew of other problems, and that won't let us focus on the topic at hand. Plus, I don't have it in me to deal with the amount of emotional shit that'll dredge up. Not right now. Not after all of this. I'm already wiped out.

So, instead, I nod and stare at my half-empty plate. "Okay."

"Please talk to me."

"About what?"

He's incredulous. "About what? About this, about why you'd take that job, about why you have hardly said a word in the past five minutes. Are you that pissed off at me?"

Yes. No. Maybe. But the truth is, my anger at him is growing. "Not everything is about you, Anderson."

"So, you're giving me the silent treatment because of my father?"

I glare up at him. "What makes you think this is about either of you?"

"Because I cannot imagine why you would willingly go to work for Andre, June. Dad is blackballing you, I know, but there has to be better places to work than the bar that aren't run by a maniac!"

When he raises his voice, I want to curl up into a ball and hide under the table. But I'm not hiding anymore. I'm not a victim. I'm a survivor. Even when the difference feels razor-thin, it's still there.

"I want respect."

He squints at me. "I respect you—"

"Professional respect. Do you think I get that at the bar?"

He shrugs a shoulder. "I don't know. It's a bar—"

"When was the last time you saw a bartender and thought, 'Gee, she's great at her job. I should show her some respect.'?"

"You're being ridiculous."

"You're being petulant."

He pauses, drumming his fingers on the table. "You want to be in your field again, I get it—"

"You don't. Not at all. You are more comfortable with me flashing my cleavage to drunk men than you are with me working for someone who wants to hire me for my brains. You would rather me use my body instead of my mind, and that is how I know you do not get it."

"June, baby, you are going around in circles on this. I know you want a better job. We will find you a better job—"

"I want *this* job." I hadn't realized it until he talked down to me, but it's true. It's not just curiosity. Andre is a fucked up sociopath, but I know where I stand with him, and that is more than I can say for any corporate job I have ever had. Strange to think of him as the secure option, but in a lot of ways, he is.

"And I want access to my money again, but some things are not options in life." He says it with such simplicity that his tone implies it's no longer up for discussion.

That smug asshole! "You don't get to make my choices for me, or was I not clear before?"

He smirks just a little, and it makes my blood boil. "This is better."

"What's better?"

"This. You being pissed off at me. It's much better than when you were giving me the silent treatment. What was that about? Are you tired? Were you regrouping? Are you just that pissed off at me? I want to know."

Years of abuse, dummy! Why else does someone shut down? But I know what he means. He wants specifics. Well, right now, he doesn't have access to specifics. I give a thin smile. "Some things are not options in life."

"And that means?"

"That I'm not getting into it right now when we have so much mess to play in at the moment."

"I do not appreciate being shut out like that, and I deserve to know why."

It's true, but it doesn't change things. There is no way I'm getting into all of that tonight. I can't handle it, and telling him that now would only mean him trying to drag it out of me indefinitely. I shrug and shake my head. "It's not up for discussion, Anderson."

"See, I tried that tactic on you, and it didn't work. So, unless you want to be a hypocrite, then you'll tell me what the fuck else is going on." The edge in his voice sends me spiraling again.

I close my eyes and try to count to ten, but I keep hearing him go on about how I need to talk to him instead of shutting him out. I should listen to his advice because he knows what kind of man Andre really is. I should, I should, I should, I need, I need, I need. My head spins, and then the room spins, too.

Can't breathe. Can't think. He's going to hit —

No. He's not. This is Anderson. Not my dad. He's upset. Not abusive.

I gulp down some water. "I'm going now."
Something latches onto my wrist when I scoot out of the booth and stand up.

His hand. It's crushing me. I can't escape. A scream builds —

Only he's not crushing me. His grasp is loose. He just wants me to stop for a minute. When I look into his eyes, I could dive right into them and happily drown. He's not my father. He's Anderson West. The man I love. Softly, he says, "Please talk to me."

But I can't. I take his hand off of me and kiss the back of it. "We'll talk later. For now, I need to go."

He sighs and takes his hand back. "I'll sleep at my place tonight."

I nod once and flee into the frozen night.

33

ANDERSON

I hate questions. Not the basic ones—what do you take in your coffee, do you like sunsets—not those. I hate questions with no answers. Questions like, why did I have to sleep alone last night? Why is my girlfriend getting weirdly territorial about Andre when he's the bastard who kidnapped her? Why has my life become a study in drama instead of a study in luck?

At one point in my life, I had thought I was the luckiest asshole in the world. I have a wealthy family, a name that opens doors, I'm good looking. All the stars aligned for me, and I loved my life.

Only it wasn't mine.

I see that now. For something to be yours, you have to work for it. I had fuck-all to do with my family's money when I was born. A name is something given to you. It's not earned. My looks are primarily thanks to outstanding genetics. I hit the gym whenever I can—or, at least, I used to—but that's such a small part of what goes into looking the way I do. I know that. The life I had before it all went to shit was not a life I had earned.

It was a gift. But right now, it feels like a noose.

All the things I had given to me are now what my father uses to pull his noose tighter and tighter around my neck, and I am sick of choking on it. But I don't know what else to do right now, so focusing on June is easier.

I huff at myself, shaking my head. *As if anything is easy with her.*

But it's not her fault. Not really. Every problem we have had can be traced back to my father. This is all on him, and I don't know how to fix that. I dig my head back into my pillow for the staring contest with my ceiling. I am losing this contest, too.

Lying in bed doesn't fix anything, so I roll to my feet and drop for push-ups. As much as I love my apartment building for having a place to work out, it's not the same as going to my old gym, and I don't want to admit to myself that I can't afford that anymore.

Bodyweight exercises will have to suffice for now.

I crank out a few sets of squats after the push-ups and burpees after that until I'm gassed. I'm off to the shower for a quick one, and then I am heading to the coffee shop down the street. Another frigid day in paradise, I see. No freezing rain, which is nice, but it might as well be. The mist is so heavy that it's almost rain when it hits my face, and the chilled breeze makes it feel just this side of not frozen. By the time I reach the coffee shop, I feel iced over.

Thankfully, it is warm inside—almost hot, actually. There's a thick line of customers, which makes sense. It's too cold not to drink something hot. The best part about the place? June won't be here. Not that I am avoiding her. I want to talk to her about last night's fucked up conversation. But not right now. It's too soon, I think. Whatever happened last night, she wasn't quite herself. I want to know why, and I want to know how I can fix it.

I need us to get back on the right track. The thought makes me chuckle to myself. Have we ever been on the right track?

By the time I reach the front of the line, I have forgotten what I wanted. Sometimes, I'm dedicated to a drink, but I'm too scattered right now. I need to switch things up. "Eh—"

"If you don't know, go to the back of the line!" some jackass says behind me.

The barista gives a pained smile and softly says, "Take your time." She must really hate that guy.

I don't want to make her day any worse by antagonizing that jerk, so I blurt the first menu item that jumps out at me. "Peppermint mocha, please." Shit. Do I want that? Doesn't matter. "Biggest one you've got. Two extra shots. Thank you." After I pay and go to the waiting deck, I spy the jackass.

White, middle-aged male with not enough hair and too many teeth. I'd love to fix that last part about him by knocking a few out, but that's just the primal part of me thinking. No. Not really thinking. That's the primal part of me planning.

Strange that. Since I've been doing ride-alongs with Moss, my mind slips into some darker, uncivilized place far too easily for my liking. I have a shorter fuse these days, and I don't like it. I need to work on it, but oddly, I don't want to. It's juvenile of me, but I like having an edge if I'm honest with myself.

I've always thought I was better than men like Moss. Men who use their fists instead of their words. After doing a few martial arts when I was growing up, I stopped because I wanted to be more erudite and more intellectual. Dad had begun to drill into me that I should be an academic more than a brawler, and if I wanted to inherit his title, I had to be better at books than fisticuffs.

Such a fucking liar.

I wonder if Mom put that in his head. She hated my martial arts classes because she worried I'd get hurt. I sighed at the thought. If she could see me now …

The grumpy jackass has no other choice but to stand next to me as we wait for our drinks. That primal, petty inner voice tells me to stand up straight to make him feel small. It's an embarrassing sentiment. I have nothing to prove to this guy. So, I stand there, waiting.

As the drink-making barista lifts a cup to the deck, the jackass grabs it before I think to, and then marches off. I ask her, "Was that a—'

"Large peppermint mocha, two added shots."

"And the next is…?"

"Large sugar-free vanilla steamer, nonfat, hold the whip."

I smirk, watching the guy outside as he takes his first sip. "This will be funny."

The barista cocks an eye up, half-paying attention. The guy spits out my drink and marches back inside. "This is not my drink!"

"No," I tell him, standing square at him. "It was mine. But you grabbed it without waiting for her to announce it."

She sets his drink on the deck, announcing his drink, before going back to her work.

I'm between him and his drink now, so I politely step aside. "I believe that's yours."

He sets mine onto the deck, grabs his, and grumbles at the barista, "You should have been faster."

When he turns around, I am in his way again, this time glaring down at him. "Apologize."

He is so frustrated that it's fucking hilarious. "Fine. Sorry for taking your drink."

"Not to me, you absolute waffle. To the barista."

He whips around to her. "Sorry."

She smirks up at me, then looks at him. Her voice is falsely cheery as she says, "Have the day you deserve, sir."

He darts around me without another word.

"Sorry if that was awkward. I hate bullies."

"Me, too." She laughs, shaking her head. "And that wasn't awkward. That was awesome. Thank you for that. Here." She passes me another drink. "A replacement. Wish I could do more for you."

"No worries. Have a good day."

"You, too."

I'm glad that guy was a commuter and not someone I have to compete for seats with. The place is packed, but I manage to find a lounge chair in the corner just as my phone rings. Without looking, I answer, "June, baby, hi—

"Not June, Andy."

My eyes squint shut in a cringe before I force them open again. "Cole, hey. How is my baby brother?"

"Are you ever going to stop calling me that?"

"The day you stop calling me Andy."

"Damn. Guess we'll be ninety, and I'll still be your baby brother."

Since he's been at the office, I have been tasked with training him. But he has no aptitude for the law, and I have no aptitude for his flakiness. A match made in hell, aka, a match made by my father. I blow out a frustrated breath. "What can I do for you?"

"Actually, this is about what I can do for you, Andy."

Fuck. Another Ponzi scheme? Not again. "Whatever it is, I'm not interested—

"I'm at the office, and Dad is pissed off. I have never seen him like this."

Everything in me tightens up. Since when does Dad show Cole his real emotions? "Something wrong with you? With Mom? What's going on?"

He takes a beat. "Did you buy June?"

If I had a mouthful of peppermint mocha, I would have spat it on my phone. "What?"

"Dad is furious because he said there was an auction, and you bought June there, which doesn't make any sense —"

"Gotta go." I hang up fast and race out of the coffee shop to return home. Home is where my car is, and my car will take me to that piece of shit's office. The longer he sits on this bit of information, the angrier he will be. And if he's angry enough to spill my illegal activities to Cole, whom he barely tolerates, then there is no telling how bad this will get. The sooner I get there, the better.

34

ANDERSON

This is a fucking nightmare.

That thought keeps ticking through my mind like one of those CNN chyrons. The last thing I need is Dad on my ass about the auction. How is he going to construe this as an insult to him? I don't know. But I'm confident he will.

Since that night, my life has been turned upside down in good and bad ways. I don't regret it, though. Not even now, as I'm driving to face my father's wrath. That night brought June into my life again. I can't bring myself to regret it. Not even if I tried.

With that thought, my heart is lighter. Just a fraction, but it is. No matter how pissed off he is, I still have her. Sure, things are weird between us

now, but I love her. She loves me. We will work
this out.

Still don't know what to do about Andre, though.

That minor detail is going to haunt me until she quits
him. I cannot figure out how she has twisted her
mind into such a pretzel that it makes sense to work
for the man who fucking kidnapped her. No matter
how fucked up it is, though, I cannot let my mouth
run away from me and mention it to Dad. Ever.

It is bad enough that he's blackballing her. If Dad
finds out, she's working for his enemy to insult him
… I don't know what will happen, but it won't be
pretty. Moss says he doesn't send him out for insults,
but this would be too personal for Dad to ignore,
and I would hate to have to start a violent fight with
my father, but if so, I will be the one to end it.

I will find a way to calm Dad down. I will get him to
let this go. If he wants to ream me out, fine. I can
take it. I've been taking that my whole life.

But he will not lay a hand on June.

I shake off the bloody thought as I park in the
underground parking of our office building.
Whatever the situation, I will not let it devolve into
something physical between me and Dad over June.
I don't want that to stain the fabric of our
relationship. As filthy as things began with her, I'd
like to keep that relatively clean.

Minus the dirty things I do to her.

I head up in the elevator, nodding politely at the people who come and go on their floors, greeting those who know me by name. It's strange to pretend to be normal when you only want to pull your hair out or run away, never to look back again. I do not like pretending. It's unnatural to me. I've never had anything to hide in my life, so it feels wrong to pretend. Until now.

Once I reach Dad's floor, I am surprised. His secretary is absent. That never happens. The woman is so dedicated that she has to be sent home whenever she's unwell, which also seldom happens. The closer I get to his door, though, the more I realize why she's gone. He must have sent her away so she didn't hear him shouting. Who is he speaking to? I listen at the door.

But it opens a moment later, and I nearly fall into the room.

"You dumbass, I have cameras on my door. You think I don't know when someone is standing there, listening in? Come in."

"Just testing you," I lie, then close the door behind myself. His office is as cold as he is, and I might feel it if I weren't dressed for the weather.

He coolly sits behind his desk, then gestures to his guest chairs. "Sit. Now."

"I prefer to—

"Sit!" His facial lines tighten, smoothing them out to mere hints. When he's angry, he looks younger than he is. I wonder if I'll have that ability when I'm his age.

If I get to his age.

I sit across from him, not wanting to make things worse. "Care to tell me about your foul mood?"

"Care to tell me about the auction where you bought yourself a fake fiancée?"

"Well." I will not squirm in my seat in front of him. I am not a frightened kid anymore. "No. Not really."

He steeples his fingers with his elbows on the desk. Every breath he takes is smooth, as if he is willing himself to calm down. "Do you recall what I have told you for your entire life, Anderson?"

"You like to hear yourself talk, so you must be more specific."

He grits his teeth. "Watch how you talk to me today. I am in no mood."

I nod my assent but say nothing.

"In all your years, I have tried my damnedest to impart one simple lesson that will echo through our family's history for all time. Every single thing you do reflects on the business."

That's what he's mad about? "I am a relatively young man who bought time with a woman for a night, Dad. This is hardly a scandal."

He stares blankly at me for a moment, then huffs a laugh. "Do you think I am so simple as to be offended by prostitution?"

"Given what I've seen of you recently, I'm surprised anything offends you."

"That mouth again," he growls before he sits back. "I am many things to many people, Anderson. A husband. A father. A boogeyman. A murderer. One thing I am not, however, is a hypocrite, and I will not pretend to be offended by prostitution, particularly when I am on the Chamberlain Museum's board."

I frown at that. "You're on the board?"

"And the auction night's committee."

Something in my gut twists. My heart beats rapidly. I think I'm having one of those out-of-body experiences because I no longer feel attached to my bones. "You mean the public auction, right? The one everyone goes to?"

He arches a brow at me. "Come now, Anderson. Don't play the fool."

My insides try to drop out of me. "You knew ... you knew this whole time?"

His smirk slowly pulls his lips sly. "The thing about me, my son, is that even after I finish my last breath in this life, you will never be free of me."

The noose tightens.

"I … I … "

"In this city, when there is an important event, or something goes spectacularly wrong, my hands are in it. My name is rarely in the headlines, but my fingerprints are on every story and bit of gossip. Some men leave big shoes to fill when they die, but, Anderson, my footprint *is* Boston."

I have no idea what to say. My mind is blank. He has known from the start. He's played his hand without even a hint that he was playing at all. In short, whatever I do, I am fucked.

Opting for glib, I half-shrug. "Congratulations."

He fakes a smile at me. "I say all this not to brag but as a warning."

"A warning about what?"

"You have no allies, no friends. It will stay that way until I say otherwise."

"What is that supposed to mean?"

Now, I get a genuine smile out of him. "You know precisely what that means. There is no move you can make, no grand scheme you can concoct that I will not thwart. If you move against me, then you move against Boston, and as you are well aware, Boston does not take kindly to such things."

My mouth is dry. "Why would I move against you, Dad? What reason could I possibly have?"

His emotions stop registering. Moments like this make my breath hitch in my chest, and the fine hairs on the back of my neck stand. When he stops being my father and shows me his true personality. The mobster. "You will stop seeing that whore."

"Excuse me?"

"What is it the kids call it these days? Oh, right. You will ghost June Devlin. No further contact from this moment onward. No texts, calls, visits. You will cease all connections. If you feel generous and choose to contact her, that is a move against me. Against Boston. No matter how you feel about the whore, you are smart enough to know better than to face me as an adversary. It is over. Wipe that look off your face and call Moss. You have work to do."

-

35

JUNE

Our fight was terrible last night, but I didn't think he would ignore my texts. Sure, we were fighting, and we both made some valid points, but I'm just shocked he hasn't texted me back. It's not like him. I sigh to myself and pull my robe a little tighter. I just wish he would respond. Thankfully, my chocolate responds.

It's much easier to eat my feelings than to think about them. An unhealthy coping mechanism. But I don't really give a shit. Right now, my heart sits on the precipice of something bad. I can feel it. I don't even want to think about whether Anderson wants to break up.

I can't let myself think about that. We will get through this. I know we will. It's just … why hasn't he texted me back yet?

Okay, what if this thing with Andre is a deal breaker? What if this is the straw that breaks the camel's back? We have hit so many skids on our road. And this is a big one, I know it is. But I won't let some man, not even Anderson, tell me what job to take. Where does that stop?

I know where it stops. It stops when you stop agreeing to it. I watched my mother give in to my father on his every whim for years because he wore her down. First, it was what friends she could have. And he was subtle about it. He said, " I don't think that person is good for you. Or I think that guy has a crush on you, so I'm uncomfortable with you being his friend. He couched it in completely reasonable terms at the start.

Then it became what kinds of movies she would watch, and he said they weren't high-brow enough or too dumb for someone as bright as her. He made it sound like a compliment. So she would agree to whatever movie he wanted to watch. And for a long time, that was how they lived.

He ate away at her for years. Her personality, the things she liked, even if they were dumb, it didn't matter. They were what she liked. But that wasn't good enough for him. Nothing ever was.

Then, it became physical. Picking on her weight, her clothes, her hair. He had isolated her from her friends and from herself, so when he started in on her physicality, there wasn't much of her left. She didn't defend herself when he hit her the first time. She thought it would be just that one time. And then, just that second time. And so on.

She never stood up to him until he started hitting me, too.

I know Anderson is not my father. He would never, ever hit me. That's not how he gets what he wants. And that's not what last night was about. Not for him, anyway.

But last night, I was suffocating in it, and now he won't text me back, which makes me feel like I'm suffocating all over again.

I just want some kind of resolution to this. I want him to be okay with me working for Andre. I want things to be normal. We may never have normal, I know that. But I want to try for it. With him.

The downstairs intercom buzzes for me. It's odd because I didn't order any food. It's probably just a neighbor's friend with the wrong apartment number. I set aside my emergency chocolate, which is dwindling at the moment, and go to the intercom. "Hello?"

"It's me, June. Let me up."

Oh shit, it's an Anderson ambush. This cannot be good. Okay, I guess we're doing this. I buzz him up and wait by the door. My heart is lodged in my throat, pounding in my ears, and waiting on my sleeve. I can't hide it from him. He will know the moment that he sees me that I feel like hell about last night, even though I was right and even though he was wrong. But when he gets here, I need to hold my head up high and stick to my points.

He doesn't get to tell me what to do about my job. He's not the boss of me.

He wraps his knuckles on the door, and I open it. Before I can open up my mouth and say a word, the way he looks shuts my mouth. My poor man looks like he has been through hell, and I have the distinct impression it's not because of last night.

I ask, "What's wrong?"

"Can I come in?"

I open the door wide, then shut it behind him, throwing all the locks. "Talk to me, Anderson. What is going on?"

"My dad knows."

I shake my head, confused. "What are you talking about?" We have a lot of secrets from Elliott West, and I need him to be more specific.

"He knows everything. The auction. The fake engagement. All of it. I wouldn't be surprised if he's behind Andre trying to hire you. But I don't know that for sure."

Suddenly, there is not enough air in the room, and I'm dizzy. "Oh my god."

"I know, I know. I'm trying to wrap my head around it too."

"Can we convince him that he's wrong? That he's just confused or that he got his facts wrong? That someone lied to him?"

"He is on the committee at the Chamberlain Museum that runs the auction. The auction where I won you."

It's as if the floor drops out from under me. "Oh fuck."

"June, there's more."

Those words hit me like a truck. "What? How can there be more? What more is there?"

Anderson pauses to look at me, and I have never seen him look quite this devastated before. The only other times have been when I was in danger, so my flipping stomach plummets. He licks his lips and takes a deep breath. "My father has forbidden me from seeing you ever again."

Those words knock all mine away. What could I possibly say to that? I knew we were having trouble.

I knew Andre was a big sticking point for him, yet I was dumb enough to think we could work that out. But this is something else entirely. How do I tell him to tell his own father no when his father has done everything to have him by the balls?

I don't have a trump card for that. This is game over. I'm sure of it.

I want to cry that it's not fair. I want to scream, and I want to vomit. And I want to pound Elliott West's ugly face in. But I can't do any of that. This obviously hurts Anderson just as much as it hurts me. Maybe more because it's his father doing it.

I gather all the courage that I have inside of me and try to ask the question that I don't want to ask. It doesn't come out easily. I can't even ask it the right way. My voice sticks around the hot ball of pain in my throat, begging me to cry to release it. But I don't. I can't make this harder on him. "I love you, Anderson. And I understand-"

He grabs me, pulling me into his arms for a kiss. I don't know if it's a kiss goodbye, but I give myself over to it. Our passion, our love, wrapped up in that kiss, sends a sharp thrill through my body, warming me from the inside out. He presses his forehead to mine. And murmurs, "My father can go fuck himself."

36

ANDERSON

"Do you mean that?" she whispers. Her breath is sweet, and it fills my lungs with her scent. This is all I ever want out of life. Being close enough to June to be surrounded by her. She is everything to me. She's my world, my air, my reason for being.

If Elliot West thought he could pry me from this woman, he has lost his damned mind.

"With everything I am, I mean that, June. I'm not going anywhere."

She tilts her mouth up to meet mine, and I hold her tighter to me, feeling her soft body against me. Each sensation is precious. When her tongue slips into my mouth, I groan. As her fingertips trail up the back of my neck, I am in ecstasy. I memorize every detail of our kiss, banking it for later.

When she pulls out of the kiss, it's like the sun is blotted out from my sky. "Your father is—"

"Not what I want to talk about right now." I yank my leather jacket off and toss it behind me someplace before I hold her again, ravishing her mouth with my own. During our kiss, I kick off my boots. My hands skate down her back until I reach her ass, and there, I grab her to pull her against me. She moans and melts on me, forming herself onto my body perfectly. I pick her up from there, bracing her legs around my waist to carry her to her bedroom.

But she pulls back. "Here. Now."

I nod once and set her down before untying her robe while I stare into her eyes. I feel like a kid on Christmas, unwrapping my present. No matter how many times I do this, it never gets old. She fumbles with my sweater, trying to take it off at the same time I'm working on her clothes, and we laugh, then trade assignments to make this faster.

Before I have my jeans off all the way, she's on her knees and takes me into her mouth. I damn near lose my balance thanks to her hot, wet tongue on my shaft. I suck in air through tight teeth, making a hissing sound. This fucking woman is going to be the death of me, and I will welcome it with open arms.

But I need more.

I hoist her to her feet by her shoulders, and for a moment, I marvel at her naked body. She's soft and curvy in every way I like, but most importantly, she's June. She is the woman of my dreams in every way imaginable. Even now, I cannot believe that she's mine or that she chooses me. What are the odds?

I can't wait any longer. I pull her to me by the small of her back, pressing her supple skin to me. My cock wedges between her thighs at the apex, and I can feel how wet she is already. Instead of maneuvering her to enter, though, I grab her hips and move her back and forth over my cock, rubbing against her wet pussy. When I do, she shudders against me. She bites her lip and stares up at me. "Tease."

"Never."

Since we didn't make it to her bedroom, I bend her over the back of the couch and swipe my hand up between her thighs from behind. She whimpers at my touch, angling herself at me for more. I tease, "You wanton thing."

"Your fault. Entirely."

My fingers are so fucking wet. I kneel behind her and bury my face against her pussy, drinking in everything she is until I brush against her clit with my chin and make her yelp my name. She rides back, working her hips up and down for more stimulation. God, I fucking love her for that. Love that she's not shy about her pleasure-seeking.

No wife of mine should ever be shy about that.

I'd be tempted to propose if my mouth weren't busy right now. She would hate me for proposing during sex. I'm sure of that. But I am on my knees for this woman, and nothing has ever felt so right. My body aches to fill hers, though. Precum coats the head of my cock, and I need to be inside of her like I need oxygen. But more than all of that, I need her to come.

I work my jaw, my tongue, my fingers. Anything to get her there. I crave her orgasm. When her thighs go tight, I know what's coming, and I throw my arm over her ass to pin her in place. She erupts in my face, kicking and screaming in the best way possible. It's not until her body goes slack that I let her go.

When I stand up, she carefully does the same and faces me. Her cheeks are rosy and sweaty, and she has never been more beautiful. I slant my mouth over hers, and we lose ourselves in the moment until she sits on the back of the couch and wraps her legs around me to pull me into her.

The second her pussy touches my cock, Anderson West is gone. There is only the animal I am.

I grab her ass and thrust into her in one shot, relishing the tight, wet warmth. Her nails drag down my chest, leaving bright red trails in my skin. Not blood, but marks all the same. Seems I'm meeting her animal, too.

I pick her up again, this time with her on my cock. With every step, I sink deeper into her body just like she has sunk into my heart. By the time we reach the front of her couch, she's shaking again, and her pussy clenches against me. I lay her onto her back and fit inside, arching my back to reach her furthest depths. Her legs tighten around me and her back arches from the couch, body tense, as she snarls out, "Fuck, baby, yes!" I reach down for her clit to wring out every bit of her pleasure, and she shrieks like a final girl in one of her favorite movies as she comes on my cock.

I have to fight the pull to join her over the edge. I am not done with her yet.

Pumping into her, I lay down onto her squirming form to kiss and toy and nibble on all her pink parts. Lips, nipples, tongue. Let her dance on my cock while I do it. I will play her body like my favorite instrument because she is, and her screams are the best music in the world.

She digs her head back against the couch cushions so she can breathe, and it happens in a strangled gasp that ends with a throaty, "Oh, fuck!" Then she hooks her hand around my neck, pulling me down for her mouth and another intoxicating kiss that sends me spiraling into our love.

I grind into her and reach her G-spot with inches of my shaft on each thrust. I can tell when I hit it because her body locks up and her eyes flutter. This is what I want. Precisely this. June, helpless to the stunning pleasure in her body. I want to do whatever I can to make this happen again and again, and why is she moving differently?

June bites my lip, stealing my focus. In a breathy moan, she pants, "Want you to come!"

I lick the sweat from her lip. "You have to—"

"I have," she says with a giggle. "A lot. Baby, I want to feel you lose control." With that, she wriggles from me and turns over. "Like this."

Grabbing her ass, I bring her up onto her knees. "Spread your legs for me."

She does so, and I'm beholden to the sight, losing my mind in the process.

"Touch yourself."

June reaches between her legs and works her clit for my viewing pleasure. Her wet body glistens as she waits for my next words.

Fuck, I love this woman.

I line up behind her and growl, "Keep touching yourself," before I mount her. It's too much and not enough. I lie on her back, pressing her to the couch so I can feel all of her on me. Her neck tastes like sweets, and I bite her there as I pound into her. Her fingers graze my cock sometimes because she is such a good girl that she's still touching herself on my order. I murmur, "Do you want me to come in you, love? To fill you up?"

"Yes!" she whimpers beneath me. "Come inside of me!"

Those words are almost enough to do it. But still, I want more.

I cock myself downward to dig against her spot harder, and she releases a throatier sound, something from her core. That's it. That's what I want. She trembles beneath me, and it vibrates through my body. I'm close—her pulse makes me throb. Each stroke makes her frame stiffen. She is almost there. But I need one more—

"Fuck!" she whines. Her body goes crazy, and I arch back to let her move. She gushes on me in a rush as she comes screaming yet again. I bear down on her, loving all the honey pouring from her body. The heat tears through me and melts my resolve. I come in a bellow, hammering into her quivering body, until I collapse onto her back, desperate for air.

This solved nothing, but it feels like the answer to everything.

37

JUNE

It has been days since Elliott put down his ultimatum to Anderson. I am surprised that we haven't heard anything about it yet. But according to Anderson, his dad hasn't said a peep about us being together. We are certain that he knows that we keep seeing each other. That man knows everything. He probably knows what I had for breakfast yesterday. So it's not like this is going to be some big surprise to him. Anderson says that maybe he respects the fact that he is doing his own thing.

But I don't think it's that. I think he's waiting like a snake in the grass. So I keep waiting for the other shoe to fall. Until then, I'm going to live my life.

Today is Monday, and it is my first day at Andre's office. I am nervous and anxious, and part of me feels like this is the dumbest thing I have ever willingly done. But I'm doing it. After losing my last job because of Elliot. And all of the other things that he has managed to have a hand in in my life. I am doing the one thing that I am sure he will hate.

Well, aside from continuing to see Anderson.

I slide out of bed, trying not to wake him. His day starts later than mine, so I decided that I will take a shower by myself for once and really enjoy it. That man hates a properly hot shower.

Under the steaming hot water, I keep thinking of things I don't wanna think about. The bruises on my throat have been gone for days. But I still see them sometimes in the mirror. Not to mention, I see Moss's face in my head, too. That man was a savior that night. Right alongside Anderson. But he terrifies me. He is a living, breathing nightmare. He reeks of death. Whatever he does for Elliot, none of it is good. I hate that Anderson has to work with him.

So many of my recent bad memories are wrapped around Elliott West. I hate that. I would love to have a boyfriend whose father was a good man. But those are not the cards I was dealt. I have to play the hand that I was dealt. That means figuring out how to deal with Elliot. And I have yet to do that.

Hopefully, Andre will give me some pointers. I will have to divest him of the idea that we're engaged. It could be a useful lie to hang on to, but the truth is, I will absolutely lose track of my lies. I am not slick like they are. It's just not in me. Once we set the record straight, things will go smoothly.

Although maybe I can wait to tell him the truth. It is a useful lie. And since I'm only doing a two-week trial run at Andre's office, he doesn't necessarily need to know the truth. I can maintain a life for two weeks. Probably.

Kelsey was not happy about me taking two weeks away from the bar. I don't blame him. I make that man a lot of money. But he knows that my working there is temporary, so he didn't give me too much grief about it.

The one I'm really worried about is Anderson. He's still not on board about this, but we've reached some kind of a stalemate. He doesn't like that I'm working for Andre, and I don't like that he's working for his father. I know it's not my place to tell him to quit working for his dad. Just as it's not his place to tell me whether or not I can take a job with Andre. But so far, Andre has only kidnapped me. Elliott has done everything in his power to depower Anderson. He's done it his whole life. My poor boyfriend has been emotionally abused and manipulated by that man for decades.

Maybe if Andre likes me enough, he'll take out Elliot for me.

It's a fun thought experiment, but that's all it is. I could never ask such a thing and would never want it on my conscience. Though if he keeps pulling his shit with Anderson, I might figure out how to deal with a loaded conscience.

Anderson knocks on the bathroom door. "You gonna be much longer, baby?"

"Give me five minutes."

"Okay, but the bagels are getting cold."

That little shit snuck out of here and got bagels? I love that man.

I get out of the shower a little faster, wrap my hair in a towel, and put on my robe before running out into the kitchen. There on the counter is a bag heavy with bagels and two lattes. "I can't believe you did this."

"Figured my girl needed some good fuel for her first day."

It means so much to me that he said that. "When was the last time I told you I love you?"

"Last night. Twice."

I giggle, with my face going red again. "Pretty sure that second time my mouth was too full to say I love you."

He grins like the devil. "That's the best way to say I love you."

"I'll remember that for next time." I don't want to ask, but I have to. "Busy schedule today?"

He shakes his head. "Nothing terrible today, don't worry. Just gonna do a quick pick up with Moss."

I have resolved not to ask about these pickups, the ride-alongs, or any other details of his side work, as I've started to call it in my head. We are not married. If I were called to testify against him, I would have to. So the fewer details I have about what he does as his side work, the better for us both.

But that seems like a shitty reason to get married.

We gobble down on our bagels and drink our lattes in relative peace, neither of us happy with the other's work. I suppose that's just the nature of things right now. Neither of us feels as if we have any other choice. But there is one thing that came to mind late last night.

What if we just moved?

It's a crazy idea, and I know it. We are both Bostonians at heart. But what else do you do when your hometown is exactly what's killing you?

I haven't brought it up to Anderson. He would just shoot it down. He doesn't see a way around his father. Truthfully, neither do I. That man has hooks

on hooks on hooks. I am sure that he would
probably send Moss after us. Or worse. And I don't.
I don't wanna know what's worse.

"You have such a look on your face."

I snort a laugh around my bagel trying not to choke.
"What's that supposed to mean?"

"Just that you look like you're deep in thought.
What's on your mind?"

I can never hide a damn thing around this man.
"Just thinking about my day, I guess."

"Hmm. If you say so." His little smirk slays me every
time.

I give him a kiss and tell him, "I have to get ready."

"Can I do one boyfriend thing?"

"What's that?"

"Pick out your armor for the day."

I snort a laugh and shake my head. "Armor?"

"Armor, outfit, whatever you wanna call it."

"Sure."

While I do my hair, Anderson digs around in my
closet for something he deems armor. I'm not even
remotely surprised when it's a black pantsuit and a
black high-necked camisole. The ensemble covers

me from neck to wrist to ankle. "What do you think?"

He's trying. I know he is. It's not easy when your partner wants to do something so big that you disagree. So he's trying, and I'm going to accept his help. "It's perfect. Thank you, sweetie."

"Happy to help."

I get dressed, and I am swallowed in black once the outfit is on me. It's the office equivalent of a muumuu. But it makes him happy, and I'm not going to give him grief today. After checking my look in the mirror one more time, I grab my bag, and we head out for our respective destinations. When it comes time to part, I take a nervous breath. "See you at my place tonight? Chinese food?"

He smiles and nods. "Good luck today, June."

"You, too, baby."

38

ANDERSON

Meeting Moss at a convenience store down the street from June's apartment feels wrong. He's been there before. He knows where she lives. Obviously. But I just don't like having him in proximity to June. Ever.

Today, though, shouldn't be that bad. According to Moss, the guy we're going to pick up from is a pipsqueak. So, having him anywhere near her today doesn't feel too dangerous. I don't want him around her any day we're going to do any serious pick up, though. He gets this edgy, unstable energy on those days. Like his gun might go off in the wrong direction at any moment.

He pulls up in his big black SUV, wearing clothes to match. The large man grins and says, "Anderson, good to see you. Get in." His typical greeting.

I get in on the passenger side of his ride, and we're off. "How did Caterina's ballet recital go?"

"I gave her the wrong name."

I laugh at that, confused. "How so?"

He chuckles. "I should have named her Angela. Not her sister. Caterina moves like an angel. I am so proud of her."

There are many things that I could say about Moss. Maybe the most important one is that he is a doting father. "I'm glad to hear she did so well. What can you tell me about our target today?"

"Today we are visiting one Mr. Edgar Jones. He is a CPA. He is afraid of his own shadow but managed to lose $100,000 to your father, and that is what we are coming to collect."

"Holy crap, How did he lose that kind of money?"

Moss shakes his head. "Never bet on the Cowboys."

I laugh hard at that. Can't believe somebody lost their life savings over the Dallas Cowboys. "Damn, if you're gonna lose that kind of money, at least bet on the Patriots. If you're gonna lose, lose on the home team."

"Jones is originally from Texas. I think he holds some sort of loyalty to them."

I sigh. "Bad call, Jonesy. Bad call."

"We get Chinese food after this?"

It is easier to talk June out of her cravings than to talk Moss out of his. There are two things, three things, to never come between Moss and (Moss and what?). His daughters. His music. And his food. That's why I ask about the recital and why we listen to opera on the way to threaten some guy. Staying on Moss's good side is a good way to stay alive.

"You think Jonesy might give us any trouble?"

"Never. He's a good client. This is a lot of money for him. But he is a good client. He will pay."

Moss takes us to a four-story average brick office building in Wellesley. It's as plain as plain can be. I'm not even sure I could find my way back here. Nothing about this place sticks out other than the empty parking lot. "Why are there almost no cars?"

"Most of the offices here do work-from-home. Makes it the perfect place to meet Jones." He parks near some trees instead of near the front, making it easier to distort what his vehicle looks like if there are any cameras around. The more branches, the better. Moss parks so that his license plate will not face any camera.

I have so much to learn from this man.

"How does a CPA come up with this kind of cash?"

"He said he takes it from 401K."

"His wife won't like that," I note.

Moss chuckles. "You tell the girlfriend everything?"

I can't tell if that's a careful interrogation or a genuine question. Does he know that I've been forbidden to see June? Does he think I'll confide in him? Every word, every sentence, every gesture means something to Moss. And those things he reports to my father. I have no illusions about his loyalty to me over Dad.

I smile at him. "Does anyone?"

He laughs boisterously at that. "Telling everything is a good way to lose a relationship. Let's go."

I can't tell if that was romantic advice or not. But I get out of the car and follow him into the building. It smells like floor wax throughout the halls. Wooden doors line the walls, and fluorescent lighting burns into my retinas. I've always hated places like this. Their garish lighting and endless halls make me feel like a rat in a scientist's maze.

I'm relieved when Moss picks a door to stop at. "Here we are." He knocks.

The chair scrapes the floor inside before footsteps carry to the door. No privacy in this place. Not if others were not working from home. Every sound carries, and I'm very, very glad that there's no one else around. The door opens, and a small man greets us. He is white to the point of being translucent. I would guess the UK is somewhere in his background. Thin nose and thinner lips. He has scant hair on the top of his head. His clothes are far nicer than I would have imagined he could afford.

But then again, if he has a $100,000 gambling debt, the man is probably making a decent living.

He nervously looks at Moss and stutters, "You brought company?"

"Do not worry about the company I keep. Can we come in?" It is not a request.

Jonesy opens the door wide for us, then closes it. "Can I get you some water?"

"We are not here for a visit, but you knew that."

The office is far nicer than I expected, given the exterior. I'm unsure if he has a habit of overspending or if a CPA makes this kind of money. The floors are hardwood. His view is of the nice pond in the back. There's even a fountain. Expensive paintings hang on the walls, and the chairs and couch are from the same designer as my Dad's private office pieces. I do not get the impression that he has the money for this. The man has cheap shoes. Spending beyond his means tells me that he is going to not want to pay up. I'm surprised that Moss calls him a good client.

He has a bit of a hunch as he walks to his desk chair. "No reason not to be friendly, right, Moss?"

Following Moss' lead, I sit in the guest chair next to him. Moss grins. "I am always friendly, Edgar."

"So then, who is your friend?"

Before he can speak, Moss puts his hand out in front of me, indicating I should keep my mouth shut. "That is not important. What is important is you pay Mr. West."

"Right." He gulps. Loudly. "The money."

"Since I do not see a large bag around here for the money, does that mean it is a wire transfer?"

I have never heard of my father accepting a wire transfer. But maybe because he's a CPA, he knows how to hide it. The intricacies of money laundering have been tricky for me to learn.

"Moss, um. I've … I've had trouble getting the money."

"Wife find out you lose money?"

He closes his eyes and shakes his head. A spouse finding out that their partner owes us money is a dangerous proposition. That means witnesses. Witnesses mean legalities. None of us want that. Jonesy says, "She … she doesn't know anything. That's how I like to keep it."

"So do I, Edgar. So do I. Which is why you must pay. I do not want your wife to find out anything. You do not want your wife to find out anything. It's much cleaner this way, right?"

"Yes, but taking that kind of money out of my 401K sends up too many red flags. I can't get the money."

Moss takes a beat. "You mean to say you will not pay?"

Jonesy gulps again, then nervously licks his lips. A bead of sweat trickles down his lined forehead. "I won't."

Moss sighs, then cracks his knuckles. "That is unfortunate, Edgar. I have always liked you. I want to keep liking you. Most important of all, *you* would like me to keep liking you. But today, you make a liar out of me."

"How ... how's that?"

"I told my partner here that today is easy day. I want easy day. He want easy day. End of the three of us, you want easy day most of all." He sits back. "So you make me liar, and I don't like that. I am a man of my word. That is difference between us. I give my word, I keep it. You give your word, you break it. That means I break things, Edgar. Things you wish I did not break. Maybe then you figure out how to pay."

He stands up, and the hackles of my neck rise. I hate this part. Moss gave him plenty of lead-up. Gave him plenty of time to back out and agree to pay. Even after he said he couldn't, Moss still tried to give him that time to figure out how to pay. But now his time is up.

I brace my stomach for the sight of it. The sight of a cowering man is terrible. It's worse when he's getting the shit beat out of him. This kind of thing is my second least favorite thing about the job.

The first least favorite thing is all the murder.

I saw you trying to keep my eyes on the target, but it's hard. I can't imagine what's going through his mind right now other than fighting the urge to run. It must be hell to be in his head right now.

But then he pulls out a gun.

39

JUNE

"What is it about first days that make people so nervous?"

I look up at the man standing in my doorway. It's not Andre. He's Latin and has a friendly smile to go with his Prada suit. "I'm sorry, have we met?"

"Carlos Perez." He holds out his hand to shake mine as he strides in. "My office is next to yours, neighbor."

Meaning, I got the corner office before he did, and I just got here. But I stifle that thought, hoping for a pleasant encounter with my new neighbor. "Oh, nice to meet you. June Devlin. And I'm not nervous, but thanks for the concern."

He smiles confidently. "Come now. Everyone's a little nervous on their first day. Even I was."

"You look like you've never been nervous a day in your life."

He laughs heartily at that. "It has been known to happen. Did you get the file drop?"

I nod, staring at my computer screen. "Yes, and I've been digging through them for two hours."

"Anything we've missed?"

I'm torn about answering him. Andre brought me in to look through the files and see what has been going on. If I tell Carlos that I've found anything, he might try to cover it up or offer excuses. Or worse, he will try to act like he's my supervisor and tell me what to do. I need to be clear about who it is that I answer to. I smile. "Anything I find will be in a report to Andre."

"Of course, of course." He glances around the room, and I'm not sure what he's noticing. It's not like I've put in anything personal here. This is just a trial run. I'm not moving into my office for real until I know that I'm keeping the job. There's no sense in bringing in personal photos or decorations until I've decided. He turned his gaze to me, piercing me with his dark eyes. "I am dying to ask a question. But I'm not sure you'll answer it."

Oh hell. "If you ask it, you'll find out."

He grins. And it's one of those million-dollar smiles. "Are you here only to consult, or will you stay?"

So that's his angle. He's worried about keeping his job. "It's debatable. That's something I'll work out with Andre." Let him be nervous. Likely, he wouldn't be this nervous if he weren't already screwing up.

But his grin does not falter. "The way things go around here, we can always use fresh eyes. Be seeing you, June." With that, he glides out of my office.

Andre's firm is a lot like others. A world full of sharks looking for blood in the water. We're lawyers. We're competitive. It's in our nature. We didn't work as hard as we did in school to skate by in life.

My office is posh. Being the corner office. I have two walls of windows, with a view over a park. The pale blue carpet is plush and goes nicely with the pale blue and gold furniture. Heavy curtains hang at either end of the windows, blocking out a little light. Similar curtains hang along the glass wall shared by the hallway. If I wanted to, I could have absolute privacy in this room, which I love.

But there's no time to revel in the majesty of my office. The client files are calling me.

I spend the better part of the morning parsing through them. It's mostly standard stuff, nothing too out of the ordinary. In fact, the whole place is like that. I had come here expecting something nefarious or treacherous or extremely illegal. But Andre's law firm is just a law firm. There's nothing for me to worry about. Or so it seems.

But then a knock at my door takes my attention away from my work. I'm a little annoyed until I see that it's Andre himself. "Good day, Ms. Devlin."

It's always so strange having a conversation with Andre Moeller. His every sentence is a little bit off.

I smile and give a nod. "Good morning, Andre." Good morning, not day. Sometimes, talking to him feels like giving him lessons in how to be an American. Or a human. I can't tell which it is with him.

He strides in and sits on my desk corner. He peers at my computer screen. "We are keeping you busy already, I see."

"No rest for the wicked."

He chortles at that. "Or for you."

Does that mean he doesn't think that I'm wicked? "How are you today, Andre?"

"Eternally curious."

That's it. That's all he says. I have no idea how to respond to that, which goes along with every other conversation I've had with the man. He's smiling, and he seems happy. But I've seen that exact same expression on his face fall away in a flash the moment anything else came to mind. It's like having a tiger by the tail. I just need to keep the tiger happy.

To do that, I will do my job. "What is it you're curious about?"

"Whatever it is that you were buried so deep in that you didn't notice me watching you for a minute."

Did he just admit to staring at me for a minute? I am not sure what to think of that. Is he just being a boss? Is this his style? Probably best not to put too much thought into that.

"Well. What caught my attention is that whoever had this client last completely overlooked the fact that they are overpaying their taxes by about two hundred grand a year."

He looks positively scandalized. "No! Show me."

"First, are you well versed in tax code?"

"Not at all." Yet he still seems just as enthusiastic as he did a moment ago.

"Okay, let's see if I can explain this." I do a deep dive into the details of the tax code for Andre's benefit so that what I'm about to tell him about the client makes any kind of sense. He listens with rapt attention, eating up every word that I tell him. I cannot figure out if this man is interested in me or just interested in what I can do for him. He is impossible to read. But it's nice to talk to somebody who appears to be interested in tax code. I have so missed this. "... so you see here if we take the right deduction, boom. They save enough money for a small yacht."

He belly laughs. "What is it you think a small yacht costs?"

"Under two hundred k? Why? What do they cost?"

He sits back, pondering my question for a moment. "Come to think of it, I don't know, either. I should look into that. In the meantime, I am very impressed with you, Miss Devlin. I know a bright mind when I see one. Keep up the good work."

"Thank you, Andre. And you can call me June, remember?"

He smiles. "In the office, I prefer to address with formalities. Do not feel it necessary to respond in kind. Enjoy your day." With that, he leaves my office.

I sit back and relax momentarily, trying to figure out what happened. I never know with Andre. One day, he kidnaps me. The next time I see him, he offers me a job. It could be anything from either end of the spectrum at any point. So, at least, I'll be kept on my toes.

But being here feels kind of wrong. I know how Anderson feels about it. He's made that abundantly clear. He doesn't get to tell me what to do with my career. But I should consider his feelings. Now, if only he would do the same for me.

I hate that he's doing whatever it is he's doing for his father. I know that there's some kind of violence involved sometimes, and that unnerves me. But until both of us can get out from underneath his father's thumb, there's not much more that either of us can do to avoid the situations we're in.

That doesn't mean that I don't feel conflicted as hell. We could leave Boston. I know we could. We can make a new life for ourselves somewhere else. Maybe someplace like Seattle. Or Los Angeles. Another big city where we can get lost in the shuffle. But then there's Moss, Elliott's right-hand goon. I'm sure he's not the only one that he has.

The more Elliott West tightens his grip on the both of us. The more I am convinced that something must be done about him. I just don't know what that is.

As things stand, I like it here. So far. It's complicated, and it makes me work my brain. And I love that. I love not working for tips. It was a relief at first, but after a week, the customers were getting annoying. Plus, I think I have a bit of anxiety and PTSD about going back to work given what happened with Neil and the fact that I met him at a bar. I love not feeling swat pour down my back while I pour drinks. I love not having to dodge grabby hands. There's money and respect here, both of which I am in short supply of.

But at the bar, things were simpler. Clients came in, had a few drinks, then left. And Anderson didn't hate what I did.

CHAPTER FORTY-ANDERSON

"I SAID, LEAVE!" Jonesy repeats, waving his gun around.

My mouth is dry, my back is wet with sweat, my head spins, and we are running out of time. I can feel it. Like sand slipping away in a tide, the seconds tick on, and this is not getting better. Our hands are up to show him we aren't a threat, but I don't think it's working. We are a threat, and we all know it.

Jonesy looks mad. As in, insane to the point of a break with reality.

By the raised brows on Moss, this is the first time he's seen the man lose his shit. In this line of work, I don't want to be along for the ride for any of Moss' *firsts'*. I like that he's experienced and can show me the ropes in any given situation. It's a comfort to think he can swoop in and fix things.

But this moment proves that's all an illusion.

How many times have I thought of Moss as my own personal Superman? My get-out-of-jail-free card? The guy who can fix anything? He handles shit. That's his job. Why else would Dad pair me up with him?

None of that matters. I got too comfortable. I know that now. Today was supposed to be an easy day. I never should have thought of any of these days as easy. Not when I'm with Moss. A grimace of uncertainty plasters itself onto his face, and I don't know what to think. All I know is we might be fucked.

Moss uses the same soothing tone he used on June the night he helped us with Green Sweater. "Edgar, put that away. Now is not the time for that. You are good man. You don't want to hurt anyone—"

"You don't know what I want!" Jonesy snarls. Sweat trickles from his brow, and he winces from the sensation. It's like anything might set this guy off.

"Calm down, eh? You make my associate nervous."

Associate. He's still not using my name, and it takes me a blink to realize why. If Jonesy knew who I was, he might kill me out of spite for my father. Even now, with a gun pointed at him, Moss is thinking clearer than anyone I know.

"You think I give a shit, Moss?"

Moss clicks his tongue. "I think you love your wife, Edgar. She does not want this for you."

The gun hand twitches, and soon, his hand goes into full-on shakes. He shouts, "Don't talk about my wife!"

But Moss presses him on it. "And your sons? What about them?" His hands drift downward. He's about to do something, and I need to be ready for it.

Everything tenses inside of me as I try to keep my face placid. If I don't react, hopefully, Jonesy won't, either.

Jonesy's gun stays trained on us as he stumbles around his desk to face us down. This isn't going right. He should be calming at the mention of his family—why else would Moss mention them? The CPA's jaw tightens, his eyes ferocious. "Get out now!"

I want nothing more than to do exactly that. But he's gone wild, and I get the sense that the moment we turn our backs, there will be holes in them. I think

Moss knows that, too—otherwise, he would be getting us out the door.

"Edgar—"

"This … this is what happens," Jonesy mutters to himself. His tone reminds me of junkies on the street when they talk to themselves. His eyes dip for just a moment, then they scatter around the room. But that gun is still aimed at us the whole time. "This is what happens when you do the wrong thing, Eddie. The mob comes to kill you—"

"I am not here to kill you," Moss says quietly.

Jonesy doesn't seem to hear him. "They come, and they bring a wet work guy for the clean-up, and then you're nothing but a stain on an office rug you overpaid for, and they roll your body in it and dump you into a river or set you on fire, and no one knows," he rambles, gun still shaking at us. I don't think he even took a breath before he starts again. "Not your wife, not your kids, you just disappear on them, and they don't know what happened, only that you're gone, that you abandoned them … " For a moment, his eyes focus on Mosses face. "I didn't abandon my family, Moss."

"You never would," he says serenely. "You're a nice man." Mosses hand is dangerously close to his gun.

"I can't … I can't let them think that of me."

"No one ever would. Everyone knows Edgar Jones is a stalwart. A pillar of community." Mosses next-level reverse psychology game is unnerving me. How many people has he had to do this with? Talk them down until he can take them out? The better question is, will this work with Jonesy? Moss continues, "You will have a long and happy life with them."

The CPA slowly nods. "I will."

Moss nods, too. "Let us figure out how to make that happen. Just put the gun down—"

"I won't." The steel is gone from his eyes.

But I get the sense this just got worse. Something inside of me tenses.

Moss says, "Edgar—"

"Don't say my name like we're friends."

If he's frustrated, he doesn't show it. Nothing but cool, calm, and collected on the surface. Other than the hand gradually getting to his gun. Moss goes on, "Think about your family. What would they want for you to do right now?"

"To live." His hand stops shaking. His eyes go completely sober and focused.

This is not going the way Moss wants it to, and I am the only one who knows it.

He tries to coax him with more words. "That's right. They want you to live. So, all you have to do is—"

"Pull the trigger."

Mosses hand jerks for his gun, but I dive for him as a loud sound cracks through the air. Something hits the middle of me, knocking me against Moss. But the man is a wall of muscle and doesn't budge from the impact, while I fall in front of him, slamming onto the expensive office rug. My shoulder hits it first, followed by the rest of me.

I'm on my side when the pain hits. I try to gasp for breath, but the wind was knocked out of me. Or it doesn't want to go into me. I can't tell which it is. My head rings with pain, but I don't think I hit it. I look down at my body. My hands are in the way of seeing what I already know. I don't really remember grabbing for my stomach. When I pull my hands back, they're covered in red.

Fucking Jonesy shot me in the stomach.

I'd always heard a gunshot wound to the gut is one of the worst ways to die. You don't necessarily die from the bullet making you bleed out. The way a bullet travels through someone's core is unpredictable. They don't go straight through—they ricochet and fragment, tearing through your delicate structures, eviscerating the viscera, and shattering the spine.

At the moment, I almost wish it had hit my spine. I might not feel the pain if my nerves were severed. There should be a word beyond pain for what I feel right now. Agony? Torment? They're just words for pain, and none of them are adequate for it.

When I can finally take a breath again, I am deafened by the sound of my own gasp. I don't know if the bullet climbed up into my lungs, but I don't think so. I'm not breathing blood. Maybe it was just the impact that stole my breath away. Hard to say.

On the exhale, though, somehow, the pain intensifies. It's not heat I feel in my middle, but the only thing I can think of is it feels like what I imagine lava to feel like. As if each nerve has been twisted into something new, and that new thing only wants your screams.

Blackness takes over, and I don't want to think of death as a comfort, but right now, it fucking would be. Anything to end this.

But I come to a second later. The sound of wet thuds brought me back around. A distinctive crunch I've come to associate with Moss follows. Bones are breaking nearby.

It takes every bit of my waning energy to send the signal to my face to open my eyes. For a moment, I don't think they're going to do it, but then my eyes pry open. I have to check on Moss.

When my eyes focus, all I see is Jonesy's battered face. What's left of it, anyway. Moses fist slams into it one more time, before he turns the man's head toward me, forcing him to look at me if he's still in there. Moss crouches over him and hisses, "You shot Anderson West. You make me do this." A shot rings out, and Jonesy's mangled forehead has a hole.

-

40

ANDERSON

Jonesy's eyes are glassy and red. His abused face had swollen in places before he died. Didn't know you swell that fast. The last time I was in a fight, I didn't feel it in the moment. I wonder if he felt it when Moss beat the ever-loving shit out of him. Or if he felt it when the bullet entered his face. I didn't really feel it when his bullet pierced me. It was an impact, not a piercing.

I don't have answers, and I never will. All I know is, I don't want that bastard's face to be the last thing I see in this life.

Moss looks at my body before my face. He snaps his fingers inches in front of my nose. "Anderson!"

I blink up at him, too exhausted to speak.

"Must get you out. This will hurt." He bends down, scooping me into his arms, and he's fucking right.

I howl my lungs out in pain.

"Sorry, sorry. But quiet is best."

Quiet? This man wants quiet? He's out of his fucking mind!

But he manages to wrap his hand over my mouth as he carts me through the building, and his palm tastes like blood as I do my best to keep the howling to a minimum. Mercifully, the darkness floods in again when fresh air hits me.

When I wake, it's because something is laid over me. I'm in the rear of a vehicle — probably Mosses SUV. I push against the shroud. It's one of the tarps he keeps in the back.

"Need to keep you covered," Moss grunts. "Cannot let others see."

But right now, it feels like death is coming to swallow me. I peel back the top so I can see and breathe. Shouldn't have done that.

For the first time since I've known the man, Moss looks terrified. He's pale. Paler than usual, anyway. His lips are tight, and those cold, dead eyes of his host sprays of wrinkles at the corners. "Okay. Like this, then."

"Where … " but the word trails off in my mouth and my mind, and the black rolls in again.

When I come to, we're moving. Every bump and turn sizzles pain through me. A scream erupts out of me, and I can't stop it.

Mosses voice is distant from me. Of course it is, he's driving. "You wake. This is good sign."

"Hospital," I plead.

"Hospital … it is not the right place for you."

Fuck. He's going to let me die. I saved his life, and he's going to let me die because I left evidence back there. My blood. One of the first things he told me after our first ride-along was to never leave evidence of our presence. He'd even told me it would be a wise idea to shave my head like him so I would be less likely to leave hair behind.

And now, because I saved his life, I'm going to die.

I swallow, my throat parched. I'm not above begging for my own life. With some of the precious air in my lungs, I rasp, "Please, Moss. I don't want to die."

"You will not die."

Four simple words that might mean so much. But I don't know that I can believe them. "Why not?"

"Because I take you where people go to live."

My voice shakes because my breaths are uneven. "Hospital?"

"I am taking you to get help, Anderson. Rest now."

Resting sounds like dying, but I don't have the energy to argue. Looking over the black tarp on my body, some morbid part of me wants to peek underneath and see my ruined flesh. Something cold sticks between me and the tarp, and something else cold has coated my back. I know what it is. The slow trickle of blood around my sides tells me everything. The details of a gunshot wound play back in my mind, but I don't want them to. I want to think about anything other than that. Yet I still want to look.

I curl up the edge just a little. The foul stench of blood and other things hits hard and fast, and I drop the edge. I am overwhelmed by the need to not see. Denial is my friend.

I close my eyes and take as deep of a breath as I'm willing to under the circumstances, then try to think about anything else. Still don't know if Moss is taking me for help or not. He could be, or he could be driving around and waiting for me to die. He likes me well enough, but I'm a liability now. I come at a cost. He is not a fan of those things. His line of work does not allow for them.

Will he feel guilty when I die? I did it to save him. He should at least feel guilty about this.

Hell, if I'm honest with myself, I'm not even sure I did it to save him. When I replay what happened in my mind, it's almost as if *I* didn't do it at all. Instinct took over. He was the man at my side. I owed him for what he did for me and June with *Green Sweater*. Of course, I'd fucking jump in front of a bullet for the man who helped to save her. It's not even a question. It was instinctual to save Moss.

Even if it kills me.

But I don't want to die for him or anyone. Not if I can help it. The rear space of the SUV is missing the internal handle to make kidnapping easier. So I can't open the doors easily. I could try to kick out the windows, but even just the thought of lifting my leg causes pain in my abdomen. Maybe if I had my full faculties, I could subtly remove the panel cover on the door and trigger the handle mechanism to open somehow, but I am far beyond those capabilities at the moment. Sitting up sounds like climbing Mount Everest.

Which just leaves me with my thoughts, because for some reason, right now I can't sleep. Probably because falling asleep is a little too close to death for comfort, and I have just enough fight left in me to hold out.

A spike of pain hits when we roll over what was probably a pothole. I grit my teeth and shout, "Fuck you, Boston!"

Moss laughs heartily. "Good to know you keep the sense of humor. Sleep now."

I huff and glare at the ceiling. It's gray to match the interior and has a fray at the corner nearest me. I wonder if some kidnap victim picked at it out of boredom or if it's there just because it happens like Boston's potholes.

Glaring isn't much of a hobby when you're dying, and it takes too much effort. So, I lean back against the floor and close my eyes. I don't quite recall how Moss got me in here when he had to bend my knees for me so I'd fit. Seems like I would have remembered the shock of pain that must have caused, but I don't. Blood loss makes my head fuzzy.

The black comes at the edges of my mind again. If it's my time, then I want to go out with better thoughts than my own blood. Instantly, June's pretty face comes to mind.

Her sweet smile. Her scent. The tender way she strokes my chest absentmindedly when we're in bed. Her taste. I have experienced every inch of that woman's skin with my tongue, and I long to do that again and again for every day of my life. I should have savored her more. Should have cherished her more.

I did what I could with the time we had, but it doesn't feel like enough. Though, to be fair to mortality, I'm not sure it could ever be enough. June and I could have been alive from the formation of the Earth until the planet is wiped out by the death of the sun, and that still would not be enough time with her. I love her with everything I am. She breathed new life into me when we met. Everything I have become, I owe to her.

I don't know if she knows that—how much she changed me, I mean. When we met, I was a spoiled, arrogant brat, hellbent on doing anything to earn my father's love. But I met June, and I didn't know what to do. She set off alarm bells in me. I wanted to hold her hand and, show her the school and introduce her to my friends and bring her to my room. No clue what I would have done once we were there—we were barely teens at the time. I might have shown her some trophy I'd won or hoped she'd let me steal a kiss. But I didn't have the language for any of that at the time. I had Dad's language, and the only way he showed affection was through cruelty …

I had a lifetime of regrets, and all the profound ones revolved around June.

I sigh into the darkness, feeling it wash over me again. But as I drifted away, I prayed she knew how I felt about her. Not just our love, but how much I wished I could take back all the mean things I'd said to her when we were young. How much I wished to make all of that up to her.

Once Dad was dealt with, I had planned to do so.

How I would make love to her over and over. How I'd worship her with my tongue. I would have made her scream with pleasure until her throat went hoarse. Even now, the thought makes my cock want to stand up, but alas, I don't think I have enough blood in my body for a proper erection.

The thought gets a grim chuckle out of me before I black out again.

41

JUNE

At the end of the day, I get a text from Callie for a dinner date tonight. I'd wanted to do Chinese delivery with Anderson, so I try to put her off. I haven't seen her in what feels like a million years, but it's my first day with Andre—sue me for wanting to celebrate with my boyfriend.

But she's persistent. "I need to see your face."

Crap. That can't be good, right? So, I relent and agree to meet her at a bar near my place. Not Kelsey's. I'd love to throw the business his way, but I already feel guilty for not working there right now. I do not need his wounded puppy eyes on me while I'm trying to pay attention to Callie.

When I walk in, she waves at me from a booth on the side. The place is the typical Boston establishment—booths along the walls, dark wood everywhere, a little too crowded for comfort—but it's nice enough. I make my way to her, plopping across from her in the booth. After we order beers, I ask, "What's wrong?"

She frowns in that uniquely Callie way. A graceful dent forms between her blond brows. That's it. Not that she's been Botox-ed to blankness. For her, it's natural to have a lineless face. Callie Brown was born without imperfections. I'd hate her for it if she weren't so damned sweet.

"It's Daniel. I think he might propose." Happy words said with a bad tone do not make my mood any better.

"And that is bad because?"

"Because I don't know what to tell him." She worries her bottom lip.

"Callie, ever since you two started dating, all you've talked about is marrying him. What's changed?"

"That's just it. June, nothing has changed."

I frown at her, significantly less graceful than she frowned at me earlier. "And that's a bad thing?"

She fidgets with her cardigan. "Think about it. Nothing has changed between me and him. Things just keep getting better. He's a divorced man. I'm pretty sure his first wife thought the same thing."

Ah. "You're waiting for the other shoe to drop."

Nervously, she nods. "I can't be naive in this. I have to go into it with my eyes open. If he's going to leave me—"

"Callie, that man thinks you hung the moon."

"But I didn't." Her eyes darken.

I shake my head. "What are you getting at?"

She licks her lips, then clenches her jaw. Her hand wraps tightly around her drink. "Daniel thinks of me in a certain way. He thinks I'm perfect."

"So? Isn't that a good thing to have in a husband?"

"I'm the other shoe that will drop."

None of this makes any sense. "You're going to have to explain this to me using very small words because I am completely lost."

"He thinks that I'm perfect, June. He's going to figure out that I am not. And then he's going to leave me."

I smile, rolling my eyes. "Okay, he doesn't actually think that you're perfect, honey. That's just a figure of speech people use."

She reaches into her purse and pulls out a note, sliding it across the table. "Oh yeah? Read that."

I open it up, and inside is a hand-scrawled note reading, "I didn't have it in my heart to wake you. But I feel compelled to tell you this. I find you beautiful, Callie. It's such a fiery, fierce beauty, like a white-hot star. You could burn me with your beauty, and I would thank you for the scar. You are my perfect angel. Never forget." A mix of emotions hit all at once.

"He really wrote you this?"

She nods nervously. "I woke up to it this morning."

"Okay, but like, he knows you're not perfect. I mean, you wake up with morning breath like the rest of us."

Her pouty lips smooth into a thin line. "Not with him, I don't."

"What does that even mean?"

Callie sighs and gazes out the window. "When I sleep over at Daniel's, I get up an hour before he does. I take a shower. Brush my teeth. Put on a full face of makeup. Then I crawl back into the sheets and pretend I was there all night long. He thinks that I wake up looking like this."

My mouth drops at first. Then I snort a laugh. "You've got to be fucking kidding me."

"I wish I were."

"Oh my God, Callie, show him who you really are. I bet you don't even burp in front of him."

She gasps. "Hell no. Of course not."

"Fuck. Are you joking?"

"How could I possibly expect him to marry a woman who burps? He's perfect."

I can't help it. I just start laughing.

"This isn't funny!"

Once I catch my breath, I point out, "You're upset because he thinks you're perfect, right? Well, you think that *he's* perfect. Any chance that he's doing the same kind of thing that you're doing?"

"Daniel is not as insecure as I am."

But I smirk and fight a laugh. "I bet he thinks the same of you."

Finally, something in her cracks. "Do you really think so? You think he's hiding his flaws from me?"

"He's human. He has flaws. If you have not seen them, then yes, he's hiding them. Have you ever heard him burp?"

"Well, no."

The snickering comes out whether or not I want it to. "Then I am pretty sure he's pulling the same con that you are. You two need to sit down and have a real talk. Especially before you go getting engaged."

She takes a deep breath and lets it out very slowly. "You might be right."

"Of course I am. Maybe do it while you drink some soda together. That way, you can get the burping thing out of the way first."

She rolls her eyes at me. "How are you and Anderson doing? When you texted me, the two of you had gotten back together. I was happy for you, but I really haven't heard back from you much. He's keeping you too busy, huh? All that make-up sex?"

I smile at the thought and realize I haven't heard from him pretty much all day. As I speak, I shoot him a text to check-in. "We're doing as well as we can."

"And what does that mean?"

I lift a shoulder, unwilling to commit to that portion of the conversation. No matter how much she already knows, I can't tell her about everything. Doing that would put her in danger. She doesn't know about Neil, and I plan to keep it that way. "We're still figuring things out. But it's external things. Anderson and me as a couple? We are really good."

"I am so glad to hear that. I have never seen you as happy as you are with him."

Nodding, I sigh. "That's because I've never been as happy as I am with him. Didn't know that things could be this good."

She gets a funny look in her eyes. "And do you think there's the possibility that you might be going down the aisle, too?"

The question flutters through me. Between my job and his father, getting married feels like something that could be a wonderful thing or a huge, crushing mistake. "Oh, let's not go thinking about things like that right now. I am focused on the present. The future will have to take care of itself."

Odd that he hasn't texted back already. Anderson is usually one of those fast texters.

"Well, whatever it is, I need a girls' night. Do you think we can catch a movie after this?"

As much as I would love to go home and curl up next to Anderson, I haven't seen Callie in a really long time. It gets too easy to neglect my friendships when I'm with a guy. Even one as wonderful as Anderson.

"That sounds great. Let's do it."

She beams at me, and I understand why Daniel thinks that she's perfect. Even if she weren't pulling off some con on him, I could still understand it.

After dinner, we hit up a romcom. Since I've been the one neglecting her, I let her have the choice of the movie. And even though I am trying to focus on the present, I checked my phone a few times when we were in the movie. Still no response from Anderson.

His radio silence has made me a little nervous.

"What did you think of the movie?" she asks as we walk out.

"It was okay, I guess."

She grins at me, giving me that patient smile of hers. "Go ahead. What plot holes were eating at you?"

I laugh because she knows me way too well. "Okay, please tell me how it was that a girl who grew up in the US South has a West Coast accent. And when the little boy went missing, and they had to chase him down, why didn't they call the cops? Also, if the vacuum of space can rip off the door, then how is it that the guy could hang on to the ladder like that and resist the vacuum of space?"

"Are you done yet?"

"For now."

Callie drops me off at my building, and I go up to my apartment. When I don't find Anderson there, I check my phone again. Still nothing. Worry roils in my gut. Given his work with Moss, I can't stop thinking about what could be going wrong.

I undress and shower, then check my phone again. Still nothing. If I had Mosses number, I would reach out to him. But I don't. His work is violent, I know that much. What if ... what if ...

An angry thought sits in my stomach like a hot rock and a life raft together. What if his father has found a way to keep us apart? I'd rather that be the case than the alternative because the alternative is too painful to think about. But I can't stop myself from thinking about it.

What if something went wrong on one of his jobs with Moss?

-

42

ANDERSON

A beeping stirs me. I don't recognize it. Why is it so fucking bright in here? The light burns through my closed eyelids. There is no possible way I ended up in heaven. Maybe I'm surrounded by the fires of hell. That feels appropriate.

But when I open my eyes, I find it's neither.

To my left, there is a big window. Someone left the blind up, and it's morning. Scanning the room, I find it's pretty nice. A sofa sits below the window. Across from me is a pair of chairs. Everything is in soft blues and grays. A sniffle catches my ear.

"Anderson, honey? Can you hear me?" It's a woman's voice off to my right.

I glance over and find my mother. Her sweater set is askew. She has a few hairs out of place. I don't think

I've ever seen her this disheveled. When I open my mouth, it feels crusty. "Mom?"

"Oh, my baby." She weeps, embroidered handkerchief in hand to wipe her eyes. She clutches onto my right forearm like she's fighting the urge to jump into the bed next to me. "What can I do? How are you feeling? Can I get you anything? Ice chips? Water?"

I nod for water, and she holds up the cup for me. It has one of those bendy straws, so I don't have to stretch my neck. I reach for the cup. "I can do it my—'

But in the middle of the reach, I feel it. The wince hits me the same time as the pain does.

Mom chides, "Let me do this."

I give up and let her hold the water cup for me. I've never tasted water that good. She sets the cup back down on the table next to me. It's then that I see her eyes catch the light. They're so red. "It's a good thing we're in a hospital."

She gives me a quizzical look.

"Those bags under your eyes need medical attention."

She snorts a laugh, then taps my arm with her hand. Her version of a swat. "You watch that smart mouth of yours. It gets you into trouble."

"What hospital are we in?"

That earns a nervous look from her. "A private one."

"Is that why I don't hear anything in the halls?"

Her lips purse as she nods. "It's state-of-the-art. You have nothing to worry about."

But I do. I worry about June. How can she find me in a private hospital? I don't ask Mom this. As far as I know, she doesn't know that Dad forbid me from being with June. That would require a lot more explaining than I think he's willing to do. It's better to keep Mom out of our business.

That makes me assume that this hospital must be legitimate. Dad wouldn't take Mom to any place where she might be in danger. Knowing this, I'm sure he's around somewhere. This moment of peace won't last forever.

Dad is coming.

"Anderson, how are you feeling? Do you need more pain medication?"

I'm tempted. But I shake my head no. Until I wonder about something. She is the one person who I know will not lie to me about this. "Am I actually gonna make it, Mom?"

"Of course you are. What a thing to ask."

At that, I tried to take a full breath. But it hurts like a son of a bitch. "You know, I wouldn't mind one of those painkillers you were talking about."

She smiles, then presses a button. It only takes seconds, but I feel it when it hits. It's like all of my muscles relax at once. Then she passes me the button. "This won't be activated for another five minutes. That way, you can't overdo it."

I nod, grateful for the button in my hand. "Thanks for that."

"Thank you for breathing."

"Well, I am fond of it."

"Don't act like this was nothing, Anderson." Her voice wavers as she speaks. "You nearly died."

"I —"

But the door opens, and it's Dad. I wish I could say I was surprised he was the one to interrupt me. But I am surprised when I see his face. He actually looks worried until he looks at me. Then, relief washes over him. It makes me uncomfortable to see that he cares. As if I weren't in this position because of him.

"Nice of you to wake up, son. I see you found your morphine drip. Can't say I'm surprised."

What he doesn't say out loud is he thinks morphine is for the weak. He won't insult me in front of Mom.

But I hear the words all the same.

"Nice of you to come visit me."

"Well, it is expected when one's son almost dies." He looks at mom. "Dear, why don't you go get a sandwich and a cup of coffee? I'm sure you could use both."

"I will if you promise not to leave his side."

He smiles warmly at her. She is the only person on earth who gets that smile. "Of course, my love."

Mom squeezes my hand one more time before she leaves us.

When the door closes, he begins. I expect nothing but insults and cruelty. That expectation has never let me down before. "How are you feeling, Anderson?"

I hate it when he swerves from our usual script. It's confusing, particularly when he pretends to care, and it doesn't help that I'm doped up right now. "Like I was shot in the gut. What do you think? Where are we really?"

"In a private hospital that I use to conduct business. The doctors here are skilled at both medicine and discretion."

Reading between the lines, I understand. It's a hospital for mobsters.

He licks his lips. It's almost as if he's stalling. But Elliott West does not stall. His tactic makes me nervous. "If—"

"Dad, am I going to live?"

"What would make you ask? You're in a hospital. Of course, you're going to live."

I snort a laugh, and it hurts. "People die in hospitals every day."

"No one dies here. That's why you're here."

I don't know what to make of that. "You're saying we're in the Disney World of hospitals?"

A glimmer of a smile hits him. That's all I ever get out of the old man. "Something of that nature, yes."

"Lucky me."

He sits in the same chair as Mom. "Moss told me what happened."

By his tone, I can't tell if I'm in more trouble with him or less trouble with him for what I did. "Yeah, I got shot. It happens when you force your son out on—"

"You got shot for *the help*."

Ah. I'm in *more* trouble with him for what I did. "I see there's no commendation for my bravery coming, huh?"

Barely checked rage simmers behind his eyes. "You had no right to take such a foolish risk! You are my heir! What would happen to the company if you died?"

I smirk at him. "There's always Cole."

"If you were not already laid up, I would slap the shit out of you for that."

No flowery language? No prissiness. Just a threat. That's a lot of fire coming out of the old man. I might have actually gotten to him. "And if I hadn't done what I did, Moss would be dead."

"Moss is a good man. I like him. But he is not my son."

"Well then, think about it this way. If Moss had gotten shot, then who would have gotten us out of there? Edgar Jones was out for blood. He would have killed us both."

Dad shakes his head. "You were not thinking of that when you jumped in front of a bullet. You were thinking of Moss as a friend, and you are just the type of sap to jump in front of a bullet for a friend."

He's got me there. "I did what I did. It's done now."

"You don't seem to get it, Anderson. I need you to understand this. No more jumping in front of bullets for Moss. Not ever again. He is a good man, but he is the help. The help will not inherit my company. You will. I need you to stay alive to do that."

"You do understand that *the help* are people too, right?"

He scrubs his hand over his face. "There is us, and there is everyone else in the world. They can die in a fire for all I care."

This man knows how to piss me off faster than anybody else. I brace to sit up, but just doing that sends pain shooting through me again. "Fuck."

"If you keep up that nonsense, you will tear your stitches again. Sit still."

"You don't even get it, do you? I am in this hospital bed, tearing my stitches because of you. I got shot because of you. You forced me into the ride-alongs with Moss. You have put me in the line of fire more than once. You don't get to pretend that I did something wrong by trying to do the right thing."

He huffs out a breath. "You still don't understand that the right thing is to save yourself. I don't know how to make you understand that. With any luck, your recovery will do that for me. Every time you hurt, and you want to scream in pain, remember this. You made the decision to jump in front of that bullet. The help are not worth it."

43

JUNE

It's unlike Anderson to willingly shut me out, which leaves two options. Either his father is keeping him from contacting me. Or something went wrong with Moss. I am going to have to track him down somehow.

I'm in the middle of freaking out in my office when I get a text. My phone dances in my nervous fingers before I calm down enough to check the text, and I nearly drop it twice before I open it up. But the text is from Kelsey, not Anderson. I let my breath loose in disappointment and open it up.

"Geiger quit. I'm out of options, or I wouldn't bother you on your two-week tryout. But June, I need help tonight, or I might have to close. Can't do this whole show on my own."

He can't close tonight. There's hockey. That's money hand over fist for him. It's going to be packed wall to wall tonight, so he's right. He can't do this alone.

Fuck, fuck, fuck.

I fall into my desk chair to think. My gut tells me to track Anderson down, but realistically, how would I manage that? I know where he works and sleeps, but I don't know where he goes with Moss. That whole side of his life has been left purposefully blank to keep me safe. Anderson decided that long ago, and now, his decision is biting me in the ass.

And he's a grown man. He can take care of himself. If I expect him to trust me with Andre, I have to show that I trust him with Moss. Maybe they're doing something somewhere, and he's out of range for cell phones ... I try not to dive too deep into that thought. No good will come of it.

The point is, I have to let him do his thing. He's letting me, so I have to let him. And right now, my thing is helping out a friend.

I text Kelsey, "I'll be there by six."

"You are a goddess," comes back fast.

If only I were. If I were a goddess, my boyfriend wouldn't be missing.

I finish up at Andre's, then zip home to change for the bar. Today is going to be a very long day, and that means energy drinks, but as soon as I reach for one in my fridge, I remember Kelsey owes me, and I duck back out. He has Roaring Lion on tap, and I plan to make full use of it. It tastes like Red Bull, but better somehow, and it definitely keeps me up when I need it.

When I walk into the bar, Kelsey's glee is palpable. He hollers over the din, "My savior!"

I chuckle and pop behind the bar, diving right in.

It's as busy as I expected—hockey nights always are. We are slammed, and I end up in the weeds a couple of times before things calm down and I get a break. At that point, I race to the bathroom and check my phone.

Nothing from Anderson. It sits like a weight on my chest.

There is a text from Callie, though. "Call me!"

Shit. I dial her up. "Hey, what—"

"I burped. In front of Daniel."

I laugh. "And?"

"He didn't seem to notice."

"That's good. He—"

"Do you think he's going to break up with me?"

I smack my forehead. "How are you this pretty and this smart and this insecure, Callie?"

"Because I'm in love."

I let out a sigh. "Yeah, okay. That makes everyone dumb. Me included."

"What's wrong? You sound off."

"I haven't heard from Anderson since I saw him yesterday morning. It's not like him." Skipping the parts about his Moss work, I'm not sure I'm conveying the situation properly. But this is all I can say to her.

"Is he ghosting you?"

I laugh at the thought. "No way, he's … " But is he? It doesn't feel possible. Anderson is not that kind of guy. Especially not after everything we've been through.

Except that he is that kind of guy.

Before dating me, he's always been a shitty boyfriend to people. At least, according to the college grapevine. He was a well-known womanizer, and now that things have settled down, has he gotten bored? Or maybe I'm too much trouble for him. How many times has he had to save me? And with his father breathing down his neck about me …

How long before Anderson figures out I'm more trouble than I'm worth?

Each thought makes my body want to turn inside out. I can't be another notch on his bedpost, can I? Not when I haven't ever even seen his bedposts. That man has never brought me to his place. Every time we sleep together, it's at my apartment.

Holy crap. Does he live with someone? Is that why he's always kept us at my place? It's always felt circumstantial at the time, but now ... now I don't know what the fuck to think.

I'm not sure if the pieces of this mystery are falling together or if I'm falling apart. Anderson bid on me at an auction. He blamed his dad for freezing his accounts so he couldn't pay me. He rescued me from my kidnappers. Or did he? Sure, Andre puts the blame for that on Elliot, but that doesn't mean Anderson wasn't involved somehow. After all he's working with Moss doing ... he keeps me from knowing about his work with Moss. He says his dad forces him to do the work, but does he?

Or does Anderson have a whole secret life that I know nothing about?

I've heard about that crap on true crime podcasts all the time. Hell, it was practically a trope in the old days. The man who has a secret family across town.

But that doesn't track—his family was happy to meet me when they thought I was his fiancée.

So, maybe he simply has a secret girlfriend he lives with. Fuck me.

"June, are you there?"

That's a very good question. "Sorry, Cal, I'm covering a shift for Kelsey. I need to go. Glad you burped." Which is not how I ever thought I'd end a conversation, but tonight is a strange night.

When I leave the bathroom, I jump straight behind the bar again, diving into the only thing that helps to keep me distracted. Work. I'm eight drinks deep when Kelsey asks, "You good, Devlin?"

"Yeah, why?"

"Because you have another twenty minutes on your break."

Oh. Huh. "I'd rather stay busy if that's okay."

"I'm not complaining." We bang out the night, drink after drink until the place cools down. When it's quiet enough, he offers, "If you want to clock out, go for it. I've got this."

But I shake my head while I roll silver. I've got a nice stack of napkin-encased silverware going, and I'm hesitant to stop. "I'm good."

"I'm sorry about calling you in."

"Don't worry about it. Anytime I can be here for you, you know how to reach me."

He smiles. "And I don't want to take advantage of that. Considering I'm sure you have work in the morning, I thought you'd like to go home."

Home. If I'm going to find Anderson's secret girlfriend, I bet that's where she'll be this late at night. His apartment. My jaw tightens without thinking about it. "You know what? I think I will take you up on that. Home sounds like exactly where I want to be." I yank off my half apron.

"Thanks again for coming in. You saved my ass, Devlin."

"Happy to." I jet out of there and march into the frozen night, catching a cab. I give the address, and within ten minutes, I'm walking up to the door of his building.

It's one of those high-end high rises. The kind of place that I could never afford in my wildest dreams. I wish I could say I was surprised this is where Anderson West would stash a secret girlfriend, but I'm not.

I may also be getting ahead of myself.

Is he a cheater? I don't know. But he is—or was—a womanizer, and those guys' relationships tend to overlap. Unfortunately, I also feel like one of those crazy women who overreact the moment something goes wrong in their relationship.

It's been a day and a half, and I'm jumping to some pretty big conclusions. But the thing is—our relationship has never been normal. It certainly didn't start out that way, and we haven't had more than ten days go by without some kind of catastrophic drama, so it's hard to not think the worst is happening.

When I walk into the lobby, I'm surprised. There's no doorman. No visible security. That makes no sense for a building like this. But when I reach the elevators, I realize why. You need a keycard to activate the elevators.

Well, shit.

Just as I'm ready to give up, a pretty blond woman walks into the lobby. She gives me a curt smile as she slashes her keycard for the elevator. This could be her. She's pretty enough for Anderson. She asks, "Late night?"

"Yeah. So late that I left my keycard back at the bar. Can't go get it, either."

"They closed up?"

I shake my head, trying my best to look pitiful. "There's a guy back there who wouldn't leave me alone."

She tips her head in sympathy. "Oh, that sucks." The doors open. "Ride up with me. I won't tell if you don't."

"Oh my gosh, thank you." I follow her in. "I thought I'd be sleeping in the lobby all night."

"We can't have that." She presses the button for the third floor. Okay, she is not his secret girlfriend. "Which floor?"

"Five, please."

After she presses the button, the doors slide open for the third floor. "Have a nice night."

"You, too." It's not much longer before the doors open again for Anderson's floor. His apartment is 522. I know this because I memorized it when I saw his license. An old bartender habit. Best to know where your customers come from. Direct those with a better address to the expensive stuff and those with a normal address to the cheaper stuff. Both get you better tips.

A minute later, I find his apartment door. It feels like a big gray blank. I have no clue what or who sits on the other side of it. But I'm going to find out.

I ring the bell and wait. But no one comes. So, I switch to knocking. Still, no answer.

Either no one is home, or no one is going to answer the door. I text him one more time, "No more hiding, Anderson. Come out, come out, wherever you are."

But I get nothing in return.

-

44

ANDERSON

The hospital's breakfast is far better than any hospital breakfast I had expected. But given the location of my injury, I have to be careful. A bullet fragment nicked the exterior of my stomach, so I'm on liquids for a while. Thankfully, today's was a meaty-tasting broth and a strawberry-flavored collagen yogurt smoothie, both designed to aid in speedier healing. Whatever the reason for the food, I like it. They warn me I'll be on something like it when I go home tomorrow.

God, I miss my fucking apartment. Almost as much as I miss June.

I hate not being able to contact her, but Dad had the phone removed from my room, and my phone has been suspiciously absent since I woke up. No doubt Dad is keeping it from me to keep us apart. I am sure he knows we have been seeing each other. There's no way he doesn't know about that. And now, he has total control over my ability to contact her, so he's going to exert it.

I've already tried to ask the staff for a phone, but according to them, Elliot West has told them no phones for me so I can focus on recovery. One doctor actually cooed, "What a good dad," when she explained that detail.

I wanted to break something.

All of this means she has no clue where I am or what's happened. It must be driving her to the brink. If she vanished on me like this, I would lose my fucking mind.

When the door opens again, I'm expecting my parents or another hot nurse. They must hire for both skill and sexiness because each one of them looks like a fantasy made of tattoos, mayhem, and a pinup model.

My breath catches in my throat when I see Moss blocking most of the doorframe. He closes it softly behind himself before he joins me at my bedside. The rigid lines on his face go slack. He is relieved to see me.

Today is a day for his Boston-blended Italian accent to be thick, apparently. "It is good to see you, boss."

"Good to be seen." Especially after I assumed he was going to let me die.

He gives a wan smile. "How you feel?"

"Somewhat better, thanks. I didn't get a chance to ask—what with nearly dying and all that—how did things go after I went down?"

His shoulders stiffen. "Edgar Jones has been taken care of."

"Yeah, I saw the bullet hole in his forehead." With that memory comes my breakfast, trying to launch out of my mouth. But I squash it back down. Vomiting after being shot in the stomach is, evidently, discouraged, per the doctors. But even the antiemetic they gave to counter the morphine is no match for the mental image of an accountant with a fresh hole in his face. "What happened before that?"

"Ah. After he shot you, he was less of a man. He dropped the gun. I stepped over you, then did what I do all over him." He stretches his hands out, and the knuckles are bruised to shit. "I fear it was not enough, but we had limited time for vengeance. Had I more time, I would have made the bastard suffer. But with you bleeding out, I could not take it. I plugged him, then took you from the office building. After, I called your father and told him I was on the way here. The doctors here are—"

"Discreet?"

"Da. It is good hospital. They have patched me up many times."

I have no doubt about that. I smile up at him. "That's not why you come here, though, is it? It's all the hot nurses, right?"

"Now is no the time for jokes," he says solemnly. Whatever humor had been on his face falls away as he comes closer. Too close for my liking.

"What's going on, Moss?"

A glint of light draws my attention back down to his hands. He's holding a small knife as he looms over me.

I start to cringe back from him, but I couldn't. Not without hurting myself more. "Moss—"

Without another word, he holds out the knife and cuts his palm before squeezing that fist tight and letting the blood run between his fingers onto the floor. "I vow to you my loyalty, Anderson West."

I'm left blinking, utterly confused. "Yeah, I'm gonna need you to explain what the fuck you just did, Moss."

"My loyalty is no longer to your father. It is to you. I do your jobs. I follow your orders. You saved my life. I am indebted to you and you alone."

Oh, shit. How the fuck do I turn that down? "Uh, as much as I appreciate this, I don't know that I can accept it."

He frowns. "Of course, you can."

I rub my temple, trying to figure this out. "They have me on some really good drugs right now, so I may need your help in sorting this out."

"Whatever you need."

"Think about it this way—if you stop listening to my dad, what will happen to you? To your family? I know you're not Dad's only ... helper."

His lips pucker to the side as he thinks. "You are wise man. I see your point."

"Good." But maybe I can use this. "That said, there's no reason we can't do our own thing sometimes, right? Until Dad passes me the reins, he doesn't need to know what we're up to."

Moss nods. "I will keep your secrets from him. Always."

That is exactly what I needed to hear. "Don't keep too much from him, though. Tell him just enough to let him think he's still on top of everything."

"Da."

"And can I use your phone?"

"A burner or my phone?"

That makes me smile. He doesn't say, "*My* burner or my phone." He said, "*A* burner," because he has several on him even now.

"A burner, if you don't mind." I don't know if Dad monitors Mosses personal line, and there's no reason to drag him into this mess in case he does.

Moss pats down his coat a few times before he finds a burner for me. "This one has never been used."

"You keep ones that have been used? That seems risky."

"Exactly why to keep." He nods once. "They make good evidence to plant at crime scene. I mark each one I have used—who I call on it, the date, where from. Much easier to blackmail someone with the right information this way."

"Good god, man. What would happen if you used your powers for good?"

He huffs a laugh and passes me the burner. "Perhaps one day, we find out together."

"I'd like that." Now, the moment of truth. Can I trust him or not? "You know I'm still seeing June, right?"

"Of course."

"And that Dad doesn't want me to?"

He shrugs. "Elliot West has been disappointed before. He will live."

"And you won't tell him."

"If that is a secret you wish me to keep, it is kept."

"It is. Thank you."

He nods once. "Whatever you need, whenever you need it."

I guess that's that. It takes a second to remember her phone number—the combination of drugs and never dialing her up doesn't help matters. She doesn't answer, but I get her voicemail. "Baby, it's me. Call this number, please." I recite the number and hang up, hoping for a quick—

Her number pops up as a call. "Where have you—"

"Fuck, it's good to hear your voice," I blurt. Something deep inside releases. Something the drugs couldn't help with.

Moss turns around, pretending to be distracted by his own phone to give me privacy.

She barks, "What the fuck is going on, Anderson?"

"I will explain everything in person." Telling her I've been shot and I don't know exactly where I am will not set her mind at ease. "I'll be home tomorrow. Can you meet me there tomorrow? Say eleven?"

"Just tell me what is going on. Please."

When her voice breaks on that last word, so does my heart. But I can't tell her about any of this on the phone. That would be cruel. "I need you to trust me. It's better I tell you in person."

"Fine, I guess. But it better be good. I'm talking about a full explanation of something big. I have been freaking out since you went radio silent on me. And whose number is this?"

"No one's, and I promise —"

"No one? How pretty is No One?"

I laugh, which hurts, but I don't care. "It's a burner, June."

"Oh."

"You'll have all your answers tomorrow. I promise."

"I'll see you at eleven."

"I love you so much, baby. Whatever I can do to make this up to you, I will."

For a moment, her end is silent. "I love you, too."

We hang up, and I already feel better from hearing her voice. "Thank you, Moss."

"You are right not to tell her on phone."

"You can tell I feel guilty, huh?"

He smiles and nods. "You are good man. You feel guilty about everything."

Good? Doubt it. But there is no sense in arguing with Moss. When he knows something, he knows it. No matter the evidence to the contrary.

"And do you ever feel guilty about anything?"

He mulls over the question. "People like me, we are born without goodness, so we feel no guilt."

But I didn't believe that for a second. Not when he came into my room on a mission to alleviate his debt to me. He has goodness, and he has guilt. There is no mistaking that. Maybe it makes him feel like a tough guy to pretend otherwise, but I know better.

To be clear, I ask, "You know I don't think of you as indebted to me, right?"

"Like I say. You are good man."

CHAPTER FORTY-SIX–ANDERSON

"I BRING you healthy foods for recovery, eh?" Moss says as he unloads paper bags of groceries on my kitchen island. "We have steaks, tendon—"

"I'm sorry, what?"

"Steaks—

"The second thing."

"Tendon."

I grimace at that. "Why would you bring me tendon? Who eats tendon?"

He laughs heartily. "Millions of people around the world. Why you think Asians age better than Americans? It's the tendon, the tripe, the offal." He points to my stomach, his face going serious all of a sudden. "You want to rebuild tendons, you eat tendons. You want to rebuild stomach, you eat stomach—"

"You got me stomach?" I gulp.

"I got you tripe." He shrugs. "Which is stomach. Tripe will make all better." He pulls out the package of tripe and through the cling wrap, it looks like a very wrinkled white bag. "See? Not scary—"

"Not appetizing, either."

"Why is the red steak appetizing, but not the white tripe?" he asks while gesturing to each. "It's all the same animal."

"I'm not going to eat hooves, but they are on the same animal."

He frowns, thinking. "Very well. But you listen to Moss. I have recovered from many bullets, stabs, falls. I know how. I will teach you how to cook all of these things."

"Is it possible you can teach me later? June is coming soon, and—"

"You know your father will give trouble for this."

I sigh. "That's why I need you to call the home nurse off. I don't want a stranger in my home, especially one who will report back to Dad."

He rubs his chin. "I will do this. But if he does not get reports on you, he will come by himself, so consider letting the home nurse come tomorrow, or you will have him to answer to. Nothing I can do to stop him."

"Thanks. I appreciate it."

"Anything for you." He goes on about the food. "Now you see, tendon and tripe go with the marrow bones—

"You brought me bones?"

"And onions, celery, carrots, garlic, and parsley. For soup. Together, they make a wonderful broth, lots of good protein to help you heal."

I grin up at him. "You sound like a grandma."

He points at me. "Grandmas know everything. You listen to grandmas, you live a long, happy life. My grandma taught me the recipe when she found me with broken arm from a fight. She say I need to know how to heal to get strong and beat those boys up." He leans forward conspiratorially, even though we are alone in my place. "I had no heart to tell her it was girls who broke my arm."

I laugh. "Must have been some tough girls to break your arm."

"I was seven and alone. They were ten, and there were four of them. They shove me from tree, I break my arm." He shrugs. "Gravity did the work for them. But I ate my soup, I got strong, and I beat them up right back."

"You picked on girls?"

"Bullies," he clarifies. "Grandma did not like that, either. Said she did not make soup for me to hurt women. She gave me roses from her garden to go apologize with."

"And what happened then?"

He smiles slyly. "Well, not then, then we were too young. But ten years later, I married the one who pushed me."

I laugh so hard that I worry about my stitches. Worth it, though. "You married your childhood bully?"

"Da. Life has been interesting ever since."

I can't help it. His story pulls on my heartstrings and makes me think of June. Could I ever convince her to do the same? To overlook the boy I was and marry the man I am now? "What convinced you to marry her?"

"How could I not? She was all I could think of for so long. Then she blossomed into a great beauty right before my eyes ... " He sighs, like talking about his wife is the only thing he ever wants to do. I understand that feeling. "My wife grew up knowing only violence in her family. They were *connected*. It's why I never share this life with her. We have agreement. I tell her nothing, give her a good life with our daughters. She asks nothing, gives me the best life I could ever ask for."

The love in his eyes lodges a lump in my throat. I clear it away. "You two sound like a perfect match."

He nods. "We are. She is the love of my life."

"And she doesn't mind the strip clubs?"

That earns his devilish grin. "I always shower as soon as I come home. If I go there, if I don't go there, always shower. This way, she is not suspicious of when I shower off glitter."

"And your other women—"

"What other women?" He shakes his head like I've offended him. "I see the tits and ass at the club, yes, but I do not do more. Maybe a lap dance, but that is all. I like pretty women, true. But I do not stick my cock in them."

Crass but honest in his own way. I notice the milk sitting on the counter is wet from sitting too long and reach to put it away, but the moment I lift it, sharp pains stab at my middle, and I growl through the pain. Moss finishes stowing the remainder of the groceries. "Thanks."

"It takes time, Anderson. When your lady friend comes, do not think to fuck her—"

"Moss!"

"I am serious. You heard doctor say no strenuous activities for at least four weeks." He pauses. "Unless how you do is not strenuous—"

"It's strenuous enough that I'm not going to." My middle throbs with my pulse. "I doubt I could even get it up right now, fuck."

He nods knowingly, then pulls up his shirt, exposing a rounded scar near his liver. That's not the only thing I notice. Moss has knife wounds and burns along his abdomen, as well. The guy's body has seen some shit. And a gym. For a man who looks like a retired football player with his clothes on, the dude has a spare tire that has its own muscles. So odd.

He explains, "It took me five weeks when I got shot in the liver. And that first time was ... let's just say, the word *gently* became my new favorite word for long while."

I chuckle at that, trying to stop from laughing harder. "Understood."

"I should go," he says, checking the time. "June comes soon, and I do not wish to dampen her enthusiasm for seeing you. I will call off home nurse and tell your father you wish for a day of quiet."

"Thank you for that. And everything else."

"Of course, Anderson. Anything you need." He claps my shoulder on the way out of my apartment, and I have a few minutes to myself before June is supposed to arrive.

God, I have missed my place. It's dark and cool and feels almost like home. But I know what it's missing. What it's always been missing. Her. Even though she has never been here, I know she is the piece that will make my home complete. Funny to think I know I won't feel alright until I see her face.

But it's always that way when we've been apart. She could walk out of the room and come right back, and she's gone for too long as far as I'm concerned.

Obsessive? Maybe. But it's my obsession, and no one will stand in the way of it. Not even my father.

I meant what I told her. He can go fuck himself.

Getting shot has been a revelation, which, honestly, I'm almost sad I can't thank Jonesy for it. My priorities have shifted completely. I'm young. I can remake my life, and I want to remake it around her. If she'll have me.

My heart pounds when I think of starting a proper life with June. It's all I've ever really wanted, and it took me a shamefully long time to grasp that fact. Now, I want to make that a reality. But I can't push. She's about to see me at my lowest. It feels like a test for the future. Can she handle me at my weakest? Some people can't do that kind of thing. No judgment—it's just that some people are not caretakers.

But I need that now.

June has never spoken much about her family, so I don't know if she has much of a nurturing instinct in her. Come to think of it, I don't know a lot about her background. Every time it gets brought up, she obfuscates.

Well, if she sticks around, I have weeks of talking-only dates ahead of me. Plenty of time to dive into it, I suppose.

Mostly, I just need to see her face. The anticipation is an itch under my skin that can't be scratched. A craving that never ends until I taste her lips. Knowing she is on her way here, I can't unwind, I can't think straight. There's a weight in my chest that won't lift until—"

Someone knocks at my door. I grin, then wince as I hobble my way to it.

45

JUNE

"Oh my god, you look like shit!" bursts out of my mouth.

He laughs, then clutches his middle. "Don't make me laugh. I'll tear my stitches. Again."

I rush into his apartment, taking in none of it. "Stitches? What the hell is going on?"

He gingerly shuts the front door, and it looks like that takes all his energy. He is shuffling. Anderson West does not shuffle. He steps commandingly, he saunters, he strides with grace, but my man does not shuffle. Slowly, he makes his way to his bed, and I'm glued to his side. He is the only thing in my vision at the moment. His face is rough with several days of growth. His skin is sickeningly pale. He even reaches out for my arm when he's getting into bed. I help him get into it, but my mind is racing.

For fuck's sake, what the hell happened?

Once he's under the covers, Anderson sighs carefully, still wincing as he does it. "I need you to not freak out or yell. Can't take that right now. Promise?"

"Yeah, whatever you need."

"I got shot."

"You what!" Okay. I yelled that.

He grimaces at the volume. "You promised—"

"You were shot? Like, with a gun, that kind of shot?" Me with the genius questions.

"Yeah." He swallows. "Can you pass me the water?"

It's only then I notice the glass of water on his nightstand. It could have been a snake, ready to bite me, and I wouldn't have noticed it, not after seeing him hurting. I pass it over. "I need explanations. Now. Why are you home? Why aren't you in a hospital? How bad is it? And who the fuck shot you?"

He sips his water, then hands it back, so I set it down. "I am home because healing does not happen in hospitals. I don't care what anyone says. You cannot get a good night's sleep with nurses coming by for vitals every two hours. That's why I'm not in the hospital."

"Okay, and the rest?"

"Well, I got shot in the stomach, so it's not fucking great, I can tell you that."

"Don't do that with me, Anderson. Don't make light of this." I am trembling right now. Feels like I'm going to lose my mind.

"Sorry. I've had a little time to get used to this. It's new to you. I'll try to keep that in mind." He shrugs a little, and even that earns a pain face. "A fragment of the bullet skimmed my stomach and kinda lodged in the middle of a few spots, but the stomach was the worst injury. I'm on liquids for now, so my six-pack might become one of those coveted ten-packs if I'm lucky—"

"No jokes! This is fucking serious!" I am in tears. I can't help it.

He takes my hand in his and brushes a kiss on my knuckles. "I'm sorry. It's just how I deal with this. I'll do better."

The words sit in my throat until I let them out. "So … you're gonna live?"

"I'm going to live. As long as I'm careful of my stitches and let myself heal, and I don't do much more than healing for the next few weeks, I will live."

I can finally breathe. "Who was it?"

"A dead guy. He —"

"A name. I deserve the fucking name of the man who shot my boyfriend."

He smiles faintly. "I am trusting you with a secret that could bite us both in the ass if you had to testify. You still want to know?"

I bite out, "Yes."

"Edgar Jones. A CPA who bit off way more than he could chew. He was desperate, and he snapped. He was going to shoot Moss, and on instinct, I jumped in the way. Moss beat him near to death, then shot him in the head."

I take his face in both hands and kiss him hard. "You stupid, stupid man." Then, I kiss him again. I can feel him smile against my lips.

"I love you, too."

"I can't believe you did that."

He sighs. "Almost everyone seems to be mad at me for it. Everyone except Moss, who has sworn loyalty to me over my father, which we are also keeping under wraps for now. As far as Dad knows, Mosses loyalty hasn't changed. I've got him as a double agent to be used as I see fit."

I try to think of how to leverage that, but right now, I'm too damn grateful that he's alive. My gratitude takes all the energy away from my scheming, and I don't care because Anderson is breathing, he didn't ghost me, and he's not cheating on me.

He was only shot.

Waves of sick terror flush through me. "I can't believe you were fucking shot, baby."

"It's kind of the same for me, to be honest. I mean, you see it on TV and in movies, and you think, hey, that doesn't seem so bad. Unless it's a headshot, of course. But then it happens, and fuck me, it *is* that bad. Do me a favor and never, ever get shot, okay?"

I giggle back tears, and snot. "I'll do my best."

He sighs and, oh so carefully, leans back. His pillows are arranged behind him to keep him mostly upright, though. "I really wanted to stay up longer when you got here, but I think my pain meds are going to stop me from doing that."

"Do we need to change your bandages? Do you need—"

"I'm fine," he says gently. There is such softness in his eyes that it makes my heart bleed. "You don't have to stay."

"You are out of your damn mind if you think I am letting you handle this on your own! You were shot! Anderson, I don't give a shit what your dad thinks about me, I am staying—"

"Please, no more yelling."

My hand covers my mouth. "Sorry. Didn't realize I was."

"I meant it, though. June. You have your new job. I don't want you to get in trouble for me about this."

"You are all that matters to me, Anderson. I am here until you don't need me anymore."

"I'll always need you." He yawns hard and tries to shake it off. "But I think I need a nap, too."

"Once you fall asleep, I'm going to go back to my place and get a few things so I can work from home and stay here. Clothes, toothbrush, that kind of thing. Do we need groceries?"

"Check the fridge. Moss stocked it. Says he'll make me soup."

The thought of the big bad gangster making my boyfriend soup is painfully adorable. The fact he needs to because my boyfriend was dumb enough to take a bullet for him … ? Far less adorable. God, I don't want to think about any of it. I could have lost him. Fuck.

"Soup is a good healing food. I'm sure gangster soup is even more healing."

He laughs, then holds his side. "No more funny stuff. Oh, and no other *funny stuff* for at least four weeks. Sorry, baby. If I knew that before, I wouldn't have been so eager to take the bullet."

I smile and watch as he closes his eyes. "I'll get going, so I can get back sooner—"

But he grabs my hand. "Please stay. Just a couple minutes until I fall asleep."

"Of course, baby."

So, I stay until I'm certain he's out, and then I take his keys from the bowl by the door and fly out of the place. All those months of running have paid off because I am not even winded by the time I get to my apartment. I gather everything I think I'll need while I call for a ride share—I'm not carrying all of this on foot. Once that's done, I scramble downstairs and jet back to his place. When I'm inside, I check that he's breathing before I unpack.

He is breathing. Now, it's my turn to do the same.

I have never lived with a man before, so moving in— even temporarily—feels strange. His place screams masculine. Everything is in charcoals and blues, or when applicable, big pieces of wood. It's dark and, in a strange way, kind of soothing. His cologne is faint in the air.

The total opposite of my grandma chic apartment, but I'm not mad at it.

I shoot Andre an email, explaining I'll need a few personal days, and within seconds, I get one saying that is not a problem. Then I take a trip through the kitchen. Sure enough, there are soup supplies in the kitchen, along with cases of protein shakes and protein bars—those will have to wait for a while. Protein powder, too. No wonder Anderson eats fries every chance he gets. He eats nothing like that at home.

I order grocery delivery for anything that's missing and to suit my tastes. No sense in me being on a liquid diet, too. I'll just eat my chewing food when Anderson is asleep so he doesn't feel like he's missing out. I'm sure he'd think that was ridiculous, but I don't care. He was shot. I can be a little ridiculous while I take care of him.

46

JUNE

A few days of taking care of Anderson, and I know some things for certain. My boyfriend is trying to hide his pain from me, so I don't worry, and he's so hilariously bad at it. He thinks I'm not watching him out of the corner of my eye, but I see every wince and every cringe. I see it every time he reaches for the remote. Every time he coughs. All of it.

But I also know Anderson is a trooper. He listens when the home nurse comes by, and he does the exercises she prescribes. He's cooperating about his liquid diet, even though he's lost a few pounds. The home nurse says he's making excellent progress, and I couldn't be prouder of him.

In other news, Edgar Jones is so fucking lucky that he's already dead. When Anderson sleeps, I'm either working, working out, or fantasizing about how I would have destroyed him if he weren't already dead. I have never torn a man apart limb from limb, but I could learn how. I'm sure Moss would show me if I asked.

I am so glad that scary big guy is on our side.

Moss has come by a couple of times and made good on his soup threat, which was, in fact, delicious. But I try to save most of it for Anderson since he's the one who is healing. I'm still not comfortable around Moss — I can't see him without thinking of Neil, but it's getting better. Especially because I know he's the one who saved Anderson. He thinks he owes Anderson, but the truth is, we owe him so much.

Speaking of owing, Andre has been great about me taking time away, but I do check in on work and get done what I can. I don't want to live off his good graces for too long. Partially because I'm just not that kind of employee but also because I don't want him to think that I owe him in any way that is not professional. I still cannot pin that guy down when it comes to his intentions with me.

In fact, since last night was rough, I've been up checking emails since around four this morning, and I got a lot done already. It hits me that I haven't made coffee yet. I had gone from playing nursemaid in the middle of the night straight to emails without a thought in between. I've gotten so used to things that this has become my routine.

Strange how fast you can adjust to traumatic situations.

When someone knocks on the door, I check the time. It's not time for the home nurse, and Moss always texts before he shows up, so I'm cautious. If it's Elliot West, this could end up as a fight, and I do not want to wake Anderson for the world right now. He had such a hard time sleeping last night. Hell, I'm still in my robe and slippers since I wasn't expecting company.

I check the doorbell cam. An older woman I recognize—oh shit. His mom. Throwing open the door, I smile, completely at a loss for what to say.

She stands there, the perfect picture of Massachusetts poise. Prim and proper and overly educated to wind up the wife of a lunatic gangster media tycoon. Her hair sits with every strand in its place in a style that was popular twenty years ago but still somehow suits her. Elegant makeup to go with her fashionable attire. Nothing too showy, yet easy to notice how effortless it looks. Everything about her screams *money*, but in a classy way.

"Kitty, come in, come in," I say, opening the door wide. "Is everything alright?" I ask, closing it.

She gives me a wan smile. "I believe that is my question for you, June."

"He's doing better. The home nurse says he's improving every day."

At that, her shoulders relax. I hadn't noticed just how stiff they were before. "That is good to hear, thank you."

I nod, wondering just how much trouble we are in now that she knows I'm here. With Elliot's stupid rule about us being together, I'm sure she will rat us out. If the home nurse hasn't yet. I almost want to ask about it, but I'm not that brave before coffee.

Kitty steps close, taking my hands in hers. "Thank you for being here for him, June. It means a lot to me that you're taking care of my boy."

Oh. Well. Wasn't expecting that. "Of course. Can I get you some coffee? I'd wake him up for you, but he slept terribly last night—"

"Actually, I was hoping to speak with you before him, if that's alright. So, coffee sounds lovely."

An impromptu conversation with the woman who, under any other circumstances, probably hates me just as much as Elliot does? That's exactly how I like to start my day. Woo hoo.

But I pad to the overpriced and confusing coffeemaker in Anderson's kitchen anyway. It's plumbed into his waterline, so no trips back and forth to the sink. I teased him the other day about how it must save him so much time and effort, and he declared that it made better coffee that way.

Somehow.

For all his tough-guy talk, Anderson can be a big baby when it comes to how he likes to spend his money. And I kinda love that about him. He puts out such an un-fuck-with-able air about himself that I love needling him about the little things. In fact, we've fallen into a bit of a rhythm in our days living together, and I love that, too.

Kitty takes a seat on one of the barstools at the island. "You know, his place has always needed a woman's touch."

"It's a little sterile in here—"

She lets out a huff, staring at the blank walls. "That is putting it nicely." Then she turns to me. "But I am not here for that. I do not know how much you know of Anderson's injury. Suffice to say, it was obtained in the line of duty while working for his father. I do not approve of these things."

I blink at her for a breath. "Oh."

"You were unaware—"

"No, I mean, I didn't know you didn't approve. I know a little about his side work with Moss."

Kitty nods. "Yes, well, I do not. I knew Elliot was going to put him under Mosses guidance, but I certainly did not know he would make him dive head-first into madness. Anderson has a great deal to learn about the business—this I understand. But Elliot was reckless in his assignments." There is an edge to this woman's voice about the topic, and it makes me like her a lot.

"Reckless is a polite way—"

"He fucked up."

I giggle at her swearing. It's like hearing the Pope swear.

Her lips curl up at the sides a little. "Didn't think I knew the word?"

I laugh. "No, I just never expected to hear it out of you."

She shrugs and sighs, still smiling just a bit. "Yes, well, Elliot did. And now, my son must pay for it, which is not something I am overly fond of."

The coffee is ready, so I pour our mugs and set out the cream and sugar. I was shocked to find it in Anderson's place, considering how body-conscious he is. "What happens now?"

"I want it to stop. His side work, I mean. The way I see it, this goes one of three ways. One, he continues in his side work and ends up dead. Two, he stops his side work and ends up CEO. Or three, something catches up to him, and he ends up dead or imprisoned, either by a client he has dealt with or during an altercation with the law." She glances up at me. "I am terrified that I have a one in three chance of outliving my son."

I can see it in her eyes. There is no bullshit there. Motherly fear crinkles her eyes at the corners. This time, I'm the one who reaches out for hands. "We won't let that happen, Kitty."

"That's right. We won't. I need your help on this, June. I want him out. May I count on you?"

"When it comes to keeping Anderson alive, I would be insulted if you didn't already count me in."

She smiles, and we drink in silence for one brief, peaceful moment. "This isn't going to be easy."

"Few things worth doing are easy."

"I knew I liked you."

"Same here."

47

ANDERSON

I don't know what time it is, but the sun is up. It wasn't the last time I was awake. June lets me sleep when I can, swearing I can get back on a normal schedule when I'm better. I'm not sure if that's the best idea, but I am too weak to argue.

Someone is humming in my bedroom. June is not a hummer.

My eyes flip open, and I have to squint because it's so bright in here. "Mom?"

She scurries to my side from the window. "Anderson. How are you feeling?"

"I'd be better if the shade was drawn."

She rolls her eyes, then goes back and closes it. That's when I notice we are alone in my room. Then she sits in the chair at my bedside. She must have brought it in with her.

How hard was I sleeping?

"I thought a little light would do you some good."

"A little, maybe. Not the whole damn sun."

"Language."

I smirk and fight a laugh. "I got shot, Mom. I'm allowed to curse."

She sighs, smiling a little as she pulls my blankets up to tuck me in. "How is your wound?"

"The home nurse—"

"I want to hear it from you." Her voice is unusually firm.

Her worry hits something deep inside of me, and I remember I'm still her first child. That's who she is tucking in right now. "It's doing better, Mom. Thanks for asking."

Only then do I see the worry lines on her face. I got shot, and now her plastic surgeon is going to buy a new boat. The circle of life. "I do not like your side work, Anderson."

I shrug and that doesn't hurt as much as it had been. "Me, either."

"Then why—"

"Dad. It's all him. He's the one who decided I have to do this, even though it's dangerous."

"He expects you to be learning. Not taking bullets for the help."

My head digs back into the pillow. "Not you, too."

"Your father, flawed though he is, is right about this, Anderson. You are the valuable person in any equation you are in, and you must act accordingly."

I know she is saying this because she loves me, and I scared her. I get that. So, I am trying to be understanding about it. "Mom, it was you who taught me everyone is valuable—"

"Not like this," she says sharply. "In general, yes, but in this? No. Not at all. We need you alive and well to run West Media. We need you breathing, Anderson. Why is that so hard for you to understand?"

"I am not special—"

"Don't you ever say that again. You are. I won't hear talk to the contrary."

I let out as big of a breath as I've been able to take lately. There is no winning this with her, and I know it. "I know you're upset, but I need you to understand my side of this. I acted on instinct—"

"An instinct to get yourself killed? Are you suicidal, Anderson? Because we will get you the best therapist money can buy, and you know that."

"No, it was an instinct to protect the man at my side."

She sits back to ponder. "How may I divest you of that instinct?"

"I'm not sure you can. You see, my mother raised me to believe everyone has value—"

"Don't get cute with me, Anderson. I'll not have it. Not now. Not when we are talking about life and death."

"Geez, you get shot, and everyone loses their sense of—"

She silences me with a look. "June is here."

A conversation swerve as hard as any Dad takes. Didn't see it coming. "What of it?"

"You are not supposed to be seeing her."

"And?"

Her eyes go sly. "Your father will not like it."

"My father can suck—"

"Anderson!"

"A lemon."

Her lips go tight with frustration while she fights a smile. "He only wants what's best for you."

"He wants what is best for the company, and that, according to Dad, is some mealy-mouthed pushover who looks good in pictures and isn't too bright. Someone who doesn't challenge me or him because someone who bores me isn't going to dig into what we actually do. He wants me to be miserable because he is afraid, and I won't have that. Not now, not ever."

Again, Mom sits back to think about what I said. She takes her time about it, and the prolonged silence makes me uneasy. Quietly, she asks, "So then. I'm a mealy-mouthed pushover who isn't too bright, eh?"

"Wait, what?"

"It makes sense that is what you think of me. That your father found his ideal woman in me, a woman who won't ask too many questions, a woman who looks good in pictures, all of it—"

"That is not what I said, Mom. You're making this about you, and it's not."

"Isn't it?" There is so much hurt in her voice that I'm sick from it.

"No. I have never thought of you like that. You're quiet, but I've seen you give him a hell of a time or ten."

She cuts a fragile smile at that. "Every man needs to be reminded of his mortality now and then."

"Mom, I promise I was not talking about you at all. Dad is determined that June isn't the right woman for me for all of those reasons and more. When it comes to me, he is only thinking about West Media. Not my safety, not my happiness, none of it. He doesn't give a shit about that if it gets in the way of the company, and I need that to change because I am never giving her up."

"You love her deeply, don't you, son?"

"More than I ever knew I could."

She sighs. "This would be easier if you did not, I suppose. Far simpler to pry a man from an inappropriate woman when he doesn't love her."

"Did you just call June inappropriate?"

She smirks. "By your father's standards, yes. She is."

She had me there. "Like I said, he can get over it. She is the one who is always there for me. Even now, when I've been miserable to deal with, she has been at my side this whole time. When the home nurse comes, she's there, taking notes so we keep my meds straight. She set a physical therapy reminder on my phone, so I do my exercises. She makes my food, helps me shower … Mom, she has been amazing. I am so damn lucky to have a woman like her. So, yeah. When it comes to June, Dad can go suck a lemon. I cannot find it in me to care about Dad's standards because she surpasses all of mine."

"I agree that she has been noble about these things. Truly, she has been. If things were different, then I could see how she would be perfect for you. But do you think she has it in her to be a CEO's wife? Or, god willing, a Senator's wife? Do you think she can stand in the background and smile until her face hurts and wear conservative clothes, all the while making chit-chat with the right people and making do while you're at work eighty hours a week? Or, perhaps the better question is, do you wish to inflict that upon her? Do you want her to face an empty bed every night? To tuck your children in by herself? And once your children move out but you're still obsessed with work, do you want her to rattle around that hollow home all by herself, day-drinking until she's a numb shell of the woman she used to be?"

I stare up at her, feeling like I just took a peek behind a curtain I never knew existed. "Mom, are you alright?"

"Right as rain," she says with a forced smile. "Why do you ask?"

I gulp, suddenly parched. When I reach for the water, she hands it to me instead. It'll be great when people don't have to hand me water. Until then, though, I'll take the help and be grateful for it.

"No reason, I guess."

"I like June. I do. But I worry you haven't thought all of this through."

For all her squabbling about June, I wonder just how much of my mom sees herself in her. Does she take Dad's side on this for him or out of concern for June? I can't tell. But in the end, it doesn't even matter.

So, I tell her, "Firstly, when I run West Media, I will not run it like Dad. Eighty hours in the office is out of the question. I will not be an absentee husband or father. That is not up for debate. Secondly, she is well aware of what my ambitions are, and she knows what she is signing up for by being with me, gunshot wound aside. Thirdly, and most important of all, it's her choice. I will not break up with her out of some misguided attempt to protect her from my lifestyle. She is here because she wants to be, and I will never take away her choices. She has had enough of that shit in her life. I won't contribute to it. I am with June. She is with me. End of discussion on that topic."

Mom stares at me in silence, then sighs, shaking her head. Then she says the worst possible thing she could ever say to me. "You are so much like your father."

48

ANDERSON

Time simultaneously flies and drags when you're recuperating. I lose whole days to sleep. Liquid diets are nowhere near as fun as they sound, and I wasn't too keen on the idea to start with. I'd give my left nut for something to chew on besides ice and popsicles. But as the weeks go on, I am getting better, and that's all that counts.

I can even answer the door myself when someone knocks. "Moss, come on in."

He lumbers in with a cursory wave to June on the couch. It's become her office over the past few weeks, and when she's there, we don't bother her. She returns the wave and then returns to her laptop, but I have the impression she keeps an eye on me at all times.

Since there is no wall between the kitchen and living room, I know she can hear us. But there are no secrets with her anymore, and Moss has been acting accordingly. We crowd at the kitchen island, but I have to take a seat.

Moss asks, "How are you feeling today?"

"Considerably better now that I've been getting sleep on a regular basis. Thanks for asking."

"Here." He passes me a piece of folded construction paper.

"What's this?"

"Marianna says hello."

I laugh, and it hurts a lot less than it used to. There's still that same pinch in my side, but it doesn't take my breath away. I unfold the paper, and inside is a skillful pencil drawing of me and his ten-year-old holding hands. Underneath, it says, "Get well soon."

"Wow. She is so thoughtful—wait. What does she think is wrong with me?"

"I tell her you were hurt at work. Had a bad fall."

"Ah." I get up and amble to my refrigerator, sticking the drawing on the side with a magnet from a downtown bar. "She really is the sweetest kid."

"She thinks you are love of her life. She was bereft to learn you were hurt. She begged, 'Daddy, take me to see him,' but I tell her, 'Marianna, he is too old for you.' She did not talk to me the rest of the night." He grins and shrugs. "Such is young heartbreak."

"I am certain she will get over it. You just have to redirect her to someone her own age."

"Perhaps." He lowers his voice. "Things with June? They are good?"

I nod. "She's been amazing this whole time. I don't know what I did to deserve her."

"We never deserve them. We just do things to make them blind to that."

That feels remarkably true. Especially now. "Yeah, maybe."

"I want you to know this. I am grateful for what you did for me, Anderson."

I frown up at him while I smile. "I know that."

There is something on his mind that he doesn't want to tell me—I can tell by the way his brow goes Cro-Magnon as he frowns. "Your father does not want you going on the ride-alongs any longer."

"Since when?"

"He tells me this morning."

"Do you think he suspects your divided loyalty?"

He shakes his head. "I do not. I have given no reason to suspect anything."

Then ... the fault lies with me. I whisper, "Do you think it's about June?"

"That I do not know. He did not speak much on the matter. Only no more ride-alongs. I do not know if he wishes you to learn other parts of the business or if something else is happening. He has been agitated. A little erratic—"

"For how long? Why haven't you told me?"

He glances toward my injury. "Why, you think, eh?"

"Fine." But it's not fine. I hate that I've been sidelined like this, and worry creeps in like a thief in the night. "Moss, are there ... worse things that get done in my father's name? Things that not even you do?"

"If there are, I do not know of them. Do you think he will send you to do worse things after what happened to you?"

"He's Elliot West. I think assuming I know what he's thinking will only get me into trouble." It always has in the past.

But Moss shakes his head. "I do not think so. This has shaken him. That is why he is agitated, I believe. A father seeing his child this way ... it is bad for him. If someone did anything like this to my girls ...

" Just starting that sentence, Moss' face goes so cold I might freeze in front of him. "Erratic behavior would be best thing that would come from me, were that the case."

"Understood." But my father isn't sentimental like Moss. He has been blackmailing me for months. That's how I got into this mess. If he wanted to protect me, then he never would have gotten me in this in the first place.

"You and your father, you have differences. But he is still your father. That does not change. And like I say before, he is not the kind of person I used to work for. There is good in him. Deep, deep, deep down. I know it is there. Something like this brings out the good in people. You will see."

"I really do wish I had your faith in that man."

He smiles and gently pats my shoulder. "He will give you a reason to have faith in him. Until then, trust in Moss."

I chuckle. "Unlike him, trusting you has never failed me. So, I can do that."

He grins. "Good. This will bring family together. You will see."

How did a man with his life experience end up this naïve? I have no idea. It's sweet in a way, but it leaves me on less than solid ground.

I cannot stop catastrophizing about this. Moss is a heavy hitter. If Dad is doing things he doesn't include Moss in on, how bad are they? And if that's the case, what terrible thing is he going to blackmail me into next? That's the worst part about being blackmailed by my own father. Not the fact I'm being blackmailed—that happens all the time in business. It's that it's my own father and his endless hoops I have to jump through to keep him happy, all the while keeping the blackmail detail to myself in front of other people.

Mom thinks he's just teaching me a new skill set. She never mentioned the fact he is blackmailing me into this life. As much as I would like to tell her that, I don't want to put a target on her back. I don't think Dad would hurt her, but the more she knows about the business, the worse things could be for her. It nearly knocked the breath out of my lungs to hear her speak as openly as she did about it in the first place.

At least I know she likes June, and she's on my side about that. Sort of.

If I'm not riding along with Moss, he *will* have me doing something worse. I can feel it. He wants to punish me for being with June. For everything I do, he doesn't approve. For still breathing.

He's never been fond of me. Eldest son or not, it's never mattered to him. I've always been what everyone else is to him. Set dressing. We are his pawns he moves about the board to maintain his tragic kingdom. That's why he doesn't like June. He can't control her.

It's not why I'm with her, but it is a definite bonus.

I want to start my life over. Why is no one passing out do-overs when you hit adulthood? I want to take June and run away from everything and everyone. To live a life free of all the trappings of the West name.

A nice fantasy, but one without teeth, and I know it. Deep down, I know it. I am Anderson West, son of Elliot West and the future CEO of West Media. This is the hand life has dealt me, and I must play it. I will play to win.

As much as he has declared me heir apparent, he has always driven home how little he thinks of me. His slights, his threats, his comments, all of them have been to mold me into what he thinks I should be. Now, with June as an excuse to drive that home further, there is no telling what he will force me to do. All I know is I better get ready.

49

JUNE

After Mosses last visit to Anderson's apartment, things are quiet for a time. It's nice getting to wake up next to him every day. In fact, it's one of the best parts about living with him. He always wakes up rumpled and innocent-looking, and I can't help but fall in love with him again right then. Even though we both know it's temporary, I can't help but think about it on a permanent basis. Living with Anderson has been challenging but rewarding, too.

He's not the world's best patient. He started out that way, but now things have been getting easier, so he forgets to do his exercises. I've even gotten an eye roll out of him on the matter. But he doesn't refuse, and he doesn't complain when I give him a nudge. Things could be far worse.

He could be dead.

Anytime we disagree about anything, it is hard not to think about how I could have so easily lost him. One night, I had a nightmare about what he went through, and he woke me up to comfort me, asking about why I was screaming in my sleep. I lied. I didn't want him to feel guilty. So, I said it was one of those nightmares where you show up naked to class, and he smiled and went back to sleep. I lay awake the rest of the night, holding his hand.

So, living together has its ups and downs, but I wouldn't trade it for anything.

Today, while getting ready, though, I find his barbs on the bathroom sink again. It's particularly bad since he's been shaving only every few days, so the barbs are long. It's like living with a werewolf. "Baby, you missed the sink when you shaved."

He sighs. He's doing his stretches in the bedroom, so I hate to say anything that puts him in a bad mood right now, but I have had to remind him so many times about that. "Sorry. I'll do better next time."

Hope so.

Once my face is on for the day, I scoot past him in the bedroom and gather my things in the living room. I have to make sure I have everything—yesterday I forgot my laptop. Going back to the office has been disorienting, so I made a checklist.

Triple-checking my bag, I do, in fact, have everything. "Okay, I'm heading out."

"Hang on." He comes to the door for our new morning routine. "Have as good of a day as you can, and remember I love you."

It still makes me smile that he's being so attentive like this. "You do the same, and I love you, too."

He carefully pulls me in for a kiss because I wait until after I leave for lipstick just so I can have my goodbye kisses. "Alright. Off with you before I make you stay in bed with me all day." He says this every morning.

"Wish I could." My scripted response.

He grabs my ass on the way out, and I'm off. I'm not sure when we became one of those cutesy couples, but I am loving it. The trip to Andre's office isn't as long as it is from my house, and with a shorter commute, I have less time for work emails on the way there. So, when I get to work, I am blindsided by Andre in my office. "Good morning, Ms. Devlin."

"Good morning, Andre. Did we have a meeting on the books?"

"No, nothing so formal." He closes my door and draws the curtains for total privacy, which sends a tight knot to my stomach. "May I sit?"

"Please do."

He sits and smiles. It's that imitation smile of his, and I can never tell when it's good or bad. "I need you on a new project. But it is confidential. Completely."

"I'm all ears."

"There is a list of companies I wish to purchase at below market value. I need you to figure out how I can do that."

"You want me to work on acquisitions? I am a tax attorney—"

"Yes, that is why I hired you," he steamrolls over my objection. "I believe the board members of these companies are cheating at their taxes, or rather, cheating at *something*. If that knowledge became public, then they would be ousted. We can either oust them, or they can sell their controlling shares for cheap with proof of cheating."

"Isn't that something a fixer would do? I'm sure you have plenty on staff—"

"Are you saying you cannot accomplish a simple audit of their taxes?"

I give him a sharp look. "If you get me their taxes, then of course I can. You know that is not what I am saying. I only mean that if you want me to look into things outside of their taxes, a fixer would be better equipped to do that. They have more connections in that realm than I do."

He smiles again. "I believe in you, June. Someone as clever as you can come up with the connections needed for the task. I want to buy these companies before the end of the quarter." He gives my desk a smack. "Let's make this happen." Then, he walks out.

He is the oddest man I have ever known.

Within minutes, the list is sent to me, and it is extensive. Along with tax information comes shareholder agreements and a barrage of confectioned documentation, none of which Andre has any legal right to have. But I am not about to dig into that aspect of it. He wants to buy their shares. My job is to find him a way. I knew going into this job that some aspects would be seedy, and this is one of the least seedy things I expected, so I am not going to complain.

Come lunchtime, though, I head home for a late lunch. It's so nice to have a freshly made, home-cooked meal at lunch. Anderson had taken to watching cooking shows so he could prepare delicious food once he could eat again. We're taking it slowly—nothing too hard to digest for him.

When I walk in, the place smells incredible. "What did you make?"

He smiles as he plates for us. "Mapo tofu—not spicy, don't make that face—and rice, with a side of sauteed eggplant and ginger. All soft, don't worry."

"You spoil me."

"Whenever I can."

We sit down at the kitchen island for lunch, and it is every bit as delicious as it smells. Anderson asks, "How is work so far?"

"Great. New project from Andre. Nothing too crazy. Have you heard from work yet?"

He takes a stiff breath. "Sort of. I got a call from Dad. He wants me to meet him at the office today so we can discuss the next steps."

I knew these happy days couldn't last. Elliot West casts a long shadow over everything, and I am so fucking tired of it. But I am not the only one. Anderson's face is tight with tension. I reach out for his hand. "We will get through this."

He smiles. "I know. He's not the boss of us. Okay, technically, he is my boss, but he's not in charge of you and me. We will get through this. One way or another."

I just hope that's true. I love this man down to my very soul, but Elliot controls so much of him, and I hate that. It's not the first time I have thought about how much better the world would be if Elliot were not in it. I'm sure it won't be the last.

"How is the tofu?"

"Excellent. What did you do differently?"

"I froze it before I crumbled it. Gives it a whole different texture."

I nod and smile, listening to him talk about his latest culinary triumph. But I can't help but worry about this situation. On the other hand, though, I should believe that Anderson will handle this. For heaven's sake, the man came back from being shot in the stomach. If he can handle that, he can handle Elliot West.

I hope.

Whatever happens, I am here until he says otherwise. I am inextricably, irrevocably infatuated with Anderson West. There is no power in this world that can stop me from being by his side other than himself. As long as we are together, I can handle anything. He makes me feel braver than I ever have. Working side by side to get him healthy again bonded us in a way nothing else could.

That aside, though, I wish we didn't have to be brave or strong. I wish we could just be. That we could take a breather that didn't involve rehab and nurse appointments. Recovery is not a vacation. It is work.

When everything settles down, I am whisking this man away to some Caribbean island where all we have to do is eat tropical fruit and, drink rum punch and bask in the sun. And that is where I try to spend the afternoon in my head instead of dreading his meeting with Elliot. I just wish I knew what the meeting was about. I have no clue what that bastard might do next.

50

ANDERSON

Been a long time since I left my apartment, and with this meeting, I have no idea what to expect. Best to put my armor on.

I pick out a black suit, nothing too fancy but sharp enough to draw attention. After a long shower and a shave, I feel closer to my old self. In my head, at least. My body is less familiar.

In the mirror, I see what that psychotic accountant did to me. I don't see myself. Not yet. One day, maybe. But for now, all I see is that little round scar and the surgical scars around the area from when they had to hunt for the particles of the bullet. I'm skinnier, too. All that time I wasted in the gym trying to get my body fat percentage lower and lower when I could have just gotten shot and saved myself the trouble … I blow out a breath and finish drying off without looking in the mirror. I've lost some muscle, too. Not much. June says she doesn't see it, but I do.

With June gone for the day, I feel less connected to my own body. She keeps me grounded and solid. But when I'm alone, I feel untethered when I see myself. Not exactly a stranger in the mirror, but definitely someone I don't totally recognize. Recovery is a strange process.

My hair has gotten a little shaggy over the past few weeks. I could use a trim. But the idea of sitting still long enough for somebody to work on me feels wrong. Like I'm a sitting duck. I'll get over it eventually. The body isn't the only thing that needs to recover after something like this. In the meantime, I fix my hair as stylishly as I can before I head out.

This is the first time that I'm leaving my apartment and going any distance further than the convenience store around the corner. It feels wrong. But I've got this. I know I can do it. I just keep putting one foot in front of the other. I was already nervous about my first trip out of the house. That trip being to go see Dad does not help.

Being taken off of Mosses ride-alongs makes me uneasy. Not that I was anxious to go back to them, particularly not after what happened last time. But a new assignment under my current condition seems like a bad idea. My recovery is going well. Trying something new sounds terrible, not that he will care about my opinion on the matter. I don't know what the old man is thinking.

Seems to me he would want to keep me on something familiar. But that's what I get for thinking that Dad would ever be predictable.

It's not like him to change things midstream, though. That's definitely got me concerned. One thing I can say for Dad is that he likes things to be consistent. He threw me to the wolves once. What the hell is he gonna do now that I'm damn near physically helpless?

I check my look one more time before I leave the house and maybe it's the stress of the situation but, I think I look okay. I've always done well under pressure. Or well enough. But this is different.

Dad doesn't want me with June, and he knows that she's living here. This meeting can only go badly, and I don't have any outs. Moss won't be there. It'll be just me and Dad, I know it. He won't want anyone around for this. When he's cruel, he doesn't like witnesses unless it can benefit him somehow.

I get to the office, and I get a few looks. I don't know what anybody has been saying about me or what the rumor mill has been churning out regarding my injury, but nobody seems to be overly surprised that they haven't seen me in over a month.

I wonder if Dad told them that I was on some kind of vacation.

Worst. Vacation. Ever.

Only his secretary seems to know. Or at least Margaret knows something happened to me. There are tears in her eyes when she sees me. The sweet old woman has been a bit of a substitute grandmother for me over the years, and she's always loved to dote on me in her own ornery way. But today, there is nothing but anguish on her face. As she takes my hands in hers, she gushes, "Oh Anderson, how are you feeling, my boy?"

"On the mend. Thanks for asking, Margaret. Is my father in?"

"He is, and he's waiting for you with bells on. Go on in, honey."

I take one last deep breath before I turn the doorknob. His office is just as cold as I remember. Not the temperature. But the feeling. It's enormous and gray, with windows overlooking the city. No piece of furniture in the room is comfortable, other than possibly his desk chair. However, I wouldn't put it past him to have an uncomfortable desk chair just to remind himself to be hard.

The one thing that does surprise me in the room is his smile. It's the same smile that he uses for Mom. I am instantly uncomfortable. What is he trying to hide?

He comes around the desk to shake my hand. He even claps my shoulder as he does it. If someone else were watching, they would think he actually liked me. "Anderson, it is good to see you. I hope the trip was not too arduous. Take a seat."

If I weren't on edge before, I would be now. I take his guest chair, and unlike every other time I have come to his office, he takes the second guest chair next to me instead of his desk chair. My father never puts himself in proximity to anyone except for my mother. He's acting like a different person, and I have no idea what to expect.

He begins, "How are you feeling today, son?"

I'm not even sure how to respond to that. I don't think this man has ever asked me that question in any serious capacity. "Uh, fine."

"No need to be nervous. This is just a friendly chat."

"We have those?"

He smiles to cover a wince. "I'm glad to see you up and about."

"I'm glad to be able to be up and about."

"I am sure that you have heard from Moss regarding the ride-alongs. You will be on them no longer."

"Can you explain why?"

He firmly says, "I want you in the office again."

"I thought you didn't want me in the office. That I'm not good enough to be in the office. That I'm training to be some new kind of dog for you."

"It was never like that in the first place, and you know it. There are many aspects to this business that I need you to learn. Not all of them will be pleasant. But those kinds of unpleasantries are in the past now. They are no longer for you. Too many bad things have happened. I cannot risk you."

I don't ... what is he up to? "Are you saying that you regret sending me out?"

He takes a breath to say something but then changes his mind mid-thought. "Let's just say mistakes were made. When we make mistakes, we course correct. That's what this is. A course correction."

It's funny. I never expected an apology from my father. And I'm pretty sure I'll never get one, but that was close to it. At this point, I'll take what I can get.

I sit back a little and try to take a deep breath. There's a tightness in my middle still that hasn't gone away with physical therapy yet. He must have seen my pained face because he makes one of his own. "I—"

"Do you need a medication? Was coming down here too much for you? I can send for a car to drive you home."

I hold my hands up for him to stop. "I'm going to need you to stop with all of this parental concern that you have going because it's freaking me out. Who are you?"

For a moment, he looks offended. But then he chuckles. "I suppose it is a bit of a change. But I don't know that I can stop it." His voice goes thick with emotion. "I nearly lost my boy."

I have no idea where this is coming from. It would be refreshing if it weren't so far out of left field. "Well, I'm here now. So let's move forward."

He scrubs his hand over his face and takes a deep breath. Somehow, that wipes away all the emotion from his face. He clears his throat and then looks me in the eye. "Moving forward is a great idea. When you come back to the office—and there's no rush on that—we will make things as easy for you as possible. I know you're still recovering. I don't want you to stress out about the office. It takes time to get past something this big, Anderson. But I also understand the therapeutic use of work. So, if you're anxious to get back at it, I can definitely send some things your way. Work has always been a great distraction for me in trying times. But that's entirely your choice."

I frown deeply at him, still unsure where this latent parental concern is coming from. "I'm supposed to meet with Elliot West. About yay tall, a bit of a bastard. Do you know where he is?"

He laughs once, shaking his head. "There's that trademark wit of yours."

I can't believe he didn't come out swinging. "Dad, are you okay? How are *you* feeling?"

"I believe I have expressed myself clearly."

Okay, he isn't gonna give me anything else on it. I asked how he was doing. His emotional wall went up. At least, this is more familiar territory to me. I know how to deal with him when he walls up. Cold and bitter, I can do. Kindness and caring are not in my wheelhouse of how to manage my overbearing father.

"Fine, fine. I don't think I'm quite ready to jump back into a full day of work, but if you wanna send me a couple of things, then I could take a look at them."

"Splendid." He pauses, looking me over. "So, how is June doing with all of this?"

51

ANDERSON

In all my years on this planet, my father has never shown an interest in a girlfriend of mine. He has also never tried to be supportive when I've done something he explicitly told me not to do, and June falls under that umbrella. As soon as he said her name, a shot of panic went up my back. I knew it was coming. I came here fully expecting to be interrogated and, once again, told to dump her. Today was always going to be a fight, but I didn't think it would go down like this.

"What would you like to know about June?"

"I thought I made that clear. I made an inquiry into her well-being."

"Yes, and since you've never done that before, I want to know what it is that you want to know about her."

He draws a long, slow breath. It seems I've irritated him. "I have tried to ask about her. How is she doing? It cannot be easy for her to deal with the fact that her boyfriend has gone through something so traumatic. So I ask how she is doing. As I understand it, that is something that people do when they care about people."

It's almost as though he is doing his best to replicate a good parent. But I can't tell if this is coming from a sincere place or not. I have a lifetime of baggage telling me that this is a trap. I'll play his game until he gives me a reason not to. "She is doing well. Thank you for asking."

"My social set is aging, and with that comes the issues of aging. Debilitation. Disability. Sickness. It happens to everyone. But not everyone can handle it. Some people are excellent caregivers. Some are not. So I suppose my real question is, has she been there for you? I wouldn't hold it against her if she wasn't. Personally, I have never been much of a caregiver—"

I try to keep it to myself, but a laugh pops out of me. "Apologies."

He waves his hand in the air as if to say it's nothing. "You are right to laugh. I'm well aware of my shortcomings. Caregiving is one of them. I could hardly hold it against her if it's something I am incapable of."

At least the man isn't a hypocrite.

"To answer your question, June has been great. When I left the hospital, she was the one who was there taking care of me. She cooked my meals. She helped me in the shower. There were even a few incidences where she had to help me in the bathroom, which was utterly humiliating, but she was unfazed. June has been there for me every step of the way. And she has taken all of it with a poise and grace that I didn't know was possible."

Tension leaves his shoulders. "I am very glad to hear that, son."

"I love her. I loved her before all of this. And I love her even more now. We've known each other since high school. I don't know if I told you that. I was in love with her then, but I was terrible to her. Cruel. In part because that was what I thought love was. I saw how you treated everyone around you, and I absorbed that and mimicked it. *That* was what I put out into the world because of you. It took me a very long time to unlearn your cruelty. When I found her again, I decided I was never letting her go. And I am glad that I made that choice."

His lips curve a little. "Then I am glad you did, as well."

It is uncomfortable to be completely honest with him. Maybe because it is so new? It feels wrong, like

I'm falling into his trap. I have no inner gauge about this. This isn't me running off at the mouth at him or saying things to make him uncomfortable. This is just me being me.

Maybe I can turn getting shot and almost dying into a good thing.

Quietly, I ask, "What do you have to say to me about how you have been about her?"

"That things are never as simple as they appear. But as it stands, I want only your happiness."

Another non-apology. I have too many years in the bank to believe that he wants my happiness. Maybe if my happiness dovetailed into a benefit for the business, he would want that. This is the same man who threatened me with prison time not so long ago. The man who told me that I had to break up with June, or I was done for. He has done everything in his power to ruin me, and now he wants to act as if we are a normal father and son. For now, this turnaround remains hard to believe.

But I'd like to. I think everyone has an inner child who wants their parents' approval. I'm not above such things. It's almost as if my near-death experience changed him instead of me. "So you're actually happy for me in regards to June?"

"I am happy if you're happy."

This is still too strange. It's like my mother is puppeting my father's mouth. In a strange way, it hurts more than if he had been an asshole. If this really is him, then this man was always somewhere deep down inside of him. That means that we have spent thirty years going head-to-head with each other for no reason. He could have been this caring, this nice, this understanding, and he chose to be a fucking bastard. It is hard not to be angry at him right now.

I know that traumatic events can change people. I am trying to be cognizant of the fact that these things can seriously alter a person, and if he is to be believed, that's happened to him. But right now, all I can think of is the boy I was who just wanted a hug from his dad and never got one. I am angry for him.

"You're happy that I'm happy? Since when?"

"People change, Anderson. Best to roll with the punches."

People don't change that much. They don't go 180° from their original personality. This is fake. It has to be.

"Is this some kind of a prank? Is this funny to you? To pretend that you care about what I'm going through?"

He sighs and glances out the window before looking me in the eye. "I want to do better by you. By everyone. But I want to start with you. If you'll let me."

I'm still too angry about this. It takes everything inside of me not to throw this in his face. But I have to think of the future. If he wants to play nice, then I should let him. I have to be strategic about this.

He's playing right into my hands.

It will be so much easier to dismantle his empire from the inside. The plan I started months ago is finally coming to fruition. I went on the ride-alongs. I learned everything I could from Moss in the time that we had together. Now, Dad wants to move me into the office. I can use this, too, if I'm smart about it.

But what if he's being honest?

That doesn't change the fact that he's involved in a lot of illegal activities that need to end. So, let him be honest. Let him try to become dad of the year. I will use every bit of this to my advantage. Even if it hurts.

Can I forgive and forget? Maybe. But I have two things to think of. June and any children we might have. If I do this from the inside, I'm going to have to walk a very tight rope. I can do this and make him an enemy. Or I can do this and keep him as my father. What happens next depends greatly on him.

So, I swallow my anger down harder than I ever have before and give a wan smile. If I make this too easy on him, he won't buy it. "Dad, if you're turning over a new leaf, I'm happy to see it."

He looked like he was stressed as if I were going to yell at him. He expected anger out of me, which means he knew that he had earned it. Or that he thinks I'm a hothead. Whatever the case, he looks more relaxed now.

"Your mother and I would like for you and June to join us for supper this weekend. Saturday night. If you don't have plans."

"Nothing on the schedule that I know of. But I'll check in with her to make sure."

"Excellent."

I wait for more of a follow-up than that, but nothing comes. No snide comment. No judgmental overtone. He simply seems glad that we are coming to dinner. It's uncanny. I really do wonder how much of this has made him reevaluate who he is. Maybe I'm not the only one in recovery.

"Was that everything you wanted to talk about, or is there something else?"

"I believe that covers our bases. Your mother said that dinner will be ready at seven. Are you still on any food restrictions for your wound care?"

"I can eat most things these days, but soft foods are still best for now."

"Understood."

I stand, and so does he. For a moment, he holds his arms up as if to hug me. But that's a bridge too far. I make up an excuse and stiffly move back from the embrace. "I'm not really physically capable of safely hugging right now."

His arms drop, but he has a sad smile. "Of course. I don't know what I was thinking."

"It's a lot to get used to. There are things that I can't do that I used to do without a thought. Now, they exhaust me. It's an adjustment. But we'll get through it."

"We certainly will."

As I leave Dad's office, I have an impending sense of dread. I don't know if it's about Saturday or about the future in general, but something deep inside is telling me that everything is wrong. Maybe I'm paranoid. But I have no reason to doubt this feeling. It's always been right in the past, and Dad's given me no reason to think it is wrong now. But I would like it to be.

52

JUNE

Digging through shareholder agreements is a slog. I've been at this all week now, and it starts to look like gibberish after a while. Sure, it's legalese and I should be familiar with this sort of thing. And I am. But, oh my god, this is not what I'm cut out for. But Andre wants to buy these companies, and it's my job to help him do that. So that's what I'm doing.

It feels like one part corporate espionage and one part extraordinarily tedious work. I always thought spying would be more fun. The movies make it look fun. But they don't show the spies going through boatloads of paperwork and the boredom that accompanies it. Corporate espionage is dull.

It doesn't help that I feel like I haven't seen Anderson all week long. This is my fifth twelve-hour day in a row, or it will be by the time I get out of here, I'm sure. But I can't complain. Andre gave me a well-paying job before anybody else would even give me the time of day. He might be a kook who kidnapped me, but he's my boss. I'm gonna do anything I can to keep him happy.

In studying these companies, I have figured out a few things. It seems Andre wants to branch out into media conglomeration, which is not something that I would have expected out of him. Most of his holdings range widely. For him to specifically target media is odd. But maybe he got a tip from somebody that their stocks are gonna shoot up. I don't know. Whatever the reason, he has a hard-on for these selections.

He asked for a report today to him and his partners in order for them to see why he is steering them to these investments. I have presented to corporate partners before. But this is my first presentation with Andre's partners, and I'm a little nervous. Out of instinct, I have drunk way too much coffee today. Thankfully, my hand doesn't shake when I reach for my mug again. It's just about time for me to head over to the boardroom to do my presentation. So, I need to get every milligram of caffeine in me that I can.

A knock on my open office door startles me, and I almost spill my coffee. When I look up, Carlos is grinning at me. He smoothly asks, "A little nervous about your presentation?"

I'm sure he'd love that. "A little over-caffeinated, but thanks for your concern."

He strolls in, confident I'm not going to turn him away. It's annoying. "I understand Andre has had you on some big secret project."

"I understand you're supposed to be working on your things before the end of the quarter." I paused pointedly. "But you're here."

He steeples his fingers. "Let me worry about me. I have everything under control. But I was curious to know something about you."

I have nothing for him to be curious about. "Oh, you know what they say about curiosity. And the cat it killed."

"What I would like to know is what your plans are for Saturday night."

Could tell him I'm going to my boyfriend's parent's house for supper. That way, he would know to leave me alone. But I want him to leave me alone because I want him to leave me alone. Not because I'm taken. "And why is that, Carlos?"

"You spend a lot of long hours in the office, don't you?"

"Don't we all?"

He grins. "I suppose that's true. That's why I should take you out tomorrow night. You need to relax. You work too hard."

"And somehow going out with you tomorrow night would be relaxing?"

He lifts a shoulder and smirks. "I cannot promise relaxation. But I can promise a good time."

"Thank you anyway, but I make my own good times."

He runs his finger along the edge of my desk. "I know you take care of your boyfriend at home. An injured man. That is a lot of work. It is admirable."

I didn't realize that the gossip mill had spread around this far during my absence. "If you know I have a boyfriend, then why did you ask me out?"

"I meant it only as colleagues. But I am flattered you think that I would ask you out."

Whatever mind games he was trying to play, I refuse to play them with him. I can't tell if he is trying to get into my head before the presentation or if he's trying to feel better about me turning him down. It doesn't matter either way. I am done entertaining him. "Carlos, unless you have business with me, there's no reason for you to be in here right now. I am busy."

"Alright, alright. No harm in asking if I can help you out, right?"

"Don't get lost on your way back to your office."

"I know my way around here. Just like I know my way around a woman. If you ever get tired of playing nurse to your broken boyfriend, give me a call sometime. I'll be happy to loosen you up." He saunters out of my office, and I just want to strangle him.

He is nowhere near pretty enough to be that fucking egotistical.

Checking my laptop, I see that I am running late. Shit. I pack everything in my bag that I'll need for the presentation and haul ass over to the executive side of the building. That side of Andre's office building is prettier than my office. On this end of the building, there are light wood floors and big open windows. It's a cacophony of brightness and a little too much for my eyes. It feels like being in a spotlight everywhere I go.

I hit the restroom, and it is just as nice as the rest of the place. The executive world really is different from everybody else's. Polished surfaces in every direction. Flattering lighting. The hand soap comes out of a warmer. There are mints in a basket. The paper towels are the softest I have ever felt.

Like they say, it's good to be the king.

Once I get out of the restroom, I head over to the boardroom waiting area. The waiting room has seating and a woman who orchestrates everybody going in and out of the boardroom. I would have thought she was somebody's executive assistant, except I've only ever seen her in this area. She wears a headset and presses her hand to it for a moment before telling me, "Two minutes."

I give a brief smile and nod and try to suck in all the oxygen in the room because it feels like it's leaving my lungs as I step into the large wooden double doors. I've got this. I know I do. This isn't any different from any other work I've done. Except that it is. But I made all the connections that I needed to get the information that I wanted. I was able to pick apart the shareholders' agreements and find some holes in them. I can do this.

My phone chooses that exact moment to vibrate, and I almost drop it when I see who is on the caller ID.

Mitch Devlin. My father.

Why in the fuck is he calling me now? Maybe it's Mom. If something happened to her, someone might have called him. I have to take the call. But I really don't want to.

"Hello?"

"Junebug. It's so good to hear your voice."

Is this a social call? Does it even matter? Feels like there's a weight on my chest. My pulse thuds in my temple. I try to keep my voice even, but I've misplaced my saliva and have to sip my coffee just to be able to speak. "What's going on?"

"Well, I'm in town, and I was hoping to get to see you."

Oh, you have gotta be fucking kidding me. I feel like I might throw up and blackout at the same time. "Since when do we visit each other?"

"Now, come on, June, you don't gotta be like that. Can't a father wanna visit his daughter?"

I am sure that some normal fathers and some normal daughters do visit each other. We are not those people. We have never been those people. I have no intention of ever becoming those people.

I can't breathe. There's sweat going down my back. If I don't start breathing, the room is gonna start spinning. I could hang up on him, but he would just call back. My father has never been one to take no for an answer. I've always fucking hated that about him.

Now, my head is pounding. My pulse is fluttering. I take a couple of breaths and try to clear the negativity out because I am not a child anymore, and I have to get my shit together for this presentation.

The thing is, I know he wants something.
Considering our history, that is never good. But if I
don't find out what it is, Mom might give it to him.
Ex-husband or not, she's still a sucker for that man.

"Uh—

The double doors open. Andre and the partners are
looking at me. Here goes nothing.

-

53

JUNE

I flash a quick smile at everyone and hold up a finger. "Sure, Dad, I'll call you back in a bit." I hang up with him. "So sorry about that. Family emergency." Strolling in, I don't get the impression that I upset Andre by having my phone on me at the moment. That's a relief.

He merely sits back and smiles. "Family is first and foremost. It's good that you're taking care of them. I hope the emergency isn't too terrible."

"Nothing they can't handle without me. Let's get started." I begin my presentation, but I'm not present for it. I can't stop thinking about Dad. Why is it that both me and Anderson have to have daddy issues? I don't understand why that was in the cards for us, but at least it helps us to be more understanding of each other's problems.

As dastardly as Elliott West is, he runs in a different league than my father. But if a man is only as good as his word, my father is terrible. The man is a philanderer and a crook. Growing up, I never knew what to believe out of his mouth. You could never take him at his word. If selling the Brooklyn Bridge made him money or got him laid, then he would have done it.

Can't think about him. "And so you see here on the report that they project the next quarter to show three percent growth, but if they fail that … "

I hate that he and I have anything in common. He was *not* the reason that I became an attorney, despite the fact that he is one himself. He tried to take credit for me picking law school, but I shut that shit down quick. I became an attorney because I thought that it was a glamorous career. When done right. They say that when you're a child, you're always looking for good examples. Heroes to follow. My father was none of those things. He was only a warning of who not to be.

Though, come to think of it, we don't have that much in common anymore. He was disbarred. It takes a lot for someone to get disbarred. But setting up a pyramid scheme and then defrauding all of your investors will do that.

Andre raises a finger to stop me. "And we could call for a vote of no confidence?"

No confidence is precisely what I feel right now. "Exactly."

"Excellent. Tell us more."

I start with him, but I can't stop thinking about Dad's pyramid scheme. I was just a kid when it happened. Middle school became hell because of it. My father didn't just defraud investors that could afford it. Some were parents of kids I went to school with. My mother's friends. A few neighbors. That bastard ruined everything he touched.

And his touch was never light. It didn't matter that I came to school with bruises. No one ever seemed to notice. Hell, it took forever for my mom to notice, and by then, Dad had started to vanish for long weekends.

The kids whose parents were defrauded by my father began to pick on me. I couldn't even blame them. I was angry at my father, too. Sometimes, I thought it was my fault that he did what he did. That I earned my bruises. That he just wanted to have enough money to spoil me and make up for the hitting. But that was not the case. Not even close.

Dad used most of the money that he got from his schemes to shower it on new women. He wined and dined them, telling them he was single with no kids. I still don't know how many women he slept with when he and Mom were still married. But I'd have to venture a guess it was in the dozens.

After his scam fell apart and he got arrested, Mom and I were left penniless. I was worried she would want to stay with him, but Mom was smart enough to divorce his sorry ass. Even now, though, I know she has a soft part of her heart for him. My father is a charmer and a snake. One of the best con men I have ever met.

A partners asks, "In your opinion, do you think they've been cheating?"

I blink, thinking I said something about Mitch out loud. "I beg your pardon?"

"Do you think they've been cheating on their taxes? I know what the report says, but I want to hear it from you. Andre says you have killer instincts."

Well, that's nice to hear, and it pulls me from my spiral down Memory Lane. "I can almost guarantee they're cheating, however, getting proof may include a trip overseas, if Andre's computer consultants cannot obtain the information digitally." A classier way of saying, "If his hackers can't get it, someone gets on a plane to prove tax evasion." And I really hope it won't be me. It is one thing to look over documents Andre had mysteriously obtained. It is another to get on a plane and likely do illegal things overseas.

Then, I'd be no better than my father. Another criminal in the family.

At least my stepfather was not a complete criminal, but he wasn't much of a step over my father. The guy was a total asshole. I don't think he was ready to become a stepfather when he married my mother. Or maybe he just didn't understand what that meant. Not that it mattered to me. I was a child. All I knew was this new man was mean to me. And he was smart enough to hide it from Mom.

I love my mother deeply. But when a man turns on some charm, she is an absolute sucker for it. When he told her that he didn't do anything wrong, she ate it up. In her mind, I was the problem. That is until I made sure that she heard him calling me names. That was a bad day. But it was the start of their divorce, and so I am glad that happened.

My relationship to parents in general is complicated. That's why I try to avoid ever thinking about it. Because even though I am an attorney standing in a boardroom and I am presenting these findings to a group of partners who are probably multi-millionaires many times over, my head is stuck in the past, and I feel like I'm that little girl again who is torn up by the adults in the room. These men don't even know me, and I feel like they're getting ready to pick me apart. I can hardly breathe.

Being an adult comes with certain responsibilities. I know now that I am not responsible for the shitty actions of my parents back then. But back then, I thought that I was, and it is hard to let go. But that is one of my responsibilities—to let this go for the sake of my mental health. Maybe one day, I'll sit down with a therapist and really dive into it. That is not today. Today, I have to get this done.

"… In closing, I think that's the way we have to go about this. It won't be pretty. There will be a lot of hurt feelings in the country clubs. But it will get you what you're looking for."

Andre smiles up at me. "You provided everything I asked for and more. Thank you for your work, June. Truly, I cannot thank you enough. This is everything I wanted."

"I am happy to help, Andre."

"Well, everyone, that's lunch."

With that, the meeting breaks up. I gather my things and head for my office to drop off my laptop before heading home for lunch. A heady feeling of completion hits. I did the scary thing today, and now, I can breathe again.

I grab my coat and bag and take the elevator downstairs, eager for another home-cooked meal before Anderson ends up back in his office, too. It is inevitable that he will end up going back to the office one day. But it feels soon. He could be home for a year, and I think it would still feel soon. I just like having him there. He's safe in his apartment. His dad won't get him killed in his apartment.

Probably.

The elevator takes too long, as always. Anytime I'm anxious to get home, it goes slower, I swear. As soon as the elevator door is open, I'm off like a rocket.

"Junebug!"

My spine locks at that voice. Everything else in me goes rigid a second later. Everything, that is, except for my stomach. My stomach has decided to become an acrobat. I turn around slowly, hoping and praying that I am wrong.

But I'm not. He's standing right there. My father.

I want to run. Or punch him in the face. I'm really torn about which one I wanna do. But if he's around long enough, I might get to vomit on him. Who am I kidding? When has this man ever stuck around long enough for anything?

"Mitch. What are you doing here?"

He winces at me, saying his first name. But he hasn't earned "Dad" from me in nearly twenty years. "You don't have to be like that. I told you I wanted to come see you. So, surprise. Here I am."

In recent memory, I have been kidnapped, my apartment was broken into, I was nearly raped, and my boyfriend was shot. This surprise is in the top five of the worst surprises in my recent life. I'm just not sure what order they belong in.

54

JUNE

"Um, yep. Here you are."

Mitch smiles handsomely, arms out.

"Well, get in here for a hug. We don't have all day. Not if I'm gonna take you out to lunch at Riccardo's."

Since when does he have Riccardo's money? That place has a two-week waitlist. But I go ahead and hug him. We are in the lobby of my office. If any of my coworkers see this, I need this to look as normal as can be. I can pretend to be normal while he's pretending to be normal.

In all fairness to Mitch, he looks good. He's in a sharp designer suit. His hair is well-coiffed. He's even freshly shaved. A far cry from the man that I saw in prison all those years ago.

Prison jumpsuit gray looks bad on everybody. But it looked especially bad on my father. We are too pale to pull off that color. Back then, he had really let himself go. Understandably. His hair was a mess. His beard was scraggly. He was gaunt. The thing that stood out the most was that he looked so tired, as if breathing was too much work for him.

Now, he has color in his cheeks, and they've filled out. He looks like his old self again, save for a few extra years. It shows in the grey at his temples and the lines on his face. He's older. But I don't know if he's any wiser.

I haven't seen him much in the intervening years. In fact, I've actively avoided the man. But he has sought me out a few times. Each time, he wanted something. It was usually money. But sometimes, it was just a shoulder to cry on so that he could whine about the latest woman to dump him between going back and forth with my stepmother. I hate that he only ever sees me when he wants something. Standing in my office's lobby, I want to choke the man just to stop him from hitting me up for something. His mere presence exhausts me. But unless I want to throw a hissy fit right here and right now, I am going to lunch at Riccardo's.

If he wants to take me somewhere that expensive, I am happy to make him pay.

"Let's go to lunch."

He leads me to his new car. It's a shiny, expensive number that I recognize from the parking garage in Anderson's apartment building. "You like the car? I just got it."

"It's nice." I am going to need to bite my tongue so hard that I taste blood. It is that, or I will ask him if he stole it.

The ride to Riccardo's is brief, and on the way there, I text Anderson to let him know I'm not coming home for lunch. Once we arrive, we are seated right away. The place is just as snazzy as I expected. Dark floors, white tablecloths, and big picture windows around the building. I nearly lose my breath when I see the lack of prices on the menu. It's more expensive than I thought. If he ducks out of this lunch and leaves me with the bill, it's going to be a problem.

"Order whatever you want, Junebug. It's on me."

He wants to play that game? Fine. I settle on the grilled veal chops and a glass of red. Once we've ordered, I want to interrogate the man. No, not that. I want to scream at him for everything that he's done, and I wanna know what the fuck he's up to. But I don't.

This is the kind of place that Elliot's friends would eat at. If I act out or show my ass here, I'm sure that he will hear about it. Anderson is trying to get along with his father for now. I cannot afford to fuck that up. So I will play nice with my father. To the best of my ability. For now.

"What prompted this visit?"

Mitch grins, knowing he has a million-dollar smile. "I wanted to catch up with my daughter. It's been a while, hasn't it?"

"Indeed, it has been. How are you doing?"

"Life is good. It has its challenges, true. But things are going great."

"How's that?"

He smiles and flirts with the server when she comes to deliver our cocktails. Then he turns his attention to me. "Well, I don't know if I mentioned it the last time that we visited, but I am working on getting reinstated."

"Wow. I didn't know you wanted to go back to the law."

"I miss the work. But for now, I am in marketing, and that pays pretty well."

"Are you with a firm?"

"Not at all. I'm working for Metasoftware in New York."

I choke on my wine and nearly make a mess of myself. "You mean the software company who's in every corporation in the country?"

"That's the one."

My father, who knows almost nothing about tech, is working for the biggest tech company in the country. I can't even figure out how he got that job. But now that I think about it, it's not beneath him to completely lie on a resume, so I suppose I shouldn't be that surprised. The man stole over ten million dollars. Of course, he can lie on a resume.

Did mom and I ever see any of that money? No. Of course not. Not a dime of it went to us. It went to his mistresses until he met the one who became my stepmother. To romance her, he bought yachts, vacations he said were work conferences and expensive hotel rooms. I was on my own for college, which was why I had to work my fingers to the bone and study until my eyes bled just to get the scholarships to pay for school. But the less said about that, the better.

Not that I'm bitter.

Much.

I clear my head of the vitriol. The wine helps. "Congratulations. That's quite an achievement. Especially considering you used to have me program the clock on your VCR. Or, for that matter, the fact that you had a VCR when I was a kid."

He laughs heartily. "That's the great thing about marketing, Junebug. You don't have to know anything about the product, you just have to sell it."

That sounds about right. Just like him to know nothing about something before he dives into it. "How long have you been there?"

"A few years. Now tell me about yourself. You're working in that nice office. How did that happen?"

I almost laugh. It's funny to think that out of everybody that I know, my father might be the one who would just breeze past the fact that the man who kidnapped me is the one who I work for now. Largely because he has no room to talk shit about criminals. But I don't plan to tell him a thing about Andre Moeller. Telling my felon father I work for a criminal would likely end up with the two of them working together, and I'd never recover from that.

"I was recruited."

"I always knew something like that would happen for you. My little girl's too smart. One day, you'll be running that place."

"Oh, I don't know about that. Being in charge is a lot of responsibility that I don't want."

"I hear that," he says with a chuckle. "And are you seeing anyone?"

Do I tell him? Do I keep it to myself? It's a hard call. But he wants to play this game, so why not?

"Yes, I am. Actually, right now, I'm sort of living with him. He had an accident at work and was really badly injured, so I've been helping take care of him."

That earns a big smile from him. It's hard not to feel good when I get that from him. I don't want to like it. I shouldn't want this man's approval.

Mitch says, "I'm very proud of you. That's not an easy thing to do. But you make sure he's worth it. Most men are not."

"I am very familiar with what most men are worth. I learned when I was a kid."

"You're right. You're just plain right. I was not a good father. And I certainly wasn't a good husband. So, that man of yours, you make sure that he is better than I am. You deserve the best, Junebug."

Any minute now. I know it is coming any minute now. The ask. He likes to loll his prey and make them nice and warm and comfortable, and then he throws *the ask*. As I'm waiting for it, I realize he's not wearing his wedding ring anymore. *Oh hell. Jenny kicked him out again. Bet he needs a place to stay.*

I give a tight smile. *Let's cut this off before he asks.* "He really is the best. I wish his apartment were a little bit bigger, though. It's just a one-bedroom. No room for anyone else."

"Why? Are you looking to start a family?"

Okay. He didn't pick up on what I was saying. Maybe that means he's not looking for a place to stay. "No, it's just sometimes it feels like we're on top of each other."

"Understandable. I've always liked a lot of room to stretch out. That's why, even though it's just me, I have a three-bedroom apartment in the city. Hell, even the hotel room I got here is a two-bedroom. I like to live large. What can I say?"

I don't understand why the other shoe hasn't dropped yet. I keep waiting for it. But he keeps dodging me. It is unnerving. But as the lunch goes on, it never comes. He's just asking me about me, so I'm returning the questions, and we're actually having a conversation for the first time in years. I dare say it's almost nice.

When he drops me off back at work, though, it happens. "Junebug, before you go, there's something I want."

"I knew it. I fucking knew it. What? Money? A kidney?"

He smiles, amused. "I want to work on our relationship. I would like to get to know my daughter. And maybe one day, I will consider myself to be in her life again. I miss you."

Either he's serious, or he's pulling a long con. I can't tell. "Oh."

"I'd like to get to know Anderson, too, if things go well with us."

My head is throbbing, but I manage to eke out, "That, um … that sounds nice."

"Glad to hear it. Knock 'em dead, Junebug."

"Yeah. Thanks. Have a good one, Dad."

His smile is megawatt before he pulls away.

It's only then I realize what I'd called him. But saying Dad instead of Mitch felt natural. That hasn't been true since I was a child. Maybe he isn't the only one who has changed.

55

JUNE

On the way to Anderson's parents' Boston apartment, I tell him all about my lunch with Dad. Mitch. Whoever he is. "… and he wants to get to know you, too."

"How come you have never told me about your father before? That man did some crazy shit."

"I never liked talking about him because, in addition to all of the fraud and other shitty behavior, he was constantly angry … " I am going to get the words out if it kills me. So, I blurt, "Back then, he used to hit. A lot. Talking about him is just very … it's hard. It's really, really hard. Sometimes, when I think about him, it feels like there's a boulder sitting on my chest, trying to stop me from breathing. I don't know how to get past that." Okay. My back is damp, and I'm dizzy, but I said the words, and I didn't throw up. Kudos to me.

Anderson gives my thigh a supportive squeeze. "You're doing really good talking about it right now. But if you don't wanna talk about it anymore, we don't have to. That said, I think it might be a good idea for you to see a therapist about it. I'm happy to listen to whatever you wanna tell me about, but I'm not skilled like they are."

"Yeah, maybe one day. Honestly, I keep thinking about that, too. I'm just not ready yet."

"Whenever you are, we will get you the best help available." He sighs. "Strange to think that both of our fathers are becoming far too involved in our lives."

I laugh at that. "You are not wrong, sir."

"Sometime soon, we should get some time alone. Just the two of us. With nobody around to pester us."

"That sounds magical. Yes, please." The worry lines on his face become clearer the closer we are to his parents' place. I bet he needs to talk, too. "Nervous about tonight?"

"I think I have good reason to be, don't you?"

"Oh, definitely. I wasn't trying to imply that it was an unearned anxiety. Do you think that he's going to drop the hammer on us or something?"

He sighs. "Honestly, after our last meeting, I have no idea what to expect out of that man."

"That's the scariest part, isn't it?"

"Yes. I liked it when he was relatively predictable. This whole … caring thing is too weird. I don't know how to handle it."

I don't know what to think, either. Elliot has always been a little combative. Hell, the first time we met, he asked me to sign a prenup. But that was when he thought we were engaged. Now that he knows everything, I have no clue how he will be. But I'm prepared for anything.

Cold Elliot gets Clever June, who sidesteps rudeness.

Snippy Elliot gets Overly Nice June, who gets far too sweet to make him sound like an even bigger asshole.

Any other version of him I will have to play by ear. At least Kitty is nice to me. I can always fall back into conversation with her. "And you said your brother isn't coming to this shindig?"

"No. Just the four of us."

"Intimate."

"Yeah, on that note, if I say the word fluegelhorn, we are out of there."

I snort a laugh. "How exactly are you working fluegelhorn into the conversation to be subtle?"

"You're right. What do you suggest?"

"Hell, I don't know. Kettlebell."

He cocks a glance at me. "Kettlebell? How do I get that into the conversation?"

"Talk about using them in PT."

"Huh. That's a good idea."

We pull up to the valet for the building, and I didn't realize just how it would affect me to be back on the street where I was kidnapped. I can't help but eye the shadows around the building. The neighborhood is one of the most expensive in Boston, and despite the security cameras and guards, I was still whisked away in the night.

A night like this one.

I cling to Anderson's arm as we walk to the building. But he knows me. He murmurs in my ear, "I've got you, baby. No one is taking you tonight but me."

"Sorry, I didn't mean to—"

"Don't apologize for it. Not ever. I'm sorry we had to come back here for what is likely the world's most awkward supper."

I chuckle, and he kisses me. "Thanks for that."

"Ready?"

"As I'll ever be."

We walk in and take the elevator up the short ride to his parents' apartment. His mother answers the door, looking as lovely as ever. I swear there's light in her eyes when she smiles at me. The woman is made of warmth. "Come in, let me take your coats."

"Hi, Kitty."

"June, it is so good to see you." We pass our coats to her, and she hangs them for us. "Well, I am famished. I hope you're hungry. I have been in the kitchen all day."

Anderson gives a questioning expression. "You cooked tonight?"

"I can, you know."

"Well … yeah, but the question is, do you?"

"You watch that lip of yours, young man. You're never too old for me to take over my knee."

He laughs at the thought. "You never even did that when I was a kid."

"And now you're a grown man with a smart lip. I should have done it back then, but that doesn't mean I can't do it now."

He clutches his abdomen, wearing a teasing grin. "I'm not going over a knee with my injuries. Guess I have to apologize instead. Sorry, Mom."

She smirks over her shoulder at us. "That's better. Now, come along."

The apartment is airy and bright in whites and blues. It's an older building, so the architecture is gorgeous. I love old Boston buildings. They have such character.

We enter a smaller dining room than the one we had eaten in with his whole family last time. This one is similarly decorated to the rest of the house, but the table set is the palest gray to set it apart from the room. Inside, Elliot sits at the four-top table, and it is disconcerting to see him smile so genuinely. His other smiles always seem as though he is merely tolerating the presence of other humans.

"Anderson, June, I am happy you could make it. Please have a seat."

Kitty says, "I'll go get dinner—"

"No, Kitty, sit," Elliot says as he stands up. "I'll fetch dinner. You've been working all day."

"Thank you, love. And bring that bottle I have chilling in the refrigerator if you don't mind." She sits, and on his way out, he kisses the top of her head before he exits.

We take seats, and Anderson quietly asks, "What in the hell has gotten into him?"

She smiles sadly. "I think it is knowing how close he came to losing you. It softened him, Anderson. I don't know how long it'll last, but it shook him up."

He sighs. "I guess we will enjoy it while it lasts."

"That's my plan," she confides. "He hasn't been like this since he lost his parents, and that faded within a year."

"But he's always doted on you," I point out.

"He's kinder to me than everyone else. I'd have to be blind not to see it. But even so, he's not normally like this, and I enjoy it. I just wish our oldest didn't have to almost die to get this side of him."

We hear footsteps, so Anderson changes the topic. "Speaking of kids, how is Cole?"

Kitty's smile grows strained. "If he weren't a little difficult, then he wouldn't be Cole."

Elliot walks in with a silver cart on wheels. On top is a domed platter, and the shelf below contains the side dishes. He sets everything up for us, then reveals the main course. "Prime rib, cooked rare. We looked it up, and from what we read, it should be tender enough for you to eat in your condition."

Kitty adds, "And then we called Lewis to see if he thought it was okay."

Anderson's smile is unguarded. "I appreciate the effort. Thank you."

"Lewis?" I ask.

"A physician friend of ours," Elliot explains. "Genius surgeon. My only regret about Anderson's care was that he was unable to attend him."

She explains, "He was in Paris for a conference at the time."

Once our plates are full, we dig in. It is surreal to think of everything Anderson and I have gone through with Elliot, and now, we are here, eating supper in his home. The man broke into my apartment to steal from me while me and Anderson were fucking on my bed in full view of him. Now, he passes me the gravy, and we're making chitchat.

Life has not been anything resembling normal since I was in that auction.

I wish I understood the purpose of this supper. It cannot be something so simple as Elliot has had a change of heart about everything Anderson related. I'm in agreement with him on that. But I cannot suss out what the ulterior motive is. We're not hiding anything from him anymore, so there are no secrets to keep track of, no subterfuge. That stress is gone now.

It's been replaced by the stress of not knowing.

The supper goes well enough, and afterward, we retire to the parlor for after dinner drinks. Kitty corners me while Anderson and Elliot stand by the fireplace. Quietly, she asks, "How are you holding up, dear?"

"It's been a bizarre week, but I'm well. Thank you for asking. What about you?"

Her smile is mischievous. "It worked."

"What's that?"

"No more side work for Anderson. Elliot was more agreeable to my demands than I had expected. In fact, he gave no pushback on the matter."

I knew that had to be her doing. "I am glad it worked out."

She nods, and her gaze drifts toward the guys. "Perhaps something good will come of this, after all."

I hoped so.

56

ANDERSON

When we walk into my apartment, June begins, "That was ... "

"Utterly exhausting," I finish.

"Yes!" Her head drops. "I kept waiting for your dad to drop the other shoe. I don't know. Blackmail us into something more, or come up with some new problem. I did not expect *charming party guest* to be in his repertoire."

"Truthfully, neither did I. But I'm glad he has it. Wine?"

"Oh, yes, please."

I pour two glasses and pass her one. The other I lift in a toast. "To a successful night of dinner with my parents. May we never have to do it again."

She giggles. "Cheers!"

We sip, and I can't stop from smiling. "You did well tonight. I think my dad might actually *genuinely* like you. Not that fake game he was playing before."

"I think that it is inadvisable to take anything Elliott West says at face value." She pauses. "But, I did get that impression from him tonight. It shocked the hell out of me. And what did your mother mean about Cole being difficult?"

I don't wanna think about him. Not when I have more important things in mind. "My younger brother has always had a penchant for trouble. Trouble that he can't get himself out of without the family's help. It's slowed down over the years, maybe because he's maturing and growing up, I don't know. I'm just glad that he's coming to a simmer instead of a rolling boil."

"You've really gotten into those cooking shows, haven't you?"

I laughed and nodded. "Maybe a little."

"That makes me very happy. I like not having to cook all the time."

"That is a pity. I love your food."

"Speaking of that, your mother is a hell of a cook."

"She should be. She took lessons in France."

Her lips quirked quizzically. "Then why were you so surprised that she made us dinner?"

"Even though she knows how to, she doesn't do it frequently."

"She doesn't strike me as the kind of woman who usually does her own dirty work."

I laughed at the thought. "Not when she can help it."

"Why are you so smiley right now?"

"I am?"

"You haven't stopped smiling since we got home."

That explains why my face is tired. "I like that you call this apartment our home." It cements exactly what is on my mind.

She smiles bashfully. "I mean, I know this isn't my address technically. But it's kind of hard not to think of it that way sometimes. I hope I'm not overstepping."

"No. Like I said, I like that you think of this place as our home." I draw her into my arms and slant my mouth over hers for a long, sleepy, winey kiss. "I want to build a life with you, June."

"Maybe I'm assuming, but I sort of thought that's what we were doing in the first place. Isn't that why you brought me to your parents' house? We're together. Couples do that kind of thing."

"I am done talking about my fucking parents for the night."

"But we haven't even dished on them. The way your father—"

I kiss her again. "No more talk of him. No more talk of her. Not tonight. Tonight is for better things."

"Like what?"

"I am recovered enough. The doctor cleared me. I love you. I want you naked on my bed right now."

"The doctor cleared you? You're serious?"

I nod. "And it has been far too long since the last time I was inside of you. I want to make love to you until I can't, and I want to propose to you, but—"

She gasps to speak, but I press a finger over her lips.

"But fucking first."

She laughs. "Gee, how romantic—"

I kiss her again, and this time, I'm not stopping until she is in my bed. I back her up from the kitchen toward the bedroom as carefully as I can without one of us slipping. It's not my usual move, and between her high heels and my gunshot wound, we both have to be careful. But we make it just inside my bedroom door frame before she stumbles. Her heel snags on the rug. But I catch her just in time.

She gasps. "Nice save."

"Maybe stand up so I don't hurt myself?"

"Right, oh god." She stands up. "Are you okay?"

A little tender. "I'm more than okay, baby. I'm here with you."

She leans up and kisses me, and it gets good fast. Reluctantly, she asks, "Are you sure about this? I don't want to hurt you."

My cock aches for her. "The only way you'd hurt me is if we stopped."

"We'll go slow, okay? No need to rush this."

I nod. "Turn around." She does, and I unzip her dress, kissing each inch of newly exposed skin. The scent of June drives me wild. I plant a bite at the nape of her neck, and she shivers against me while I scoot her dress down the rest of the way. Left in her bra, panties, and tights, she is a vision.

"Now you." She tugs my sweater off and unbuttons my shirt. Her eyes linger on my wound. Just a faint scar now. A little dip into my abs. I'd be more self-conscious about it, except that I see the love in her eyes. And the tears.

"What is it?"

"I can't believe I almost lost you."

"But you didn't. And I'm here now."

She kisses me harder. More desperately. I understand it. That need to connect. I felt it ever since she came here to take care of me. As we kiss, I unclip her bra. She strips out of the rest of her clothes. I've seen her naked over the past few weeks, and she's seen me naked, too. She's helped me in the shower many times. But now it means something else.

Coming back together after all this time, it means the world to me.

Gently, I lay her on the bed and crawl up next to her. June is breathtaking. All soft curves and sweet smiles. I skim my hand over her tits, grazing her nipples with my fingertips. God, I love the way she squirms and moans when I do that. Still, I can't stop staring.

She asks, "Why are you looking at me like that?"

"Sometimes I see you, and I still can't believe you're mine."

"Flatterer."

"Just honest." I kiss her again, and this time, she turns and wraps her legs around my hips. Her hot warmth caresses the head of my cock, and it's been so long I'm worried I'll come as soon as I slip inside of her. But I'm not stopping now.

Carefully, I lean myself over her. As much as I want to thrust home, I know how badly that could go. Earlier today, I'd practiced the maneuver a few times on the bed by myself just to see if I could do it. I was mostly successful in my test runs. Thankfully this time, I end up on top of her with minimal discomfort.

"You okay?"

I nod and kiss my way down her chest, taking my time to lavish each nipple with my undivided attention. Her breaths heave them to my lips, and when I meet her eyes, they're half-closed and blissful.

God, I've missed this.

I take my time on my way to her core. Kisses, nibbles, bites, anything to make her writhe for me. I want her undone. Out of her mind with pleasure. There wasn't much I could do the same as I used to, but tasting her? That I could do, and this one had a goal in mind.

Had I proposed? Sort of. And there was no better way to get someone to say yes than to make them come.

I parted her thighs, or rather, she eagerly spread them for me. Once between them, I took my time. My fingers brush the wetness that pooled there, and I swear under my breath. She is so aroused right now that my cock would slide straight in. I drag my tongue up her center reverently and fight the urge to rub my cock on the sheets for some kind of relief. At this rate, I won't make it a minute inside of her. I devour her, licking every part that makes her shudder before I settle on her clit. Her moans fill the bedroom, but she does her best to hold still.

Safety first, I suppose.

I plunge a finger into her tight core, and she loses that control. Her hips lob up at my face, but I weather the attack and remain fixed on her clit. She bunches the sheets in her fists. She pants my name, and it's never sounded so good. When she breaks on my tongue, I almost follow her over the edge. But she pulls my hair and uses my face just as I hoped she would.

When she's half-recovered, she coaxes me up by my hair for a kiss, tasting herself on my tongue.

57

JUNE

With Anderson on my mouth and between my thighs, I'm tempted to go for it right now. But this is a delicate situation, and I am in no mood to be delicate.

"Lay on your back for me."

"I can do it this way. The doctor —

"I know you can. It's not what I want. I want you … " I gently roll him from me. "… on your back."

He smiled. "You're in a mood?"

"I am." After that orgasm, I was in all the moods. It had been so damn long that I had thought I'd go out of my mind the first time we were together. I knew I would have to be careful with him, but fuck, I don't want to be. The slow and gentle thing is making me crazy.

That said, breaking him would ruin sex for me forever.

So, I take my time and follow the same pattern he did to me. Velvet kisses on his chest. Patient licks and barely noticeable bites all the way down to his cock. He pants, "Damn. Baby, I don't know how long I can hold out."

"And if you don't, that's okay. We're getting reacquainted. Our bodies might take—"

"I can't wait. I need you now."

"You're sure I don't get to torture you in kind?"

He laughs flatly. "Please."

So, I twirl my tongue around the head of his cock and pull back. "Sorry. Just needed a taste."

"I see that smirk. You're not sorry at all."

I giggle as I climb atop him. From there, he looks so fucking good. All muscles and hunger. I might not get to suck his cock until he's mindless, but I'm taking my time here. Sliding myself up and down his shaft without letting him enter me is enough to get us both going. As I do it, I bend down for another kiss that makes me dizzy.

In my mouth, he growls, "No more waiting." He cocks his hips up and enters me, and swallows my elated groan.

It feels too good. Too fucking good. I can't believe I've managed to hold out this long. He's only halfway in, so I roll back for the rest of him. It's almost too much. He lets out a scary grunt, and I have to force myself to slow down. Breathlessly, I pant, "You okay?"

"Fuck, yes," he murmurs as his eyes roll back. He grabs my hips and methodically drives into me.

I'm going to lose control. It's what I've feared the most about this, and I don't think I can help myself. I clutch his shoulders for something solid to hold onto, to not lose myself in the moment.

"That's it, baby, come for me."

I burst on him, barely turning my head in time not to scream in his ear. He pumps up into me to make it last. His sounds go deeper like they pull up from his very soul. Injured or not, he bucks up into me. His cock pulses inside. When his body goes rigid, I come again and kiss him. Anderson roars into my mouth as he comes inside of me.

I go boneless on him and pry myself off his body to lie next to him. I'm sweaty and sticky, and all I want to do is clean up, but I've misplaced my legs. Or they're numb. Whatever the reason I can't get up, I'm sure it's his fault.

Anderson rolls onto his side. "I'm not finished with you." He reaches between my thighs for the most sensitive parts of me, and I squeak from overstimulation. "I have wanted to touch you for over two months now."

"But," I mumble, "you had that secondary stitch tear—"

"And I behaved long enough for it to heal." His fingers dip inside of me. "This is my reward."

The sounds that come out of me aren't normal. Not when he strokes my G-spot. My back arcs off the bed, and there's a firework in my brain. "Fuck!"

"That's my girl." He works me over with his hand, and I can't hold still. I do everything in my power not to wriggle too hard against him, but he doesn't make it easy. Then again, when has anything to do with Anderson been easy?

I still can't believe he brought up marrying me. Certainly not right now. Tonight is for sex. For reconnecting. Anything else is on the back burner. As much as I want to marry this man, I can't get distracted and hurt him because my mind was someplace else.

His fingers are drenched with us. Each stroke echoes against my last orgasm. I tremble from his touch, and he slides his tongue into my mouth just as I crest up to another. I give myself over to him. There is nothing I wouldn't give this man.

It's been a long time since I wasn't in control. Every doctor appointment, every medication timing, all his shopping ... I have had to run the show for us both. It didn't seem like much at first, but over the weeks, it wore on me. Always being in charge of everything. Always managing. I didn't realize the magnitude of it until now.

And now, it feels so good to let him control me.

Anderson is in full control. Dragging my orgasm to the edge, making me wait for it. He knows exactly how to make me shake for him, how to bring me close without bringing me on. My body goes taut from his work, and I'm on the verge of begging.

His lips press to the sensitive edge of my ear, and he whispers, "Come for me, baby."

I shatter on his words, and my body goes wild. I can't hold still. I can't hold back. There is nothing but the pleasure between my thighs and the man who makes it possible. I kiss him ravenously, unable to contain myself as ecstasy courses through my veins.

Slowly, I go limp again. No more air in my lungs. No more thoughts in my head. I am utterly spent and quivering. He pulls the sheets up to cover us. I gasp, "I love you."

"Was that for the orgasm or because you were cold and I covered you?"

I giggle. "Both."

He grins and kisses me. "Valid."

I lay my head on his shoulder, happy to be in his arms again. "Anderson?"

"Yes?"

"I don't want you to joke about proposing again, okay?"

"Not a problem." He rolls over and stuffs his arm deep under the pillow.

"What are you doing?"

When he returns, he has a small black box in his hand, which sends my heart racing.

I sit up. "Seriously, what are you doing?"

"June Devlin," he says as he opens the box. Inside is the biggest damn diamond I have ever seen. "I was not joking earlier. I hope this proves that. You are the woman of my dreams. Not a day goes by that I don't want to spend with you. If you'll have me, I want to spend the rest of my days with you. Marry me."

I can't even say the word. I'm speechless. So, I kiss him instead. It's a reckless, messy kiss, and I end up on top of him again. Too many things are trying to come to life in my head, but his fingers wiped out the computational skills in my brain, and I have lost the capacity for rational thought.

He laughs and pulls back. "Is that a yes? You're leaving me hanging here—"

"Yes!"

Anderson wraps me in his arms, and we continue to kiss until I feel him harden up again. Just as I wriggle back to meet him, he grunts one of his pain grunts, and it shakes me out of my stupor.

"Oh my god, are you okay?"

"I'm good. Just ended up on the box."

"Give me that!" I swipe it from him and pull out the ring. The damn thing nearly blinds me. "It's too much, Anderson."

"I can get you something smaller—"

"Don't you dare!"

He laughs again. "I promise not to." Then he slides the ring on my finger, and my breath catches in my throat. "God, I love you."

"I love you, too, baby," I say with a sigh. There is no other man in the world for me. I've known that for a long time. Right now, I mean to show him.

58

ANDERSON

Some insecure part of me thought for sure she would say no. Maybe I worried about my karma. Or the fact that my luck had gone to shit in the past six months. Whatever it was, I didn't know if she would say yes. But I'm so glad she did.

Everything is going right. For the first time since I've gotten with June, everything has started to go right. Dad has me back in the office. I am evidently in his good graces now. June has agreed to be my wife. Something I never truly let myself believe would ever happen. Nothing could diminish this high.

As she kisses me again, I get lost in her mouth. This time, I want to be lost in her body, too.

I roll her over with a renewed sense of confidence. Now that we've established I can handle sex, I want to go for more. There's no pain to slow me down, either. Maybe it's the sex talking, but I don't feel anything but her right now.

She stares up at me, looking mystified as I thrust into her. She's so fucking wet with both of us that there's no resistance. Her back arches, and her eyes flutter back as her throat blushes pink. I bite her there, and she groans for more. It's perfect. She's perfect. I can't get enough of her.

I don't think there could ever be enough.

June is my home. My person. She is my better half in every way. I am so lucky to have found this woman. I took a chance at that auction, and it was the best risk I have ever taken in my life. I bury myself to the base and promise, "I will do everything in my power to take care of you, June."

She pants, "I know that."

But I have to show her. I hook my arms around her shoulders from underneath and pump into her. We are as close as two people can be, but I wish we were somehow closer. More connected. I am addicted to this woman. Her body, her scent, her taste. I want it all. I need it all. There could never be another.

I arch myself at that angle that hits her spot just right, and she tenses beneath me, purring. I know the signs, and I keep pounding on her there. I have to make her mine. Forever.

I growl, "That's it, baby. Come for me again."

This time, her trembles are an earthquake. She gasps loudly, like a scream in reverse. Clawing at my back, her thighs squeeze around me as she comes on me. When her pussy clenches rhythmically on my cock, she brings me with her. My balls seize, and my spine lights up as I come again. I know everyone must think such things, but I feel bad for every other man who exists because none of them will ever have June. No one else will get to feel this way. I could weep for them.

But she's mine. All mine. I smirk to myself as I roll off of her.

Her voice is thrashed. "Pretty proud of yourself there, eh?"

"You could say that."

She nuzzles my shoulder. "You should be. Injured or not, that was amazing."

"Same to you." I kiss her forehead. "I know there's a ton of things to figure out going forward, but right now … I am here with you. In the moment. And it's been a long time since I felt this good, so I am going to enjoy it and try not to overthink."

She giggles. "Good luck with that. I find multiple orgasms will do that for you."

"Multiple? I know you came a few times, but —"

"I lost count."

I kiss her again. "You know, just what to say to a guy."

She laughs. "And with that, I have to go clean up, and we probably need to change the sheets when I come back. You game?"

I hate changing the sheets. "Not sure if I can. I got shot a while back, and —"

She laughs harder at that and heads for the bathroom. "If you have the strength to dirty the sheets, you have the strength to change them with me, you big faker." She closes the door behind herself.

I lay back and discover she has a point. There are wet spots everywhere. Still, life is good. With work getting back to normal and June as my bride, things feel complete. Like I am on the right track.

She emerges, naked and sated, and the sight of her stills the breath in my chest. "What?"

"You. Always you."

She smiles, then bails for the closet. "The blue set or the other blue set?"

"I like consistency."

"So you bought three sets of identical sheets?"

"Yes."

She snickers and comes out with her selection. We change the sheets out and bed down for the night. "Aren't fresh sheets better?"

They are, but I'll never admit it. "The others were fine. You could have slept in the wet spot, and I —"

She slugs my shoulder and giggles. "You asshole!"

I clutch her to my chest. "But I'm your asshole."

"Ew."

"That was supposed to be romantic and took a turn for the worse. Sorry."

She giggles again, and I drift off to that perfect sound. In the morning, I wake up to the sunlight refracting in the diamond on her hand. Gotta get used to that. I hope to have fifty or sixty years of practice. A tug of sadness hits me, though.

Fifty or sixty years is just not enough. I need lifetimes with this woman. But, for now, I'll take what I can get.

She stirs in her sleep and mumbles, "Morning."

"It is. Coffee?"

"Yes, please."

"Coffee is for ladies who leave the bed."

She whines but scoots off the bed for her robe, and I follow suit. Sunday mornings had been for cuddling and doing the Times' crossword together. But today, I feel good. Like I have too much energy. After last night's fun, I am refreshed and invigorated.

June, however, appears to have lost energy during her sleep.

"You okay?"

"You fucked the daylights out of me last night."

I grin as I make coffee. "Why don't you go sit on the couch, and I'll bring the coffee when it's ready."

"Okay. But only if you promise to be less chipper when you bring it."

I laugh. "Promise."

She toddles off to the living room, still half asleep, and I turn my attention to my task. She likes her coffee light and sweet when it's regular and not espresso, so I set out the cream and sugar. I'm in such a good mood I find myself humming as I do so. On rough mornings, she tinkers with her ratios of cream and sugar, and I can't assume anything. So, I set everything on the tray she used to bring me my meals for weeks.

Fuck. I owe this woman everything. Which works out since I want to give her everything.

Once the coffee is ready, I set the mugs on the tray and tote it into the living room. Just as I come around the couch, she gasps. "Fuck!"

"What—"

But she points to the screen. She has it on the news, which I always advise against. It's nothing but sensationalism—

Why does that dock look familiar?

"A grim discovery at the docks is our lead story this morning. Johnny Green is live on the scene, where homicide investigators are searching for answers." The newscaster speaks to the onsite reporter on a split screen. "What can you tell us, Johnny?"

"I am here at the Marina Bay dock of Squantum Channel where police have identified the body of Neil Johnson, a missing hedge fund manager from Nebraska—"

The tray slips from my hands as I lose my grip. It crashes to the floor, but neither of us moves to clean it.

"... Police suspect foul play due to the injuries found on the body. At this point, there is no word on the person or persons who may have been involved."

They show a blurred image of his body on the shore, and even with the blurs, I recognize that fucking green sweater.

"How was the body discovered?"

"Police say it washed ashore sometime in the night. Fishermen were aghast at what they saw, though sadly, this is not the first time they have found such a gruesome discovery."

The video went to a fisherman who rambled on about having found other bodies in the past, but his words fall on deaf ears. All I can hear is the roaring of my blood in my veins.

When the reporter comes back on, though, I tune in. "Johnny, you said Neil Johnson had been declared missing?"

"That's right, Carl. He was reported missing almost three months ago. Police say identifying evidence will be difficult, as he was in the water for that entire time. They are asking the public for help in identifying the culprits. Back to you."

"And in other news … "

I just stand there. Dazed. It's a minute before I realize June's hand is waving in my face. Tears stream down her cheeks. "What do we do?"

I wish I knew.

THANK you for reading Bidding War! Can't wait to find out what happens next? **1-click Winning Bid now!**

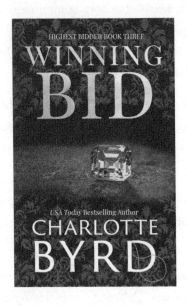

He ended a life to save mine. Now the walls are closing in.

They hunt us, seeking our weaknesses. I may have to sacrifice myself to save him.

I never meant to love him.

Yet now I'm enthralled, ensnared by his every word, his every look.

The way he moves, the way he undresses me with his eyes.

I can't let go. Not when his touch sets me ablaze.

My job with his father's worst enemy is an existential threat. I'm undercover in enemy territory and I can't trust anyone.

If we can endure the gathering storm, our bond might save us.

Yet a betrayal whispers in the shadows, one that could shatter us for good.

1-click Winning Bid now!

WANT MORE of June and Anderson (and another STEAMY chapter)? **Read the FREE Bonus Chapter now!**

PLEASE TAKE a moment to leave a review on Amazon! Reviews help me find new readers and they can be as short as a sentence. Thank you!

IF YOU FIND any mistakes or typos, please write to me directly so I can make changes immediately instead of through Amazon. My email is charlotte@charlotte-byrd.com

ABOUT CHARLOTTE BYRD

Charlotte Byrd is the bestselling author of romantic suspense novels. She has sold over 1.5 Million books and has been translated into five languages.

She lives near Palm Springs, California with her husband, son, a toy Australian Shepherd and a Ragdoll cat. Charlotte is addicted to books and Netflix and she loves hot weather and crystal blue water.

Write her here:

charlotte@charlotte-byrd.com

Check out her books here:

www.charlotte-byrd.com

Connect with her here:

www.tiktok.com/charlottebyrdbooks

www.facebook.com/charlottebyrdbooks

www.instagram.com/charlottebyrdbooks

Sign up for my newsletter: https://www.
subscribepage.com/byrdVIPList

Join my Facebook Group: https://www.facebook.
com/groups/276340079439433/

Bonus Points: Follow me on BookBub and
Goodreads!

amazon.com/Charlotte-Byrd/e/B013MN45Q6

facebook.com/charlottebyrdbooks

tiktok.com/charlottebyrdbooks

bookbub.com/profile/charlotte-byrd

instagram.com/charlottebyrdbooks

x.com/byrdauthor

ALSO BY CHARLOTTE BYRD

All books are available at ALL major retailers! If you can't find it, please email me at charlotte@ charlotte-byrd.com

Highest Bidder Series
Highest Bidder
Bidding War
Winning Bid

Hockey Why Choose
One Pucking Night (Novella)
Kiss and Puck
Pucking Disaster
Puck Me
Puck It

Tell me Series
Tell Me to Stop

Tell Me to Go
Tell Me to Stay
Tell Me to Run
Tell Me to Fight
Tell Me to Lie

Tell Me to Stop Box Set Books 1-6

Black Series
Black Edge
Black Rules
Black Bounds
Black Contract
Black Limit

Black Edge Box Set Books 1-5

Dark Intentions Series
Dark Intentions
Dark Redemption
Dark Sins
Dark Temptations
<u>Dark Inheritance</u>

Dark Intentions Box Set Books 1-5

Tangled Series
Tangled up in Ice
Tangled up in Pain
Tangled up in Lace

Tangled up in Hate
Tangled up in Love

Tangled up in Ice Box Set Books 1-5

The Perfect Stranger Series
The Perfect Stranger
The Perfect Cover
The Perfect Lie
The Perfect Life
The Perfect Getaway

The Perfect Stranger Box Set Books 1-5

Wedlocked Trilogy
Dangerous Engagement
Lethal Wedding
Fatal Wedding

Dangerous Engagement Box Set Books 1-3

Lavish Trilogy
Lavish Lies
Lavish Betrayal
Lavish Obsession

Lavish Lies Box Set Books 1-3

Somerset Harbor
Hate Mate (Cargill Brothers 1)

Best Laid Plans (Cargill Brothers 2)
Picture Perfect (Cargill Brothers 3)
Always Never (Cargill Brothers 4)
Kiss Me Again (Macmillan Brothers 1)
Say You'll Stay (Macmillan Brothers 2)
Never Let Go (Macmillan Brothers 3)
Keep Me Close (Macmillan Brothers 4)

All the Lies Series
All the Lies
All the Secrets
All the Doubts

All the Lies Box Set Books 1-3

Not into you Duet
Not into you
Still not into you

Standalone Novels
Dressing Mr. Dalton
Debt
Offer
Unknown

Made in the USA
Monee, IL
12 February 2025